THROUGH THE SEASONS OF THE SUN

CHESS CAPINO

Introduction

Shrouded in the mists of time, in the so-called "Dark Ages",
our forebears lived, loved and found their way, just as people
had been doing for centuries and are still doing to this day.
This is the story of one boy's journey to manhood; meeting
exceptional people along the way to finding himself.

WINTER

Chapter 1 - I Remember

I sit here on the edge of the village square, in the last patch of weak sunlight on this autumn day, a day like so many others. Now I measure the passing seasons by the movement of those patches of sunlight, sometimes bright and to be avoided, and other times, like this moment, to be treasured and enjoyed.

Around me, the people of the village carry on their lives, coming and going to the market place, the women visiting the home of a sister, cousin or friend, the men going to and from the tavern, or, the older ones, sitting here beside me in the shrinking patches of sunlight. How many have sat for a while then left this world, while I sit on, and on, and on. Sometimes I think I have lived long enough on this earth. I am ready for the next journey or infinite rest, whichever it may be.

Here come the children. There are always children. They cannot be the same children, because, unlike us older folk, they change and grow. But always at this time of day they come, roaring home from their adventures in the fields to be safely snug at home by the time darkness falls. They are lucky to live in a time of peace; to be free to run into the woods and fields, safe in the knowledge that they will return home to their families when the day is done. Times were not always so secure. But I don't want to remember those days. And I do not need to remember. I didn't even consider remembering. Until yesterday.

What happened yesterday? A little girl. There so many children. I have watched my own children grow up and have children of their own. These in turn have made me a great grandfather many times over. At first I knew all of them, which little ones belonged to each of my children. But now, all the children in the village call me Grandfather.

As everyone's Grandfather, they show me respect, but I can't say I feel much warmth. They have games to play to pass their time rather than visit with a tired old man. And, in truth, that is fine with me. Although a man may not be allotted a certain number of breaths or heart beats, I think I was given a fixed number of words and I used them up long ago. Or I thought I had, until yesterday.

What happened yesterday? A little girl. I'd noticed her before, watching me from the side of the fountain. But each time she saw me looking at her, she turned and ran away. Sometimes she played with the other children but several times I saw her going into the woods alone; strange for such a little one. Would she be safe, I wondered? But she always came home before the sun set like the others. Except yesterday.

What happened yesterday? Yesterday, the evening was warm. I dozed off as I sat in that last patch of sunlight in the square. When I awoke, it was already past nightfall and a full moon had risen. A shadow moved over the cobblestones and I heard the sound of footsteps running nearby. I opened my eyes and saw the girl. At the same time, she stopped and looked at me. Our eyes met and she smiled. The moonlight had robbed her of her colors but I remembered the reddish gold highlights in long brown hair, curling wildly around her shoulders, never bound in a kerchief like the other girls. Her skirt looked grey in the moonlight but I knew it would be some bright color, red or orange or green. No, no, it wouldn't. The girls in this village wear somber colors or blue on feast days…but I knew I'd seen this girl twirling in colors bright…

"Grandfather," she said, tentatively taking a step nearer.

"Grandfather," she said again, "it's late, can I help you to go to your home?"

I roused myself out of my vision and looked at her again.

"Grandfather," she said with a warm smile as she reached out and offered me her hand. "Come with me, I'll take you home."

Did she think I couldn't find my own way? I, who have lead men in battle; I who was respected as a wise leader; I who have traveled farther than anyone else in this sleepy village? I shook off her hand and grumbled,

"I can do it".

"Of course you can, Grandfather, but it would be my pleasure to go with you and hear your tales".

"Who are you?" I asked. The sound of my voice was rough to my ears. What I heard seemed much more curt than I intended.

"I'm Anna," she replied.

"They called you 'Milada'," I said, shocked at my own words.
"No, I am simply Anna; but I've heard of this Milada," the girl replied. "I was hoping you would tell me about her **someday**. Won't you, please?" she begged clutching both my hands, her deep brown eyes pleading.

I wasn't sure that I could remember or wanted to, but seeing this young girl who was so like my darling friend, how could I say no.

"Why do you want to know about her?" I asked.

"Many of the older folk have told me that I am like her; that she was born here but then went to live with some people who didn't live in a village; they traveled around all the time. I think I would like that! They say you lived with them for a time, too. Did you? Is it true?"

"Did anyone tell you that she was always asking questions?"

The girl smiled, understanding the connection.

"No; no one remembers her very well. They say it was a long, long time ago, and that you are the only one who really knows her story. I think she was related to great-great grandma," she added.

"Are you one of my grandchildren? You know they all call me Grandfather now."

"Yes, well no. My mother's father was one of your grandchildren. I'm a great-great something," she giggled.

The sound of her laugh tinkled like the ringing bells of sheep returning from their high mountain pastures. It was like having Milada beside me once again. Without noticing it, my lips had curled into a smile.

"So will you tell me about her, Grandfather? Please!"

How could I say no? The girl must have seen something on my face as we waited together in the moonlight.

"So you will? Oh, thank you, thank you!" her shadow danced behind her as she jumped in excitement.

"Yes, my child, I will tell you the story of Milada, and my own, if you have patience to hear the ramblings of an old man".

"Yes, oh yes, I do!" she exclaimed.

"But not tonight," I told her. "Let me rest tonight and who knows, maybe I will dream of those days so long ago".

Together we walked slowly back to the home I shared with my granddaughter and her family. Anna left me at the door. She spun around once and called, "See you tomorrow, when you will tell me your story. Until then, sweet dreams!"

And with that she was off. That is what happened yesterday. And today, my tale will begin.

Chapter 2 - The Story Begins

I never sleep deeply any more. It's just as well. I have nothing important to do. I can doze in the sun or by the fire whenever fancy takes me. I was roused by the sounds of morning; cocks crowing before the dawn, smaller birds joining the chorus as the sun rose, the soft footsteps of my granddaughter stoking the fire to prepare breakfast for the family. I sleep under a goose down quilt on a soft bench by the hearth, snug in the warmth of the cozy stone house that once belonged to Milada's uncle, a very long time ago.

Milada. It has been a very long time since I've thought of those days. Did I speak to her last night? Or was it just a dream?

"Good morning, Grandfather!" Mirianna nodded when she saw that my eyes were open.

"Good morning, my girl," I replied as she helped me rise from my bed. The family would need it soon, as a seat for the breakfast table.

Mirianna's two daughters appeared from the back room, rubbing the sleep from their eyes.

"Say good morning to your Granddad, girls," their mother said, "and then come help me with the meal. We can have some boiled eggs for breakfast; that is if the hens have laid some for us. One of you, go and have a look".

There was always a bustle around the house in the morning. I missed the days when my old woman was still alive and the two of us lived here alone. We took our time, those last years together. Now, I was pleased to finish my meal and leave for my day in the village square, watching the people or just sitting in silence. After the meal, I put on my jacket, left the house and headed toward the center of the village.

Before I reached the main road I felt a warmth in my hand. I looked down and saw that a little girl had placed her small hand in mine.

"Here I am!" she chirped. "You promised to tell me your story today – and Milada's".

So it wasn't a dream. Here is that child. And in the light of the morning she looks even more like the girl I knew so long ago.

"Yes, my girl," I said, wondering why she wanted me to tell her and if I had the energy and desire to do so. "I will tell you what I can remember. Let's sit over there in the sun and I will begin."

We found a bench on the west side of the square, not far from the church steps. The village square was alive with people as usual at this hour of the morning. The early service had finished and somberly clad women chatted outside the church before continuing to the market place and getting on with their bartering. I smiled, thinking of the day I met Milada. It was in a market place. I'll never forget the taste of that cheese....

"Grandfather, grandfather...where are you? You said you would tell me your story. I'm ready!"

Where am I? Oh, yes. Here in the square. An old man. For a moment I was that clever youth, streetwise and sassy; hungry and alone...

"I was staying in a big village, the time I first met Milada," I began. "It was after my mother had gone."

"Where did you mother go? Where was your father? Did you have any brothers and sisters?" she asked.

I should have known she would have many questions. Now I would have to speak about things I thought I'd long forgotten.

"I never knew my father," I began. "I never knew any family except my mother. No brothers; no sisters, no grandparents. I hardly even remember my mother. She was never very well. She worked in a tavern, serving meat and ale until late every night in exchange for room and board for us two."

"We slept in the storeroom between sacks of flour and dried beans. Often at night I lay awake, listening to the sounds of rats running on the shelves above my head and my mother's dry, and labored coughing."

"Didn't they have a cat?" the girl asked? "It could catch the rats!"

"I do remember one cat," I said, surprised at the recollection. "It was all black and slept in the corner, like a shadow. I heard him running in the night, as well. Maybe he did catch some rats, but there were always more."

"So, why did your mother leave you? Did you stay by yourself in the tavern with the cat and the rats?" she asked me.

"One morning, it was winter and very cold, I woke up and heard nothing. No rats, no cat and no coughing. I felt strange and didn't know why. I guess I was so accustomed to the sounds that silence was actually frightening. I moved closer to my mother to cuddle up to her for warmth but when I touched her she was as cold as the chilly winter air in the room. I got up and ran into the tavern. The master was just stirring the embers to rouse the fire for breakfast."

"Come quick," I said to him, "There's something wrong with my Ma".

He followed me into the storeroom and bend down to take a closer look.

"This girl is dead," he said, brushing the dust from the ground off his apron.

"Dead!" exclaimed Anna. How awful! What did you do?"

"I sat there beside my mother's body for what seemed like a very long time. Eventually some people came and took her away. No one said anything to me. The next day the tavern master told me that my mother had a brother and that he would come for me when he could. Until then, I needed to earn my keep by wiping down the tables in the tavern and making myself useful as best I could."

"I was small, but strong for my size. I helped stir the porridge at breakfast time and carried plates to and from the kitchen for the noonday meal. I liked listening to the men talking and making deals to exchange their produce and livestock. Sometimes travelers would pass through bringing news from other villages. I wasn't really unhappy then, but I missed my mother."

"One day a man dressed in smelly sheepskins came to the tavern. The master called me over. "Goran," he said, "this man is your uncle. You will go and live with him now."

"Without a smile, the man told me to follow him out of the tavern. There was snow on the ground and it was very cold. He took another sheepskin from a pack on his back and wrapped it around my shoulders. We walked for a long time, higher and higher into the hills above the village until we came to a rough stone hut. He pushed the door open. First I felt a rush of welcome warmth, but the price of the heat was the smell of a dozen sheep, all turning to see who had arrived."

"I stayed with my uncle the shepherd, helping him tend his flock and bring the sheep to market until I was old enough to live on my own. The shepherd was a man of little words, with more time and affection for his sheep than he felt for me."

"It was after that time that I met Milada and traveled for a while with the gypsy band."

The girl Anna looked up at me, with a smile. She seemed content to sit and listen to the ramblings of an old man.

Chapter 3 – The First Time I Saw Milada

I was hungry. I'd been living on my own for two months, doing odd jobs when I could find them. It was summer and the air was warm so I could sleep comfortably out of doors. I'd just come to a large village, hitching a ride on a wagon. I'd heard that the village was a prosperous one and would have many opportunities for me to earn my keep. But now I was hungry and there was no time to go looking for work.

Luckily for me it was market day! It was a much busier village than any I had ever seen. The market square was full of people, buying and selling. Voices haggled loudly over the price of each exchange. The morning sunlight gleamed off polished copper plates, their brightness set off by the dark black cast-iron cooking pots. In one corner of the square tanned hides and furs were piled up high alongside richly colored rugs and woven woolen blankets, colorful ribbons fluttered in the light wind. The day was warm, but the first touches of the coming autumn tinged the breeze.

I quickly moved deeper into the market square, looking for something to eat. I followed my nose, the smell of grilling sausages leading me on, even though I had no money to buy even one.

I spotted some vendors selling cheese. There were two stalls side by side, with a large pink-cheeked lady serving at each. I knew from experience how I could get some breakfast.

As I stepped up to the first stall the lady behind the counter called, "Good day, young man. Buy some cheese – it's the freshest in the market!

"I need a taste before I buy. How do I know that your cheese is any good?" I told her, looking as serious as I could with my tummy rumbling underneath my shirt.

I watched as the woman took a huge round of cheese off the shelf and cut me a small piece. A VERY small piece, I thought!

"There you go," she said.

I took the cheese and popped it in my mouth. "Mmm, it's not bad, not bad. I'll think about it."

Then I went to the next stall and called to the plump lady at the counter, "Your neighbor's cheese is very good, but I have heard that yours is better."

"Here, have a taste," she said, cutting off an even tinier piece of soft white cheese.

"Make a little bigger so I can taste it!" I said.

She gave me another piece, I was happy it was a larger one!

"Very, nice, very nice." I told her, as I spotted my favorite cheese, a drier one shaped into a large yellow wheel. "What about that other kind, that one there?"

I was happy when the woman cut me a slice without question.

"There you are," she said, "why don't you buy some of each?"

"Maybe I will," I told her, enjoying the second piece and feeling the edge coming off my hunger. "Maybe I will."

I smiled at the woman and walked back to the first seller. "Your neighbor's cheese is excellent," I told her. "Let me have another piece of yours so I can choose whose is best, and a piece of bread too if you can spare it."

The woman looked at me for a moment, then cut me another piece of the yellow cheese. There was a loaf of heavy brown bread beside it on the table. The woman tore off a chunk and handed it to me without another word.

"This is such a hard choice," I said, "I'll have go away and give it some thought."

Afraid of pushing my luck, I turned and started to walk away from the cheese sellers, wondering if I could play the same trick and get some sausages.

Both of them started shouting at me, "Eh, boy - you eat my cheese and buy nothing!" said one. "If everybody were like you I would have no cheese to sell!" said the other. I knew I had better get out of there fast in case the other vendors heard them and got wise to me!

As I moved quickly away, I felt like I was being following. Would the city guards arrest me for stealing cheese? But I didn't steal anything! Those nice ladies were happy to give me the cheese!

I felt a hand grab my arm. It wasn't hard, but strong enough to stop me. I turned to look, fearing the worst. Instead of a burly guard, a pair of kind brown eyes met mine. Holding my arm was a young man, not much older than I was. He was dressed differently than anyone I'd ever seen, with a richly embroidered waistcoat and wide black trousers tucked into a pair of shining riding boots.

"Are you hungry?" he asked me, with a kind smile in his eyes.

"Not so much anymore," I told him, feeling myself smiling back, "I've had some cheese".

A beautiful young woman came up to us. I could see a resemblance between her and the boy. They both had the same kind, dark eyes and jet black hair that framed their serene and lovely faces. Two young girls holding baskets with fruits and vegetables from the market stood back a little way, watching. One of then had wild reddish-brown hair that flowed untamed in all directions. I was thinking how unusual it looked when the dark-eyed beauty said, "Do you have a home?"

What a question! I felt something move in my heart as she looked at me with concern. No one had ever looked at me like that before.

"Not really," I told her. "I'm free. I come and go; do odd jobs for food."

The boy touched my arm and said, "We are camped in the forest not far from here. Tonight we will have a celebration. Come with us and eat your fill."

I looked at him to see if he was serious. He smiled and nodded as did the dark haired girl. I saw the other two girls smiling and giggling together. I had nothing to lose if I went with them, I thought. If I didn't like it I could always move on. So I told them, "Why not?"

I guess that was the first time I saw Milada.

SPRING

Chapter 4 - Introductions

I had a hard time keeping pace with the young man as we walked out of the village toward the nearby forest. He didn't seem much older than I was, but he was taller and very fit. He said that he was called Dragan.

"My name is Goran," I told him. "I grew up in a nearby village but when my ma died I went to live with her brother. He has no children of his own - but if he did they would probably run away! It's not that he is a bad man, he just forgets things, you know, unimportant things, like feeding me!"

"He has a flock of sheep. The *sheep* he loves! *They* never go to sleep hungry. He is out in the fields with them all day, talking to them, playing them music on his flute. Sometimes he remembered to come home and give me some supper, sometimes he didn't. Now I do odd jobs, run errands, help the ladies beat their rugs - that's one dusty job! But that way I get enough to eat."

Dragan listened to me rambling on. I don't know why I was talking so much. Maybe I was nervous. Or maybe, I thought, I'd been lonely and this young man really seemed to be interested in my story.

"It looks like you have had to work hard," Dragan said. "It's not easy to live by yourself without the support of a tribe."

"What is a 'tribe'?" I asked him. I had not heard that word before.

"It's like a big family," Dragan replied. "I live as a part of a gypsy band. We all share the chores and the celebrations."

"Do you all live in one big house?" I asked.

He let out a hearty laugh. "We don't live in houses at all," he said. "We live in wagons and travel with the seasons of the sun."

"How do you make your money?" I wondered out loud,

"We don't need too much money to live," he replied. "On our travels we hunt and collect the wild fruits of the forest. When we stop near a village we help the people there and they thank us with gifts of food."

"How do you help the people? Do you do odd jobs for them, like I do?"

"Sometimes we help in that way, but mostly we help people when they are ill. Our tribe carries many herbs from far off lands and our people know how to use them to heal the sick," Dragon told me.

I had come across men in the village who claim to have healing powers. I'd seen the village barber pulling out a tooth to cure a person's toothache. And heard their screams! I remember my mother asking for a special tea to help her cough, and the man in the tavern saying he had none left.

"I heard about a tea that helps with coughs. Is that what you mean?" I asked Dragan.

"Yes," he replied. "We carry herbs that can sooth a cough or lower a fever or relieve stomach pain and others that can help with many ailments."

"How do you know about these herbs?" I asked, wondering why everyone didn't possess this useful information.

"My tribe holds this knowledge. We are just one band of four. Each travels in a different direction. When we meet we exchange herbs, news and knowledge," he explained.

"Why don't the people in the village know these things," I asked, puzzled.

"Some of them know some things," he replied, "especially about the herbs that grow close by. We have a wider knowledge because we travel. And we remember."

I was about to ask "remember what?" when a big black horse pushed its head between us and nuzzled Dragan's face.

"Dobro, my boy, good boy," he said. He turned to me, "We are almost back to our camp."

When I turned back to look at the horse I noticed that the beautiful young woman and the two girls were not far behind us.

I watched the one with the wild hair. Our eyes met briefly. She seemed to be laughing at me. The other girl ran up to me and took my arm.

"I'm Tanya," she said. "Do you like animals?"

What a funny question! "Animals?" I replied, "Well, sure," But then I thought a moment and added, "I really don't like sheep very much!" thinking of the smell my uncle brought back with him from his days tending his flock.

We'd arrived in a clearing in the forest. Long tables were set up and many people bustled about preparing the meal. There was a delicious aroma of meat roasting. My eyes followed my nose to see a whole deer turning on a spit above a low fire.

Dragan led me over toward the roasting meat. He introduced me to the men who were tending the fire and turning the spit. There was a boy there with them, about my age, holding a wooden bowl. He gave me a big, welcoming smile.

"I must see my father now," Dragan said. "Make yourself at home!"

"Is it a special occasion?" I asked, "I haven't seem this much food in one place at one time except for very special occasions."

The boy with the bowl, whose name was Bora, said, "Yes, it is a special occasion. Our friend Radko has died and we are celebrating."

"But no one looks sad," I said.

"It's true that we will miss our brother," Bora told me, "but this is a start of a new journey for him; one that will bring us back together again someday."

I didn't understand what he was talking about. Rather than go on about it I asked, "What's in that bowl you're holding?"

"It's to make the meat tastier!" he answered, pulling out a bunch of herbs tied with a string.

"This is rosemary," he said. "I dip it in a mixture of olive oil, salt and other herbs and put it on the meat as it roasts. Like this."

I watched as he painted the deer's flank with the mixture as it turned around. It certainly smelled wonderful. Maybe I was very hungry, but it seemed the best thing I had ever smelled. My tummy rumbled at the thought of eating some of the delicious meat.

I was embarrassed, but Bora laughed. "It's not quite ready yet or I'd give you some now. Be a little patient and you can eat your fill."

Looking out beyond the roast I could see the wild haired girl preparing some vegetables with her friend.

"Who is that girl?" I asked Bora.

"Tanya," he said.

"No, I met Tanya," I told him. "The other one, the one with the hair."

"They all have hair," Bora smiled. "I guess you mean Milada. She never ties hers up or braids it like Tanya does. She isn't one of our tribe, but we all love her as if she were."

Before I could ask any more questions, the man who was turning the spit tapped me on the shoulder and asked me to relieve him for a moment. The job was harder than it looked, but I knew the work was worth it. The sooner the meat was done, the sooner we could eat! The delicious aroma made my stomach rumble some more.

Soon the feast was ready. I moved aside as two men carved the deer right off the spit and set the succulent meat on platters that the women carried over to the long table. A distinguished looking man with black hair just touched with grey stood at its head; on either side of him stood Dragan and the dark eyed girl. I could see a resemblance between the three of them. He must be their father and, from the look of things, the leader of their tribe.

We all took a place along the sides of the table. Each person held a beaker out to be filled from large jugs that were passed around. A serious looking young girl gave me one and then smiled.

"Here," she said, "use this while you are with us. And here is a plate a knife and a spoon. Keep them with you and bring them when it is time to eat."

When we each had a full glass, the leader raised his and said, "Tonight we celebrate our friend's passing. May his

15

journey be a smooth one. May we meet again when the time is right. Radko – farewell!"

We lifted our cups and drank a toast to Radko. Then Bora picked up a viol. At first he looked a little awkward with it but the moment he touched it with his bow a beautiful, happy song came forth. I was surprised at how a boy of my age could play so well.

And, finally, it was time to eat! I was absorbed in Bora's music and didn't notice that my plate had been stacked high with food, and bowl of aromatic soup placed beside it.

I fell to it, trying to appreciate the wonderful flavor of the soup, but once I started I couldn't stop. I drank the soup in almost one go and then started in on the succulent meat.

My mouth full, I heard someone whisper, "That boy is really hungry."

I looked up to see the wild haired girl, Milada, sitting opposite me.

"My name is Goran," I told her feeling a little embarrassed that our first conversation should start like this. "This is the best food I've had in my life!" I noticed she was blushing, too.

"Thanks to Zora's herbs," she said. "My name is Milada."

"Pleased to meet you," I replied, "You were at the market today, too, weren't you."

"Yes, I liked watching you with the cheese sellers!" she said.

Oh, no! Does she think I'm a thief? "You saw that?" I asked. "I really did plan to buy some cheese." I lied.

"Yes, of course," she said with a grin. I knew she didn't believe me, but I don't think she cared. She was smiling, and I had no trouble smiling back.

Chapter 5 – A Strange Feast

When my first plate of food was finished, I was offered more from the serving platters that were passed along the table. I was vaguely aware of different music being played as I enjoyed the delicious meal but my concentration was on my food, and on the girl sitting opposite.

I saw her watching me, but every time our eyes met she looked away. The music grew louder and louder and just as I finished mopping up every last bit of juice left on my plate with some of the crusty brown bread I had sampled that morning, the men started to clear the tables and move them to make a space around a roaring fire.

I could see Bora playing with the other musicians. They were smiling at each other, daring each other to play faster and louder. Soon people started dancing. I had never seen people dance like this! In the village, people danced at festivals and at wedding feasts, but always together in a circle, moving as one. These people danced two by two or in small groups or even alone, moving their bodies to the pulsating beat of the music. I sat by the fire and watched.

Dragan danced with wild abandon, clicking his heals and raising dust on the dry earth, adding another rhythm to song. The women wore brightly colored skirts with sparkles that reflected the light of the fire as they spun and twirled. Where was Milada? Did she know how to dance like this? Her hair, already wild, would be swinging around her shoulders. Who are these people? What am I doing here with them, enjoying their food, their music and their company?

I was lost in thought, when I felt someone next sit down next to me; someone breathing hard.

"Come and dance with us!" I looked to see who was sitting beside me. It was Milada.

"What were you thinking?" she asked me, once she had caught her breath.

"I was thinking by what luck or twist of fate I am here tonight among these people, people who dance at death,

17

having eaten the best food in my life, listening to the most beautiful music, feeling accepted," I told her.

"Will you stay with us?" she asked me.

Would I stay? I felt welcome, I was well fed; I liked this girl who had come over to talk with me. I had nothing to keep me in the village.

"If they will have me, yes, I will," I told her, wondering at my luck. "I can't think of any reason not to."

At that moment the music faded. Only Bora continued. He played a song that was almost sad, yet hauntingly beautiful. The people stopped dancing and made a circle around the dying fire. Everyone else also drew up and joined the circle and we all joined hands. Milada's was cool and soft. I held it tightly in mine. The song ended, but nobody moved. They all just stood there watching the fire die.

Then the men left the circle and started to shovel the embers to the side. I didn't know what to do. I saw that some of the boys stayed in the circle. Milada held on to my hand. I didn't want to let it go, so I stayed where I was and watched as the men dug a hole where the glowing fire had been. What a strange thing to do, I thought to myself.

But then I realized what was happening. Two men carried something wrapped in a light cloth and laid it in the hole. It was the body of a man. The hole was quickly covered up and the embers pushed back on top.

People started to wander away. Dragan was coming over. Milada dropped my hand as he approached.

"We will move camp at first light, just as we always do when someone dies," he said to me. "Goran, will you come with us?"

So, I was asked. I knew what I wanted to do.

Yes," I told him, "I would be honored to join you."

Bora, having wrapped his viol in a soft piece of leather, came and joined us by the dying embers.

Dragan said, "You can share a wagon with Bora. He will show you how we live."

Bora appeared with a smile. "I was hoping to have some company in my wagon." He said, Todor is taking Radko's place with the older ones so I would have been alone."

"When one leaves," Dragan said, "another comes. Go now and make your preparations. We will leave at first light."

I followed Bora into the forest, a little ways distant from the large clearing. We passed several wagons on the way to his. I wondered which one was Milada's. Did she share with the girl with the braids, Tanya? Or with the serious one who gave me a plate? Oh! Where was my plate? She told me to keep it with me.

"Bora," I said, "I was supposed to keep my plate and my knife! I forgot to take them."

"And you beaker, too," Bora said with a laugh. "It's all right. Someone would have picked them up. You can collect them tomorrow when you're settled in our wagon and have a place to keep them."

"Why do you all keep your own plates and things?" I asked.

"It's a way we divide the work," he replied. "If we all take care of our own things then no one person has to wash them all. And we always have them when we need them," he added.

That made sense, I guess. It was my mother's job to wash all the beakers and plates and pots and pans at the tavern. She was always very tired at the end of the day.

"Here we are," Bora said, indicating a fine wooden wagon with bright green trim. It was different from any wagon I had ever seen. It looked like a little cottage on wheels. We climbed up the steps and Bora pushed aside a curtain to reveal the room inside. There were two neat bunks, one on either side with shelves above them. Bora placed his viol one of them.

"This one bed's mine," he said. "You take that one. There are more blankets in the chest there if you feel cold."

A real bed! Extra blankets! A full stomach! New friends and a pretty girl that held my hand. I hoped that this wasn't all a dream but the start of a new life, a new adventure.

Chapter 6 – My First Morning

I slept soundly that first night in the wagon, maybe more deeply than I had ever slept before. A cool breeze riffled the curtains that covered the windows but I felt snug under my warm woolen blanket. At first light I heard Bora get up from his bed.

He looked over at me and saw that I was watching him.

"Good morning, Goran," he said. "It's time to get up. We will leave soon."

He pushed aside the curtain and I saw that the sun still hung low over the horizon as I followed him out of the wagon. Bora splashed some water on his head from a large bowl set on a chest beside the wagon. He rubbed his face, then shook his head sending droplets of water in all directions. Then he emptied the water at the base of a tree and filled the bowl up again from a large earthenware jar.

"Here you are," he said." Give yourself a rinse and then we can get some breakfast before the cooking wagon packs up for the journey.

I wasn't used to washing, except on Sundays sometimes or holidays. I wondered if this was another special day, but I didn't want to ask. I would hold my tongue and observe. I cupped my hands and dipped them in the bowl then rubbed my face with the refreshing water. When I put my hands in the bowl a second time the water turned a pale brown color. Was my face so very dirty! I rinsed it one more time, then dumped the water at the base of the tree as I'd seen Bora do, but quickly so he wouldn't see how dirty it was.

I followed Bora back to the clearing and enjoyed a breakfast of brown bread, cheese and delicious wild berries. This time, when I was done, I took a plate, knife and spoon with me. Bora told me to take some extra food, too, since we would be on the road until nightfall. People were bustling around me, collecting the large pots and pans and loading them onto a wagon. I heard some music playing in the distance, a lively tune that seemed to accompany the activity in the clearing. I caught sight of Tanya rounding up some young goats. A small dog following her, scattering the kids as she tried to tether them to a wagon. I went over to her to see if I could lend a hand.

"Good morning, Tanya," I said. "Let me help you with those goats. You catch one and the puppy scares the others away."

"Thank you!" she said, "That would be a big help. I love my animals, but sometimes it's hard to be with them all at once."

Together we managed to tether the six kids. The puppy never left Tanya's side.

"I remember that you don't like sheep," she told me as we sat for a moment on the lowest step of the wagon, "but how about dogs? How could you not love this one?"

I looked at the active ball of fur at Tanya's feet, busy nipping at her bare toes. I really didn't have time for dogs. My uncle had one who helped him herd his sheep; this little one did just the opposite. But Tanya was looking at me expectantly.

"He's active," I said, though it was pretty obvious. But then I had a question for her.

"Where is your friend Milada today? I didn't see her here."

"Milada sometimes has trouble waking up in the morning, especially after a night of dancing!" she told me. "We share a wagon with Zora, too. I'll bring her some food for now, and for later. Did Bora tell you we'll be on the road until nightfall?"

"Yes," I said, "he did. Do you know where we are going from here?"

"We go where the Baron leads us," she said.

"Who is 'The Baron'?" I asked.

"The Baron is the leader of our band. You saw him last night. At the head of the table," she explained.

"Is he Dragan's father?"

"Yes, and Layla's, too."

"Is Layla the beautiful girl with the black hair who sat beside him last night?" I asked.

"Yes, she is a little older than Dragan and ever so nice," Tanya replied. "Look! Here she comes now!"

I looked up and saw the girl coming toward us. The sun was still low, silhouetting her shape and giving it a glowing outline like an angel I saw once, painted on a church wall.

"Good morning! Good morning!" she said. The puppy pranced over to her and was licking her toes feverishly. "Are you ready to go? It's time to hitch up the horses and depart."

She bent over and scooped the pup into her arms, nuzzling it against her cheek. Then she handed it to Tanya.

"Take this little one with you. He's so active he might startle the horses," she told Tanya as she handed over the wriggling puppy. Then she turned to me.

"Goran, Dragan told me that you will be travelling with us. I want you to know how welcome you are!"

She took both my hands and drew me close to her in a hug. My head rested on her breast and I felt secure in a way that was half remembered half dreamt. I could have stayed there all day, but gently she let me go with a smile that touched my heart. My mother's face came into my mind. Not as it had been when she was ill, but from the time before when she would hold me in her arms and sing me to sleep, when there was time to take me by the hand and show me flowers blooming in the fields or angels on church walls. That seemed a long time ago. I'd missed that feeling and thought it was forever gone, and now I had it once again.

Chapter 7 – On the Road

      We went back to Bora's wagon. I put my plate and beaker on the shelf above my bed. I hadn't really looked around the night before, it was dark and I was tired after a long and unusual day. There was a high window at the back of the wagon covered by a thick brown curtain, now drawn to one side to let in the morning sunlight. Besides the bunks that lined the long sides of the wagon there was not much other furniture. A piece of wood hinged under the window could be rotated to provide a table, but now it lay flat against the wall secured for our journey. I noticed that the bunks could be opened like trunks providing storage beneath their straw mattresses and that there was a third one hinged closed above mine. Shelves over Bora's bed added more space to hold things as did rail hanging from the ceiling.

      I felt the wagon jerk and realized that Bora had hitched up the horse.

      "Let's go!" I heard him call and rushed out to join him on the wagon's high seat. Bora pulled the horse's head around and joined a line of wagons that were making their way out of the clearing to join the main road. Others fell in behind ours.

      "Where are we going?" I asked Bora.

      "We are traveling west," He replied.

      "West?"

      "Yes, where the sun sets," he said.

      I was expecting to hear the name of a village or town, not that we were heading toward sunset. I noticed that our wagon cast a shadow in our path.

      "Why are we going west and not in another direction?" I asked. "Are we going to a particular village?"

      "We go where the road takes us and stop when the Baron tells us we have arrived," he replied.

      There wasn't much to say to that. We bounced on in companionable silence for a while. One or two times Dragan or Layla rode by, waving and encouraging us on.

      When the sun was high, the wagon in front of us slowed down. We did the same, and the one behind us followed. Soon the whole line was stopped. The track was wide here and lined with tall trees on either side, providing shade for our midday meal and a short rest before continuing our journey to wherever it was we were headed.

Bora unhitched the horse. It moved to the side of the track to graze with the others. Then he brought a jug and bowl from the wagon.

"Here," he said, "I'll pour and you can rinse. Then you pour for me".

We washed our hands Bora returned the jug and bowl to their place just behind the bench in the wagon. He brought out a basket and handed me some bread and dried sausage.

"I have some apples, too, if you want them," he said.

"I'll have some later, thanks," I replied.

As we ate, I couldn't help myself from asking, "How come you can play the viol so well? Have you been playing a long time? You don't look much older than I am."

"I just picked it up the other day," he said. "Radko, the man we buried last night, was a great musician. He gave me the viol the day before he was killed."

"He was killed? Who killed him?" I asked, wondering if there was some secret violent tradition among these people. Maybe I would be next!

"It was an accident," Bora said. "He was fixing an axel on a wagon and the support slipped. He was crushed beneath the heavy wood. I guess it was his time to go."

"And he taught you how to play so well in just one day?" I asked.

"He didn't teach me. He put the instrument in my hands. It just felt right and I started to play."

I figured he was pulling my leg. "Can you all play like that, with no lessons and all?" I asked, regretting that some of my doubts might have come across in my voice.

"No," he laughed, "Milada tried to but it sounded like an angry cat!"

"But Milada isn't one of your tribe," I said, remembering what he'd told me the night before.

"True, I forget sometimes because she's been with us so long," he said. "Some of us can play music, others have other talents."

"Like what kind of talents?" I asked him.

"Some excel at the bow and never miss a target, others have knowledge of herbs and healing plants, some, like Tanya, are very good with animals," he replied.

I wondered what my talent was. I couldn't think of anything I did particularly well. As if he were reading my thoughts, Bora said, "I didn't know that playing the viol was my talent. I always liked listening to music, but everyone does! But when Radko placed the viol in my hands I just knew I could play it."

Maybe one day I would find my talent, too.

After we finished our meal we lay on our bunks and had a rest until thin rays of sunlight pushed their way through the weave of the curtain at the front of the wagon.

"Time to move on," Bora said as he hopped out of bed and down the wagon's steps to hitch up the horse.

I followed him outside and saw others doing the same, up and down the line.

"How did you know it was time to move," I asked him.

"I felt it was the right time," he said. And soon we were on the road again, the horse's hooves raising dust beneath the leafy green canopy with its first touches of gold. I munched on an apple, enjoying the rhythm of the movement of the wagon and the late afternoon sun on my face.

After a while I saw that we were veering off the main path and following a narrower track. It led down a small slope and then wound along beside a stream.

"We must be getting close to our new camp," Bora said. "We usually stay nearby a river or stream so we have fresh water for drinking and bathing."

"Do you wash every day?" I asked, thinking that this was a strange thing to do.

"Yes, of course," he replied. "We wash often and like to swim in the streams even if they are cold."

"But people just wash for special occasions," I told him. "Some say it isn't healthy to wash too much."

"I didn't really think about it. It's something we always do. I don't feel well if I don't wash, especially before we eat."

"Well I guess I'll have to get used to it," I said, remembering how refreshing the water felt on my face this morning. I wondered what else I would have to get used to on my journey with these strange yet wonderful people.

Chapter 8 – Life Among the Gypsies

Just as the sun was setting, I could see the wagons in front of us veering off in different directions.

"Where are they going?" I asked Bora. "They aren't keeping the line?"

"We have arrived." he said. "Here is where we will make camp."

"Is it just for tonight?" I asked wondering. "Will we move on again tomorrow?"

"The Baron will tell us tonight at the campfire," Bora replied as he guided the horse into a small clearing where two other men were unhitching horses.

"We'll make camp here with Vlada and Nico," he said as he hopped down the wagon's steps and released the horse.

The three horses wandered off together.

"Aren't you worried that the horses will run away?" I asked him, as I watched them disappear into the woods.

"They are going to find their friends," he laughed, "and something to eat. They are part of our band and don't want to be anywhere except with us."

I didn't know much about horses, but I did know that in the villages people kept their horses tied, or fenced, or in a stable. I'd never seen horses wandering free like this. I remembered Dragan's horse following him around the camp like a pet dog.

"Do you ride them or just use them to pull the wagons?" I asked.

"Some people like to ride. Some have a real talent for it, like the Baron and his children. The ones who do act as scouts and hunters for the band," Bora explained.

"But what about you? I have never been on a horse, myself," I told him.

"I play around with them sometimes, but I'm not always successful at staying on a horse's back," he confessed. "If you'd like to try it one day I'll ask Vlada to give us some tips."

"It must be fun to see the world from horse's height," I said.

"Well then, we can give it a go!" he told me with a grin. "But not now. Now it's time to get us a good hot meal!"

We grabbed our plates and followed our noses through the woodland until we came to a clearing bordered by a fast flowing stream. I was surprised at how quickly the fire had been lit and food set out to warm. Men tended the fire while the women chopped vegetables and bustled about their preparations. I saw Dragan coming toward us from the direction of the stream, his longish hair dripping with water.

"Been for a dip in the river?" Bora asked him when he got close to us.

"No," he said with a smile, "I just splashed some water on my face. It's refreshing after our journey. I thought about diving in, but the sun is down and soon it will be chilly. And besides," he added, "I'm very hungry!"

"Will we stay here for a while?" I asked him.

"We will stay for as long as we stay," he replied. "It is a pleasant spot."

"Is there a village nearby where we can get food to eat," I wondered out loud.

"The woods and the stream will provide us with plenty of food," Dragan replied. "Tonight we'll enjoy the remains of last night's feast. Then we'll see what tomorrow brings.
***

The next day I awoke to the sound of raindrops pattering on the wooden roof over my head. I could smell the damp earth and figured it must have been raining for some time. I looked over to where Bora slept, but his bed was empty. Even though I had eaten well the night before, I was very hungry. I got up and pushed open the heavy curtain. Someone had set up an awning in front of the wagon that sheltered its bench and a little space in front from the rain. The jug and bowl were there on the floorboards. The water in the jug was still warm, so it couldn't have been too long since Bora got up. I rinsed my face, took my bowl and spoon and followed my nose to breakfast.

I saw Milada sitting with Tanya and another girl at a long table. At its head, a woman dished out steaming porridge. She smiled at me when I held out my bowl to be filled. I smiled back, appreciating the way she filled it right up to the top!

I didn't think to look and see where Bora was; instead I sat on the bench next to Milada.

"Good morning, girls!" I said.

"Good morning, Goran," Tanya replied. "Did you have a good night's sleep?"

"I like the sound of the rain on the roof of our wagon," Milada said. "Do you like it or did it wake you up too early?"

"I like the sound of the rain, too," I told her, even though I had never really thought about it. "I slept well but woke up hungry!"

"The porridge will warm up your tummy," Tanya said. "It's made with milk fresh from the goats and honey from the woods."

I had eaten porridge before but this was different.

"What other magic ingredients are in it?" I asked.

The third girl, the one with the serious face, answered. "There is no magic ingredient," she said. "We use cinnamon and turmeric, spices from the east; they help to keep you warm and reduce dampness in your body on rainy days like today."

"This is Zora," Tanya said. "She knows all about spices and herbs."

"Hello Zora," I said. "I've never tasted anything like this before."

"These spices come from far away. We get them when we meet with the other bands of our tribe," Zora explained.

"Zora's teaching me," Milada interjected.

"Bora told me that you are not one of the band," I said, "that you have been with them for a long time, but, like me, are not one of them."

Maybe that was not a good thing to say, for Milada's cheeks turned red and she remained in tense silence until she got up and left the table with Tanya, who said she needed to tend to her animals.

After they had left, Zora turned to me and said, "Milada feels as if she is one of us, and we care for her as if she were. But there are some things that only people born to the tribe can know and understand."

Then she collected her bowl and spoon and was off. I felt as if I had really got off on the wrong foot with Milada. I wondered why I cared.

Chapter 9 – I Learn To Hunt

The coming days and months brought plenty of opportunity to learn the ways of the gypsy band. We travelled throughout the countryside, never staying for long in any one place. I watched how the villagers welcomed the gypsies; always bringing them gifts of nuts, dried fruits and fresh cheese. I enjoyed Bora's company, spending our days exploring the woods with the other boys. One of them, Nico joined Bora and me in the wagon. He taught me how to make snares that were great for catching rabbits.

At first, I hardly ever caught anything. I didn't understand how Nico, Bora and the others always managed to contribute to the cooking pots. I could see that my snares were as good as theirs; but still, no luck.

"Nico," I asked one morning, "Why can't I get any rabbits with my snare. I know I'm making it right; you even said so, but I never catch anything!"

"Are you calling the animals?" he asked me.

"Calling the animals?" I said, confused. "No, I stay really quiet so they don't know where I'm putting the trap."

"Ah," he said, "no wonder you aren't catching anything."

"I don't hear you calling any animals, either," I said. I figured he was pulling my leg.

"I call them with my mind," he told me.

"And they hear you and jump into your trap, I suppose."

"Yes," he said. Could he be serious? After all, he always caught a rabbit or bird in his snare.

"What do you say to them," I asked.

"I call to their spirit and ask them to come, to give themselves to help our band survive, "he replied.

"And they come?" I asked.

"You see that they do," he said with a smile, holding out the morning's first catch.

"Why would they come to get caught?" Talking to animals was strange enough, but expecting them to walk into a trap was hard to believe.

"We honor every living creature; everything in nature. All is provided for survival of the whole. Sometimes one needs to sacrifice a life to help others to live and thrive. We are always grateful for what we receive. The little animals are happy to be of service to us in this way. We take only what we need to live and respect all that lives around us."

What did I have to lose! Later that morning, when I lay my snare I whispered, "Hey, rabbits! It's me, Goran. I'm putting out a snare to catch you for our supper. I'd be happy and grateful if you come and get caught."

I hoped no one heard me talking to rabbits! I felt very foolish as I walked deeper into the forest. But when we came back to check our snares I found a very plumb rabbit caught in mine! The other boys gathered around and complemented – the rabbit!

I expected praise for finally catching one, and such a big one, at that. But no one said anything to me! Nico exclaimed to the rabbit, who sat there very calmly, "Well look at you! Finally you have come!"

Bora whispered in my ear, "we've been seeing that one for the last couple of days, but he didn't want to come. You must have been very persuasive!"

This was all too strange for me. I watched in silence as Nico quickly dispatched the rabbit. He removed its skin as if he were taking off its furry jacket and put it into one basket and the bare carcass into another.

Back at the camp I came across Milada and Tanya playing with the puppy. It had grown, though still not as big as the young goats, grazing contentedly nearby. Tanya tossed a ball make of wound rags and the puppy caught it and brought it back to her, wagging his tail with delight.

Milada saw me and waved, "Hello Goran, what have you been up to this morning?"

"Finally catching a rabbit," I said sitting down beside her to watch the pair play ball. I always felt more comfortable with Milada than with the others. Maybe because I knew that she was not one of them either, even though she had been with them so long and really wanted to be part of their band.

"Milada," I said. "Do you know they talk to animals?"

"I know Tanya does!" she replied. "Just look at them!"

I heard Tanya complementing the pup, "What a good dog you are," she cooed, "so cute and so clever, as well!"

"They call them to come to their traps," he whispered. "Then they kill them when they come."

Milada looked at me, wide-eyed, "They are our food, Goran," she said. "They offer their lives so we can live."

I thought of the stories I'd heard in the tavern. Hunters would come and tell about how they had stalked and killed deer or wild boar, bragging about their bravery. What would they say about inviting an animal to be caught?

I was thinking about it when I heard a rustle in the bushes. I turned to see Dragan mounted on his black horse coming into the sunny clearing. A blush tinted Milada cheeks when she saw Dragan lithely hop off his horse.

He gave one of Tanya's thick braids a playful tug, then picked her up by her waist and kissed her forehead. He waved at Milada and me, and then joined us on the mossy ground.

I didn't know what to make of this tall boy with regal bearing. In the towns and villages the nobles seldom mixed with the ordinary people. We would sometimes see them riding out to hunt or passing through the village on their way from one castle to another, mounted on fine horses, wearing richly decorated clothes, with little time for the likes of us.

For this band, Dragan and Layla were like the prince and princess. Yet, they were also just like us. Dragan and his father both wore black riding boots, polished to such a shine that they reflected the light from the evening fires. Some of the other men also had boots, but none took the time and effort to polish them as Dragan and the Baron did. In the towns, the nobles had servants to do their bidding; to do the jobs like polishing boots; but I'd often come across Dragan and his father, polishing their boots together, side by side, sometimes deep in conversation and other times lost in their own thoughts in companionable silence.

I looked up to see Dragan watching me, as if he knew what I had been thinking. Who were these strange people and what was I doing here among them?

Chapter 10 – A Mother Lost

We fell into a rhythm of travelling for a day, staying for a while near a village and then moving on again. On the days that we moved, we rose with the sun. Breakfast was whatever we had saved from the night before; the cooking pots were already packed in the kitchen wagon. At first I was worried that we would leave something or someone behind but after a while I realized that, for these people, moving around was as natural as breathing. Everyone knew what they needed to prepare, even the small children took care of themselves. I wondered about the old people. In the village there were always old people, old like I am now. Did they need help to get about? After a while I noticed that none of the members of the band were very old. I guessed that when someone got too old to move along with the band they stayed in a village somewhere along the road.

I enjoyed sitting on the high seat at the front of the wagon, chatting with the boys and watching the fields of ripening grain as we travelled down the dusty road. Every so often Dragan or Layla would ride by, waving a greeting. I was very curious about those two.

"Bora, who are your parents," I asked one day as we rattled down the road. I had noticed that the children lived together in their own wagons as soon as they were big enough to control the horses. Men and women sometimes shared a wagon together, but some lived with their friends. Only the very young ones stayed with their mothers.

In the villages, families lived together; the old ones, the grownups and their children. Of course, the children spent much of the day playing with their friends once their work was done, but they always returned home for their evening meal.

"Darko is my father," Bora replied. I thought for a moment and then the man called Darko came to my mind. He was a huge fellow with a thick black beard. He worked with metal, keeping the knives nice and sharp.

"And you mother?" I asked.

"My mother is traveling with the band of the South," he told me. "I haven't seen her for many years."

"What's the 'Band of the South'?" I asked him.

"Our tribe has four bands," he replied. "One travels in each of the four directions. Once in a while we all meet up to exchange knowledge, stories, herbs and often, people."

"Don't you miss her?" I asked, thinking how I missed my own mother now that she was gone. "How could she leave you like that?"

"She felt it was her time to go; that she had work to do with the band of the South," he explained. "I don't really miss her. I feel as though every woman in the band is a mother to all of us."

I remembered the feeling when Layla held me in her arms that first night. It reminded me of how I felt with my mother. I felt tears welling up in my eyes.

"I know that the Baron is their father, but who is Dragan and Layla's mother?" I asked, not wanting to dwell on that feeling and risk crying in front of Bora and Nico.

"That's a long story," Nico said. Bora nodded, "a very long story."

"The sun is still high, so we have a way to go yet," I said, hoping that they would tell me.

"You know that the Baron is the leader of our band," Nico began.

"Yes," I said. "Which band are you?"

"We are the Band of the West. In autumn we journey with the sun. In the spring, we head East; back to our center." Nico said.

"It is the leader's responsibility to keep the band safe. The leader decides when to move on and where to go," Nico explained.

"Something happened many years ago that endangered our band," Nico continued. "I was very small and don't really remember, but I know the story."

"Our band was camped for the winter not far from a prosperous town. The people there were very friendly and hospitable to us. Often, they would join us around our fire, enjoying our music, our dances and the stories we had heard about places far away. They brought smoked meat, preserved fruits and wine in return for the entertainment."

"The Baron was a great story teller. With the Baroness, Dragan's mother, by his side he could go on for hours, on those long winter evenings, telling of their travels. Her long black hair had highlights of red that came to life by firelight, and her smile had a light of its own. Layla watched over Dragan, who was just beginning to walk, and put him to sleep in the wagon that they shared. Sometime she returned to sit by her mother's side at the fire. But she was very young, too, and often fell asleep with her little brother."

"One afternoon, a man from the town came to our camp. "I need help," he cried, "Our king has been injured. He fell off his horse while hunting and the wound is bad. He sent me to ask if one of you would come with your healing herbs to help him.""

"The Baroness heard the request. " I will go," she said and went to collect her bag of herbs."

"She mounted her ebony mare and followed the man back to the King's castle, her long black hair flying behind her as they sped down the track."

"The king's wound was very bad indeed, but the Baroness knew how to treat it. She stayed at the castle by the king's bedside for many days, using her knowledge to set his broken leg and compresses of particular herbs to keep the open wound from festering. With her own hands, she prepared a special soup to regain his strength and helped him pass the time by telling him stories of her travels. Soon he was well enough to move around with a walking stick and was grateful for all her help."

"She returned to the camp as the preparations were being made to move on. The camp was packed up, the horses all hitched to the wagons. The Baron and Baroness rode down the line of wagons, as Layla and Dragan do now, to make sure everyone was ready to leave."

"When the last of the wagons took its place onto the road, instead of moving forward, they all stopped. No one knew what was happening. A hunting horn sounded and, as if out of thin air, archers appeared from the woods with their bows drawn."

"In all the stories the Baron told, there was nothing as frightening as this moment. There was nowhere to run. If the archers shot their arrows the whole band would be wiped out. The horn sounded again. The archers lowered their bows and melted back into the forest. The line of wagons began to move again."

"I can still remember that moment." Bora said, "even though I was very little. All those arrows pointing at us are not easy to forget!"

"What happened?" I asked, wondering why the archers were there in the first place and why they stood down.

"When the band stopped for the night, the story was told. The King sent the archers to stop our band from leaving."

"Why," I asked.

"The Baroness," Nico replied. "The King wanted her to stay with him."

"She left the Baron and her children to stay with the King?" I asked.

"It was not her choice," he answered. "The band needed to survive."

"You could have fought them!" I said.

"It is not our way to fight. The Baron and Baroness tried to reason with him but he was a King and was accustomed to being obeyed. He had the band surrounded and there was no doubt that we would all have been killed if the Baroness refused to stay."

"Do you go back to that place?" I asked.

"No, the King said that our band was no longer welcome there," Bora answered. "I'm sure he was afraid that the Baroness would want to come back to us."

By this time the sun was low on the horizon. I watched as the wagons in front of us turned off the main track and then spread out in a clearing. I sat in silence, thinking about how both Dragan and I had lost our beloved mothers and felt less wary of the dark-haired boy.

Chapter 11 - A Shadow in the Woods

"Grandfather," Anna said. This is a good story but I want to know about Milada!"

I realized my mind had wandered. I focused on the child and seeing her brought back my memories of Milada.

"One morning, I found her sitting alone under an oak tree, lost in thought," I began.

"What are you doing here, all by yourself?" I asked her.

"I'm just thinking," she said.

"Mind if I join you?" sitting down beside her.

"It looks like you already have!" she said with a grin.

We stated there for a while without saying a word. She was different from the other girls in the band. They all seemed to be very confident and wise beyond their years. Milada was a little younger that I was and curious about everything. She wanted to know all about me, where I came from, what I liked to eat; she even asked what I dreamt about. She was different, too, from the village girls I knew from the marketplace. She let her brown hair curl freely around her shoulders, not plaited in neat braids or tucked under a kerchief like they did. An unusual girl; and I felt very comfortable sitting there beside her.

"No hunting today?" she asked after some time had passed.

"We have enough for now," I replied. "Everyone seems to be taking it easy; enjoying the warmth of the morning. What about you? You girls always seem to be busy with something."

"There is so much to learn," she said. "Zora is teaching me about herbs. There are so many of them and a lot of them look alike! I don't know how I'll ever remember them all!"

"Zora," I said, "she's the serious girl who shares the wagon with you and Tanya?"

"Yes, that's Zora!"

"She must be about my age," I said. "How does she know so much about herbs?"

"I don't know, but she does; and it's good of her to teach me," Milada replied. "Especially since I wasn't born into the band," she added quietly.

"How did you come to be with them," I asked her.

"I was a very, very little girl. It's hard for me to remember the time before I came to live with the gypsies. I always loved being out of doors. I would run off into the fields and remember being told off by my by grandma. I don't remember my parents. My mother died when I was born and my father went away. I thought my grandmother was coming with me to the gypsies. I realized later that she had died."

"I had another name before I came here, but Layla called me 'Milada" and I liked it. The gypsies have many names in their life; one that they are given at birth, one that they choose for themselves as they grow up. When they marry, the Baron gives them a new one for their new role in the group."

"I love my life here. I can't imagine living in a house and never moving, never seeing different places, meeting new people and learning about the treasures of the forest," she exclaimed, looking into my eyes.

"I like it for now," I told her. "I've never meet such nice people. No one argues or raises a voice in anger. But it's strange, too. Parents don't live with their children; no one really knows where their next meal is coming from. I think that someday I'd like to find a nice village and make a life there."

"Not me!" Milada said.

She was about to continue when we heard someone calling her name.

"Milada, there you are," exclaimed Tanya, as she ran ever to where we sat in the shade. "I've been looking for you for ages."

"Here I am!" Milada said.

"So I see," Tanya said, "and look who else is here!"

"Only me," I said, with a grin. "Why are you looking for Milada so desperately?"

"Zora wants to show us something," she replied.

"I'd better come then," Milada said.

"Can I come along?" I asked. I wasn't sure I liked that Zora girl but I was curious about her.

"Yes," said Tanya. "Come on!" She grabbed Milada's hand and off they went; Tanya's braids swinging from one side to the other and Milada's wild mane trailing behind her.

I hurried to stand up and follow them before they disappeared into the darkness of the forest. I still wasn't used to spending so much time there. I was always told to stay on the roads, not to venture deep into the woods where there were unspeakable dangers. To see these two girls and the other children of the band being so comfortable here made me wonder if maybe the forest wasn't as dangerous as people thought.

But, no sooner than that thought crossed my mind, I needed to think again! Not far from the clearing I saw the girls standing, frozen. Tanya must have heard my footsteps because she slowly turned her face toward me. The look she gave me made me stop in my tracks. She moved her eyes to the right. I knew that she wanted me to look that way.

When I did, what I saw took my breath away. This is why we were told to stay out of the forest! A huge brown bear stood not ten paces away. It was looking right at us. Tanya turned back to face the bear.

I was ready to run, but I suddenly had the feeling that it was better to stand still. Then I heard Tanya say something. I couldn't make out what she was saying. Her voice was soft, but strong and in a language I had never heard before.

She still had Milada by the hand. Slowly, Tanya took a step backwards, taking Milada with her. She never stopped her soft chanting as slowly, step by step they came to stand just in front of me. The three of us slowly backed up into the clearing. When we were well away from the shadowy forest, Tanya said, with a smile "He was a big one!"

Milada exploded into a peal of laughter. "Did you see his face? I think he was falling in love with you!"

I looked at the two girls, giggling as if they had just come from a celebration rather than from a frightening encounter with a huge, wild bear.

Tanya caught her breath and looked at me. "Did you see the bear?" she asked me. "He was in the shadows."

"Yes, I saw it," I replied. "I'm glad it didn't see us!"

"Oh, but he did see us!" Tanya said.

"What?" I asked.

"He saw us, alright," said Tanya. "That's why I spoke to him."

"I heard you, but I couldn't understand what you were saying," I told her.

"That's because she was speaking *bear*, silly!" Milada said, giving me a playful punch.

I noticed the way her eyes sparkled. She must be pulling my leg, I thought.

"I told him that we would not hurt him and that he could continue his grazing in peace, "Tanya said.

"But aren't you afraid of bears?" I asked. "You know they can kill a full grown man; eat children like us for breakfast."

"I respect the creatures of the forest, but I am not afraid of them," she replied. "I know that they will not harm me if I do not threaten to harm them, or surprise them. I let them know I am a person, not another bear, by speaking to them. You know, they can't see very well, so they can be frightened by an unfamiliar shape."

I had never thought about bears being afraid of *me* and not the other way around!

"When you have knowledge," Tanya said as if reading my mind, "you don't need to have fear to protect you."

Chapter 12 – The Magic Cauldron

We skirted the wood and approached the wagons from the other side. I saw Zora's back hunched over a big copper pot. It was balanced on a tripod over a smoldering fire.

"I found Milada," Tanya called. "And Goran's here, too."

Zora looked over her shoulder at us as we approached. She was about my age, but her serious expression made her seem much older than her years. I noticed that she rarely smiled and joked like the other gypsy children. She always was busy with some concoction or other.

"Milada," she said, as she kept on stirring whatever was in the bubbling cauldron, "please come and keep things moving in here while I go fetch some more dandelion greens. Goran, will you please bring me some medium sized pieces of wood for the fire?"

Milada took the handle of the wooden stirring stick from Zora's hand while continuing the circular movement.

"That was a smooth move," I said, admiringly.

"It took me some time to learn!" she replied. "I don't know how many times I dropped the stick into the pot!"

"I'm going to check on the baby goats," Tanya said. "I'll see you later! Goran, you'd better go get that wood, if Zora comes back and find you here still chatting to Milada she'll be angry with you."

"Do you think she will be angry with me if I stay here with you for a while?" I asked Milada. "The gypsies never seem to get angry. But that Zora seems more serious than most; and she is just a girl! Imagine what she will be like when she grows up!"

"I don't think that she will be angry," Milada responded. "Maybe a little annoyed. If you hadn't come she would have collected the wood herself or asked Tanya to bring it. It may be important for the fire to stay at a constant heat."

"What is she cooking?" I asked, peering down into the pot. "If it's soup it's really thin!"

"Goran," she said, giving me a little push, "go and fetch the wood and I'll tell you when you come back."

I didn't like the idea of going back into the forest to find wood. After all, *I* didn't speak bear! Zora said to bring medium sized pieces, so I looked under the trees shading the wagons and soon collected an armful of twigs.

Milada was still stirring the pot when I returned. I was disappointed to see that Zora was back, feeding spiky green leaves into the cauldron.

"Just put the wood down over there," she told me, hardly looking up.

"See how the leaves turn a bright green," I heard her telling Milada. "They are releasing their oils. Then we keep the water moving until the color fades. And, as you know, as we stir we send our love and healing intention into the pot."

"What are you making there?" I asked.

Zora looked up from her work and said," We are making a tonic. Now that we have so many fresh greens we can prepare a large batch."

"Will you put it in a big barrel?" I asked.

"No, "she replied. "That's why we need the steady fire. We will boil it down into a concentrate and then strain and store it."

"How long does Milada have to keep stirring?" I asked, thinking that it would take a long time for so much water to boil down.

"Until her arms get tired, "Zora said. "Or until someone else comes along to take a turn to stir it."

"I can do it!" I told her, thinking it would be nice to give Milada a break.

"I don't know if you have the right intention," she said. "But you can put a little wood on the fire while I go and get more herbs."

When she had gone I asked Milada. "What did she mean about 'intention'?"

"The gypsies believe that all things are alive and carry and hold energy. Your thoughts are also energy," she told me.

"How can a thought be energy?" I asked. "Thoughts are not real things."

"That depends on what you mean by real," she said. "Before you do anything you have a thought and the intention to do it."

"What do you mean?" I asked, feeling confused.

"Goran, put your arm up in the air!" she said.

"Why?"

"Just put it up!" she said.

I raised my arm to my side. "Like this?" I asked her.

"Yes!" she said. "How did you do it?"

"I just put it up!" I said.

"Did it go up all by itself?" she asked.

"No, I wanted to raise my arm, so I did!" I told her. "Can I put it down now?"

"So you wanted to put it up; you had that desire; that's a thought" she said. "First comes the thought and then the action."

"I guess so," I said, letting my hand flop down by my side.

"If you touch another person, you can have many intentions," she went on.

"You could touch someone with care and affection" she said and stroked my arm. I felt a shiver of electricity pass through her fingertips. It ran right up my spine.

"Or you can punch someone," she said, punching me playfully. "It's a very different energy!"

"What kind of energy are you sending into that pot while you are busy punching me?" I asked her with a grin.

"Oh, my!" she exclaimed, "I forgot! I'm so busy trying to explain things to you that I am not doing what Zora asked of me."

She turned her face away from me and focused on stirring the pot. I could hear her murmuring in a low voice and suddenly, she looked very serious.

"Shall I go?" I asked her.

She looked at me again and said, "You can stay, but only if you are quiet!"

I added another twig to the fire then settled down beneath a tree to watch Milada at her work. Her skirt swished around her calves as she moved. I liked watching her; the way her wild curls picked up and reflected the filtered sunlight coming through the overhanging branches. I must have dozed off because I felt something warm besides me and when I opened my eyes I saw it was Milada.

"Who's stirring the pot?" I asked, sleepily.

"Tanya is taking a turn," she said.

I looked over to see Tanya's long braids swinging to and fro as she kept up the circular motion.

"Tell me again what it is you are cooking there?" I asked.

"It is a tonic to help people to stay healthy," she said. "In the autumn when the days turn cool, often people feel unwell. If we have a little tonic made from these springtime greens our body gets stronger and won't fall ill as easily. The gypsies say that it is easier to support health than it is to cure disease. We just need to be prepared!"

"What about the 'intention'?" I asked. "Is it one of their magic spells?"

Milada laugh rang out, "Magic spells?" she exclaimed, "Is that what you think?"

"Well they say the gypsies can do magic; that they can cast spells and bring luck – both good and bad!" I said.

"In all the years I've lived with them I haven't seen any magic!" she replied, hopping up from where we were sitting. She skipped over to where Tanya was stirring and singing. She placed her hand on Tanya's shoulder and the two girls had a short, whispered conversation.

Milada came back and plopped herself next to me again.

"I asked Tanya," she began, "I asked her is the tonic works without the intention we put into it."

"What did she say," I asked.

"She said that of course it would work," Milada replied, "but not as well as it works when it is infused with the energy of love."

Chapter 13 – A Surprise in the Pond

As the days, then seasons passed I felt more at comfortable with the gypsy band. One beautiful sunny morning I went with Nico and Bora to snare some rabbits. We quickly caught six fat ones and returned to the camp. Some of the women were already slicing onions and crushing garlic cloves for the thick stew.

"Greeting, boys," said one of the woman, "Bring those rabbits over here!"

"How did she know we've got rabbits?" I asked Bora, under my breath.

"Mother Miriana knows everything!" Bora whispered, raising his eyebrows.

"Come on, boys!" she said, "No time to lose! The longer the stew simmers, the better it will taste."

I was a little bit afraid of this woman who really did seem to know everything. She seemed older than most of the other gypsies. In the village, there were many old men and women, their hair gone white with age. In the gypsy band, Mother Miriana was the only woman whose hair was white like snow. But though her hair was white, her face was unlined and her step was as quick and supple as a young girl's.

Maybe because it was such a beautiful day and I was emboldened by the success of our hunting as I handed over the rabbits I asked her, "Mother Miriana, how did you know we were catching rabbits?"

"Ah, my boy," she said, looking so deeply into my eyes I found myself gazing down at the dusty ground beneath my bare feet, "a little bunny told me!"

I looked at her and saw a wide grin. I couldn't help but smile back even though I had no idea if she was joking or if she thought that rabbits could really talk to her. Were these people a little crazy? If there were, at least they were happy. And also very good cooks!

I stayed around the kitchen wagon for a while and helped tend the cooking fire. I wondered where Milada was. I usually ran into her sometime in the morning and often we shared the mid-day meal. But on this day she was not about. Maybe that Zora had her out collecting some wild plants. Tanya was nowhere to be seen either, though Zora was here, adding her herbs to the cooking pot.

When the stew was ready we all gathered at the long table. Milada and Tanya still did not appear. While Zora ladled some thick stew into my bowl I asked her, "Do you know where Tanya and Milada are today?"

"Tanya was tending to a sheep that is giving birth," she said. "I'm surprised that she's not here. It must be a difficult one. "

"Is Milada with her?" I asked.

"I don't know." Zora replied. "I left the wagon early this morning and haven't seen her."

I took a seat with Bora and Nico. The stew was very tasty but I missed Milada's good-natured joking and comments.

"Hey, Goran," Bora said, "Look over there."

He indicated the far end of the table. I saw a lady with bright red hair sitting next to one of the young men of the band.

"Who's that lady?" I asked. "I'm sure I would have noticed her before, with hair like that!"

"Todor wants to marry her," Nico reported, "He told me about her."

"Is she a gypsy," I asked.

"I don't think so," Nico answered. "They met in the village."

"Can he marry someone outside your tribe?" I asked.

"He can marry anyone he wants," Nico answered. "But whether or not the couple can stay with the band is the Baron's decision."

I saw that the both the Baron and his son were sitting with the couple. The young people looked happy, but the Baron's face was grim.

"Do may people join the band through marriage?" I asked.

"No, not many; it's a difficult adjustment for most people," Bora replied. "Unless they join us when they are very young," he added.

After we finished, we rinsed our bowls and spoons and returned to the wagon to put them away. I had a short rest and then wandered towards the brook. I followed it upstream a little ways from the camp until I came to a deep clear pool. The day was still very warm and the cool water was inviting. I left my clothes on a high rock and jumped in, making a big splash!

Floating in the clear water, I observed the overhanging branches and the creatures that shared the pond with me; birds chirped above, brightly colored dragonflies buzzed the surface of the water, little fish tickled my back from below. After a while I began to feel chilly so I got out and dried myself in the sun. As I was getting dressed I noticed movement in a small rock pool a little downstream of the pond. I moved closer, staying in the shadows so I wouldn't disturb whatever was it was.

At first, it was hard to see what was there. The pool was in the shade and the water flowed fairly quickly but I could see there was something moving and wanted to know what it was.

I kept very still and waited and watched. Slowly, my eyes could focus on what was happening beneath the water's surface. Salamanders! Lots and lots of slimy salamanders were wiggling and squiggling in the pool. They must be mating, I thought. I didn't realize that they would do this in such a big group. They found safety in the rock pool. The swimming pond was too deep and the water was flowing too fast in the main stream for them to congregate there.

So lost in thought was I that the sound of nearby footsteps startled me. I looked up to see Milada walking along a path beside the stream.

"Milada!" I called out to her forgetting, for a moment, the mass of salamanders. "Milada! Is that you? What are you doing here?"

"It's a long story," she said quietly. "Tell me what you are doing here instead."

When Milada approached I could see that something was wrong. She looked very tired, her hair had bits of weeds in it and her palms were red and raw. But I could see from her expression that it would not do to ask. Better to answer her question.

"I'm watching these salamanders," I told her, pointing to the rock pool. She came and sat beside me and we watched together in silence. I noticed another salamander slithering over a rock, bent on joining the others in the pool.

"Look! Here comes another one," I said. We watched as it skirted the edge of the group and, eventually pushed its way in to

47

join them. I thought about how this one creature had been all alone, but now was part of the group.

"Now it's one of them. It's not alone anymore," I whispered, more to myself than to Milada.

We sat watching the watery creatures, both of us lost in our own thoughts. I sometimes felt like that lone salamander. Wanting and needing to be a part of something bigger. I had enjoyed these months with the gypsies, but their ways were strange. They were always very kind to me, but I knew that I was not one of them; nor was Milada.

"Do you think that the gypsies really accept us as one of their group?" I asked her, thoughtfully.

Milada replied immediately, "Oh yes!"

"Do they, though? I see them talking among themselves and then stop if you or I come near. All right, I have only been with them for a little while, but you have been with them since you were small, haven't you?"

"Yes," she said, "Since the day my Grandma died, and that was a long time ago."

"And some of the things they do are strange," I said.

"Like what," she asked.

"They use funny words and sing those strange songs and they dance when someone dies. They are not like other people," I said, throwing a small stone into the stream.

It entered the water with a plop.

"No," she said, "They are happier. They know how to keep from getting sick, from getting old. They understand death in a different way."

"But that's strange," I told her.

"It may be strange," she said, "but it's good! And I can't imagine staying in one place like other people do. I like the way we move around seeing new places, visiting old friends and bringing them news. It's always a celebration when we arrive."

"Yes," I said, "I like it for now. But I don't know that I would always want to live like this. I'd like a place of my own somewhere, a little land to grow my food."

I saw some movement out of the corner of my eye. I'd forgotten all about the salamanders. The force of the stream pushed them all over the edge of the pool and the whole mass of them was flowing down the stream.

"Look at that, Milada" I said, "They don't even notice that they aren't protected anymore".

Chapter 14 – Hidden Words

We watched the mass of salamanders until they disappeared downstream.

Milada said, "I'm really, really, really hungry!"

"Let's go and find something to eat, then," I told her as I stood up and brushed the dust off my trousers.

I reached down to Milada to help her up, but when I took her hand she flinched with pain. I gazed down at it and saw that her palm was full of scrapes and dried blood. I reached out and took her other wrist. I turned it so I could see her palm. It was cut and bloody, too.

"Milada, "I said, "What happened to your hands?"

"I was lost in a field of millet," she said. "I wandered off the path. I thought I was heading toward the camp, but I walked and walked and didn't come to the road. The millet grew so high above me; I lost my sense of direction and couldn't find the way out for a long time. My hands are cut from pushing through the stalks of the tall plants."

"No wonder you looked so upset," I said. "But here you are; you managed to find you way."

"I saw some light coming through the millet and thought that I had come to the road," she said. "But it wasn't the road at all; it was this stream. At first I didn't know which way to go, but then I remembered what Layla told me once. When you don't know what to do, just sit quietly and wait until you can hear the answer in your head. Somehow, the answer is always there, but we need to be still to hear it."

"I sat by the stream and let my thoughts flow away with the tinkling water. After a while, the water seemed to say 'go, go, go with the stream...go with the stream.' I decided to follow the direction of the water. I remembered that it flows to the river. The village is on the river and our camp is near the village. And here, I found you!"

"Do you feel better now?" I asked her.

"Yes," she replied. "Just really, really, really hungry!"

We walked back to the camp together. I could smell some meat roasting and noticed that Milada was picking up our pace. She must have noticed it as well.

"I hope the meat is ready." she said, licking her lips.

"Me, too," I told her as we hurried on.

We joined the others congregating near the venison, turning slowly on the spit. I noticed Tanya sitting near the fire with something cradled on her lap.

"Come and see," she called to us. As we approached I saw that she was holding a tiny lamb.

"The mother sheep gave birth to two lambs but would only give milk to the first-born," she explained. "It happens sometimes."

Milada reached out to touch the little lamb. Its fleece must have felt soft against her lacerated palms.

"Look at your hands!" Tanya exclaimed, "What have you been up to all day!"

"It's a long story," she sighed.

"Zora's over there. Go ask her for something to help your hands mend quickly," Tanya said, still looking at the baby lamb sleeping contentedly on her lap.

Milada went off to find Zora.

"What can Zora do to help Milada's hands?" I asked.

"Zora knows many remedies that can help the wounds to heal faster and take away the pain," Tanya said.

"How does she know?" I asked. She's not much older that you, but seems to know so much about plants and things."

"Each of us has a talent," Tanya said, "something that we are naturally good at."

"You are good with animals," I told her. "I've noticed that you are always taking care of them and that they respond to you,"

"Yes," she said, "I love them and they can feel it. I know how to care for them. Zora has a talent for healing people. Mother Miriana also has that talent."

"And Bora can play the viol and hunt rabbits," I said.

"What is your talent, Goran?" she asked.

I had never really thought about it. I knew it wasn't taking care of sheep. This little lamb was cute and all, but it would soon grow up into a woolly, smelly beast!

"I don't really know," I told her.

"One day you will," she said with a grin. "Look, they are slicing the meat. Let's go and eat! Will you hold the little lamb so I can get up without waking her?"

I awkwardly tried to lift the lamb without disturbing its slumber. For sure taking care of sheep was not my talent! Once Tanya was standing she held out her arms for the lamb and disappeared in the direction of the wagon she shared with Milada and Zora. I saw them passing the Baron's colorful wagon. He and his son were deep in conversation and didn't look up when Tanya passed by. I thought that was strange, since Dragan was obviously very fond of her.

I went to my wagon to wash up and get my plate and knife. Soon Tanya and I were back at the long table, anxious to enjoy the succulent meal. I was happy when Milada and Zora joined us. But, though the food was delicious, there was a strange atmosphere at the long table that night. The Baron and Dragan eventually took their places at the head of the table, but they were both lost in their own thoughts.

Milada was quiet, not even asking her usual barrage of questions, and for once, even I could think of nothing to say. When we'd finished eating, the Baron, Dragan and some of the other gypsies moved away from the table, still whispering between themselves.

"I wonder what is going on today," I said, as I watched the gypsies get up and join the group that was gathering by the embers of the cooking fire.

"I know the Baron called Dragan to see him this morning when we went out for ride on Dobro," Milada said.

"You went riding with Dragan?" I exclaimed, surprised she hadn't mentioned it before. "How could he leave you to get lost in that field?"

"I didn't plan on getting lost," she told me sharply.

"You planned to spend the day with the Baron's son?" I asked.

"Well, I like his company. I like riding with him," she said, defensively.

"So why didn't you ride back with him when the Baron summoned him?" I said.

"It was such a beautiful morning. I didn't want to go back," she replied. "I really didn't think I would get lost. I told you. Can we talk about something else, please?"

I knew she liked that boy, Dragan. What girl wouldn't like a boy like that; so self-assured and charming? Maybe a little too charming. I wasn't sure if I trusted him. I glanced over and saw that he and the Baron were still deep in discussion with the group by the fire.

"What do you think they are talking about over there?" I asked Milada.

"I really don't know," she said, "but it must be something important. Let's go and see."

But when they noticed us approaching, people went quiet, until no one spoke at all. Then the Baron broke this strange silence.

"Good evening, my children" he said. His voice was calm, and he was smiling but his eyes looked very serious.

"Please would you two go find Mother Miriana?" he asked. "We would like some of her special tea. Tell her we need the *very special* brew. She will know what you mean."

"Certainly, Baron." Milada said. She grabbed my hand and turned toward Mother Miriana's wagon.

"Ouch!" she exclaimed, letting it go. She must have forgotten about the cuts on her palms.

"What's the rush?" I asked, running to catch up with her.

"The Baron wants his tea," she said.

"I think he just wanted to get rid of us," I told her.

Milada stopped running and turned to face me. "Why do you say that?" she asked.

"Because it's true. Haven't you noticed that lots of times they stop talking when you or I come near? We live with them but we are not trusted like the others."

"That's not true!" she exclaimed. "Maybe they don't trust *you*. You've only been with us for a while, but I've lived most of my life with them. Why wouldn't they trust *me*?"

"If you don't believe me just observe," I said. "They are different from us. We will never be totally accepted in their lives."

"If I marry Dragan they'll have to accept me!" she snapped, then dropped her eyes to the ground as if she regretted her words.

"They'll never let you marry Dragan!" I said. "And besides, I always thought you would marry *me*."

"What!" Milada exclaimed and raising her eyes to mine. I'm not sure what she saw there, but after a moment she said, "Ha, you're joking!" and slapped my shoulder playfully.

"Ouch!" she had forgotten her hands again. We both burst out laughing.

Milada said, "Let's go find Mother Miriana and see about the Baron's *special* tea.

Chapter 15 – Magic Dust

Through the darkness of the evening, I could make out the shape of the white haired woman sitting at a small fire beside her wagon. I was getting over my fear of Mother Miriana, but I was less than comfortable running the Baron's errand. The woman looked up as we approached the crackling fire. Steam rose from a big black pot suspended over it.

She looked up at us and said, "Good evening, children."

"Good evening, Mother Miriana," Milada greeted her in return.

I wondered what strange potion she had brewing in that cauldron.

"I'm preparing tea," she said, as if she read my mind.

I tried to hide my surprise at her comment and quickly told her, "The Baron would like you to make some of the special tea."

"The *very* special tea, please." Milada added.

"It will be ready soon. Would you like to sit by my fire for a while until it brews?" she said.

Milada and I joined Mother Miriana by the fire on the worn, once colorful carpets that covered the bare earth. While we waited for the tea to be ready a young man in a red jacket and high riding boots approached from a path through the forest.

"Good evening, Madam," he said, addressing the old woman. "I seek Mother Miriana. Are you she?"

Mother Miriana observed him for a moment and then replied, "Why do you seek this woman?"

"I have been told that she has magic," the young man replied.

"Magic?" Mother Miriana said without taking her eyes off his face.

"That she can cure the sick. Help people solve their problems...," he said.

"What you speak of, young man, is knowledge, not magic," she told him very seriously. I was surprised when she glanced in our direction and gave us a quick wink.

"I am she," she said, turning back to the young man. "Tell me what you want and I will help you if I can."

The young man knelt down beside Mother Miriana and said, "My father died two years ago. He left me an estate with much land. I have men who work the land for me, but although they seem to have enough to eat there is nothing coming in for my family or me. I have debts to pay. If I don't make some money from my land I will be ruined. I heard from my cousin that you have magic dust that can make the land produce more. Please, Mother Miriana, can you give me some of that magic dust to make my land more fertile?"

"And what will you give me if I give you this magic dust?" she asked him.

"I have a gold ring that my father left me. I will give that to you." With these words he took a gold signet ring off his finger and offered it to Mother Miriana.

"Just a minute," she said, taking the ring and disappearing behind the curtain of her wagon.

The wagon blocked his view but I could see Mother Miriana climbing out the back of it. She scraped some dirt from the ground and put it in a small box. I saw Milada watching her, too. I gazed over at the young man; he touched his finger where the ring had been. It must be very valuable, being real gold and all. Looking more closely at his face I remembered having seen him before.

"I think I've seen you in town; in the tavern," I said.

"I sometimes go there to hear the news from the other farmers," the young man replied, still rubbing this finger. I could see that the skin was whiter there. He must have been wearing it for a long time. I wanted to ask him about it, but before I had a chance to continue the conversation Mother Miriana returned.

"Here is your magic dust," she said, handing him the small box.

I saw that it was the one she had just filled with dirt! Milada looked at me. I wondered if she was thinking what I was thinking; that this man had given a valuable gold ring in exchange for a box of common dirt!

"Now here is what you must do with it to make it work," Mother Miriana continued. "Every morning as the sun is rising and every evening as it is setting you must sprinkle some of this magic dust in the four corners of your land. You must not miss even one day or the magic will be undone. Is that understood?"

"If I do this I will prosper?" he asked, hopefully.

"If you follow my instructions, yes, you will," the woman assured him.

"Thank you, Mother Miriana, I will do as you say," said the young man as he stood up to take his leave.

"One more thing," Mother added. "When the box is empty come back here and tell me your experience."

"Certainly I will. A thousand thanks!" The young man disappeared down the path. He seemed relieved to be done with his business here and to return to the safe familiarly of his village.

I looked over and saw Mother Miriana smiling.

"Mother Miriana, that was clever of you to take that man's gold ring for a box full of dirt! I mean *magic dust!*" I said with a laugh.

"I know of that young man. He is lazy, a wastrel. His father left him a large inheritance and he spent most of it on drink and gambled the rest away," Mother Miriana said.

"I've seen him through the tavern window playing games of chance," I said, realizing why he looked so familiar.

"Although his land is good he never checks on the farmers who work it. Of course, they keep everything for themselves since their landlord cannot be bothered to do any work himself. There is no magic. I told him at the start; there is only knowledge. When he goes around his land sprinkling the *magic dust* the farmers will see him. He will get to know them and keep up with the day-to-day doings on his land. And he *will* prosper," she said, "through knowledge, not magic."

"That golden ring must be very valuable," I said.

"To the young man it is," she said. "I could have just given him the "magic dust" but then he would not value it. He would not make a point of following my instructions to visit his land."

Mother Miriana turned away from me and back to the steaming pot.

"The Baron's tea is ready. Will you help me carry it?" she asked.

She poured the hot tea into three smaller pots. We took one each and followed Mother Miriana back to the main fire where the conversation continued. She told us to leave the tea on the table.

"Hey, Goran," Bora called, "Some of the lads are playing a game. Come and join us!"

I looked at Milada to see if she wanted to play.

"I'm going to find Tanya and see how the little lamb is faring," she told me. "You go play with the boys!"

"Come on Goran," Bora said, "Let's go!"

Bora and I ran to catch up with the others. We ran for a while on a path through the woods then the trees opened up into a grassy field. There was no moon, but the stars shone brightly and soon my eyes became accustomed to the darkness and I could make out the shadows of children moving.

"What is the game?" I asked as we reached a group of around twenty boys and a few girls, too.

"We try not to get caught!" Bora said. "Look, Nico is starting."

I saw Nico running around the children while they tried to avoid him. But he was too fast for Jolay! The two of them clasped their hands and, as a pair, began again to try and catch the others.

"There are still two hands that catch," Bora explained, "but now one is Nico's and one is Jolay's!"

The boys were coming our way so Bora sprinted to the center of the field. I went the other way and was able to avoid capture!

One by one the children were joining the chain. Only the two at the end could catch people. It was funny to watch when one end went one way and the other end went the other way, but the children never released their grip. We were all laughing hard. Then I felt a hand on my shoulder. I was caught! It was fun being on the end of the chain, running around trying to catch one of the few children left. Soon I tagged one of the little girls. She giggled and took my hand and off we went again.

Before long all the children had been caught. The last one to be captured led the others in a sort of dance, spiraling the line into a tight circle. We all came closer and closer together, still laughing. I found myself wishing it was Milada's hand that I held in mine, and her hair tickling my ears as we all stood shoulder to shoulder, back to belly under the stars. When we couldn't get any closer, Nico let out a loud whoop. We all joined in and the circle broke with all of us running out from the center.

"That game has worked up an appetite!" I told Bora. "Let's go see if there is anything left from the meal that was can munch on."

We hurried back to the camp.

"Look there!" said Bora.

I looked over to where the Baron and his son sat. They weren't alone. I knew the gypsies liked their animals but I'd never seen anything like the scene before me. Dragan's horse, Dobro, lay beside the boy, with his massive black head in Dragan's lap! Bora went over and had a few words with Dragan; they both broke out in laughter.

We found some meat and bread on a small table near the kitchen wagon and had our snack. We were heading back to the main fire when I noticed Milada, Tanya and Dragan's beautiful sister, Layla, chatting nearby. Bora and I went over to where they sat.

"'Evening, ladies," I told them with a little bow.

"You all seem happy, boys," Layla said, laughing herself.

"What's so funny, Goran?" Milada asked with a smile.

"It's that Dobro," said Bora, his eyes sparking. "You know the Baron wanted to speak with Dragan today about a matter of importance to the group."

"Yes, he was called back from our ride this morning for some important matter," she said.

"Well, you know how much that horse loves him," Bora continued. "He kept looking over Dragan's shoulder. When Dragan told him to go, instead of going he just sat down next to the Baron and put his head on Dragan's lap!"

The girls must have been sitting there for a while because Layla said, "We've had enough talk for one night. Bora, play us a tune on your viol to soothe us into a good night's sleep."

Bora ran to our wagon and brought back his instrument. As he played by the fire the gypsies listened for a while then headed to their beds. It felt good, sitting under the stars with Milada. We stayed until Bora put down his viol and bid us both good night.

"It's been a long day," said Milada. "It's time for bed."

When I helped her up I saw that her hands looked better. As we companionably walked to our wagons, I put my arm around Milada's shoulders. When we reached her wagon, without thinking I

59

planted a little kiss on her cheek. Then I hurried on to my wagon, without a word.

When I entered, Bora was just getting into his bed. I heard Nico's soft breathing and could tell that he was already fast asleep.

"I can see you like Milada," Bora whispered, "and that she likes you, too."

"There's something special about her," I said. "I've never known a girl like her before."

"Love is in the air these days, it seems," he said. "Todor is madly in love with the redhead. People have been talking about them all day; wondering if the Baron will allow her to join him in the band."

"Do you think he will?" I asked.

"It's a serious decision," Bora replied. "We have many secrets."

"Why do you keep secrets from people? I thought the gypsies wanted to help people and to share their knowledge," I said.

"We do," he said, "but there are some things that we need to keep to ourselves. It's for our own safety."

"Do you think that Todor would leave the band; stay in the village with this woman?" I wondered aloud.

"If he had to decide today," Bora said, "yes, I think he would. But that's because he is in love."

"Being in love makes you crazy!" I said.

"Sometimes it seems that way," Bora quietly commented, drifting off to sleep.

I lay there in the silence of the night, wondering if I was crazy to be falling in love with Milada.

Chapter 16 – On the Way to the Village

I woke up the next morning to the sound of birdsong, feeling happy and hungry. I got up and rinsed my face with the water that one of the boys had thoughtfully left for me in front of our wagon and then went to find some breakfast.

I was very happy to see a huge wheel of cheese on the long table. I cut myself a large slice, thinking how lucky I was to be invited to share the gypsies' abundant food.

I had my mouth full when I saw Milada approaching.

"Are you going to eat all that cheese?" she asked me. "I remember that you like cheese, but that's a lot!"

I felt my cheeks flush. She must be thinking about that first day we met in the market and how I tricked the ladies into giving me some cheese to eat.

"Yes, I like cheese," I quickly said, to hide my embarrassment, "but I'll share this with you."

I sliced off a generous piece of the cheese and passed it to her.

"I'm going to the village with Zora," she said.

"I'm coming, too," I told her, thinking that it would be fun to spend the day in the village with Milada.

When we finished our breakfast we went to find Zora at the wagon that they shared.

When she saw us, she said, "Are you ready to go?"

Milada replied, "Yes, and Goran is coming with us, too!"

"Good. Please, would you both help me carry these things?" Zora said, handing us each a bundle wrapped in vibrant colored cloths.

On our way to the village, Milada asked about them.

Zora explained, "It is a special color made from the stamens of the crocus flower, called saffron. It takes thousands of flowers to get enough stamens to make the dye, and the flowers grow very far from here and are hard to come by. It adds to the healing power of the herbs."

"Each color has a particular vibration. By storing the herbs in different colored cloths I am subtly enhancing their properties. It makes them work better to help people recover more quickly."

Milada looked at me as if she thought I couldn't understand what Zora was saying. It's true that I wasn't sure what she was talking about, altering properties and vibrations and how colors could make someone feel better. I knew Milada was interested to learn all these things, but I can't say I was. But, as usual, Milada wanted to know everything.

She asked Zora, "Can you explain how a color can help a person get over a sickness? I don't understand how that can be."

Zora thought for a moment then replied, "I will try to explain it to you. Things seem solid, but they are not. Think about water. In the winter when it is very cold, we have icicles hanging off the roof of our wagon, right?"

"Yes," Milada replied and I nodded, starting to pay more attention to her words.

"Usually water is a liquid. It takes the form of whatever container it is in. When we put it in the pot and heat it up for tea, have you noticed the steam that rises above the pot?" she asked.

I had some experience with that! I said," Yes, I burnt myself on the hot steam more than once."

"That steam is water, too, but in another form."

"But what does all this have to do with color and healing?" Milada asked impatiently.

"I want you to understand that everything that appears to be solid, like the icicle, is really not solid and static but is a pattern of movement, like steam," she explained. "In things that appear to be solid the movement is slower, in liquid faster and in gas or steam even faster."

"But what about color?" she asked.

"The colors we see are a reflection of the light on a surface. We see different colors because different colors absorb and reflect different frequencies of light," she told us.

Here she started to lose me. "This is too complicated," I told her.

"Shall I stop?" replied Zora.

Milada said, "No, no, please go on."

"At night we don't see colors" Zora continued. "Everything seems to be different shades of gray. That is because there is no sunlight to reflect and produce the colors we see."

"What about the rainbow," Milada asked. "There is every color in a rainbow!"

"We see a rainbow when there is moisture in the air while the sun is shining," she said. "The tiny drops of moisture separate the white light of the sun into all its seven colors. Each color holds a particular vibration. When the colors are separated we see each one side by side in the rainbow."

"I always thought the rainbow was a magic sign," I told them. "That's what everybody thinks. I don't know about this air moisture business…"

"Call it magic if you like," Zora said.

For a while Zora stopped talking. What she was saying didn't make any sense. But how can a rainbow be made of sunlight? Where do all those colors come from? It has to be magic of some kind. She just isn't telling us how it works. Probably, she doesn't know.

After a while, of course Milada had to ask a question.

"Zora, please tell me how the color makes a difference to your herbs."

Zora replied, "Just like everything else, our bodies are not solid as they appear but are also a pattern of movement. Different parts of our body resonate with different frequencies of color and also of sound."

Now this was really crazy talk. I only half listened to their conversation and amused myself by kicking a little stone as we walked.

Zora continued, "When someone gets ill it means that their body is out of balance. It could be from something outside of them, liking eating food that is spoiled or poisoned or it could come from a strong feeling like sadness, anger or fear. With herbs, with color and with sound, too, the body can be brought back into balance. The body is a very subtle system. It responds to subtle treatment. A bit of color applied in the correct spot, the right sound, the right tea can all help a person to heal."

"How do you know which is the right color, sound or herb?" Milada asked.

"You learn from observation and experience, Milada." she replied.

"Why this special yellow and the blue?"

"Yellow is good for the stomach and spleen," Zora told her. "It helps to calm a person's worries and fear. The dark blue is for the head. It soothes a headache and can help bring down a fever."

"Zora, how do you know all of this?" Milada asked.

This conversation went on and on, all the way to the village. I almost wished I had stayed back at the camp, or gone hunting with the boys.

When we were at the village gate, Milada asked Zora, "How do you know all of this?"

"It is the wisdom of our people. I have always known it," Zora replied.

"Do all the gypsies know?" she asked.

"All have some knowledge about how to heal. I seem to have a talent for it, like Bora has for the viol. But we all understand the true nature of things," she said.

Chapter 17 – A Trip to Market

As we entered the village a group of people hurried over to us.

"There you are at last," a woman said, taking Zora's arm. "Come quickly, his fever is rising."

We hurried along to the woman's house. When we reached the doorway, I hesitated. I felt out of place among these women.

"This isn't a job for me," I told them. "I'll find you later."

I gave Milada the herbs that I'd been carrying and headed off to the market square. I passed the cheese stalls and the sausage sellers. It felt strange not to be plotting how to trick them into giving me something to eat! I wandered between vendors selling all sorts vegetables, onions, fresh greens, strings of garlic. There were stalls selling bright trinkets and colorful ribbons. I thought about buying one for Milada but I didn't have any coins. I didn't need any money now that I was living with the gypsy band, but it would be a good idea if I could earn some to put away for when the time came for me to leave them and settle down in a village.

I sat in the sun beside the fountain and watched the people going about their business; children running to and fro, women with large wicker baskets doing their morning shopping, men hawking their wares. Across the square, I saw a flash of red hair and realized it was the young woman who had been at the gypsy camp. She was sitting outside the tavern with another woman. Todor's girl was pleasant looking but there was something I didn't like at all about her dark-haired friend, who was doing most of the talking. The redhead seemed relieved when the other woman got up and left. A moment later I saw Todor join her at the table. Her face brightened when he sat down beside her.

I watched a pretty girl hurrying past, then realized it was Milada! She was waving at me. Before she could call my name I put my finger to my lips to signal her to stay quiet.

She sat down next to me and said, "Hello! What's going on?"

I pointed at the tavern.

"I think that's the woman Todor wants to marry!" I whispered. "Look at that hair. Have you ever seen such a color?"

"I like it. It's red like fire," she said. "Once on our travels we stopped at a village where many people had hair that color; men, women and children, too. The little ones were so cute with their red hair and little brownish dots across their noses. Maybe she is from that village."

"Shh. Don't let them hear you." I told her, pulling back behind the edge of the fountain as Todor looked our way.

"Why not?" she asked. "We all know about the woman."

"I don't know. I just think it's better if they don't know we're watching, that's all," I said quietly.

"Well, I'm not watching. I'm on my way to the market place. Do you want to come with me or are you happy here, in hiding?" she asked.

I was startled when she held out two large silver coins.

"You can buy a lot with that much money," I told her, fingering the two heavy disks.

"Please come with me. You know better how to buy things in the marketplace," she said.

She told me that the woman in the house asked her to go and buy bread, cheese and some vegetables for soup. She said that she had never bought things in the market before. We followed the smell of freshly baked bread to a bakery stall. A fat man was just removing the bread from a large clay oven. The hot loaves looked and smelled delicious!

The baker's red-faced wife stood at the front of the stall. Milada said, with a big smile, "I would like to buy one of those, please," indicating the freshly baked bread.

"That will be three Florins," she said.

I was shocked to see Milada offering one of the coins! I quickly grabbed her hand and hoped the woman hadn't seen it.

"I can see you don't know how to shop," I whispered, "You never pay the first price!"

I turned to the baker's wife and said, "Madam, although your bread smells good it is hardly worth the princely sum of three Florins. We will give you one."

Milada looked shocked. I elbowed her ribs so she wouldn't speak.

"Young man, our bread is the finest in the village. And you can see it is fresh; it has just come out of the oven. For one Florin I can give you a loaf from yesterday. If you want a fresh loaf then you must pay the price," the baker's wife replied.

"Thanks for your offer, but day-old bread is not for us, " I told her, taking a step away from her stall. "I will find another baker. I've heard there is a much better one on the other side of the square. Come on, Milada. Let's go to the other baker."

I took Milada's arm and led her away from the stall.

"Come back," the woman called to us. "I can let you have the fresh loaf for two Florins; save you the walk to the other side of the square."

"Wait, Milada," I said, as if it were she who had quibbled about the cost, "two Florins is a fair price."

Milada gave me a coin and I paid the woman for the bread. She handed it to Milada who stowed it safely in her basket while I counted the change.

"Thank you, ma'am. I'm sure your bread is delicious; certainly the best in the village," I told the baker's wife with a smile. She was shaking her head, but couldn't help smiling back at me as we went on our way.

"I think I'll let you do all the shopping," Milada said, with a sigh. "This is too much work for me!"

"You'll get used to it. It's a game we all play," I told her as we headed for the vegetable sellers.

Soon we'd purchased all the items that the woman had asked for. We still had one of the silver coins and several copper florins.

I smelled some nuts roasting over hot coals.

"Shall we buy some of those roasted nuts to eat on the way back?" I asked Milada.

"This is not our money," she said. "We need to bring the change back to the lady."

"I don't think she would mind," I told her. "My careful shopping saved her money!"

"No, Goran. I wouldn't feel right using her money to buy something for ourselves," Milada said. "Come on, she's waiting for these vegetables to make the soup."

I didn't see why we couldn't buy some nuts with the extra money, but I didn't want to argue with Milada. We headed back through the main square on our way to the woman's house. Todor was still sitting with the red-haired woman. He recognized us and waved.

"Hello there, you two," he called. "Come and meet Emilia."

We ran to the tavern.

"Goran, Milada," Todor said, "I would like you to meet Emilia. I am hoping to make her my wife."

"I am happy to meet you both," the redhead said, "Are you part of Todor's clan?"

Todor said, "My clan has adopted these two. Milada has been with us most of her life, young Goran for a year or so, isn't that right?"

"Yes, just about a year, "I replied, I couldn't help staring at the woman's hair. She was sitting in the sun and close up it looked even brighter than it had in the light of the campfire. Milada seemed more interested in a strange shaped bundle at the woman's feet.

"Todor, I know that is your instrument wrapped up in the rug, but what is that other thing next to it?" Milada asked, with her usual curiosity.

Todor told Emilia, "Milada is famous for her questions. She is always asking questions! Why don't you answer this one? "

Emilia said nothing but reached across Todor and picked up the bundle. It was another musical instrument.

"This is my lyra,' she said, plucking its short strings.

"Oh! Would you play us a song?" Milada asked.

I was beginning to feel hungry and didn't really want to sit around listening to music now.

"Don't we have to deliver those vegetables," I said, knowing that Milada would feel guilty for keeping the woman waiting.

"Yes, we do. But can I come back later for a song?" she said.

Emilia said, "We will be here for a while, won't we?" looking at Todor. "I told my friends to come and meet us here."

Todor nodded. "This is as good a place as any to enjoy the sunshine."

Milada and I left them there and hurried back to the woman's house to deliver our shopping. I hoped that Milada would forget about coming back!

Chapter 18 – Good Soup and Magic Rocks

Soon Milada and I were back at the house where we'd left Zora. We knocked on the heavy front door but no one answered. I noticed that it was a very well-made door, with shiny brass hinges and lock. We knocked again. Lucky for us the door was not bolted shut so when no one came to the door we let ourselves in to the dimly lit room.

When my eyes grew accustomed to the shadows, I was amazed at the richness of the furnishings. Heavy drapes hung from the ceiling to the floor, keeping in the warmth of the hearth but also keeping out any daylight. The fireplace had a mantelpiece of polished wood, very smooth to my touch. There were fine silver plates lined up on it and delicate vases and bowls placed around the room.

"These people must have a lot of money," I said.

"Maybe they do, but all the money in the world won't help the man get over his fever. Only Zora's knowledge can do that," Milada replied.

"Does Zora take money for her healing?" I wondered out loud.

"She doesn't ask for any," Milada told me. "She says she is just sharing her gift. Sometimes people insist on giving her money or presents of food for our group."

I guess she heard our voices, because the woman of the house entered the room. "You are back," she said. "Good. Did you find everything?"

Milada placed the basket on the oaken table and started to hand over the coins, change from the money the lady had given her to buy the food.

"You keep those for doing the shopping for me," the lady said.

I was happy to hear those words! After all, it was my careful bargaining that saved those coins from the greedy vendors!

"Thank you ma'am. We appreciate it," I said, taking the coins from Milada's outstretched hand and putting them in my pocket before she could change her mind.

I picked up the basket and followed the woman into the kitchen as Milada hopped up the stairs to see what Zora was doing.

"Let me help you," I told the lady when we reached the well-appointed kitchen. Maybe she would give me another coin or two for my help.

"I usually have a girl to help me in the kitchen," the woman said as she took the vegetables out of the basket. "But with my husband ill, the girl clattering about the kitchen just annoyed me so I let her go. Sometimes I regret it, though," she added, "so thank you for your offer of help."

"The first thing we need is some water for the soup," she said. "Take this pot and fill it half way full of water from the well outside."

I took the heavy cast iron pot and was happy that the lady had her own well close beside her house. The black pot was heavy enough empty. I wouldn't want to have to carry it back all the way from the central fountain when it was full of water!

When I returned to the kitchen, the lady was kindling the fire at the large hearth in the corner of the kitchen.

"Please hang the pot on the hook over the fire so that the water can start to warm up," she told me.

I did as she asked and then joined her at the long wooden table where she had laid out the vegetables for the soup. Distractedly, she handed me a sharp knife. I figured she was thinking about her husband; wondering if Zora's magic would help him to recover. I thought that it was foolish of her to hand a stranger a sharp knife in a house full of valuable things. I would not harm her, but many a person would.

I started to chop up the carrots and was ready to tell her that she should be less trusting when Milada burst into the kitchen and said, "Better hurry with that soup! Your husband is very, very hungry!"

When she heard Milada's words, the lady's worried expression brightened into a smile. Without a word, she ripped off her apron and ran to her husband's bedside.

"Is he really better," I asked Milada. I found it hard to believe that Zora's magic could work so fast, or work at all, for that matter.

"He looks better," Milada told me. "Zora says that he had the fever to make him rest; that his illness is from worrying too much about money."

"But he must have lots of money!" I said. "Just look at the things in this house!"

Before Milada could continue the woman returned to the kitchen, beaming.

"I don't know how Zora's magic cured him so quickly," she said. "My neighbor told me he would be dead in a few hours and here he is asking for bread and soup!"

"Let me take him a piece of bread," Milada said, and ran back up the stairs while we continued to prepare the soup.

After a little while the girls joined us. The soup was beginning to smell good and I realized how hungry I was. Zora added some of the herbs we had brought along with us and my mouth really started to water!

We cleared the long table, and the woman set out a bowl, plate and spoon for each of us. She opened the larder and brought out a selection of cheeses and dried meat.

When the soup was ready, she filled our bowls and urged us to eat but did not sit down herself. Instead, she filled another bowl and took the steaming soup upstairs to her husband.

"Don't wait for me," she told us. "You've all had a busy morning and must be very hungry."

And we were! After I had a few spoons of soup and some of the delicious fresh bread I told Zora that we had meet Todor in the square, and the woman he wanted to marry.

"She has very red hair and plays the lyra," Milada said, as if it were important to know that.

"Did you hear her play?" Zora asked.

"Not yet," Milada said. "We'll go and see if they are still there when we finish our meal."

I had hoped that Milada wouldn't want to go back and sit with those people. I didn't have a good feeling about them. Maybe if I changed the subject she would forget about going back!

"How did it go with the man upstairs?" I asked.

"He will recover," Zora replied, "this time."

"What do you mean, this time?" I asked her.

"I think he really doesn't want to live anymore," she said.

"Why not? He has everything money can buy," I said.

"Yes, but his sons do not respect him for the many years he spent travelling the countryside, trading. He provided everything money could buy, but he was never home," she told me. "His children do not know him. Even his wife is like a stranger to him. He is tired from all his travels, yet feels lonely and useless staying at home without the adventure of the road."

"But it's good to stay in one place sometimes, isn't it?" I said, thinking that I was getting tired of the gypsy band's constant travels. I could see from Milada's eyes that she disagreed with me. She always said that she would never want to settle in one place.

Soon the woman came back, carrying an empty bowl.

"What magic have you worked, my girl?" she asked Zora. "My husband was so hungry he ate the whole bowl of soup and is asking for more."

"One bowl is enough for now," Zora told her, seriously. "He can eat another in a few hours. Now he needs to sleep and regain his strength. And don't forget to infuse the herbs I gave you. The lighter colored one in the morning and the darker one at sunset."

"I won't forget," the woman said.

"It's time for us to go now," Zora announced, collecting her things and preparing to depart. "Thank you for your wonderful meal."

Milada and I thanked the woman and stood up to leave.

"You hardly need to thank me, young man. You did much of the work, chopping all those carrots and onions. And one meal is not enough to thank you for healing my husband," she said turning to Zora. "Please let me give you some coins."

The woman reached up to the top shelf of the cupboard beside the fire place and took down a plain looking, wide mouthed earthenware jug. She removed its wooden cover and took out a handful of silver coins. I had never seen so many coins!

"Here," she said, "Take these. Please."

I expected her to offer something for Zora's help and mine, too, but not a handful of silver coins! That was a small fortune!

"No, that is not necessary. It is my path and it is my pleasure to help when I can," Zora told the lady. She wasn't going to take even one coin!

The woman pressed her to accept payment but to my amazement and disappointment, she staunchly refused.

"I really cannot take your money," she told the woman.

"Well then, let me give you a gift. What will it be, a china vase?" she said, picking up a delicate vase from the sideboard.

"I don't think that would survive very long in Zora's wagon," I said. Much better to take some silver coins!

"You are right, young man," the woman said.

"We really have everything we need," said Zora. I could see that she was ready to leave the confines of this house and get back to the freedom and open space of the gypsy camp.

"I know something you may like," the lady said. "It is a curiosity that my husband brought back from his travels. It's like nothing I had ever seen before. Wait here a moment."

She left the kitchen – and the jar of coins, but soon returned carrying a small but seemingly heavy parcel, which she put on the table and slowly unwrapped.

Gold coins, maybe, I hoped. But instead of shiny gold metal, sitting there on the cloth was a funny looking black rock. No, there were two rocks stuck together. What were they supposed to be? Zora was crazy not to take the coins when the lady offered them. The lady was smarter than she seemed, giving Zora a couple of rocks for her services instead of something valuable!

"What's so special about those rocks?" I couldn't help asking.

I saw Milada blush. I guess I sounded rude, but, by the quizzical look on her face I thought Milada was ready to ask the same thing. But there was something strange about Zora. She looked different; younger. I realized she was smiling!

"Do you know what these are?" the woman asked Zora.

"I have seen something like them once before, many, many years ago," Zora replied. "It was at a gathering of all the gypsy bands. A woman from another band had some and showed them to me. No one in our band has any. They are very hard to come by."

"Yes, they are rare indeed," the woman said, "and I insist on giving them to you."

"But what are they?" I asked, wondering why these ugly rocks were making Zora smile so.

"Try to pull them apart," the woman said.

What's all the fuss about, I thought, taking a rock in each hand. But when I tried to separate them they wouldn't budge.

"They are stuck together," I said. "If we get a hammer and awl I can get them apart."

Zora reached out and picked up the pair of rocks. She jiggled them a bit and then easily pulled them apart.

"We don't need a hammer," she said, giggling.

Zora never giggled! Milada looked at her with amazement.

"Watch this," Zora said.

She turned one of the rocks around and then moved them close together. But instead of getting stuck like they were before they seemed to jump away from each other! Like magic! I needed to see for myself.

"Let me try that," I said, reaching out for the rocks.

"Be careful with them," Zora said, "Don't drop them!"

"This is so strange!" I said, amazed when no matter how hard I tried I couldn't bring the two rocks close together. "Here, Milada. You try it."

I gave her the rocks so she could see for herself how strangely they behaved. When she tried to push them together one of them turned itself around clamped on to the other nearly catching the skin of her finger. After that she quickly handed them back to Zora, who stood by with a big grin on her face.

"Can I really have them?" Zora asked the woman.

"Yes, my dear. They have been sitting 0n the shelf for years. My sons played with them when they were small, but got bored as they grew older. You can play with them on your travels; show them to the children. I think my husband got them from some gypsies, a long time ago. That's why I thought you might like them."

"I do. I like them very much," Zora said, "and I can use them in my work."

She wrapped the stones up and slipped them into the pocket of her skirt.

"Thank you, so much!" she said.

"I always knew they were magic," said the lady. "I just didn't know how to use them."

Chapter 19 – Music and Unpleasant Strangers

As we left the house, Zora said, "You two can stay in the village, but I'm going back to camp now," and skipped away before we had a chance to comment.

Milada headed the other way, back to the village square. I hesitated for a moment. I really didn't want to go and sit with those people, but then turned to follow Milada. I sensed that it wouldn't be good to let her go there on her own.

I ran to catch up with her, thinking maybe I could persuade her to see if any of the market stalls were open instead of going to the tavern, but by the time I caught up with her, Todor and Emilia had already seen her and were waving at her to come and join them.

"We wondered if you would come back," Todor said, moving over so we could sit with them on the long wooden bench.

"Will you play for us?" Milada asked. "I'd love to hear you play."

The lady reached down and took her instrument. "And I would love to play for you!" she said.

She played and Todor clapped his hands to the rhythm. Milada swayed happily back and forth, enjoying the music. I guess she played well, but I wasn't really listening. I noticed some men sitting at a table across the way. They were close enough to hear the cheery music but they looked tough and serious. One, with wobbly jowls and greasy black hair hanging limply to his shoulders, was scowling at us. I had a heavy feeling in the pit of my stomach. Somehow I felt that these men were watching us; and that it meant trouble.

The sound of Milada's voice brought me out of my thoughts.

"That was wonderful!" Milada said to Emilia. "Could you always play like that?"

"No, it took me many years of practice to learn," she said. "I lived with a gypsy band for some years, like you Milada. One of the gypsies taught me to play. But it never came as easily to me as it seemed for them."

"But you were a very good student," Todor said, with a love-sick smile. "Let's have another song!"

He picked up his instrument and the two played song after song into the twilight. The men at the other table didn't move. They still sat there, sometimes glancing in our direction and sometimes looking toward the square as if they were expecting someone to come.

I was starting to feel cold and it felt good when Milada snuggled up next to me. I thought she was feeling chilly, too and had come close to feel warmer, but then I realized she wanted to tell me something without the others hearing.

"Look over there. Do you think those people are watching us?" she whispered.

"I noticed them some time ago," I told her. "At first I thought they just liked the music. But look at their faces. They don't seem to enjoy the music at all."

"Maybe they don't like the music. Maybe it disturbs them," she said.

"Then why don't they leave? There are other taverns they can sit and be miserable in!" I whispered.

Finally, Todor put down his instrument. "I'm ready to go back to our camp. Will you join us for our evening meal, Emilia?" he asked.

"I would like to," Emilia replied, "but Vesna has not come back yet. She asked me to wait for her."

"We've been here for hours. Night is falling. She won't come now," Todor said, "Let's go to my camp".

We were all standing up to go when a high pitched voice called out.

"Emilia! There you are, my friend!"

I turned to see who was calling. I saw a slender woman with long, dark hair. She was smiling, but when I saw her eyes I got that heavy feeling in the pit of my stomach again. They were cold and shifty like a snake's.

Emilia looked up from packing her lyra. "Vesna, there you are!" she said. "We've been here all day waiting for you."

Emilia didn't sound very happy to see her "friend".

"Well, I'm here now and looking forward to a long chat," said Vesna. "Is this that man I've been hearing about? The gypsy? Just couldn't stay away from them, could you?"

"Very good looking," she said, right in front of Todor. "I'd like to find a handsome gypsy boy of my own."

Then she fixed her snake-eyes on me.

"This one might turn out to be a looker when he grows up!"

The nerve!

"And what's your name, boy?" she asked me.

"None of your business," I muttered. I wanted to get away from her as fast as I could!

"Come on, Milada, it's time to go. See you later Todor, Emilia," I said, taking Milada by the arm and making a move away from the others.

Milada thanked Emilia and Todor for the music but neither of us said a word to that Vesna woman.

"I like Emilia," Milada said while we walked back to the camp. "She seems like one of us. I think it would be great if she marries Todor and comes to live with our band."

Milada always talked as if we were part of the gypsy band. I knew she wouldn't like it, but I couldn't keep my mouth shut.

"They are not *our* band," I told her. "We will never be a part of them. They see us as visitors, passing through. And that is what we are."

"Don't say that, Goran. They are the only family I have now," she said.

"How do you know that? You told me you had a grandfather. Maybe he still lives. What about aunts and uncles or cousins your own age?"

"Some children came to our house on feast days. Maybe they were my cousins," she told me.

"Have you ever been back to your village?" I asked her as we approached the camp.

"No, I haven't," she replied.

"You never asked the Baron to lead the group back there?" I asked.

"I would never ask the Baron such a thing! It's up to him where we go. He knows best what is good for us," she said.

"Do you really think he does what's best for everyone?" I asked. "How do you know that he doesn't have his own agenda to satisfy?"

"Goran, you have been here only for a year," she said. "But even you can see that we are happy, and well cared for. Why are you so suspicious?"

"Because I know more of the real world," I told her. "You are the one who is living in a dream. And one of these days you will wake up!"

Oh, I went too far! I should have known not to say these things to her. She pulled away from me and ran to her wagon. I didn't mean to upset her, but she needed to face the fact that we were not part of the gypsy band. I wondered if she had family back in the village of her birth. It was fun to travel around the countryside, but I knew this life was not for me. I dreamed of having my own house in a friendly village with fertile fields. I'd have some animals for meat and milk. I wouldn't need anything as fancy as the house we visited today, just a snug stone cottage to keep Milada and me warm on cold winter nights.

Chapter 20 – The Gypsies' Secret?

I went to the wagon I shared with Bora. I thought I would just rest my eyes for a moment, but I must have dozed off. When I opened them it was dark outside. I had probably slept through supper, but I had eaten my fill of that tasty soup so I was not very hungry. While I lay on my bunk, half asleep, I remembered something I'd seen in the marketplace that morning. I needed to tell Milada.

I found her sitting with Tanya by the fire, waiting for the musicians to play. She looked serious and I wondered what they had been talking about.

"Milada, I need to tell you something," I said, sitting down next to the girls, their faces glowing in the warm light of the fire. I liked Tanya very much, but I wanted to speak with Milada alone. I had an idea.

"Tanya, have you seen Zora's new toy?" I asked her.

"I saw her showing something to Layla but I didn't see what it was," she replied.

"Go and ask her about it. I'm sure she would love to show you her magic rocks!" I said, knowing that she would want to go and see what I was talking about.

"Magic rocks?" Tanya said, "Sounds intriguing!"

My plan worked! Tanya was getting up; I would be able to talk to Milada alone and tell her about what I had seen.

"What is it Goran?" Milada asked. I could hear from her tone of voice that she was still cross with me.

"Do you remember those people in the tavern; the ones who were watching us?" I asked her, as soon as Tanya had gone.

"Yes," she said, "I remember them well. Why?"

"You know when we were in the market buying vegetables for the soup?" I asked.

"Yes."

"I saw two of those men with Emilia's friend Vesna!"

"Really? Where were they?"

"They were standing in an alley," I told her. "They were talking, and then looking around as if to see if anyone was listening to their conversation."

"Why didn't Vesna greet them in the tavern?" I asked him.

"That's what I was wondering, too. I know they saw each other. But she totally ignored them."

"I like Emilia but didn't have a good feeling at all about her friend," she said.

"The red-haired woman is all right, I guess, but I didn't like that Vesna person either!" I replied.

"That was obvious. You were so rude to her!"

"Well, now you know why," I replied to her tart comment. "And she was rude to us, too," I added in my defense.

"Emilia didn't seem to like her much, even though she called her a friend. I think she wanted to come back here with Todor."

"No wonder the Baron isn't sure if he should allow Todor to marry the red-haired woman," I said.

"She has a name!" Milada replied curtly, "And she lived with the gypsies like we do. I'm sure she would fit in".

"It's the Baron's decision, not yours," I told her. "And you said yourself, "he always knows what's best"!"

Milada remained silent, watching the dancing flames. Oh no, I went too far again! I sat beside her for a while, listening to the musicians playing as they did every night. I don't know why, but tonight there seemed to be sadness in their songs. Once or twice, Milada looked over at me as if she wanted to say something, but then turned back to the fire. After a while, I stood up, gently patted her shoulder and went back to my wagon without a word.

~

Since I knew my way around the market place well, if something was needed at the camp I was often requested to bring it. One day, Layla asked me to bring some yeast from the baker. I was wondering if the women were going to make bread, and if so, how without an oven? Certainly it was easier to get some from the market. Usually the bakers would each offer a loaf or two for me to take back to the camp.

Lost in thought, I bumped right into Tanya.

"Where are you off to?" she asked me brightly.

"Layla asked me to fetch some yeast from the market," I told her. "Are you planning to bake your own bread now?"

Tanya giggled, "No, it's for blackberry wine', she said.

I liked that idea! I'd tried it once and found it delicious. I hurried into the village. I wanted to finish my errand and get back to the camp soon since I'd offered to help out with the berry picking as well. When I reached the village square, I took a shortcut through the narrow alley that ran behind the tavern. It was dark and smelled of the cows that were stabled there. I used this short cut now and again but I usually avoided it, preferring the longer, more pleasant walk to the marketplace from the north side of the square.

The alley curved so that when I entered it I could not see that there were people there. First, I heard voices echoing off the cobblestones. As I got closer, I saw it was that woman, Vesna, and the unsavory men. I could not help overhearing their conversation and when I did, I slowed my pace to listen, keeping my head down in case they recognized me. I didn't like what I heard.

When I got back to the camp I found Milada with the other women and girls by the cooking wagon. There were several crackling fires with large pots of bubbling berry juice hanging over them from iron tripods. I handed the block of yeast to Layla. She thanked me with a smile then crumbled a little into her palm and inhaled its earthy aroma. Satisfied, she scattered some into each of the fragrant vats of berry juice. I wanted to tell Milada what I had overheard, but I didn't want to share it with the others. I guess my news would have to wait a while.

She asked me, "What is that grey block that you brought?"

I told her, "It's what makes the bread rise when they bake it and it makes the juice turn into wine."

"Is it magic?" she asked, "It sounds like it!"

"It's not magic, everyone knows about it," I told her.

"I didn't know about it," she said.

"Well, now you do," I told her, grabbing a berry basket and heading for the bramble bushes, hoping that she would follow me, but when I looked back, I saw that she was deep in conversation with Layla; she was probably asking her innumerable questions about the "magic' powder.

There were so many berries that I quickly filled my basket. Deep in the woods, I found Bora and some of the other boys sitting in the shade by a creek. I joined them, watching the water flow by. They were munching on the blackberries that they had collected.

"Aren't those for the wine?" I asked them.

"The girls picked plenty," Bora replied.

We stayed there together for a while, chatting and eating our fill of blackberries. I wondered if I should tell them what I had heard, since it concerned the gypsy band; but even though I'd known them for a year, I didn't feel as comfortable talking to them as I did with Milada. I decided to go and see if I could get her alone.

She was sitting where I'd left her with Zora and Tanya.

I called out to them teasingly, "You picked all the blackberries in the woods already? There are no more left to collect? Is that why you three are just sitting around?"

"Shhhh! You'll wake the fawn," Milada said.

Fawn? I put down my basket and went over to have a look. I saw the young deer nestled in Tanya's lap. One of its legs was bandaged.

"What happened to its leg?" I asked as I settled myself on the mossy ground.

"I don't know how, but she broke it," Tanya told me. "I put it in a splint and Zora is using her rocks to help it mend faster."

Zora's rocks? "How can those old rocks help heal the deer's leg?" I asked, looking at how Zora held the ugly rocks close to the fawn's injured leg.

"Remember the force you felt pulling the rocks back together?" she said.

"Yes, it was strong!"

"Well that force, when it passes through the damaged bone, helps it to heal faster," Tanya told me. "Wait and see how quickly the fawn will be able to walk again."

Milada asked, "Will she walk in time for Todor's wedding?"

"So the Baron decided to let it go ahead?" I asked.

"I thought you liked Emilia," Milada said.

"I don't trust those friends of hers," I replied.

"We don't know that those men even know her!" Milada said.

"Well that weasel Vesna does," I said, knowing I had to talk to Milada alone.

"What are you two on about?" Tanya said, her attention focused on the fawn.

"Nothing, really," Milada said. "I like Emilia, and Todor seems to really love her."

It surprised me when Zora spoke, "Sometimes it takes more than love to make a marriage work".

Here was my chance to ask a question that had been on my mind since I the overheard the conversation in the morning. "Do you have love potions to make people get on better? Gypsies do, don't they?" I asked Zora, seriously.

"Yes, we have love potions," she said, "and wealth dust and all sorts of magic rocks."

That was not the answer that I was expecting! I wondered what had got into Zora. I'd never heard her make a joke before, yet I knew that she was not being serious; there was a mischievous sparkle in her eyes.

With the mood lightened, I gave Milada a friendly punch on her shoulder, "Come on lazy bones," I said, "Let's go find more blackberries before it gets too dark to see them."

I helped her up, our eyes meeting as she rose from the ground. Milada had beautiful eyes.

"Where's your basket?" I asked her.

She pointed in where it lay, tossed in haste to the ground. I ran and got it.

"My lady's basket!" I said, handing it over to her with a little bow.

We walked toward where the brambles grew, but as soon as we were distanced from the girls I grabbed Milada's arm and steered her down a different path to a place where we could speak without being overheard. I pulled her down to sit close beside me under a spreading oak tree.

She looked at me with curiosity and a little impatience, "What is it?" she asked.

"I went into the village today; to the market square," I told her.

"Yes, and?"

"I saw that Vesna again. She was with those men."

"Did she see you?" I asked.

"No, I was careful to stay in the shadows. I pulled my cap down low over my face and got close enough to hear what they were saying."

"And what were they talking about? The rising price of carrots?"

"No, they were talking about the gypsies!"

"About us?" she said.

"About the gypsies' secret."

"What secret? I don't know about any secret!"

"I told you we don't know everything about the gypsies!" I said.

"What did they say about this secret?" she asked.

"They were saying that the gypsies never get old so that they must have a secret potion that keeps them youthful. And that potion would be worth a lot of money!" I told her.

"There's no secret potion!" she exclaimed.

"How do you know?" I asked. It seemed plausible to me. I knew the gypsies had secrets; that they knew things that other people did not. It wouldn't surprise me if they had a magic youth potion, or at least some secret herb that kept them all young.

"I just know," she said, "But I will ask Layla. She will tell me the truth."

On our way back to the camp I took Milada's hand in mine. In the gathering darkness, we walked together in silence, each lost in thoughts of our own.

Chapter 21 - I Get a Job

The next day I walked to the village. I had an idea. I knew that the lady we visited with Zora would be busy tending her husband and might be in need of a hired hand. I went to her house and knocked.

She opened the heavy wooden door with a curious expression, looked at me for a moment, puzzled, and then smiled.

"Hello!" she said, "You are that helpful boy who was here yesterday."

"Yes, Ma'am," I said cheerfully, "that's me. I was wondering if you need any help today. I could go to the market for you, or help you to prepare your meals."

"That is kind of you," she said, "With my husband feeling better, I would like to spend time with him instead of going out to the market or being busy in the kitchen."

"There is not much work for me to do with the gypsy band," I told her. "I miss living in a village and enjoy the marketplace."

"Please, come in," she said, opening the door wider to let me pass across the threshold into her pleasant home.

I followed her into the kitchen and smelled the familiar aroma of Zora's herbs.

"I was just going to take some tea upstairs to my husband," she said, "and then start preparing the food for lunch."

I saw some sausages and vegetables on the kitchen table.

"Would you like me to cut these for you, Ma'am?" I asked.

"That would be very helpful" she said. "Oh, I'm sorry. I've forgotten your name!"

"I'm called Goran," I told her.

"Thank you, Goran," she said, as she left the kitchen. She didn't tell me her name and I didn't ask. "Ma'am" would be good enough.

I began to cut the onions, fighting the tears that came to my eyes as I did so. I had to stop several times to let my eyes recover so I would be able to see what I was doing and not cut myself with the sharp knife. Looking away from the onions my eyes came to rest on the earthenware jug that I knew was full of silver coins. I was hoping the lady would pay me for my work even thought I didn't ask her to. Maybe I should have said that I wanted a job, instead of just offering to help!

What if I dipped in my hand and helped myself to some silver coins? There were so many I'm sure she would not even notice. I took a step in that direction, but then stopped. It did not seem the right thing to do. But why not? These folks were rich and had more money than they needed. I had no money and without money I had no way to start a life away from the gypsies. I knew I didn't want to stay with them forever, even though Milada did. If I had enough money for a house of my own, maybe I could convince her to stay there with me.

I took another step toward the jug. Certainly it couldn't be wrong to help myself to at least a few of the silver coins. Once again, I stopped myself. Could I offer Milada a home built with stolen money? Wouldn't it be better to ask for payment in exchange for my services? I knew the lady would be generous and that I would work hard for her.

I turned my back on the jug and resumed cutting the onions. Then I made short work of the carrots, finishing them just as the lady returned to the kitchen with an empty tea cup.

"How is your husband feeling today?" I asked.

"He's much, much better," she replied. "Do you know about the gypsies' magic potions?"

"I have never seen one of them ill," I replied," and if someone is hurt in an accident they recover very quickly".

"They must have powerful magic," she whispered, as if frightened by the idea.

"Zora says 'it's knowledge, not magic' that cures people," I told her, repeating what I had so often heard.

"Well, whatever it is," she said, "I am very grateful that it saved my husband!"

The lady thanked me for cutting the vegetables and started to prepare a stew with them and the sausages.

"Some fresh bread would go well with this stew," she said. "I was going to do without because I didn't want to go out to buy some, but now that you have come, may I ask you to go and get a loaf? You are welcome to stay and eat with us when you get back."

"Certainly, I'll go," I replied; "Is there anything else that you need from the market place, Ma'am?"

"Come to think of it, yes," she said, "While you are there, please buy some hard cheese and some more of these sausages. Here, let me give you some money."

She went to the jug and took out several coins.

"Here you go," she said. "These should be more than enough. Please keep what is left for your trouble."

"Thank you, Ma'am," I told her, and taking a large basket from a shelf near kitchen door, off to the market I went, ready to drive some hard bargains so I would have lots of change left over from my purchases.

I made it a habit to go every day to the lady's house. I never asked her for money, but she always gave me more than I needed for my trips to the market. The last days of summer drew in to early fall. The gypsy band had stayed in this place for a longer time than usual, but it suited me well. Over the weeks I collected a purse full of coins. I thought about getting a jar of my own to keep them in but I preferred a soft leather pouch. I liked the feel its increasing weight. I knew that this money meant freedom for me; I was on my way to my dream of building a home for Milada and me.

I enjoyed going to the market square. I was getting to know the vendors and their wares. I took my time, tasting and prodding, and learned which of them had good products at the fairest prices. I always bought the best quality goods for the lady, even if they cost more. Of course, I could pocket more money for myself if I bought cheaper products, but if the lady was unhappy with what I brought home she might well decide to do the shopping for herself.

Sometimes I thought about stopping in at the tavern by the fountain for a drink and to watch the people go about their business, but those unpleasant looking men were usually sitting there, scowling over their mugs, so I hurried past.

Over the weeks, I learned about the lady and her husband. Her name was Mrs. Dushanka. She was from this village but her husband, Ivan, came from another town. He was trader, as had been his father before him, traveling far and wide to bring people goods that were hard to come by. When he met Mrs. Dushanka here in the village, he tried to stay and make a living as a farmer with her family, but he soon became restless and started his travels once more. He agreed to spend the winter months in the village with his family.

But as he got older, it was harder for him to keep up the hard life of a trader. Neither of his sons wanted to join him in his work. Because of their wealth, they were sought after as husbands and had both married girls from other villages. Mrs. Dushanka told me that in a way it was a good thing that her husband had fallen ill.

"I hope he will stay home with me now, "she told me one day while we were companionable preparing a meal. "It's time that he enjoyed the comfort that he provided for us all these years."

One day when I returned to their home with the shopping I found Mrs. Dushanka sitting with her husband in the kitchen. They were laughing together and looked up as I came in. I was happy to see that his health had returned.

"Is there anything else that I can do for you, today, Ma'am?" I asked.

"We are fine, Goran," she said.

"I'll be going, then," I said.

"Greetings to Zora and that other little angel," her husband said. "I don't know what we would have done without them!"

"I will give them your message, Sir," I replied as I headed out the door, thinking of my little angel and the change from the day's purchases weighing down my pockets.

Chapter 22 – My New Friend, Mladen

As the day of Todor and Emilia's wedding drew near, there was plenty of activity in the gypsy camp. Besides preparations for the wedding feast, the summer's bounty needed to be preserved for the cold winter days ahead. I was surprised at how much food the villagers gave to the gypsies, but also was aware that Zora, the one they called Mother Miriana and some of the other women were tending the villagers, bringing them herbs and potions to keep them healthy. Milada told me that she often accompanied Zora and was keen to learn from her. I went to the village to work for Mrs. Dushanka, often not returning to the gypsy camp until the evening meal.

One night, some days before the wedding would take place, as I was waiting my turn at the stew pot, Milada came up beside me.

"Where have you been?" she asked.

I was very hungry and the aroma of the wild boar and vegetables stew was beckoning. We both filled our bowls and then settled ourselves near the fire. Although the days were still warm, the evenings were chilly and it felt good to sit by the warming fire.

I could feel Milada watching me while I ate.

"So where have you been these days? I hardly ever see you around the camp," she said, curious as ever.

Did she miss me, I wondered, hopefully. "I've been in the village," I told her. "I found a job!" I don't know why I hadn't mentioned it to her before.

"A job?"

"Yes," I said. "I went to the house of the woman whose husband Zora helped. I figured she wanted to stay home to nurse her husband and offered to run errands for her and do odd jobs around her house."

"But we are so busy here, now, preparing for the winter and for Todor's wedding," she said. Maybe that's why I didn't tell her. I had a feeling that she wouldn't approve!

"There are many people here to do the work. The lady, her name is Mrs. Dushanka, needed help," he said, "and she pays me well!"

"You take money from her?" she asked.

"Why not? She has lots of it!"

"Why do you need money? Everything we need the gypsies provide for us."

"I may not always live with the gypsies," I said. "In the real world people need real money."

"Are you planning to leave us?" she asked, her voice dripping to a whisper.

"Not now, but one day the time will come when it feels right to move on," I said. "Maybe you will want to leave with me?" I added, hopefully.

"I will never leave the gypsies," she said, too quickly.

"Never is a long time," I replied.

We sat in silence for a moment. I knew that Milada always said that she wanted to stay with the gypsies; that she could never settle down. I thought of Dushanka's husband, how he couldn't settle in the village after his life on the road. But, she was still young; who knows what the future might bring. Maybe if we travelled back to her village, I could persuade her to stay there and make a life with me.

"Have you seen Vesna and those strange men?" she asked, changing the subject and pulling me back for my revelry.

"Yes," I said. "Every day I go to the market for Mrs. Dushanka. And every day I see the men sitting in the tavern, talking and drinking. I've never seen Vesna with them in the tavern, but I *have* seen her talking to one of the men in the alley near the market square a few times."

"Could you hear what they were saying?" she asked.

"I wasn't able to get close enough again without them seeing me," I told her. Then I had an idea.

"Why don't you come to the village with me tomorrow? Maybe the two of us can find a way to get close enough to overhear what they are talking about," I said.

She smiled at me and nodded. I knew that she would be up for an adventure!

The next morning we met at the breakfast fire.

"I'm ready to go," she told me.

She was dressed in a flaming red skirt and purple waistcoat with golden embroidery, looking very fine indeed, but not for our stealthy mission.

"Go back and change your clothes into something less bright," I told her. "We don't want to be noticed. You will stand out in those colors."

The villagers dressed much more simply in homespun browns and greys, the natural colors of the sheep that provided them with wool.

"I don't think I have anything less bright, "she said.

With a sudden burst of inspiration I said, "Come with me!"

I took her hand and we ran back to my wagon. I shooed away the lazy dogs in our path, pulled her inside, took some of my clothes from the chest by my bunk and tossed them to Milada.

"Quickly, put these on and meet me outside," I told her.

As I hopped out of the wagon she shouted, "But these are boys' clothes!"

"Today you'll be one of the boys!" I said, laughing.

She soon stepped out of the wagon, and I had to smile. She stood on the top step, awkwardly looking down at her feet. She had on my shirt and brown britches but with her wild hair streaming around her shoulders she looked nothing like a lad.

"How do I look?" she asked, "Like a *Mladen*, not a Milada?"

"With that hair? You must be joking!" I said. I pulled my knife out and took a step toward her as if I intended to cut off her radiant halo.

"No way am I cutting it!" she said raising her hands to her hair.

"Just kidding," I said. "I like your long hair. I'll get you a cap and you can tuck all that lovely hair under it."

I went back into the wagon and found a faded blue cap.

"Hold your hair up," I told her. She twisted it up and I slipped the cap over her head. I felt her shiver when I touched the soft spot on the back of her neck. I wondered what it would be like to plant a little kiss right there. But instead of doing so, I spun her around by her shoulders.

"There you go," I said, looking her over, "not half bad. I think you'll pass. Can you walk like a boy?"

"How does a boy walk?" she asked.

"Like this," I stuck my hands into my pocket, striding confidently forward.

"Like this?" she said, trying to copy what I had done. Comically, she stuck out her chin and took a few quick steps.

I couldn't help laughing. She moved nothing like a boy would.

"No, not quite," I said. "I hope I don't look like that. Try it again!"

She tried again, sticking her hands deep into the pockets of my britches, like I had done.

"What is it!" she shouted, pulling her hands out of the pockets. Something went flying out as she did so.

I looked over to see what it was.

"Oh, that's where Lizzie went!" I said, looking down at the creature, lying still on the ground.

"Lizzie?"

"Lizzie is a lizard I found last week. I was going to show you, but then she disappeared! I guess I forgot her in my pocket."

"Is she dead?" Milada asked, coming a little closer. Knowing the ways of lizards, I didn't think so. As we watched, it turned over and scuttled into the underbrush. Milada jumped back screaming.

"Come on, Milada, you have lived in the woods for years. I can't believe you are afraid of a little lizard."

"I'm not afraid of them," she replied. "I just don't like when they make sudden movements like that or when I stick my hand in a pocket and touch something I don't expect to be there!"

"Let's get going. You can practice walking like a boy on the way to the village. And if we run into any lizards, snakes, bats, whatever, remember you are a *boy*!"

Chapter 23 – A Conversation in the Alley

We strode toward the village. I had to suppress my smile, watching Milada trying so hard to walk like a boy, trying different gaits and postures. As we neared the village, she was getting the hang of it; she even kicked a rock that was in our path. I'd never seen her do that when she was a girl!

But just as we reached the first house, she stopped abruptly and said, "I'll never fool anyone with this outfit!"

She looked like she was ready to turn heels and run.

"Come on. Milada, I mean *Mladen*!" I told her, "You'll be fine".

I started to take her by the arm but then remembered that she was supposed to be a boy and dropped my hand.

"Come on Mladen! I'll race you to the fountain!" I said and started to run toward the village square.

There were many children playing in the square and we blended in with the crowd. I pulled Milada behind the fountain, on the side away from the tavern. Using my eyes, I signaled her to look there.

The three men sat at their usual table in front of the tavern.

"They always sit there." I whispered. "Look! Here she comes. And here comes the Baron and some of the other men of the band".

We both slumped down so as not to be seen.

Vesna's voice carried across the square.

"Good day, Baron," she said. The woman stood very close to the Baron; too close! She stuck out one hip and twiddled a lock of her hair. It looked like she was flirting with the gypsy Baron!

"And what brings such a handsome man to our village square this day?" she continued. "Looking for someone to show you around? I'd be happy to."

"Thank you, madam," I heard him say as he took as step away from the unpleasant woman, "but I have many tasks to attend to."

He strode off, followed by the men. When they had passed one of the men at the table spat on the ground, muttering.

Milada watched, and whispered to me, "How can they be so disrespectful to our Baron?"

"To them he is a 'dirty gypsy'," I said. "They cannot fathom his wisdom and kindness."

"Where did Vesna go?" she said. I looked and saw that she had left the table.

"Look, there are only two men there now. The skinny one is gone. I bet you we'll find him in the alleyway with Vesna," I said. "Let's go and see if we can find them. But first we need a plan."

What could we do? We needed to get close enough to hear, but I sure didn't want them to catch me. I don't think they would have any qualms to kick children, or do worse.

"You could pretend to be a beggar," I told Milada. "You could sit in the alley and pretend you are blind. Set your cap out for people to put coins in."

"That won't work for two reasons," she said. "First no intelligent beggar would sit in a quiet alley. It's much better to sit in the square where lots of people pass. And second, if I take off my cap my hair will fall down and it will be obvious that I am not a boy!"

"You're right," I said. "Let's think of something else."

I thought some more then said, "What would make two boys linger in an alley?"

"They could be trying to catch something. Or to collect insects?" Milada suggested.

"That might work in the woods, but not in an alley."
We thought some more.

"I have another idea," she said. "What if two boys dropped the coins from their pocket? They would stay to pick them up."

"What if Vesna and the man tried to pick up the coins the boys dropped?" I said. "It seems something they would do."

"But stopping to pick something that we drop would give us a reason to stay in the alley. It has to be something that wouldn't interest the others, though, definitely not coins!" I added, liking the idea.

"What do we have that we can drop?" she asked. "Not our caps…"

"We don't have anything, but I have some coins. We can buy something and then drop it," I told her.

"What shall we buy? Apples?" she suggested.

"We would pick them up too fast, unless we bought more apples than we could carry. We need something that would take time," I said, going through the market stalls in my mind's eye.

"What about grapes?" Milada said, "They're small and will roll off in every direction.

"The ones that come off the stem will roll all right. I guess we could take them off the stem before we go into the alley. But it might seem strange and attract attention. And grapes squash so easily. When you drop grapes you often just leave them." I told her, thinking that grapes were pricy as well.

"Let's walk around the market and see if we get any ideas," she said. "And we can pass in front of the alley and see if they are there. Maybe they aren't even meeting today, so we'd better buy something that we can really use."

We walked to the market square. The red-faced baker's wife called out, "'Morning Goran! Your usual today?"

"No, thank you!" I called back.

"Who's the lad?" she asked with a smile.

The *lad* was Milada. I saw her smiling, knowing that her disguise worked.

"A friend from the camp," I told her. "I'll see you tomorrow."

As we went past the cheese sellers, several vendors called out their greetings to Goran.

"Does everybody in the market know you?" Milada asked me, surprised.

"Most of the vendors do," I replied. "They know I'm helping Mrs. Dushanka. And they know that she has money to spend."

"Why is money so important to these people? The gypsies never worry about money?" she asked.

"People give the gypsies gifts of food, wine, tools, clothes, everything. In the villages, people need money for those things. Sometimes they exchange things they make or food they grow for other things that are needed. But money makes trading easier. You don't have to find someone who has what you need and also wants what you have to offer," I explained, thinking how little of the practicalities of life she knew.

We passed the alley but from our vantage point we could not see if anyone was there.

"Maybe they are farther back, in the shadows," Milada said.

"Let's not walk over there to look," I told her; "if they are there it might make us look suspicious."

"All right, let's see if we can find anything good in this part of the market," she agreed.

We went to the section of the market that sold produce, ignoring the apples, pears and other large fruit. We saw some berries and our eyes met in an unspoken question. They were small, but they were squishy like grapes so we kept walking. We then came to a stall displaying dried fruit and nuts.

At the same time, Milada and I exclaimed, "Walnuts!"

"Walnuts won't break when we drop them," I said.

"And they don't get squashed!" Milada added. "And they roll really well."

"And we can buy a lot of them, they are not expensive," I commented, thinking of my savings.

"And I love them, so even if Vesna and the men aren't there we can enjoy eating the walnuts!" Milada said with a smile.

I bought a big bag of walnuts. Then, slowly, we approached the alley.

"Walk quietly and don't talk too much," I whispered to Milada. "I think I can see them over there, a little way down the alley. When we get close enough I'll drop the nuts. You go after the ones that roll away. I'll stay close to Vesna and the man."

"Then you'll be able to hear them, but I won't," she complained.

"If you stay too close they might see that you are a girl," I told her, practically. Milada frowned. "Don't worry. I'll tell you everything I hear. Now, try not to talk. Follow my lead."

She followed me into the smelly alley. The tall houses and stables on either side didn't let much light filter down to the cobblestone pavement. I felt the heat from the cattle's breath passing though the iron grates set into the thick stone walls.

I was startled when a huge rat ran across our path. I jabbed Milada in the ribs and mouthed the words, *"You're a boy!"* I was relieved when she acted like one and kept any reaction to the rat to herself.

Now we were really close to Vesna and the skinny man. He stunk like rotten meat. It was difficult to be this near to them, but it was the only way I'd be able to hear their conversation. I let the bag of nuts fall open. The sound of the many nuts clacking on the paving stones echoed through the narrow alley. I crouched down and slowly started to collect the ones nearest me while Milada move further down the alley, just out of earshot.

The skinny man looked over at me with a sneer and said to Vesna, in a gravelly voice, "Clumsy children! Now, where were we?"

"About that woman," Vesna said, "She is the key to a chest of gold!"

What 'chest of gold' I thought, as I picked up the nuts, slowly one at a time. As the conversation continued, I realized that it was not a golden treasure that they wanted, but the secret to the gypsies' eternal youth; and they we making a plan how to get it. At their whispered words, I felt the color draining from my face. I couldn't believe that they would put their plan into practice; it was too cruel! But looking at these people, I thought that they might just be capable of such cruelty. How could I tell Milada?

I looked down the alley and saw her picking up the last of the fallen walnuts, watching as the foul man walked passed her. He looked like he was about to kick her as she knelt on the cobblestones. I held my breath. If he touched her I would kill him!

He looked down at her as he passed. I let out a sigh of relief when he trudged on by her and out of sight. Vesna had gone in the other direction, back to the village square.

When the coast was clear, Milada ran over and knelt down beside me. I could see my face reflected in her eyes. I didn't know how to tell her what I had heard, and, for once, she didn't ask.

Chapter 24 - A Dark Plot?

Milada broke the moment of silence. "Goran, tell me what they said".

"Not now," I whispered as if the people were still there and could hear us. I think I was in shock from what I had just overheard. Should I tell Milada everything? Could I tell her?

I dropped some walnuts as I stood up; the racket they made when they hit the cobblestones brought me back to the here and now.

"Come on, let's go," Milada said. She forgot that she was supposed to be a boy and took my arm. "Tell me when we get to the woods."

I shook off her arm before anyone could see us. We hurried out of the alley and though the square. Todor and Emilia were sitting in the tavern and that snake, Vesna, was with them. They were all laughing. I noticed Milada pulling her hat down tight and walking even faster. Todor was gazing at the red headed woman looking all love sick. I don't think he noticed us as we hurried by.

As soon as we were back in the sheltering woods, Milada pulled off the cap and shook her long hair free. She ran her fingers through the shining tresses, rubbing her scalp, and then plopped down in the shade of a tree beside the stream that led to our camp.

"Tell me, Goran," she said. "It can't be *that* bad."

I took a deep breath, "It can be *that* bad, and worse," I said, "they are determined to find out the gypsies' secret. They will stop at nothing to get it."

"But there *is* no secret," she said.

"Maybe there isn't," I replied, "but those people think there is and they will kill one of the gypsies to get it!"

Milada gasped in disbelief. "Kill one of us?" she exclaimed. "How can we tell them a secret that doesn't exist?"

"Apparently, Vesna asked Emilia to get it out of Todor. But Emilia told her there was no secret."

"Is Emilia in on the plot with Vesna?" she asked, looking concerned.

"I don't think do," I replied. "Vesna said that Emilia was a fool to believe there was no secret when it's obvious that there is, and that they will have to try another way to get it."

"What other way, did they say?"

"They will kidnap one of the gypsies," I told her. "If they find out the secret the gypsy will be released. Otherwise…"

"Did they say which of us was the target?" she asked.

How could I tell her? Maybe there was nothing to this plot. Looking into her expectant eyes and seeing the worry there, I couldn't bring myself to tell her who that evil woman wanted to take. No, I couldn't tell her something I knew would disturb her even more than the news of the plot itself.

I lied and said, "No. I didn't hear any names mentioned."

"Maybe it will be Todor, since he goes to the tavern everyday it would be easy to trick him into a house and lock him in. Should we warn him?" she asked.

"No, I don't think we should say anything yet," I replied. "Maybe they are just talking and will not do anything."

Milada moved around so that we were face to face. I felt like she knew that I was holding something back. For the first time, I saw fear in her eyes and I had to look away.

She sat back beside me and said, "I think even if it is only a possibility we should tell someone what we heard. We should tell the Baron."

"Do you think he would believe us?" I asked her. "We are not a part of their band."

"Why would we say something that wasn't true? We should tell him what you heard!"

Maybe she was right. He was the leader of the tribe and could make a decision about this situation, whereas we were powerless. But, I knew that often the person who brings bad news is blamed for what he has to say. I really wasn't sure that the Baron would believe what I had heard. What if he thought I was making it up to get attention? On the other hand, if the threat was real, something had to be done, and fast!

Milada stood up and held out her hand for me. She said, "We'll tell him tonight after the evening meal."

Milada went to change back into her colorful girl-clothes. I met her later at the table by the fire. We looked for the Baron but couldn't see him or Dragan at the campfire. Milada went to ask Tanya if she knew why they were absent. I followed her. I didn't think we should tell anyone else about what we had heard; not even Tanya.

As I approached, Tanya was saying, "The Baron heard that there was another band of gypsies related to ours camping in a nearby valley. Todor's brothers travel with that band. The Baron went to tell them about Todor's wedding and Dragan went along to keep him company."

"When will they be back?" Milada asked.

"I don't know exactly, a few days maybe," Tanya replied. "For sure they'll be here in time for the wedding."

"Goran and I went to the village today," Milada told her. Before she could say anything else I interrupted her and finished her sentence;

"And bought some lovely walnuts," I said, taking some out of my pocket and tossing one lightly to her. "Try one!"

Tanya caught the nut with a grin and cracked its hard shell. I gave Milada a look that I know she understood: *don't say anything!*

She looked back at me and raised her eyebrows as if to say *why not?*

I just shook my head and was happy when she let the subject drop.

"This walnut is delicious, "Tanya said. "May I have another one?"

"Certainly," I told her. "I'm going to see what Bora is up too. Maybe we will have music tonight." I gave Milada a questioning look, suggesting that she come with me, but she shook her head. One more glance passed between us, confirming that she wouldn't mention the overheard conversation to Tanya.

I joined Bora by the fire. I hoped Milada would join me, but I could see her deep in conversation with Tanya. *What were they talking about?* I wondered. After a while, I saw Milada getting up. I thought she was coming over to me, but she went the other way, back toward her wagon. I could see the by the way she was dragging her feet, raising dust on the dry earth, that she was very tired. I longed to go to her; to hold her in my arms and reassure her that Vesna's evil plot would come to nothing. The gypsies had been good to me and I would hate to see them hurt. Maybe it's a good thing to tell the Baron. Maybe he would order us to move on now, before those people could put their evil plan into action.

Chapter 25 - Preparations

In the morning, the camp was busting with activity. I was helping the boys erect a wooden frame to hang a canopy for the wedding. I saw Layla watching us, looking more serious that she usually did. I wondered if she was thinking about a wedding of her own. It was unusual for a girl of her years not to be wed. She held a large empty basket; maybe she was going to the village to collect supplies for the feast. When she walked away from us, I ran after her.

"Layla," I cried, "Are you going to the village?"

"Yes, I am" she replied.

"I'll come with you," I told her, "and help you carry your basket back when it is full." We had nearly finished the canopy frame. I figured if I went into the village I could keep an eye on those people.

As we walked along in companionable, I asked Layla, "Why are you not married? Has the Baron not chosen someone for you?"

"Why do you ask?" she said.

"I don't know. I guess with the preparation for Goran's wedding, I was just wondering." I told her.

"Marriage is not my way, this time," she said, with a faraway look in her eyes.

This time? I didn't know what she meant, but it didn't seem right to ask her any more questions.

We quickly finished our errands in the market place. No money was exchanged, only Layla's beautiful smile and kind words for all she met. As we walked through the village square on our way back to camp, I felt the skinny man and the other two watching us as we passed. My skin crawled. I moved closer to Layla, glad that we would soon be back in the safety of our camp and hoping that the Baron had returned; but by sundown he and his son had not come back.

Although there was still much work to be done in preparation for Todor's marriage and our journey, I went into the village every day, but not to help Mrs. Dushanka. I sat in the square, keeping an eye on those men.

Sitting there all day gave me time to think. I had spent one year travelling with the gypsy band. It had been a happy one; maybe the happiest of my life. These people took me in; fed me, provided me with clothes and a comfortable bed, asking nothing in return. It was natural for me to help when I could. But, at the end of the day, I knew that I didn't belong with them; that this was not the life for me. I missed the routine of life in the village. Seeing Mrs. Dushanka's cozy house, I knew I wanted a home of my own, not to spend all of my life traipsing about on dusty roads. But I also knew I wanted to be with Milada. I could see that she liked Dragan by the way she watched him at the campfire. I wished she would look at me like that.

I knew that Dragan was not right for Milada. He would succeed the Baron as the leader of the tribe and would need a woman beside him who knew their ways, who was a part of the band. One day, Milada would realize this, too; and I would be there for her and make her feel wanted; and loved.

A few days passed and I was really beginning to think that Vesna's plot was just idle talk. I'd seen the men in the tavern as usual, but not her. The Baron had still not returned, but wedding preparations went on. I knew that the marriage could not take place without him. The band planned to leave for lower ground the day after the celebration. Nights were already getting cold and soon the first snows would come.

I felt more relaxed when I sat at the campfire the night before Todor's wedding. The camp was in a festive mood, decorated for the wedding in the morning. Garlands of bright leaves from the forest were hung in preparation for the feast and the air was already scented with the aroma of roasting meat.

Nothing had happened. The morrow would bring the wedding celebration. All the gypsies would be here, together; safe. I hadn't seen much of Milada since I overheard the disturbing conversation in the alley. I watched her sitting with Tanya and Zora, picking at her meal, with furled brow. I missed her bright smile and could see she was still worried about what we had overheard. I hoped that she had kept her promise and not told anyone. Our eyes met. As she got up, I did, too, and drew her to a spot near the fire well out of earshot of the others.

"What if the Baron isn't back before the wedding?" she asked me. "We won't be able to warn him."

"The more I think about it," I said, 'the more I think we ought to mind our own business and keep our mouths shut."

"Are you saying that we shouldn't tell the Baron?" she asked, her eyes widening in shock.

"Can we be sure we heard right? We don't know that the gypsies have a secret. And anyway, why would the Baron believe us?" I said.

"They *do* have a secret!" she exclaimed. "What if we don't tell him and then someone is hurt? We have to tell him. It's up to him if he believes us or not."

"Well, we can't tell him if he isn't here," I said.

"We can tell someone else. We can tell Mother Miriana," she said.

"If we tell her, what will she do? She'll tell us to tell the Baron," I reasoned. I could see that she knew I was right.

"We'll be leaving this camp in a day or two," she said. "What can they do tomorrow? It's the wedding. We will all be together so how can they kidnap anyone? And then we leave. Maybe you are right and we won't have to tell anyone."

"Let's enjoy this evening and the wedding tomorrow. I'll be sorry to leave this place and my job with Mrs. Dushanka; but I won't miss Vesna and her "friends," I said.

I took Milada's hand in mine and lead her to where the musicians played a cheerful tune, without any concern about the heavy thoughts that weighed on our minds. We saw Layla next to the musicians, swaying to the rhythm and tapping her foot. Milada dropped my hand and ran over and sat beside her. I was hoping that she would stay with me, but I watched as she and Layla chatted. Milada looked very earnest, as if the subject were something serious. I hoped that she wasn't telling Layla about the plot. Certainly nothing would come of it now. Soon I saw a smile return to Milada's face as she and Layla got up to dance. I went to my bunk, happy that she was happy and looking forward to festivities that morning would bring, convinced that there was no more cause for worry.

Chapter 25 – The Wedding Day Arrives

The sun shone brightly the morning of Todor's wedding to the red-haired woman. I had been looking forward to the delicacies that had been prepared, but not as much as I was to leaving this place, Vesna, those men and their evil plot. I looked for Milada as the sun rose higher. She probably had been up until the wee hours of the morning, dancing by the fire. She was not an early riser at the best of times, but if she didn't get up soon she would miss the marriage ceremony!

The camp was crowded with gypsies massing for the wedding, their ranks swelled by the bride's people who had come out from the village for the event. I scanned the crowd for Milada. Finally I spotted her, running beside her friend. Tanya had threaded bright green ribbons into her neat long braids. Milada's hair was wild, as always, but sported a red ribbon to match the red skirt that danced around her legs as she ran. I could see that the bright ribbon was only for decoration and not restraining her chestnut mane in the least. Our eyes met across the crowd but before we could reach each other loud drumming commenced.

This was the first wedding that had been celebrated since I began my travels with the gypsy band and I did not know what to expect. In the village, the priest would say some words to the couple outside the village church and then everyone would go inside for a special liturgy. This celebration was much more noisy, with men beating drums and women playing tambourines.

There was the Baron, standing under the canopy. He must have returned in the middle of the night. There was no way we could talk to him now, even if we wanted to.

Todor was approaching the Baron, riding on a black horse, surrounded by the drumming men. The bride was coming from the other side, riding on a pure white horse lead by the women with tambourines. What a racket they were making! When they reached the canopy, they dismounted and stood beside the Baron.

He addressed the couple, and I guess us as well, as "Friends"; then said a few words and gave them his blessing. Todor looked happy and his bride had tears in her eyes; tears of happiness,

I hoped. Then the drums started again and the Baron called out, "It is done! Come now to the feast!"

I was wondering how I could reach Milada. The crowd was moving towards the wagons, creating a river of people impossible to ford and I gave up trying. I watched the red ribbon in her hair moving away from me as the group of women lead the procession to the village. Not far behind her I saw a dark-haired woman. Could it be that Vesna?

I had forgotten that the wedding celebration would take place in the village square and not in the gypsy camp and was beginning to wish that we had found the Baron and told him about the plot, after all. I didn't think that anything could happen in the forest camp; those people would look too out of place and arouse suspicion; but in the village, things were different. I decided to find Milada and the Baron as soon as we got there and tell him what I heard.

The wagons loaded with food had already started down the road leading into town. Nico ran up to me and said, "Come with me, Goran. We can ride in the wine cart!"

I had seen Milada near the front of the procession with the woman, so the sooner I got to the village the better. Nico and I ran to catch the cart just as it was pulling onto the road. We hopped on the back of it, with the barrels of blackberry wine and baskets of wooden beakers. There was a mischievous glint in Nico's eyes.

"We picked all those berries to make this wine," he said. "We deserve to drink some!"

"Shouldn't we wait for the wedding feast?" I asked him.

"I think we had better try some now," he replied, "just to make sure it is good!"

He drew a mug full of wine from the tap on a barrel, lifted it to his lips and drank deep.

"Mmmm," he said, "this is very tasty. Here you go."

He handed me the mug and I took a sip. It was good. I took another sip and then finished off what was left in the mug.

"Delicious!" I said, licking my lips. I hadn't had any breakfast knowing that there would be plenty to eat at the feast and the tasty berry wine went down well.

Nico drew another beaker and then another and before we knew it the wagon was stopping in the village square. I saw long tables set up, already laden with food. Before I could go and find Milada, Bora joined us at the cart. He started filling earthenware jugs and putting them on the trestle tables.

"Come on, you two," he said to Nico and me, "give me a hand here"

Nico waved at him, "Here's my hand!" he said.

I thought this was really funny and waved, too, laughing.

"You two have had enough wine!" Bora said, shaking his head.

"Enough for what?" I replied. "Enough for a wedding toast?"

"Enough to know better!" Bora said. "Come down from there before you fall off the cart."

I thought about climbing down and finding Milada; I'd go look for her soon, after one more mug of wine.

But before I could go looking for her, she found me. She wanted to look for the Baron, but, I am ashamed to say it, I just wanted to stay and drink more blackberry wine. I don't remember anything more; I must have passed out, but not before I let it slip that it was the baron's beautiful daughter, Layla, who was the intended victim of the kidnapping plot!

The next thing I remember is feeling the chilly hardness of the ground beneath me. Why was I lying on the cold ground instead

of on my nice warm bunk? I stretched out my arms and hit something. Looking through unfocused eyes I realized that the 'something' was Nico. How long had we been lying there? Maybe we'd decided to take a nap in the sun, but that must have been some time ago because now the sky was dark and it was cold.

Slowly, I was beginning to remember. It was Todor's wedding day. We were here to celebrate with food and wine. Wine! Oh no! There was something I had wanted to do; something important. But what was it?

I stood up on wobbly legs, looking for some water. I was very thirsty. I saw Bora sitting and laughing with some of the boys from camp. He watched me staggering towards him, trying to keep my balance.

"Goran!" he cried, his voice echoing in my head.

"Not so loud, Bora," I told him as I neared the bench where he sat. "Is there some water?"

"You sit here and rest," he said. "I'll get you some. I'll get you lots; you look like you need it! And some food would do you good as well."

I didn't think I could eat anything. My head was pounding like the rhythm of the wedding drums. Bora brought me a jug of water and a piece of bread dipped in olive oil. After drinking down all of the water I did feel hungry and wolfed down the delicious bread. Then I began to remember. I needed to find Milada and the Baron. I tried to stand up, but my legs still felt weak.

"Bora, would you please get Milada," I asked. "There is something I need to tell her".

"Now?" Bora said.

"Yes, please," I told him. "I'd go myself but I'm still feeling wobbly."

Bora smiled, shook his head and ran off to find Milada. Oh, what had I done! I looked around me. The square was full of people, the noise from their chatter and laughter feeling like a hammer in my poor head. I lifted the jug, hoping that more water would help but it was already empty.

After what seemed like an eternity I saw Bora coming, relieved that Milada was with him.

"I found her," Bora said, plonking himself down on the bench next to me, sending new waves of pain to my aching head.

I looked down at Milada's feet, ashamed to meet her searching eyes, "I'm so sorry," I told her. "I don't know what happened."

"What happened is what happens when somebody drinks too much blackberry wine!" she said and Bora laughed.

"I told you to stop," Bora said. "That happened to me once. The wine tasted so good, but it's not like drinking too much juice! It makes you crazy and then comes the headache."

I just groaned. Milada shook her head and said to Bora, "Please go get some water for Goran. I think it will help his head."

As soon as Bora left she sat close beside me and whispered, "They've got Layla. Why didn't you tell me it was she that they were after?"

Oh no! It wasn't idle talk after all. And now the lovely Layla was in danger; a danger we could have prevented.

"I really didn't think they were serious," I said, realizing how wrong I was. How did they get her and when? Maybe she wasn't really kidnapped. Maybe she just went off somewhere and is taking a rest in her wagon or helping one of the villagers in a house.

Hoping that was the case, I asked Milada, "How do you know they've got her?"

"I saw it all!" she told me. What? I felt the color draining from my face, my head suddenly clear. I sat up and listened, seeing the pain on Milada's pretty face as she continued.

"Vesna tricked her! She said that a friend had twisted her ankle and heeded help, so, of course, Layla went with her. I saw them lock her in a basement room. They slapped her and cut her arm. Vesna said that they will cut her face and then cut off her fingers and toes tomorrow if she doesn't tell them the secret. We need to tell the Baron!"

"Let's go," I said, feeling the strength coming back to my legs. It was time for action.

Chapter 26 – A Parting

I took Milada's hand and together we ran toward the sound of the celebration. Loud toasts and laughter competed with the music. We spotted the Baron in the center of the crowd.

"How will we get to him?" she asked.

"Let's go around and see if we can get there from the other side," I said, trying to make our way through or around the crowd any way we could. The band started a new tune and people were moving here and there, some starting to dance and others making their way back to the tables for more food and drink. For a moment I felt hungry, but then I remembered what we had to do and all thought of the delicious food was forgotten.

"Where is he now? I can't see the Baron?" Milada said.

I'd lost sight of him, too, as all around us people spun and whirled in a lively dance. We moved out of the way, watching for the Baron. Milada squeezed my hand as a group of the bride's friends from the village walked by. That snake-eyed Vesna was with them. Before I could speak to Milada, Tanya appeared from the crowd of dancers, her eyes shining with happiness. She grabbed Milada's free hand and laughingly pulled her into the dance.

I tried to see where they went, but the sea of dancers had sucked them into its depth. I skirted the edge of the crowd, hoping for a glimpse of the bright red ribbon in Milada's hair. Eventually, on the far side of the square I found the girls. Milada was sobbing in Tanya's arms.

"There you are!" I said, "You disappeared!

"Did you find the Baron," Milada asked me.

"No, I was looking for you." I said.

Tanya looked up at me brushing the tears from her eyes. "Please tell me what has happened," she said.

"A couple of days ago we overheard some people talking in the village," I began just as Milada exclaimed "They've got Layla!"

"Who has Layla? And why? You said before that they want to kill her? Whatever for?" Tanya asked, confused.

"They want to know the secret herbs that keep the gypsies young," I replied.

"There are no secret herbs," Tanya said.

"There is a secret, though," Milada said quietly.

Tanya looked serious, "It isn't something that can be told," she said as another tear made its way down her now ashen cheek.

"We have to find the Baron and get him to save Layla before it's too late," Milada said with resolve. "Let's all go and look for him."

I climbed up on one of the trestle tables to see if I could spot the Baron over the sea of dancers.

"Can you see him?" Milada shouted.

"No, I don't see him anywhere," I answered.

Milada climbed up on the table, too. "There he is - over there!" she said pointing toward the fire.

"That's not the Baron," I said, "It's Dragan."

"Let's tell Dragan, then. He'll know what to do," she said, hopping down from the table before I could say anything.

I jumped down beside her. Milada grabbed my hand with one of hers and Tanya's with the other. The three of us ran together in the direction of the fire. We found Dragan sitting on a bench, drinking and laughing companionably with some men from the camp. He looked up as we approached and must have seen the concern on our faces. Quickly, he stood up, excusing himself from the group.

He put his hand on Milada's shoulder and steered her away from the fire. I bristled a little, seeing this intimate gesture, but shook off the unwelcome feeling as I follow them, Tanya by my side.

"What is it, Milada? Has something happened?" he asked.

Before she could reply I told him, "Layla's been kidnapped. We heard them planning it but didn't think it would actually happen."

Milada interrupted, "Dragan, you've got to come now, quickly. I know where they are keeping her. You've got to get her out of there tonight! Come, now. We have to hurry."

I was watching Milada, and the way she was looking at Dragan. "Don't you think we should consult the Baron?" I said.

"We don't have any more time," Milada shouted. "Come on. Please! We have to save Layla."

I was surprised when Dragan didn't react. He reached out at touched the amber beads that hung around Milada's neck. I had never noticed her wearing them before, but they looked somehow familiar. Then I remembered. They belonged to Layla!

"I think it is already too late," he said gently fingering Layla's beads. "I think she has decided to go."

"Go? Go where?" Milada said in tears. "Come on!" she said, pulling on Dragan's arm. "They sliced her arm once and said they will cut her again and then kill her. I can show you where she is."

I don't know if it was her tears that moved him or the fact that she knew where Layla was that spurred him into action.

"Let's go," he said, and the four of us left the celebrations in the square. Dawn was breaking as we hurried through the narrow alleys. Milada held Dragan's hand, taking comfort from his firm grip. I wished that she had taken mine instead.

Her steps slowed as we entered a particularly dark alley, the early morning sun was still too low to shed any light into its narrow depth.

"This is the place," she whispered indicating a window set low in the wall.

She and Dragan knelt down and peered inside. Tanya and I squatted behind them, trying to see, too, but the opening was very small and it was dark in the room below the level of the road.

Dragan sighed and sat back on his heels and I had a better look. I could see Layla stretched out on a simple bed. It looked like she was asleep.

Suddenly, voices rose from the room below, shattering the silence of the alley. Someone was coming! I heard a door creaking on its hinges. I pulled back from the window as the voices inside rose.

"Shut the door," Vesna hissed. "It's time to do this before all those fools go home to bed."

Milada looked expectantly at Dragan but he did not move from the window.

"Wake up, my girl!" said Vesna with false good humor, 'It's time for us to talk. Well, actually, it's time for *you* to talk!"

Apparently, Layla did not respond. Vesna yelled, "Wake her up, Xeno!"

I heard the sound of a slap and Milada gasped. I couldn't see into the room, but I could guess what had happened and shuddered at the thought.

Still, Dragan remained motionless.

Then Vesna gasped. "She's dead! You idiot! I told you not to kill her before she told us the secret," she hissed; "or maybe she told you the secret and then you killed her before she could tell us. Xeno, get him!"

She set one man against the other. They were all yelling and swearing.

I heard one of them say, "If I killed her, where is the blood?"

At that, they all fell silent. Then Vesna said, "Maybe she took poison. We should have searched her before leaving her alone. She's no use to us now."

Dragan pulled Milada back from the window. He put his arm around her shoulder and whispered, 'It is over. Come."

He took Milada's hand in one of his and Tanya's in the other and led them away. I watched them go, but I wanted to stay and see what the people would do next. My eyes met Dragan's and he nodded, understanding. His sister was dead, and maybe I could have prevented it. The least I could do was wait and watch her beautiful body and try to make sure that nothing happened to it.

I moved closer to the window now that the others had gone. Vesna was pacing back and forth. The big man was straightening Layla's body. It must have been knocked off the bed by the heavy blow. He looked at her lasciviously, caressing her arm as he placed it by her side. He moved closer to her face as if to graze her cold lips with his hot ones when Vesna slapped the back of his head. The skinny man leaned against the wall, watching.

"What are we going to do now," he drawled. "I thought this one would tell us. Shall we go get another one?"

He talked as if the gypsies were trout in a stream; that if one got away they could cast their net for another.

"It's almost morning. It will be dangerous now. This one might be missed and they may be wary. If you had done your job right," she said, giving the big man a swift kick as he crouched by the bed still stroking Layla's motionless body, "we would have the secret by now!"

"What will we do with this?" The skinny man said, indicating Layla's body.

"Throw it in the river, for all I care," Vesna spat; "or just leave it for the rats to enjoy. Let's get out of here."

The skinny man moved to the door. The big one was fingering Layla's skirt.

"Now!" hissed Vesna, grabbing his meaty ear and pulling him to his feet. The three of them disappeared through the door. I scuttled around the corner in case they came my way, but I heard the sound of their footsteps scuffling off in the other direction.

I moved back to the window, wondering if they had locked the door. They had taken the last bit of the candle with them and even though light was beginning to filter into the alley it was too dark to see anything in the room below. Then, in what seemed to be moments later, the door cracked open and the room was illuminated by a faint light.

Who was here, entering the room in silence? It seemed to be a woman, her silver hair reflecting the dim light. As my eyes grew accustomed to darkness, I recognized the woman. It was Mother Miriana! How did she know to come here? It didn't seem enough time had passed for Milada and the others to have found her and for her to arrive so soon. Two other women followed her in. I could hardly believe what I saw next.

Chapter 27 – Moving On

After the three women left, I sat by the window in a daze. What were they doing? I was standing up to go when I heard someone else entering the room below. I crouched down again, wondering if Vesna had decided to move Layla's body after all. But instead of seeing her I gazed down at the Baron, followed by two men from the gypsy band. He looked at his beautiful daughter then tenderly picked up her body himself and carried her out of the room in his arms.

I felt tears in my eyes, the first I remember shedding since the day I was taken from my mother's corpse. I didn't understand how this could have happened. We knew about the plot but we could not prevent it. And Layla? How did she die? Was there really a secret? Was it worth dying for? All these questions played around my brain as I walked slowly back to camp to find Milada and tell her what I had just seen.

I approached her wagon and saw that she and her friends were making their preparations to leave.

'Milada, there you are," I called to her, "come here, I want to tell you something!"

Tanya saw me and said, "Go on, Milada. We are almost done. Zora and I will finish packing."

Milada ran over to me, her red-rimmed eyes full of expectation. "What happened after I left?" she asked me, settling herself next to me on wooden chest waiting to be loaded onto a nearby wagon.

"They talked about taking someone else, but Vesna thought it would be too dangerous now. They were going to take Layla's body and throw it into the river but then decided just to leave it where it was. They have no idea that we know about them."

"What will they do now?" she asked.

"Nothing. The townspeople will think we just moved on. Maybe they think Layla won't be missed? There is nothing to connect them to her," I said.

"Nothing except us! Does the Baron know?" she asked.

"Yes," I told her. "Vesna and the others didn't stick around for long. If they had, Mother Miriana would have caught them."

"Mother Miriana?" she asked, puzzled. "What does she have to do with it?"

"Maybe Dragan or Tanya told her," I said. "She arrived very soon; almost before the others fled."

"And the Baron?" she asked.

"He came to take Layla's body just as Mother Miriana was finishing," I replied.

"Finishing what?" she asked.

"She and two other gypsy women entered the room. They each had two wax candles about as long as my forearm. They put Layla's body in the middle of the room."

"On the floor?" she asked.

"Yes. They put a candle at her feet and two on either side of her body. One woman sat on each side. They were whispering something together. I could feel the rhythm but could not make out the words. They sounded very strange. Mother Miriana lit the sixth candle from an ember. She used that candle to light the others and then placed it at Layla's head. She knelt down beside it, gazing down at Layla's face with the palms of her hands hovering over it."

"Then she started to sing a strange song. Her voice was very low. Maybe I was just tired but I thought I saw light coming from Layla's body as Mother Miriana sang, moving her hands down the body and back up again three times. Then all the singing stopped. Mother Miriana placed her hands on Layla's head and bent down close like she was kissing it. Maybe she was kissing it. But then something really strange happened! All the candles went out! All by themselves! I'm sure no one blew them out," I told her. My words sounded so strange. If I hadn't seen this with my own eyes I would not believe it had happened.

"Maybe there was a draft? Did someone open a door?" she asked.

"No," I said. "They just went out. Then Mother Miriana and the others got up, took the candles and left. Just like that."

"And left Layla there?" she asked in disbelief.

"Yes, but almost as soon as they went, the Baron arrived with two men. They wrapped Layla up in a blanket and brought her back here. They are digging the pit under the fire now."

"How did Layla die?" Milada mused, not expecting an answer.

"Maybe she *did* take poison. You know they know all about herbs. I bet there are some that can kill you," I said.

"Layla wouldn't kill herself. She loved life. Why would she carry poison leaves around, anyway? She didn't know she would be kidnapped," she said in Layla's defense. She fingered the amber beads around her neck, thoughtfully.

Some men came to pack the crate that we were sitting on. "Move along, children. It's nearly time to go," one of them told us.

So we were going. And leaving the Baron's only daughter here, alone in the cold earth.

"Time to move on," I said to Milada. "They just throw her in the ground and leave. I don't know if I'll ever get used to the ways of the gypsies."

"I am sad and I am confused," she said. 'But I know the body that we are leaving behind is not Layla. Her spirit is somewhere else, free, maybe travelling with us. Somehow I feel I'll see her again."

"When you die, you die. End of story," I said. But is it? I had a feeling that the gypsies and Milada didn't think so.

I went to my wagon and found that Bora and Nico had packed all our things. I could see by their expression that they knew about Layla. A day that had started so happy had ended in grief. No one said a word but somehow everyone knew that it was time to

gather around the spot where our campfire had been. Men were just finishing burying Layla's body, patting down the earth and raking the ashes from the campfire over the spot. A once beautiful, smiling girl was no more. There were no words, no ceremony. Last year, when the man died, there was a feast, but Layla would not even have that. Slowly people drifted back to their wagons and the signal to move was sounded.

I felt the weight of my purse full of coins in my pocket and thought about the happy days of our stay in this place, now marred by the sadness of Layla's passing.

Chapter 28 – Women's Mysteries

Once again, we were on the move, travelling down dusty roads; passing through forests and fields, never stopping more than a night in any one place. I guess we had stayed too long near the village, preparing for the wedding. What a day that had been! I missed seeing Layla's smiling face. Now only Dragan rode up and down the line of wagons, making sure we were all together and safe.

During these days, I didn't see much of Milada. She rode with Tanya and Zora in their wagon while I stayed with Bora and Nico in ours, watching the horse's tail and the back of the wagon in front of us from morning 'til nightfall.

We still gathered for our evening meal and some music by the fire, but the group was subdued, knowing that we would be on the road again the next morning. Todor and his bride seemed happy at first, but soon I saw him sitting with the other young men at the campfire, his wife nowhere to be seen.

Days were getting shorter and cooler now and still we kept moving. One day I didn't see the newlyweds at the evening meal. The next day on our long ride, I asked Bora, "Where are Todor and the red- haired lady?"

Bora sighed. "Gone back to live in the village," he said. "Emilia wasn't as happy with us as she thought she would be. She missed her life in the village."

I wondered if she missed that weasel, Vesna, her "friend"!

"And Todor went back, too?" I asked; "to stay or just to bring her there?"

"He didn't say," Bora replied. "Maybe he will live there with her, but I don't think he will".

"Why not? If he loves her, why wouldn't he stay with her?"

"She loves him, but wasn't happy living like we do. As a man of the band, Todor will have difficulties with the men in the village."

"Why is that?"

"We do things differently; we think differently," he told me.

I had never thought about it before, but now that Bora mentioned it, I could see he had a point. In the village, the men work at crafts or on the land. They go home to their wives at midday, expecting a meal on the table. After a rest, they go and find their friends in the village square or in the tavern and drink together, or maybe have a game of chance until nightfall.

There is a very different rhythm in the gypsy camp. We all eat together and gather together by the fire in the evening. Generally, men go off to hunt and the women collect food from the forest. Sometimes a woman joins the men hunting and, as we did with the berries, sometimes everyone harvests wild fruit together.

Bora and I continued down the dusty road in silence, measuring time by the movement of the sun, entranced by the rhythmic beating of our horse's hoofs until the signal was given that we'd reached the place to rest for the night.

We unhitched our horse and she wandered off to join the others grazing in a nearby meadow. I spotted Milada sitting alone beside her wagon, lost in thought. I went and sat beside her, without a word.

After a few moments of silence, she said, "Why didn't the Baron do something? We knew who took Layla, we told him, but all he did was to have her body brought back to us and then we left. Didn't he care?"

"That's what they always do when one of the gypsies dies," I said. "In the villages people cry and tear their hair in mourning. They bring flowers to the graves of the people who have died. They remember them and pray for their souls".

"What's a soul?" she asked.

"I don't really know. I remember my mother saying that you have to be good or your soul will burn in hell when you die," I told her.

"What is "hell"? How can you burn when you are dead? Maybe a soul is something people get when they grow up and people burn it when they die. But what does that have to do with being bad or good?" she asked me.

I didn't really have an answer. I had never thought about it. I just knew that everyone in the villages seemed to believe this.

"When you are good, your soul goes to heaven," I told her.

"Heaven? Where is heaven?" she asked.

"It's up in the sky. The angels live there. They sing sweetly all day long," I said, "That's what people say, anyway. I've never seen an angel. I don't think that they are real. I think people just say these things to make children do what grow-ups want them to."

"Children here don't know anything about hell and heaven. We do what we are told because we understand that the grown-ups know better and want to help us to learn," she said. "Isn't it funny to tell children their souls will burn up if they aren't good!"

Milada got up and moved toward the cooking wagon. I went to find the boys and to fetch some water for our horse. I'd never really thought about what I'd been told about angels. If they were real, I think Layla was one, never raising her voice in anger, always having a kind word for everyone; finding a way to escape the evil plot and not give away her people's secret. If there was a heaven, I'm sure she'd be there now.

That night at the evening meal the Baron announced that we would be staying in this camp for the winter. I was happy to hear it. In the morning we hitched the horses and moved the wagons into our little communities around the central fire. It was like building a new village at each campsite, with the fire as the central square and the cooking wagon as the tavern. Maybe I could get used to this life if I thought about it like that.

But, still, as winter set in, I dreamed about having my own snug house and my own fields. I thought about learning a craft to earn money to buy the things I could not grow or make for myself. I was handy at helping the boys do odd jobs, but I knew I was not a craftsman; I could not make anything without the help of others.

But as much as I dreamt of a better life in a village, others preferred the life of the gypsy travelers. I don't know how he found us, but before winter had passed Todor was back with the band.

"I loved Emilia," he told us one night by the fire, "or thought I did. It was so nice to share music with her. I loved the way she looked at me and her smile. But life in the village was different. I thought she had learned the ways of our women; the way we share our love, but she had different expectations and I could not satisfy her longings."

Bora nodded in agreement, but I didn't know what they were talking about. Later, in the cozy darkness of our wagon, I asked him, "What did Todor mean about the way gypsies share their love?"

"Goran," he said, "our ways are ancient. They come from a different, older tradition than people here know. It is hard to explain."

Here we go again, another secret that they won't tell me.

As if he was reading my thoughts, Bora said, "When the women go into their moon tent, the men meet and learn the sacred traditions. If you want to come, you may."

"What is the moon tent?" I asked. "Why do only the women go there?"

"Have you never noticed that when the moon is dark most of our women are absent for a few days?" he asked me.

I hadn't really thought about it. The food was still prepared, Milada, Tanya and Zora and the other young girls didn't disappear.

"They have a special place for their special time," he continued. It's called the Moon Tent."

"What's so special about it?" I asked. If it were so special, wouldn't I have noticed it?

"From the outside it looks like one of the big tents we use for meals when the weather is not good. They fly little pink flags on the tent ropes," he said.

"And inside?" I questioned.

"I have never been inside, but I heard that it is lined with the softest cushions and fine carpets," he said.

Fine carpets? Soft cushions? I wondered what for! "What do the women do in there?" I asked.

"I think they rest together and get information for the Baron," he replied.

"How do they get information?" his words did not make any sense.

"Sometimes they play their tambourines together in the tent," he said, and then they sit in silence and listen".

"Listen to what?"

"Listen to the sound of silence and hear the words of wisdom from places beyond," he said, with a faraway look in his eye.

"Can only women hear these voices from beyond?" I asked him.

"No," he said, "men can, too; but it's easier for the women, especially at that special time of the month; the time when their blood flows."

Blood? What weird ritual do they do in that tent? Did Milada know about it? I didn't want to ask her, afraid of what she might say. Better to ask Bora.

"Do they cut themselves to better hear the voices?" I asked him?

"No, it's nothing like that," he said looking shocked! "Every month a woman's body prepares itself to carry a child. If she doesn't receive the seed from a man, her body cleanses itself of the cushion it has prepared. They call it their 'moon blood' and the time when it flows is the time for them to rest, to listen and to learn.

"Not all the girls go into the moon tent," I said. "Milada and her friends don't."

"They must still be too young," Bora said, "but I'm sure they will be old enough soon."

Maybe when Milada starts to go to the moon tent, when her body is ready to make a child, maybe then she will think about settling down with me in a cottage of our own.

Chapter 29 – Another Magic Rock

When the snow started to thaw we were on the road again, staying for a few days at each village we passed, welcomed by the people who generously shared the last of their winter provisions with the gypsies who, in turn, offered their healing herbs and their knowledge, helping to cure the sick and tend to injured people and their animals, too.

The warmer days brought a smile to my face. The forest was coming alive with fresh, bright green leaves. Tanya's she-goats had given birth to kids, which meant there was delicious fresh cheese made from their surplus milk for us to enjoy.

One morning after a filling breakfast, Nico came up to me and told me that we would be leaving soon and to spread the word to the others. I went to Milada's wagon to let her know and found Zora sorting fresh forest herbs. I watched as she separated them into small bundles and hung them upside down from a beam in their wagon.

"Hello, Goran," she said when she saw me watching her.

"Hello, Zora," I said, "What a lot of herbs you have!"

"People will be needing these," she said. "This is the season when their potency is the highest so I pick many and dry them now."

I looked at the bright green leaves with serrated edges that looked like a row of teeth.

"Why will people need this herb?" I asked. "What it is good for?"

"It is known as 'lion's tooth'. Making a tea or tonic from it will help digestion and stomach upsets," she explained. "Used fresh, its juice will help heal wounds, and its root is good for people who drink too much wine."

Her eyes sparkled, and I felt color rising to my cheeks. I guess everybody in the band knew about my experience with the blackberry wine.

"Nico said that we would be moving soon," I said, swiftly changing the subject.

"Yes, I know," she said, hanging the last of the bundles.

Where's Milada?" I asked,

"I think she's in the forest," Zora replied.

"I'm going to find her and tell her that it's almost time to go," I said. "See you later!"

I followed a path that led into the forest. I was no longer afraid of the dark mystery of the woods and of things that I only imagined. I'd learned to be more observant so I could sense if there was a real threat and I knew how to take the appropriate action.

I saw Milada sitting with Tanya in a sunny clearing.

"Hello Milada, Tanya!" I called, "What are you doing out here?"

"We're watching Layla's stone," Milada said.

Watching a stone? I wondered why they would be sitting and watching a stone; and Layla's stone at that.

Tanya said, "Let's go have a look".

I followed her to a circle of pebbles where a small fire burned. Above the fire, on a tripod made of twigs, was a clear crystal sphere. Very strange. Were the heating up the stone? If so, why? And how did they light the fire?

"Did you take an ember from the fire this morning?" I asked them.

"No," Tanya said, "I made the fire with this crystal."

Milada's eyes opened wide. "It's a magic crystal! That was the secret that those people wanted! Layla could have given them the stone and she would still be with us today!"

She seemed angered by the thought. I was wondering how the rock had made a fire. Was it really magic?

Tanya put her arm around Milada and answered my unspoken question, "No, my friend, this is not a magic rock. Its round shape gathers the rays from the sun into a small point. It becomes very, very hot and that heat makes the dry leaves burn."

Carefully, she took the stone and put it in the shade. She covered the small fire with soil, putting out the flames and scattered the circle of stones so there was no trace left.

"It is very useful to have one of these in case you need to make a fire and don't have an ember. But it doesn't work at night or on a cloudy day!" she said, wiping soot off the stone with her skirt and putting it in a protective pouch.

I told them, "I was looking for you to tell you that we are moving on now. We should be at our new camp by nightfall."

Tanya skipped over to a spreading oak tree and bent down, her long braids swinging at her back. When she turned around I saw she had gathered a bunch of squirming kittens in her wide skirt.

"Somebody please bring the mother cat!"

Milada picked up the cat and followed Tanya. It hissed at her and batted her with its claws, nearly scratching her.

I ran after her and said, "Nobody told us about these stones before. See, they still don't think of us as a part of their group."

"Don't be so sensitive," she said, struggling to keep hold of the angry cat. "We just didn't have the opportunity to see one."

"How did Tanya know what to do with it, then? Someone must have shown her," I said.

"Maybe she saw Layla using it, or Mother Miriana. Tanya said she has one, too," she replied.

"I don't like Mother Miriana. I think she's a witch," I whispered. "She's always talking in riddles."

Milada stopped and stared at me. "Don't say such things!" she said. "She helps so many people with her knowledge."

The cat was writhing in her arms.

"Here, take this cat, will you?" she said, holding it out to me.

I reached out to take it but it clawed its way free and ran off into the forest.

"Stupid animal!" I yelled. "It scratched me! Look, I'm bleeding."

Milada touched my arm gently and said, "Come on. Tanya will have some salve for it. Hopefully the cat will find her way to her kittens and not get left behind."

I hoped that it *would* get lost and we'd never see the darned thing again as we made our way through the woods.

When we got to their wagon, Tanya was already tidying the water jug and mats in preparation for moving on. I saw a wicker basket full of fur on the floorboards. The kittens were there, fast asleep. Somehow the mother cat had already found them. She was in the basket, too, glaring up at me with her evil yellow eyes.

"Look," said Milada, pointing at the cat, "she knew exactly where her kittens were!"

"Stupid cat,' I muttered. "Tanya, look what it did to me!"

I showed Tanya the scratch. At least it wasn't bleeding anymore, but it was swelling up. Tanya took a very small bottle from a chest beside her bunk.

"Sit here," she said. I sat on the wagon's step while she gently rubbed something cream on the scratch. Maybe it was made with that herb Zora had collected. I watched as the swelling magically went down.

"That's better," I said. I had been thinking about riding in the wagon with Milada, but I didn't want to be near that devil cat in case it decided to attack me again.

"I'm going to ride with the boys," I told them and ran back to my own wagon, just as the signal to leave was sounded.

Chapter 30 – Bora's Tale

We were on the road until nightfall. I was glad that I went back to ride with Bora and Nico. The fine spring day put us all in a good mood and I soon forgot my encounter with that cat.

As we travelled down the road I told the boys about Tanya starting a fire with the clear stone.

Bora said, "I saw Mother Miriana do that one time when I was small. It was in winter. There was a terrible storm. Rain pelted down like arrows. I was in our wagon; my mother and her friend cuddled with me in a warm quilt. I remember being comfortable and warm with the two women, listening to the wind howling outside and the rain beating sharp, uneven rhythms on our wagon's wooden roof."

"But this storm was like no other," he continued. "Our camp was in a valley that offered some protection from the normal winds of winter, but this was no normal storm. The wind came from the north and not the east as was expected. The excessive rains ran down the sides of the valley, swelling the trickling brook that provided us with water into a raging torrent."

"I felt a blast of cold air and realized someone had pulled open the heavy curtain at the entrance of our wagon. It was the Baron himself."

"You must come now," he said in a steady voice, "There is no time to lose."

"He held the curtain open for us. I saw many of the others of our band already outside, bracing themselves against the wind and the rain."

"Follow me," the Baron said.

"He led us away from the stream, up a hill behind the camp. The ground was very muddy and my feet slipped as I tried to keep up. I felt someone lifting me. I never did find out who it was!" he said.

"The next thing I remembered was being set down inside a big cave. We were all wet and had no fire to dry ourselves or keep ourselves warm. We spent that night huddled together, taking what warmth we could from each other's body heat."

"Eventually, the wind died down and the rain stopped. I could see light at the mouth of the cave. Still shivering in our wet clothes the Baron led us back down the hill to what was left of our camp."

"Some of the wagons lay on their side in the mud. One had been completely washed away. There was no trace of our campfire. Usually someone kept an ember from the fire so we could easily start a new one but the storm blew up unexpectedly in the middle of the night and it was all we could do to get ourselves out of there before the water could wash us away."

"We changed into dry clothes, those who had some sharing with those who didn't. As the sun rose, the horses and other animals found their way back to the camp," Bora said.

I thought of the animals in the villages. We kept them fenced and tethered. If a sudden flood came they would drown for sure, not being free to find their own way to higher ground.

Bora continued his story. "The early morning sun was weak and we were still cold and very hungry. Everybody was helping to clean up the camp as best as possible. The women were at the cooking wagon, looking for provisions, but there was no fire and no dry wood to collect."

"Then I saw my father approaching, his arms full of wood. He and some of the other men had been out collecting fuel for the fire before the storm had hit. They had been on higher ground and had managed to protect the timber that they had chopped earlier in the day."

"I ran to greet him. He looked relieved to see that I and the others in the band were alright. He must have been worried, knowing that we were camped by the stream."

"The Baron greeted him and the others. "Do you have an ember so we can start a fire?" He asked. The men all shook their heads."

"Then I saw Mother Miriana coming toward us. Her hands were full of dry hay, probably taken from the mat on her bed. "Dry wood," she said with a smile, "just what I was looking for! Please put it near the cooking wagon so we can make some nice hot breakfast."

"Did you manage to keep an ember alight?" the Baron asked her."

"No," she said, "but there is enough sun to start a fire."

"I watched her place some flat stones on the ground in the sun. On top of the stones she put the hay. She reached into her pocket, took out a clear round stone about the size of a hen's egg and placed it on top. She looked up to the sky. "Lucky that there are no clouds coming," she said, glancing down again at the stone and the hay."

"I was watching it, too, wondering what was going to happen," Bora said. "Soon I heard a crackling noise and realized that the hay had caught on fire! How could that be?"

"Mother Miriana explained it to me. "The stone's clarity and shape condenses the heat from the sun into one point. That heat makes a fire."

"Soon the cooking fires were lit and before long we were all well fed and feeling better," Bora concluded.

His story helped pass the time on our journey. Talk of their breakfast was making me hungry.

"Will we stop somewhere to eat?" I asked the boys.

"No," Nico said. "We will travel until nightfall. Are you getting hungry?"

"Yes!" I said.

Nico went into the wagon and came out with a wooden plate full of sliced sausages and fresh goat cheese.

"I'm glad that someone remembered to bring a picnic!" Bora said, with a grin.

We enjoyed the food and then each took a turn holding the reins while the others had a nap in the wagon. We stopped once or twice to let the horses rest but kept a brisk pace until twilight.

We made our camp by the light of the stars, not far from a quickly flowing brook. I couldn't help thinking about Bora's story; how the life-giving water had turned murderous overnight. I looked for Milada to tell her Bora's tale but she was nowhere to be found. She was not at the long table when we had our evening meal. I didn't see her dancing by fire that night.

I sat alone, gazing up to the sky and was relieved to see myriads of bright stars.

Bora came and sat beside me. "The stars are beautiful tonight," he said.

"I was looking to see if there were any clouds gathering," I said. "After the story you told me today I'll never look at a stream in the same way again!"

"Can you see the river in sky?" he asked.

"How can there be a river in the sky?" I asked him, puzzled.

"Look there," he said, pointing to a dense line of stars making a bright path. "Some say that it is a road to guide the birds on their long migrations," he said. "It is also a path that can guide us home."

Chapter 31   Strange Ways of the Men

The following morning, I awoke with the sun, expecting to be on the road again. I looked over to Bora's bunk and saw that he was still fast asleep. When I got up, I noticed that Nico was also asleep in the bunk above mine. Usually, they were up early, especially on days when we were travelling. I pushed aside the curtain and stuck out my head. All was quiet.

I jumped down from the wagon and, after relieving myself behind a tree, went to find the cooking wagon and some breakfast. The camp was very still, with only a few of the gypsies going about their morning business. I found Dragan at the cooking tent, deep in conversation with the silvered haired woman. When he saw me, he greeted me warmly.

"Hey there, Goran," he said with a smile. "You're up early!"

"I thought we were moving on today," I said. "But no one looks ready.

"My father wanted us to keep going. We are going farther than we usually do this year, back to camp near one of our favorite villages," he said. "The people there are very hospitable, grateful to us for helping them during a time of great sickness many, many years ago."

"Why did he decide to stop here, then?" I asked.

"The winter was long and we were late starting our journey," he said. Now, it is the dark of the moon and we must stop to let the women have their moon time."

I remembered what Bora had said about a special tent. After I had something to eat I wandered around the camp and, sure enough, a little ways off I saw a large tent with pink flags flying. It must be their special tent.

By now, more people were stirring. Back at our wagon, Bora and Nico were preparing their slings and traps.

"Coming with us?" Nico asked. "There should be some fat birds in these parts."

"Yes!" I said, happy to be off the wagon to move around the woods and fields after the long, bumpy ride.

We spent the day hunting, returning when the sun was low in the sky with a bag full of plump grouse for the cooking pots. At the cooking wagon, I noticed that there were not many women around; only Mother Miriana, her friends, and some young girls. Todor was tending the fire while Tanya stirred fragrant herbs into the broth. Where was Milada? I was just about to ask when Bora and some of the other young men came near the fire.

"You did well today," he said, clapping me on the back. "How many birds did you catch? Four?"

"I only caught three," I said. "But they were the fattest ones of the bunch!"

I still found it hard to believe that calling the birds and animals made them come to our snares. But, believe it or not, I called them and it seemed to work!

Nico had plucked the fattest grouse and was roasting it on a spit. Some of the other men were doing the same thing with birds or rabbits that they had caught. We enjoyed the succulent meal, flavored with mountain herbs and the taste of the fire.

When we'd finished, Todor came and sat beside me.

"Bora said that you wanted to learn the way of the men," he said.

"I was wondering about it," I said, not sure if I really wanted to know or not.

"We will meet tomorrow night," he said. "We'll make our own fire a little way off from the camp. Come along with Bora if you want to."

Did I want to? So many of the things the gypsies did felt strange to me, and not quite right. Yet, I was curious.

"Thanks, I told him. "Maybe I will."

The next morning I looked for Milada. There was no one in her wagon. Once again the camp seemed quiet. I saw Mother Miriana's silver braid reflecting the morning light where she stood over the cooking pot.

"Excuse me," I said, "Have you seen Milada today?"

"Good day, my lad," she said with a twinkle in her dark brown eyes. "Milada is with the women".

I started to move away, to go and find her, but Mother Miriana called be back.

"Lad, would you please take the pail and fill the barrel with water from the stream?" she asked.

I knew better than to say 'no' when asked to do something for Mother Miriana. I followed the brook to a place where I could scramble down the bank and fill the bucket. It took me several trips back and forth to fetch enough water to fill the barrel.

"Thank you, lad," Mother Miriana said when the job was done. "You have grown into a fine strong young man!"

I hadn't thought about it, but looking down at my hands I saw that the sleeves of my lightweight shirt were half way up my forearms. It had been too cold to wear it during the winter, so I must have grown so much since I put it away in autumn. I noticed that Bora and Nico had grown taller, but somehow I hadn't realized that I must be growing taller, too. I felt some down on my upper lip and on my chin, signs that I was soon to be a man and no longer a boy.

That evening, after the meal Bora told me that he was going to the men's fire.

"Will you come?" he asked me.

I hesitated, but then decided I had nothing to lose by going along to see what they did there.

We walked into the woods together, drawn by the smell of smoke in the distance. Most of the men were already there, sitting in a circle around a blazing fire. Instead of music or the usual companionable chatter they sat in silence, the only sound being the crackling of the flames and the sound of our footsteps as we drew near and took our places in the circle.

"First we will breathe together," Bora whispered, straightening his back.

We always breathe I thought, so when we are together, we breathe together. I remembered the time that Milada and I tried to see who could hold our breath the longest. It was hard *not* to breathe. And so my mind wandered as the men sat in silence around the fire.

No one seemed to be leading the group as, one by one, the men, who all sat up straight, raised their right hand to their faces. Bora looked at me as if to say, *you can do this, too.*

Bora faced me so I could see him place his index and middle finger on his forehead. Using his thumb, he closed his right nostril and inhaled through his left. Then, using his fourth finger, he closed his left nostril as well. I did the same, opening my mouth so that I would have plenty of air. Bora's lips curled into a grin and he shook his head.

I closed my mouth, hoping that we would not be holding our breath for very long and wondering why we were doing it at all. Then he released his thumb so the air could flow out the right nostril. Closing his eyes, he then inhaled through the open, right nostril, and then closed it again with his thumb. Once again, we were holding our breath. I counted to myself, wondering how long I was supposed to stay with my nose and my mouth firmly shut. When I reached the count of six, I saw Bora lifting his fourth finger for the air to escape. After another count of six, he inhaled through his left nostril, repeating the sequence. I followed along as best I could, watching the other men continue, left, right, right left until I found my eyelids falling shut as well. I lost track of time while we were breathing in this strange way. When I opened them, the fire had died down. The men still had their fingers pressed to their foreheads but they were no longer touching their noses. Their eyes were open and they gazed at the fire, but seemed to be looking beyond it rather than at it.

Slowly, the men dropped their hands to their laps. Dragan stood up and added some more wood to the fire.

Sitting back in his place in the circle, he started a low chant that the other joined. Slowly the sound began to grow and grow. I felt too self-conscious to join in at first, but the sounds became so powerful I could feel them resonating in my flesh and then it seemed natural to just open my mouth and let the sounds come forth.

"eeeeEEEEEEEEEEeeee......ahaaAAAAAAAAAaaaa ah....ohooooOOOOOOoooh..." we chanted, "eeeeEEEEEEEeeee......ahaaAAAAAAAAaaaaah....ohooOOO OOOoooh..."

The sound rose and fell as of its own accord. I felt my voice join with the others until I could not tell which sound was coming from me. We were one unit, one voice. In a way, I liked the feeling, but it also scared me. I couldn't tell where I stopped and the other men began. I felt I had lost myself; I was lost in an unknown world, a world that was not mine.

As the fire once again died down, so did the sound. The men sat for a while in silence then they began to disperse and return to the main camp and their wagons. No one spoke. Bora and Nico got up and I stood with them. The three of us returned to our wagon in silence. I had many questions, but sensed that this was not the time to ask them.

Chapter 32 - Was I Dreaming?

The morning dawned as any other, but I could not drag myself off my bunk. I had an amazing dream! I usually could not remember dreaming, but what I'd seen that night was unforgettable. I was on a craggy mountain peak, looking down at the tops of the tallest trees. In the distance, I could see fertile valleys with rivers running through them and fields of ripening grain. I scrambled down a narrow path and found myself on a rocky ledge. There was a nest there. In it I saw a small boy, not more than four years old, curled up as if asleep. He stirred, and looked up at me with sad eyes. I realized that this boy was me! At once I found myself looking out of the boy's eyes gazing down from the high cliff to the valley far below. Where was my mother? Why was I high on a mountain top? As I stood up, wondering how I could get down, I looked at my feet and saw that I was no longer a child, but the young man I am today.

Then I saw Bora and Nico, hopping down from a crag a little bit higher in the mountain.

"Hi Goran!" Bora said. "Come on and jump!"

With that, he launched himself off the cliff. He spread his arms and soared away, wheeling and dipping in the clear sky.

Did I dare to jump? People cannot fly! Would I crash to the valley floor? As I watched Bora, wondering if I could fly like he did, Nico came and stood beside me.

"Coming, Goran?" he asked and then threw himself off the ledge.

Like Bora, he was gliding on the currents of air, with a big smile on his face.

I took a deep breath. If they could do it, so could I! I moved close to the edge and jumped.

At first, I plummeted down toward the valley floor. Maybe only the gypsy boys could fly! I was frightened; I thought I would die when I hit the ground. But then I spread my arms wide like I'd seen the other boys do. Immediately I felt myself being lifted, carried upward on the warm air. It lifted me to where Bora and

Nico were gliding. I heard them chanting the strange song from the fireside,

"eeeeEEEEEEEEEEeeee……ahaaAAAAAAAAAaaaaah….oh ooooOOOOOOOoooh…"

I joined in with them, our chant merging with the sound of the breeze. It seemed like we were flying for a long time, soaring back over the fields, scattered villages and woods in the clear morning sky. We spiraled down lower and lower, finally landing gently on our feet in a clearing near our camp. We ran to our wagon and hopped into our bunks.

I wanted to go back to sleep and see if I could fly again. I shut my eyes tight, but I could hear the other boy stirring.

I looked over at Bora.

"I had an incredible dream last night," I told him.

"I know," he said. "You were flying with us!"

How did he know?

"And we were chanting," he added.

"How do you know what I was dreaming?" I asked; was this more of the gypsies' magic?

"There are many kinds of what we call 'dreams'," he explained. "Some of them come from our own head and are very personal too each of us. Others are shared."

"Did you see me as a little boy in an eagle's nest?" I asked.

"No," Bora replied. I saw you standing on a ledge looking down at the valley. Nico and I like to go there and fly. It was good to see you there, too."

"How did I get there?" I wondered aloud.

"You joined us in the men's circle," Nico said, joining the conversation from his top bunk. "When we connect with each other through our breath and through our chant we can often meet in our dreams."

"Does that chant mean anything?" I asked.

"Yes," Bora replied. The sounds are from words in an ancient language. The EEEEE is from 'Ignis' which means 'Fire'".

AAAAAh is from 'Aqua' which is water and OOOOO if from 'Origo' which is the 'source' of all things, seen and unseen."

"Mixing fire and water make steam; a union of the male and female elements. We are conscious of this when we couple with a woman. It is part of the men's teaching to learn to be with a woman without spilling our seed. This practice of sacred union helps us to be strong and healthy. It also prevents us from having too many children. We need to keep our band small and only bring new life into it when someone leaves us."

"How can you do that?" I asked.

"Learning to control our breath is one thing we do," he said, "and reciting this chant when we are coupling. Before we are able to control our seed we are careful to couple only when the moon appears less than half its full size in the sky. If you come to the men's fire you will learn other ways."

"But now, I'm hungry after all our nocturnal travelling," Nico said, stepping on my foot on his way down from his bunk.

"Hey!" I said, knowing he did it on purpose.

"Hey, yourself," he said hitting me with his pillow.

I retaliated with mine, then Bora got in on the fun and we had a full scale pillow fight, down feathers flying in every direction. We collapsed on the floor laughing. I liked this play much better that talking about breathing and 'coupling'! And now I was very hungry!

We rinsed our faces then went to the cooking wagon with our bowls and spoons. A big pot of porridge was simmering on the fire. I helped myself and then looked for some sweet honey to put on the top.

"Where is the honey," I asked Tanya. "The porridge tastes so much better with a bit of honey on the top".

"Finished," she said. "It's time to find a honey tree and collect some more. Here, have some chopped walnuts," she said, passing me an earthenware jar.

I shook some out onto my porridge, thinking that I would prefer honey.

"Here is something special," Tanya said. "Hold out your bowl."

She took a pinch of a brown powder from a small velvet pouch. Only very precious things were stored in these rare containers.

"What is it?" I asked, inhaling its unusual, pleasant aroma.

"It is a spice from lands far from here," she said. "They call it 'cinnamon'."

I tasted a spoonful of my porridge topped with nuts and this unusual spice. It was delicious!

"It's a little bit sweet," I said, "not sweet like honey, though."

"It is very good for you, too," Tanya said. "It helps you not to become ill."

"I never tasted it before," I said, with regret.

"It's hard to come by," she said. "When we have honey, we use it as it has similarly benefits for our health, but now that the honey is finished we can have a little cinnamon as a treat."

"Can we find more of it when it runs out?" I asked.

"We always get more when we have a gathering of the clans," she told me.

"What's that?" I asked.

"It's when the four clans of our band meet. You know we each travel in a different direction each year. When we can, we meet in a central place on midsummer's day."

"Not since I have been traveling with the band," I said.

"No," Tanya said, "it had been a while since the last big gathering. Hopefully, we will meet together soon. I would like to see my mother again."

This was the first time Tanya had mentioned her mother to me. I thought she was one of the women in our band. It was usual for the girls to share wagons with each other so I hadn't given it much thought.

"Your mother is not here?" I asked.

"No, she travels with another clan," she said.

But before I could ask her more, Bora and Nico called out to me "Hey, Goran! The birds aren't going to wait while you chat with Tanya".

"I've got to go!" I said, finishing my delicious breakfast. Indeed, the birds would not wait!

Chapter 33 – Back from the Moon Tent

We had another successful hunt and returned to our camp early. I left the grouse I'd trapped with Mother Miriana, filled my belly with the delicious stew that she had prepared and then went to have a nap in our wagon. Closing my eyes, I wondered if I would be taking flight in my dreams again.

But my cat nap was undisturbed by dreams or by the sound of the wind gently blowing through the leaves that shaded our wagon.

I heard the boys coming in at nightfall. I knew that they were going to the meeting with the men. The more I thought about it, the more uncomfortable I was about what they were doing there.

"Goran," Bora whispered. "Are you awake? Do you want to come with us to the men's fire?"

I opened one eye. I thought about pretending to be asleep but I suspected that Bora knew I was awake. I got up slowly and followed the boys to the distant fire. Once again the men sat in silence. This time, the Baron sat with them. When we were settled, he spoke in a low voice.

"As I have said before, it is crucial to cultivate love with your woman. One way to do this is to sit opposite your partner. Have your left hands facing up and your right hands facing down on top of hers. Focus on the area in the center of your chest, connecting it with the spot between her breasts. Visualize a bright green sphere of light emanating from that place. Feel love growing there and radiating out from the center of your chest, the center of the energy of your heart; see the sphere in your heart merging with hers and expanding out so the two of you form the center of a larger sphere, radiating your love into the world."

"When you focus on your heart center," he continued, "you take power away from your lower, sexual center, the center that drives animals to mate and procreate. For them, it is a good thing to be driven by their lower center, but for us, there is great benefit to couple on a higher plane."

I looked at the circle of men around the fire, eyes closed and lips curved into gentle smiles. I felt very uncomfortable and out of place. I slipped from the circle as quietly as I could, but not before the Baron's eye caught mine. I didn't care if he saw me go. No one could make me stay at the men's fire. I wasn't one of them, I never would be and I could do whatever I wanted.

When I heard Bora and Nico's footsteps on the wagon's wooden ladder, I kept still in my bunk. I didn't want them to ask me why I'd left. I didn't have a good answer.

I lay on my back, looking up at the bottom of Nico's bunk, thinking. The ways of the gypsies were too strange for me. I knew Milada liked being with them, but she had hardly known any other way of life, having come to live with them at such a young age. Mother Miriana told me that she was with the women. Maybe what they were telling her was as strange as what I heard at the men's fire. Maybe it would put her off the idea of staying with them. She must know that she is also different; that she is from another, normal, world.

The next morning at the cooking tent I heard that we would be moving on. I was glad to be leaving this place where I had sat at the men's fire. Once again, I spent my day hunting with the boys. They didn't mention the men's circle or my escape from it, and neither did I.

Milada was still nowhere to be seen and I was missing her. I'd been feeling closer to the boys but, since my experience at the men's circle, I remembered again how different we were. Milada and I came from the same world, even if she wanted to forget it.

That evening, I was finishing my bowl of stew when I saw her crossing the camp, heading in the direction of her wagon.

"Hey! Milada!" I said, running toward her, "Where have you been? I was worried about you, but the old witch said you were with the women. What have you been up to?" I asked. "Learning new tricks?"

She stopped and looked at me in a strange way. I regretted referring to the gypsy with the silver hair as a 'witch'.

"I spent some days with the other women," she said quietly, "now that I am old enough. Do you ever spend time with the men?"

At her words, I felt as if she'd touched an open wound. "Todor asked me if I wanted to join them at their fire'" I told her, wondering how much she knew about what went on there. "I

143

stayed for a while but the things they talked about were so strange I left and did not return."

I looked down at my feet, feeling color rising to my cheeks when I thought about 'coupling'.

"They say we will be moving on tomorrow," I told her, happy to see her. I'd really missed her company over the past few days. "Are you hungry? Let's go see what's cooking."

"I want to go to my wagon and see what Tanya is doing," she replied.

I'm sure my face fell.

"Then I'll meet you at the fire," she added with a smile, brightening the night.

I went to sit by the campfire with the other boys to wait for her to come. Bora was playing his viol, the woman and men once again sitting together and enjoying cheerful music by the light of the fire. Slowly, it burned down to the embers and still Milada did not appear. Where was she?

I heard the kitchen wagon being packed for the journey and looked that way. Milada was helping the other women to stow the cooking pots and vessels. I got up from the fire to go to her, but she turned at went in the direction of her wagon. I started to follow her.

But then I stopped in my tracks. Our eyes had me. She knew I was waiting for her to come, yet she went the other way. What strange things had she been doing with the women, I wondered. Better to leave her to herself tonight. Tomorrow would be another day.

Chapter 34 – A Familiar Village

I thought I would find Milada at the breakfast wagon but she wasn't there. We didn't have a hot breakfast, only bread, cheese and olives to eat now and also take for the journey. I saw Tanya putting some food into a basket.

"Where's Milada?" I asked her.

"Still in her bed!" Tanya replied. "You know she's not an early riser! This food is for her."

"Shall I take it to her?" I asked, but just then the signal to leave sounded.

"We are leaving now," she said. "Better get to your wagon! See you when we camp this evening."

She ran off before I could say anything else. I grabbed some food and hurried back to my wagon.

We travelled all day, mostly on a dirt track that ran through a deep forest. Although the days were warming up, we put a blanket on our laps to keep out the damp chill of the forest. Late in the day, we left the darkness of the woods and caught the last of the spring sunshine as we passed through fields of ripening wheat, dotted with bright red poppies, our wagon casting long shadows on the road ahead of us. I heard the signal indicating that we had arrived. We set up our camp in a clearing close by impressive village walls.

Before we could even light our fires, people from the village had come out to greet us, waving and carrying baskets of food. We were often made to feel welcome when we arrived in a village but I had never seen a display such as this. But I had other things on my mind. I wanted to find Milada!

I left Nico and Bora to decide on where to park our wagon while I went to look for Milada. I quickly found her wagon. She was there with Tanya and Zora, unhitching their horse so it could go and graze with the others.

I waved at the girls and said. "Come on! This looks like a great village. Let's go and explore."

Tanya nodded and said. "I'll finish off here and come and find you later," Milada and I ran off in the direction of the village gate. As we passed through it and followed the road towards the village square Milada cheeks grew pink. She took my hand in excitement and I felt a tingle coursing through me.

"This is my village, Goran!" she exclaimed "This is where I was born. I'm going to find my grandfather. He said he would leave a light on in the window for me!"

How could she know that this was her village, I wondered? She seemed certain it was the place, but less certain which way would bring her to the house she once knew. She looked down at her feet, took a deep breath and kept on walking. We walked in silence all around the village. I was beginning to think that she was mistaken. She looked at the dark windows as we passed one after the other; not one had a candle burning on its sill.

Finally, she stopped before a house near the square. I could see a dim light coming from inside, but no welcoming candle at its one window.

"I think that this is the one," she said quietly.

"Knock on the door and see who lives there," I told her.

She rapped on the door timidly but here was no answer.

"Maybe the people went out to greet the gypsies," I said. "They don't expect them to come knocking at their door!"

I rapped harder, but no one came to answer it.

"Let's go," she said, dejectedly, "There's no one home."

We had taken a few steps away, when the door opened a crack. In the faint light of dusk I thought my eyes were playing tricks on me. It looked as if Milada had opened the door! But there she was, standing next to me.

'Who's there?" the girl inside asked, looking right and left. I stared at the girl and then at Milada.

"What's the matter?" she asked me.

"That girl," I said, "she looks just like you." And she did! Her hair was the same color but where Milada's floated freely around her face, this girl's was mostly contained in a white kerchief. She was paler than Milada and looked more serious, but their features were nearly identical.

"She doesn't look like me!" I thought I heard Milada say, but I was heading back towards the house.

"Good evening," I said to the girl. "I am Goran. I travel with the gypsy band. This is my friend, Milada. She thinks she remembers this house."

The girl smiled at me and then looked Milada up and down.

"I'm Dunia," she said. "This is our house."

"Who lived here before you did?" Milada asked her.

"I don't know why I should tell you," she said, abruptly.

"Go on," I said, giving her my most dazzling smile. "Was it an old man?"

"Well, yes. Actually this house belonged to my great-grandfather," she replied.

"Is he at home, can I see him?" Milada asked, trying to look beyond her into the house.

"Granddad died years ago. We moved in here when I was a little girl," she said, moving to block the door with her body. "I live here with my parents and pesky little sister".

I took Milada by the shoulders and moved her to stand next to Dunia. "You two must be related. You could be sisters."

"The only sister I have is the one inside," she said. "Yagoda, come out here a minute," she called over her shoulder.

A second girl appeared in the doorway, a bit younger than Dunia. She looked like a little vixen with mischief in her eyes.

"This is my sister, Yagoda. Say "hello," Yagoda".

"Hello Yagoda," she said as if bored, turned and went back into the house.

"There was talk of a cousin. My father's brother had a daughter. When his wife died he left the village. He comes back now and again, looking for his daughter, but by the first time he returned Granddad had already passed away. I don't remember what happened to the girl. I think she was called Anna," Dunia said, ignoring her sister.

Once again, I looked at Dunia and then at Milada. "Well then," I told her, "maybe you're from some other house, or some other village. But you sure look like this girl."

She took my hand in hers and said, "Let's go. This has been a long day. I'm tired and hungry."

Happy to have Milada's hand in mine, I tipped my hat to Dunia and made a little bow.

"Good night, then," I told her. "We'll be staying here a while. I look forward to making your acquaintance."

Dunia smiled at me and waved goodnight. She looked less serious when she smiled. And even more like my Milada.

When we were out of earshot I said, "She seems nice".

Milada was silent. What was she thinking? "Too bad it's not your grandfather's house," I said, "or is it?"

I turned to look at her as we walked along. There were tears in her eyes.

Chapter 35 – Milada's Family?

Milada was silent as we walked back to the camp but my mind was full of questions.

"I can't get over how much that Dunia girl looks like you; and the younger one, too," I said. "She looks like you did when I came to live with the gypsies. Seeing her made me realize how long I've been travelling with the band. And you've been with them even longer. Can you remember your life before that?"

"A little," she said.

"Like what?"

"I don't know; playing in the fields, hating to be cooped up in the house; sitting in my Grandma's lap and feeling warm and loved," she said.

"I don't think I ever met my grandparents". I told her, trying to image what it would have been like to have a family. "I can't even remember my father. My mother worked hard, cooking for the tavern. We slept in the back room, on a mattress of straw on the floor. At least it was warm there."

"Why did you leave?" she asked me.

I realized that I had never told Milada my story.

"When my mother got sick and died the landlord of the tavern told me I had to go. I stayed with my uncle for a time, but when summer came I lived by finding odd jobs in other villages, helping at farms or just from the charity of people I met and sleeping wherever I was when night fell. That autumn when it was starting to get cold, I was lucky to meet the gypsy band; and I've travelled with them, and with you, ever since."

"It's hard to remember the time before you came," she said. "One year is so much like the next, moving, following the seasons. Only we get too big for our clothes and need to get bigger ones."

"I don't know how much longer I will stay with the gypsies," I told her. "It's time for me to think of my future, of what I want to do with my life."

"Why not stay with us?" she asked.

There she goes again; thinking that she is one of them! I put my hands on her shoulders and looked her straight in the eye.

"What do you mean with 'us'? You are not one of them any more than I am," I told her. "We are different. We will always be different. Why can't you understand that?"

She pushed me away from her and shouted, "You joined later. I was just a baby. I don't want another life, stuck in one place all the time!"

"You weren't so young that you don't remember your life before the gypsies," I said, "that house, your Grandpa…"

"Just leave me alone!" she yelled and ran off in the direction of the camp.

I shook my head. I knew I was right, but she couldn't or wouldn't accept reality. I looked for her when I got back to the camp but did not see her anywhere. Most of the gypsies had gathered around the cooking fire and as I moved closer I understood why. There was a delicious aroma of grilling meat in the air thanks to the generosity of the villagers. I ate my fill of succulent sausages and vegetables, then went to sit by the fire in the hope that Milada would be there.

I didn't see her sitting with the others. I watched as the musicians tuned up and began to play. After I while I saw Milada and Dragan coming from the woods. They joined Tanya at the cooking fire. Where had they been? I wondered if Milada was still mad at me for trying to make her see reason. Our eyes met and I was pleased that she didn't look away. She smiled at me and I went over to her.

"I had a little shock," she said, by way of an apology for running off. "This is the village where I lived before".

"I knew it!" I said and sat down beside her. "Those girls are so like you. I knew you had to be related. Why didn't you stay and talk with them? Why didn't you tell them that you were Anna?"

"I was just so surprised," she said, "and shocked. What do I have in common with them now? I don't remember them at all."

"Dunia is your age," Dragan said. "Didn't you play together?"

How did Dragan know the girl's name? Milada must have confided in him. I felt a pang of jealousy at the thought of them together.

"There was one girl who was often in our house," she said, "but she liked to stay indoors and I hated to stay in the house. I was always outside unless the weather was so bad that my Grandma would not allow it."

"Let's go back tomorrow and tell them," I said.

"I don't think I want to do that," she murmured.

"Why not?"

"Soon we will be moving on again," she said. "What difference will it make if they know I am their cousin? They don't know me at all."

"What if your father comes back again?" I asked. "Don't you want to meet him?" I was thinking that I would give anything for the chance to meet my own father.

"I never knew my father," she said. "The gypsies are the only family I need."

At her words, I couldn't suppress a sigh. I held my tongue, not wanting to say anything in front of Tanya and Dragan.

"Let's all go meet them," Tanya said, breaking the silence. "Maybe when you get to know them you will want to tell them that you are cousins."

Dragan smiled at Tanya and took her hand.

"That is a wise suggestion," he said. "It's usually preferable to let a situation develop and then respond rather than forcing it."

~

The following morning Milada, Tanya and I went to the village. The main square was full of activity. It was market day and people from the countryside had gathered to sell their wares.

We passed some cheese sellers and Milada's eyes sparkled.

"Remember how you used to steal the cheese?" she asked me with a little giggle.

It was good to see her looking happy and relaxed again.

"I never stole any cheese," I told her with a grin, "Those nice ladies where happy to give it to me! Look over there; it's Dunia and her sister."

They stood at a stall selling brightly colored ribbons.

"Look at those pretty ribbons!" Tanya said, stepping up to the colorful stall. "I think I have a few coins. I'll buy some for our hair."

"I like those bright red ones," Milada said, reaching out to touch them.

"I like the green ones," Tanya said.

I approached the girl from the house.

"Hello Dunia, hello, uh…I'm sorry, I've forgotten your name," I said to the younger girl.

"Hello," Dunia said, "You are back! My sister's name is Yagoda. Say 'Hello', Yagoda".

I think she heard but Yagoda ignored us, focusing her attention on the ribbons.

"Hello! I'm Tanya," Tanya said brightly. "Aren't these ribbons lovely? Which color do you like best?"

"I don't like all these bright colors," Dunia said. "Yagoda wanted to come and have a look and it's my job to keep an eye on her."

"I think they are beautiful," Milada said, "the brighter the better."

Tanya took out her coins and selected two of the long ribbons.

"I will cut mine into two pieces, one for each braid," she said as she handed two copper coins to the vendor.

"I may leave mine long to flow when I dance or cut off some small pieces to make bows," Milada said when Tanya gave the red one to her. "Thank you so much".

She gathered her hair into a bunch at the back of the head, playing with the ribbon, but not leaving her hair tied back even for a moment.

"Do you have another coin? We can get a ribbon for Dobro's mane?" She said, shaking her hair free, and wrapping the bright ribbon around loosely around her neck.

"Who or what is Dobro?" Dunia asked.

"Dobro is our Baron's son's wonderful black horse," she replied.

I caught myself feeling annoyed that she was thinking about Dragan.

"You will spend money to buy a ribbon for a horse?" Dunia said, shocked. "It's bad enough buying them for yourselves, but ribbons for a horse, well I never heard of such a thing."

Tanya and Milada looked mischievously at one another. I could see that they thought Dunia's outrage was comical.

"What color do you think Dobro would like," Tanya asked, fingering an orange ribbon, "the orange one or the blue?"

"Definitely the blue," Milada said, her eyes shining and the corners of her mouth twitching as if she were trying to look serious but wanted to break out laughing.

I felt a little badly for Dunia, being the brunt of their joke. I changed the subject, turned to her and said, "As you are from this village, show us where we can find the best cheese."

"The best cheese comes from the shepherd who takes his sheep to high pastures. It is early in the year, though. There is still snow up there, but he may have some cheese from the last season preserved in brine," she told me. "I'll show you where to find his stall."

"Come on, Yagoda," she said, tugging on her sister's sleeve.

"Can't I buy a ribbon?" the young one said.

"Do you have any money?" Dunia asked her.

"No," she replied.

"Then how to you expect to buy a ribbon?"

"You have money," Yagoda snapped.

"I was given money to buy food, not frivolous things," Dunia replied. "Let's go".

Yagoda combed through the bunch of ribbons with her fingers, gently at first, but then she roughly yanked a handful of them and they fell to the ground. She ran off as the stall keeper muttered in anger before bending down to pick the ribbons from the dust.

I kept pace with Dunia as she strode purposefully to the cheese sellers' stalls.

"Try this one," Dunia said, handing me small piece of cheese.

Milada and Tanya had caught up with us. Milada asked, "Can we have a taste, too?"

The cheese seller looked at Milada and said, "You are from the gypsy band, yes?"

"Yes, we are," she replied.

"Here, have a taste of these two. Tell me which one you like and I'll give you a piece to take to your camp."

"Thank you very much," she said with a grateful smile.

"Thank you, madam, you are very kind," said Tanya, taking the proffered pieces.

"I like the soft one," she said. "It is only made at this time of year when the young lambs are being born and the ewes have much milk."

The cheese seller said, "Good choice! Here you are. When will the gypsies come and play music in the village square?"

"Thank you, so much," Tanya said. "I don't know when we will come but it will be soon, I'm sure. Thank you for your kindness and generosity."

Dunia bought three small pieces of different cheeses. As we walked away from the stall she told me, "We in the village have to pay for what we buy, but your gypsy band gets everything free".

"I am not one of the gypsies," I told her; "I am just living with them for a while. Not all villages are as welcoming as this one."

"Our village isn't always so welcoming. Yours is the only group that gets such treatment," she said.

Tanya overheard her and said, "Do you know why that is?"

"No," Dunia replied.

"Many years ago, they say, the people of this village fell gravely ill and were dying." Tanya began, "Many had died and many more lay in their beds close to death. Our band arrived and camped near the village. When we came to the square it was empty. The streets were deserted; the market had closed down because vendors feared catching the illness."

"One of our elders knocked on the door of the headman of the village to find out what was happening. Up until that time people mistrusted the gypsies, but the situation was so bad that the headman explained about the illness that was decimating the village."

"Later that day many gypsies came into the village with a broth made from healing plants and roots. They went from house to house, giving people the rich soup and tending to anyone who was already suffering from the illness. After three days, people started to recover. After a week everyone in the village was fine."

"A feast was held to celebrate and thank the gypsies. And from that day forward the people in this village have always welcomed us."

Dunia murmured "magic…" I hoped that the girls hadn't heard her.

Milada asked Tanya, "When did that happen?"

"It was a long time ago," Tanya replied. "Mother Miriana was a young woman then. She must remember."

Chapter 36 - The Village Girls

After we'd stowed the packets of cheese in Tanya's basket, she said, "I am going back to camp. I'll bring the cheese to the cooking tent".

She reminded Milada that the women from the band had taken some bread dough to the baker that morning. "Why don't you pass by there and see if they need help carrying the loaves back to camp?" she suggested."

"Alright," she said, "I'll see you back there in a little while".

She asked Dunia, "Can you tell me where the baker's shop is?"

Dunia said, "Go down that street, turn left at Rico's house, then turn right until the cross street…"

Milada looked confused. I was surprised when the younger girl said, "I'll show you the way".

"Thank you," Milada told her, "that will be very helpful."

I wanted to go with Milada, but I felt bad leaving the other sister alone. I could tell that she was anxious to get back to her home.

The elder sister wasn't so bad. She was Milada's cousin after all; I figured it wouldn't hurt to be polite. "And I'll walk Dunia home," I said to Milada. "I'll see you later at the camp."

Dunia gave me a surprisingly bright smile.

"Let me carry your basket for you," I said, smiling back.

"Thank you," she said, passing me the basket. When our fingers touched on its handle for a moment, she didn't pull away. She stopped to make some more purchases on the way back to her house. Unlike Milada, she knew how to drive a hard bargain. I winked at her when she managed to get an extra measure of dried beans by threatening to take her business elsewhere and she gave me another dazzling smile.

When we arrived at her cottage, she held out her hand for the basket.

"I would love to invite you in," she said, but if my father comes home and finds a gypsy boy in his house he would tan my hide!"

"I'm not a gypsy," I told her. "I am from a village like you, and one day I will settle down in one."

"But you live a life of a gypsy now," she observed, standing on the threshold.

"I have no family," I told her. "I was hungry, cold and alone when the gypsy band offered me the chance to stay with them. I am grateful for what they have giving me, but the older I get, the more I know that their life is not for me. It is only a matter of time before I settle down somewhere."

"That, may be," Dunia said, but my father would still not be happy to find you here alone with me."

She looked to the left and to the right and then blushed.

"You had better go now," she said, waving at a face that had just vanished behind a curtain in a nearby house. "The neighbors are watching and may tell my father that we were talking."

"Since when is it a crime to talk?" I asked her.

"You don't know my father! Go now, please," she said, taking a step back into the house.

"Bye, then," I said, tipping my hat. "See you around."

I took my time returning to the gypsy camp. I liked the look of Milada's village. The people seemed friendly, except for the thought of Dunia's dad!

When I returned to the camp, I heard that we would stay for two turns of the moon. Maybe I could find some odd jobs to do here to fatten my bag of coins.

The days passed pleasantly. There was no need to hunt; the villagers provided us with more food than we needed. Sometimes the boys and I went fishing in the stream. We spent hours sitting in silence. I was happy that they no longer talked to me about what they did at the men's fire and I surely was not going to ask!

At the end of the day, we hung the fish we'd caught on a rack where they slowly smoked over a low fire. We didn't need them now, but preserved this way they would last well into the following winter.

Often I went into the village. The vendors recognized me now as the boy who travelled with the gypsies and were very generous with their wares. I noticed a group of boys watching me. Every afternoon they passed the time sitting on the shady side of the square, talking and playing amongst themselves. Not one of them ever called out a greeting as I passed. The group went strangely quiet as I walked by. Once, I thought I heard one of them spit on the ground and mutter what sounded like "dirty gypsy". I wasn't sure I'd heard right so I kept my eyes down and walked on.

Sometimes I ran into Dunia and her sister in the village square, either hurrying to do the shopping, or, more rarely, enjoying a chat with the other girls. One sunny afternoon I approached a group of them gossiping with each other near the fountain where they went to collect water for their homes.

"Good day, ladies!" I said. My eyes met Dunia's and she blushed when I walked toward her.

"Hello, Dunia; Yagoda," I said. The girls all went silent, casting down their eyes and skittishly moving aside like nervous birds.

"Is he a gypsy?" I heard one of them whisper.

"Hello, Goran," Yagoda said, boldly. "Yes, he's a gypsy!"

"Well, actually, he's not," Dunia clarified. "He lives with them, but he is from a village, like we are."

I saw that she had filled a large jug with water from the fountain.

"Let me help you with that," I said, lifting it to my shoulder. I could hear some of the other girls giggling. Dunia smiled, and looked even more like Milada.

"I can manage," she said. "I fetch water every day at least once. Yagoda is finally old enough to help."

"I don't doubt that you can do it yourself," I told her, "but it would be my pleasure to do it for you today."

Her blush deepened. "That's very kind of you, but no," she said.

I realized that I was embarrassing her in front of the other girls and held out the heavy jug for her to take. Things were simpler at the gypsy camp! Boys and girls, men and women, all did things together without blushes and embarrassment. I waved them goodbye and headed back to the camp, hoping to find Milada and tell her that I'd met her cousins in the village.

Chapter 37 - A Sweet Hunt

Very early one morning I heard something buzzing around my head. I wasn't ready to wake up yet! There was hardly any light filtering through the high window above Bora's bunk. I half opened one eye and saw a honeybee flitting around in the air. I was surprised to see it in the wagon; bees usually don't like being too close to people.

The buzzing must have woken Bora as well. He whispered, "Where there are bees, there is honey!"

He slowly rose from his bunk and motioned for me and Nico, who was also stirring, to do the same; his finger over his lips to keep us silent. He reached under his bunk and took a bucket from where it was stored. Nico took a second one and I grabbed the last, making a little noise as I did so.

At the sound, the bee lit on the edge of Nico's bunk. We all stood stock still and waited. I wasn't sure why, but I knew I'd better follow Bora's lead. After a moment, the bee was in flight again. Bora slowly opened the curtain that protected the entry of the wagon and the bee flew right out.

"Come on!" Bora said, taking off after the bee. The three of us ran after it, stopping when it stopped on a flower and then starting again when it took to the air. Eventually, the bee led us to a big tree in the forest. Bora motioned for us to stop before we got too close. I could see why. The air around the tree was darkened by thousands of bees flying in and out of a hole about halfway up the tall trunk.

Nico and Bora smiled. I whispered, "Where there are bees there is honey!" I remembered that the band had used all the honey they had stored so it would be great to replenish the stock.

"We have buckets to put the honey in," Bora said, "but we can't just take it from the bees."

"No," said Nico. "First we need to ask their permission and then we'll need some smoke to encourage them to let us collect some of their delicious honey."

"It's not far to go back to camp," Bora said. "I'll stay here and charm the bees. You two go and bring an ember and a bowl to hold a smoky fire. Bring some rags and, Goran, see if you can find some lighter color trousers to wear."

I noticed that my pants were dark brown and the other boys' were beige. I wondered what difference the color of my trousers made. As we walked quickly back to camp Nico explained, "Bees are attracted to darker colors. Hopefully, they will allow us to take some of their honey, but if they feel disturbed they might want to sting us!"

We approached the cooking fire to get an ember. Mother Miriana was stirring the pot with breakfast porridge. I ran back to our wagon, changed my trousers, pulling on a pair of Bora's lighter colored ones, and took my bowl. I was hungry! I held it out and she filled it. I was thinking how nice it would be with some honey!

"Tomorrow we'll have porridge with honey!" I said, with my mouth still a little full.

Mother Miriana looked at me with a smile, "Is that wishful thinking or did you find a honey tree?" she asked.

"We found a honey tree not far from here," I said. "We are going now to take some honey."

"Take only from the very top of the hive," she said. "Be careful not to disturb the Queen bee and her children. They live in its heart."

"I don't think I'll be taking honey at all!" I said. "I'll leave that to the boys who know how to get it. I'll just help carry it back."

"A wise decision, I'd say," she replied.

"Come on, Goran!" Nico said. "Bring your bowl since you have it with you and let's go."

We made our way back to the honey tree, slowing and lightening our steps as we got nearer to it. Bora sat beneath the tree, swaying a little and humming to himself. When I got closer I could hear that his humming was very much like the buzzing of the bees.

Nico handed him some long, thin rags and the boys tied each other's sleeves and trouser legs close to their bodies. Nico motioned me to come closer and likewise bound the openings of my clothes. He motioned to tie the neck of my shirt as tightly as it would go. He took my bowl and filled it with straw that he pulled out of his pockets. He shook the ember out of a small metal container and immediately the straw began to produce a choking cloud of smoke.

He waved the smoke about me first, then around Bora, then passed him the smoking bowl. Bora blew some smoke around Nico then started to climb the tree. He ascended from branch to branch until he could reach the hole where the bees busily flew in and out. I could hear his gentle humming as he wafted the smoke into the hole.

The bees dispersed, some settling on branches of the tree, others flying off. Nico climbed part way up the tree, carrying one of the buckets. He handed it up to Bora and took the smoking bowl in exchange.

He whispered, "Goran, here, take this and bring me another bucket."

I did as I was told, placing the still smoking bowl on the ground and handing up another empty bucket. Soon, one bucket was full. Bora handed it down to Nico and Nico passed it to me. I put it on a flat piece of ground a little bit away from the tree and handed up the third bucket as Nico passed me down the second one.

Soon Bora was back on the ground and we each had a very full bucket of honey and honey comb.

"Let's thank the bees for their generosity and get out of their way," he said.

I smiled at the tree and the bees flying around it, mentally thanking them. After all this time with the gypsies, I didn't find it strange to talk to animals or even insects anymore! There were some bees buzzing around the buckets full of honey. I was concerned that my hand might be stung, but as we slowly made out way back to camp, there were fewer and fewer bees buzzing around us.

Returning to the cooking wagon I was happy to see that Milada and her friends were there, helping to prepare the midday meal.

Here come the boys," she said to them when she spotted us coming.

"Hello!" she said. "Have you been hunting?"

"Only hunting for hollow trees," I told her, "filled with honey!"

As if we'd planned it, each of us held out our full bucket of honey.

"Come give us a taste!" Milada said.

I moved closer to where she was cutting up some onions for the stew. She reached out her hand to scoop some honey with her finger, but I pulled the bucket away before she could.

"I don't need onion flavored honey!" I said. I dipped my finger into the bucket and held it out for her to have a taste. Anxious for the sweet taste, she took my finger in her mouth. Many times she'd tasted things this way, but this day something was different. When she put her lips on my finger and drew it into her mouth I felt a stirring deep inside of me. I didn't recognize this peculiar feeling, but I liked it!

I looked down at Milada's hair, wanting the feeling to last but Zora spoke to me and I felt I'd been awaked from a particularly nice dream.

"Go fetch a ceramic pot for the honey and let us get on with our work," Zora scolded.

Reluctantly, I set the bucket down and went to look for the honey pot. As I turned to go, I heard one of the girls say to Milada, "He's cute. Is he your boyfriend?"

I could not hear her reply. By the time I located a large ceramic pot and returned to the fire the girls had gone. Only Mother Miriana and Zora remained, stirring aromatic herbs into the stew.

"I finally found a honey pot," I said, placing it on the trestle table beside the buckets. "I'm glad we have more honey now! I've missed its sweet taste!"

"Do you know, young Goran," Mother Miriana said, "that honey is more than just a tasty food. It is also a life saver."

"How is that?" I asked.

"Honey is a wonderful substance for healing," she said. "It will help relieve a cough very quickly. If you have a wound, placing honey in it will help it heal much faster and prevent the wound from becoming septic and spreading poison to the rest of the body."

"All of this from the little bees!" I mused.

"Yes," Zora said, "We have a lot to thank them for!"

I spotted a small jug hanging from the kitchen wagon.

"May I take a little honey to some friends in the village?" I asked, thinking of Dunia and her sister. "We can take some more tomorrow."

"You may take some honey," said Mother Miriana; "but tomorrow will be too soon to collect more. Give the bees some time to replenish their hive. We can take a bit more before we travel on."

Her words made sense. I ladled some golden honey into the jug, placing a small wooden plate on top. Zora was watching what I was doing and handed me a clean square rag to wrap the jug to keep the plate firmly on top.

"You don't want the honey to spill," she said; "it's precious; and spilled honey makes a sticky mess!"

"Thanks, Zora," I said. I put the jug carefully into my pack and headed toward the village. The sun was hanging low in the west. If I hurried, I'd catch Dunia at the fountain.

Chapter 38 – Another Hunt, Less Sweet Indeed

On my way to find Dunia, while passing the group of boys loitering in the shade as usual, I heard one of them mutter "free loader". The others sniggered.

I stopped in my tracks. "What did you say?" I asked, not directing my question at anyone in particular since I had no idea who made the comment. But looking at them one by one, I could guess who had spoken. One boy was obviously the leader. Though not the biggest, he had a cocky stance and sharp eyes.

I wasn't surprised when he opened his mouth to speak.

"I said 'free loader'," he replied, "because that is what you and your people are."

Part of me wanted to keep on walking, to not engage in any conversation with these boys. There were many of them, and if provoked they could easily gang up on me. But I couldn't let them call me names or throw insults at the generous people who had taken me in and helped their village in its time of need.

I had a split second to decide; do I walk by or do I say something; and, if so, what? In the moment I hesitated, two of the boys sauntered in front of me, blocking my path. Now I would have to speak.

"It's payback," I said. If the girls didn't know the story of how this band of gypsies had helped the village, probably the boys didn't either. But would they care?

"Payback?" the cocky boy inquired, sticking out his chin.

"Yes. Payback," I said. "You know what that means."

"You hit me and then I hit you back harder," he said, looking at me from the corner of his eyes. "And?"

"And a long time ago the gypsies helped the people in your village," I told him. "*Some* of the people here remember and are still grateful," the implication being that these boys were not.

"And what have *you* done for us?" he sneered. "What can *you* do?"

"I can do anything I set my mind to!" I said, wondering where he was going with this.

"Can you hunt?" he asked.

"Sure," I told him, "the gypsy boys showed me how when I went to live with them."

"You aren't one of the gypsies," he stated rather than asked.

"No," I said, "I've lived with them for a few years and learned some of their ways."

"So you *are* a freeloader then," he concluded, to another round of chortles from the other boys.

"Ok," I said. "I have no problem to work in exchange for what I am given. What do you want me to do?"

The cocky one glanced at the others, then looked back at me. "You know how to hunt," he said, "let's go catch a boar. The girls can make some sausages for the feast that this village always throws when your lot comes. Luckily, it isn't too often."

Boars are very dangerous creatures. I'd seen them in the woods from time to time and was surprised at how fast they could run on what looked like stubby legs. The gypsy boys never hunted boar on their own; this was a job for the strongest of the men. But I couldn't back down now.

"Fine," I said, let's go.

The boy dropped his chin a little and seemed to be surprised at my response. The boys who had been blocking my path fell back into the shadows with the others who had gone very quiet.

"What are we waiting for," I asked, emboldened by their response. "We need to get to the forest before it gets dark. Dusk is the best time to hunt for boars. Their eyesight isn't very good, you know, so we will have an advantage if the light is low".

"Let's go," he said. "We need to take our spears. Misha, Stanyo go; bring one for me and one for this boy, too. Then meet us on the way to the woods."

"Are you sure you want to do this, Jelko?" the boy called Misha asked.

"I told you! Go and get the spears. This boy will catch us a boar," he spat.

I was going to catch a boar? What kind of trick is this? Catching a boar requires team work. I couldn't face one alone! I was beginning to feel frightened, but I couldn't let it show!

But then, I had a thought. We probably wouldn't even see any boars! I just needed to prove I was willing to go and hunt one. Why did it matter? I knew that if I was going to be staying in this village, even if for a short time, it would be better to not to have these boys as my enemies. If I showed them I was brave enough to go into the woods to look for wild boars, it might be enough to earn their respect.

We left the safety of the village by the gate on the opposite side from where the gypsies were camped and headed into the forest twilight. Although the sun was still above the horizon, the leafy trees cast us into deep shade. The other boys soon caught up with us and handed that Jelko boy and me each a long wooden spear tipped with a bronze point.

Without thinking I did what the gypsy boys had taught me. I called out with my mind and invited a beast to offer itself to us. Almost immediately, I regretted it and stopped, but not before I heard a rustle in the dense bush not far from where we stood.

I motioned for the others to be quiet. I saw the color drain from their faces when they became aware of the noise in the bush. Jelko, who seemed braver than the others, signaled me to step forward. He and the two boys with spears fell in behind me. The others spread out, away from us. I knew that if we wanted to catch the boar they should move around behind it and flush it out of the bush. I remembered that the gypsy men used nets, not spears when they hunted boar, but it was too late now to tell the boys.

I felt the boys backing off. Was this all a trick to get me hurt? Some of them started to run. The sound of their feet crushing and cracking the small twigs that littered the forest floor must have startled the boar. It came roaring out of the bush at phenomenal speed. Jelko stood transfixed as the beast headed directly for him! I quickly stepped aside and as it ran past me I shouted and threw my spear. I knew it wasn't hard enough to even wound the raging animal but it might startle it and give the boy a chance to get out of its way.

My spear hit the boar and fell to the ground as the animal kept running. Jelko ducked to the side but didn't have time to move fully out of its path. He yelled out as one of the boar's sharp tusks gorged his thigh.

Swearing, he fell to the ground, writhing in pain. I ran up to him, sure that the boar was long gone, escaping into the densest part of the forest.

"My leg!" Jelko cried! "There is so much blood!"

As the other boys slowing gathered round, I knew what I had to do. I had seen Mother Miriana deal with situations like this. I need to slow down the bleeding. Shrugging off my homespun shirt, I ripped off one of its long sleeves.

Kneeling down beside the boy, I put my palm on his forehead, to reassure him and stop him from thrashing around.

"Lie still," I told him. "Try to steady your breathing."

The boar had done a good job of tearing his trousers. I ripped the fabric so I could see the extent of the wound. There was a deep gash on the outside of his left thigh and it was bleeding profusely. I took the sleeve and tied it as tightly as I could around the boy's thigh, higher up than wound. I saw that although it was still bleeding the cut was so longer spouting blood; now it was just slowly oozing.

The next thing to do was to clean the wound. I often carried a water skin with me and today I was glad that I had. I ran to where I'd dropped my pack and took out the water skin. I noticed the small earthenware jug wrapped in a cloth. Carefully, I removed the square rag and poured some clean water on it. Gently, I mopped up some of the blood from the boy's leg. Then I remembered what Mother Miriana had told me about honey.

"Someone bring me some leaves from that chestnut tree," I yelled, pointing at the tree that shaded us.

I ran some water over my fingers then reached into to the jug and took a big daub of honey. Forgetting that this boy probably had wanted to do me harm, I told him, as I had heard Mother Miriana say, "Take a deep breath in..."

I held my hand with the honey near his wound. "Now exhale," I told him as I packed the honey into the cut. He winced, but I knew from my own experience that the pain was less when you exhaled.

I saw that Misha was beside me with the chestnut leaves. Holding the wound closed, I placed them on top of it to seal it. I knew the leaves were cleaner than the other sleeve of my shirt that I then used to tie the leaves in place and keep the wound closed. I placed my hands on the boys thighs like I'd seen the gypsies do time and again and willed the cut to heal and the bleeding to stop. The few boys who had not run back to the village stood around in awe.

When I felt the time was right, I loosened the sleeve I'd tied to slow the bleeding. Waiting until I was sure that the wound was closed, I removed it altogether. Jelko looked up at me. I had seen the fear in his eyes when he was first hurt. I could see that he was still in pain, but the fear had gone and some of his old cheekiness was returning.

"Well," he said, "that was all very unexpected!"

I took a chance and smiled at him. "You'll live," I said. "Boys, can you carry your friend back to the village?"

The two biggest boys held each other's forearms, making a kind of seat. Misha and I helped Jelko up, careful not to put any weight on his left leg.

We walked back to the village in silence. At the square, I kept going straight, heading for the other gate that would take me to the gypsy camp. I'd need to get some fresh honey for Dunia, but not today; the stars were already starting to come out. Before our roads parted, Jelko beckoned me to come close to him.

"You're alright, boy," he said with a wink. "See you 'round."

Chapter 39 – Girls in the Market Place

I hurried back to the gypsy camp, lost in thought. Had the boys planned for me to be the one to be gored by the boar? I didn't think so. They were just testing me to see if I was brave enough to go looking for one. I was surprised that one actually came! Was it because I called it, like the gypsies had taught me? No; it must have been just a coincidence.

But it wasn't a coincidence that I was able to help the wounded boy. I realized that I had learned useful things from my time travelling with the gypsy band. I wondered why people in the villages didn't have this knowledge. I remember people dying after being wounded by wild boars; that's why only the bravest and strongest men even attempted to catch one, even though the meat is delicious.

By the time I got to the camp, the stars were shining brightly. I had something to eat and then joined the others at the fire. Milada was deep in conversation with the girls. I watched the golden light of the flames reflected in her unbound hair. She cocked her head at something that Tanya said, her lips breaking into a big smile. I considered going to join them to see what was making her smile, but before I could get up I saw Dragan emerging from the shadows. He sat down between Milada and Tanya, putting one of his long arms around each girl.

As I looked on, Milada blushed at his touch, her eyes shining as she looked into his. I longed for her eyes to light up like that when they looked into mine. I couldn't bear to stay any longer and made my way back to my empty wagon.

The next morning, I didn't see Milada, or the other girls at breakfast. In the distance I noticed the tent with the pink flags had been erected. Only Mother Miriana and some of the very young girls were at the cooking wagon. I stirred the last of the honey from the jug in my pack into my porridge. It tasted wonderful. When I'd finished, I added some fresh honey to the jug, wrapped it in a cloth to keep it safe and set off to the village.

First I went to the village square to see if Dunia was at the fountain, but at that time of day the square was empty except for the old men sitting in the sun. I continued on to the market place, greeted the vendors and eventually spotted Dunia and her sister at the sausage stall. Yagoda stood a little ways behind, scuffing her foot on the dusty ground, humming to herself.

As I got closer I heard Dunia arguing with the vendor.

"We agreed on the price of one copper for six sausages," she was saying' "the six sausages that I chose."

The butcher crossed his husky forearms. "Young lady," he bellowed, "we agreed the price, now take your sausages."

"These six that you have given me are much smaller! This will not do at all," she exclaimed thrusting the packet into his hands.

"Give me back my money, I will buy my meat from someone else!"

"Take your sausages and go!" he said, shoving the packet back at her and turning away.

A small crowd was beginning to gather around them, "Give me the sausages I chose and I'll go," she said, "or else I want my money back."

People began to murmur, asking each other what was going on. The butcher couldn't help noticing. Concerned with his reputation and seeing that Dunia was not about to back down he grudgingly opened the packet, took out the small sausages and wrapped up the six larger ones. He practically threw the packet at her, then busied himself arranging his wares.

Dunia put the sausages in her basket, turned on her heel and strode off, calling Yagoda to follow. I was impressed at how she stood her ground, refusing to let the butcher take advantage of her. I caught up with her at the edge of the market.

"Hello, Dunia! Yagoda!" I said coming up beside the girls.

"Hello, Goran!" Dunia said.

"That was impressive," I told her with a smile.

"What was?" she asked.

"Your little show with the butcher!" I said.

"Oh," she said, with a becoming blush. "You saw that?"

"Yes," I said. "You were right not to give in to that cheating brute."

"He did that to me once before," she told me, "but I didn't notice until I got home! So this time I checked before accepting the goods."

"Why did you go back to him?" I asked. "There are other butcher stalls in the market place".

"Well, he does make the best sausages," she said, "and I wanted to warn others that he is tricky. If he had given me the ones I'd chosen this time I would have let the other time pass, but no one cheats me twice and gets away with it!"

"Are we going home," drawled Yagoda, bored by our conversation.

"Yes, it's almost time to start the midday meal," she said, heading in the direction of their cottage; the home that once was Milada's.

"Before you go," I said reaching out and lightly touching her arm as she moved past me, "I have something for you."

At my touch, she stopped and lowered her eyes to the cobblestones, blushing again. She looked up at me through her long eyelashes and gave me a shy smile. Where was the bold girl willing to do battle with the huge butcher?

I took the small parcel with the honey from my pack and tucked it into her basket.

"A little something sweet," I murmured as she smiled once more and then hurried on her way.

"Did you bring something for me?" Yagoda asked.

I hadn't noticed that she'd stayed behind.

"I brought the honey for both of you?" I told her.

"MMM! I LOVE honey!" she exclaimed. "Did you steal it from the bees all by yourself?"

"No, not at all," I said. "My friends climbed up the honey tree while I held the buckets."

"Oh well," she said. "I still love honey."

"Shouldn't you be on your way?" I asked her, seeing Dunia waiting in the distance.

"I'd rather stay here with you," she said. "I hate being in the house all the time."

"You sister is waiting," I told her, beginning to feel uncomfortable. I don't know what it was, maybe that she looked so much like Milada but spoke and acted so differently, but I wished that she would go on home.

"Let her wait!" she said, smiling at me and kicking up a little dust with her toes.

"I need to get going now," I told her firmly. "Go along now before your sister gets angry."

"I don't care if she gets angry," she said planting herself more firmly with her hands on her hips, her basket swinging from her elbow. "Where are you going?"

"That's really none of your business," I heard myself saying. I turned away and moved into the crowded market place, hoping that she would not follow me. When I knew I'd lost her I realized how silly the situation was. I was running away from a little girl! But a little girl who made me feel very uncomfortable!

Chapter 40 – The Village Boys

As I passed the cheese vendors they called out to me to take some fresh cheese back to the gypsy camp. The bakers also offered me some loaves of bread and I filled my pack. I wasn't surprised when the burly butcher did not offer anything! The sun was already past its high point and I realized that I was hungry. I didn't think that anyone would mind if I tore off a piece of crispy crust to go with a bit of cheese. I enjoyed my little picnic in the square, washing it down with fresh cool water from the village fountain.

As the sun moved behind the houses casting them into shadow, the boys began to gather in their accustomed place on the edge of the square. I wondered how that boy, Jelko, was doing. I didn't have to wonder for long. I watched as he limped into the square to join the other boys.

When he saw me sitting beside the fountain he motioned for me to come over.

"Hey, boy," he yelled.

Slowly, I walked across the square to where the boys sat. They did not look so threatening today.

"I have I name," I told the leader.

"What is it?" he asked with a jaunty smile.

"Goran," I told him. "You are Jelko, I think."

"That I am!" he said. "Goran, eh? Let's call you Gogo for short."

'Gogo' wasn't much shorter, in fact not shorter at all, but if calling me 'Gogo' would make me more accepted it was alright by me.

"And this here is Misha," he went on, indicating a stocky boy with light brown hair and a dusting of freckles across his turned up nose."

"Hello," Misha said with a shy grin.

"And this is Stanyo, my little brother".

I didn't know if he was teasing me. Stanyo was at least a head taller and much broader than Jelko was!

"Hello, brother!" I said, playing along in case it was a joke.

The other boys laughed and I began to relax. Jelko told me the names of the other boys, too, but I could tell that Misha and Stanyo were his closest mates.

"How's the leg'" I asked him.

"Not so bad," he replied. "My mother was very surprised when she saw what you had done."

"Did you tell her how you got the wound?" I asked him.

"Are you kidding!" he exclaimed! "If she knew I was out looking for boars she's have Papa skin me alive!"

"So you don't go boar hunting often, then," I asked with a grin.

"Well, not so frequently, really," he grinned back.

"We could have been killed," I told him. "Look what happened to you? It could have been a lot worse."

"What were the chances of actually seeing a boar?" he said.

"Pretty high, I guess," I replied. The boys were chuckling at our exchange, but not in a nasty way.

Misha said, "How did you know to put that thing around his leg to stop the blood?"

I learned it from the gypsies," I told him. "They know a lot about healing. It was lucky I had that honey with me, too."

"My mother told me that a long time ago these gypsies helped people in our village," Jelko said.

"I tried to tell you that yesterday".

"When she saw my leg wrapped up with leaves, she remembered how they came when she was a little girl and fed everyone magic soup and tended the sick people with leaves and things."

"The gypsies say that they don't have magic, only knowledge," I told the boys who were listening with attention.

"I don't know about that," Stanyo said. "I've seen less deep wounds than Jelko's fester and turn black. When he uncovered it this morning to have a look the skin was pink and starting to mend and he's already able to walk around."

"Yeh, it looks like magic to me," said another of the boys.

"Whether it is magic or not," Jelko said, "I have to thank you; first for distracting that boar so it only got my leg and not my belly and second for dressing the wound so well."

"When your leg is better we can go hunting for other things, rabbits, birds, if you like," I told him.

"That would be great," he said. "I know some good spots to look for rabbits."

"Where did you find the honey," Misha said, "It's one of my favorite things!"

"We found a honey tree in the forest," I said.

"We can bring all our buckets and clean it out!" Misha said, patting his belly.

"Unless the gypsies take it all first," one of the boys said, darkly.

"They took a few bucketfuls, but no more," I said.

"Why didn't you take it all when you had the chance?" Jelko asked, looking puzzled.

"They say if we take a little, the hive stays strong and the bees will make more. Then we can go back and help ourselves." I repeated what Mother Miriana had told me. "If we take it all, we may kill the bee colony or the queen might fly away and start a new hive somewhere else, far from us."

"Hummm, I guess that makes sense," Jelko said, absentmindedly rubbing his wounded thigh.

"Enough of this talk," Misha said. "We won't go looking for honey today. Let's have a game of bones!"

"Bones?" I said.

"It's really fun," Stanyo said. "But you need some coins?"

"Coins? What for?" I asked, fingering the few I'd brought with me to the market, even though I never seemed to need to pay for anything.

"To place bets," he said.

I must have looked perplexed because Misha slapped me on my shoulder and said, "Don't tell me that you've never played 'bones'!"

"I've not only never played it," I told him. "I haven't got a clue what it is."

"Look here," he said, taking four odd shaped bones from his pocket. "These are the bones."

I could see that they were from the legs of sheep. All four fit in the palm of his hand. He took one and gave it to me.

"See the shape?" he said. The bone had six sides. Two of them were rounded, two were narrow and two were wide.

"When we cast the bones," he went on, "the way they fall determines the number of points we get. They cannot land on round side. You can see that the one of the narrow sides curves inward and one curves outward. It's the same with the wide sides."

At first I couldn't see the difference; but when I looked more closely and felt the sides I understood what he was talking about.

Squatting down close to the cobblestones, he took back the bone I was holding, cupped the four of them in his two hands, shook them around and then threw them to the ground.

"Look here," he said. "It's the 'dog'. He pointed at the narrow side of the bone that curved outward. "That's only worth one point."

"This is better," he continued, pointing at the two bones that had fallen with the narrow sides curved in. "These are worth six points each."

The remaining bone showed a wide side that curved outwards. "How much for this one?" I asked him.

"That one is worth three," he said. "If a fat one curves inward it is better, it's four points."

"So this throw would be sixteen points?" I asked, counting off the points on my fingers, hoping I didn't miss any after ten.

"That's right," Jelko said. "We throw the bones three times each and whoever has the most points wins."

"Why do we need coins?" I asked.

"If you want to play, you have to pay, of course!" Stanyo said.

"And if you win, you take all the coins," Misha added.

"We only play two at a time, so if you aren't throwing the bones you can still get in on the fun and maybe make some money by betting on who will win," Stanyo added.

"Let's go!" said Misha. "Just watch a while and you will understand. Now who will take me on? I have five coppers to say I will throw the highest score."

"I'll play," said one of the shorter boys. "I have five coppers and I'd like to make them ten!"

The two crouched down on the ground. The each threw a bone to see who would go first.

"Ha, ha, Loris!" said Misha, "You threw a 'dog'! Whatever I throw will be higher!"

"Unless you throw a 'dog', too!" the short boy whose name must be Loris, replied, with a grin.

Misha threw his bone. It was narrow with an inward curve. Now how much was it worth?

"Ha, ha; SIX," Misha cried, preempting my attempt to remember. "I throw first!"

He gathered the four bones and threw them down. Quickly he added his score. It came to twelve.

"Not so bad," one of the boys said.

"Not so good, either!" another one commented. "Will you bet on him?

"Yes," the first replied. "I'll put a copper on him to win".

"And I'll put one on Loris," the other boy said, taking a coin from his pocket and setting it next to the boy who was preparing to throw the bones.

He shook them well, spat on his hands for luck and threw the bones down. I saw one 'dog' and thought that the boy had made a bad bet, but then I saw that the other three bones were also narrow but curved inward; the ones that were six points each! I had trouble adding so many big numbers but the boys did it quickly.

"Ha! Nineteen points!" Loris cried. "Joko, you were right to bet on me! Misha, I'm upping the ante." He put another coin down beside him.

"And I'll put another coin on you if anyone will take my bet!" Joko said with a smile.

No one took his offer. Misha looked serious as he took out another coin to match Loris's bet, then he rolled again. This time his total was sixteen. How could they keep track of the points over three roles? I noticed Misha making some scratches in the dust.

"What are you doing?" I asked him.

"Keeping a tally of the points" he said. "See, I make one line for each point up to four. When I get to five I make a line across, like this."

He showed me his first score of twelve. There were two groups of four lines plus one across and two lines by themselves.

"Now I'll put my second throw" he said. He counted out sixteen, making two more lines next to the two from the first throw and then, as he counted three, drew a line across them and started another set. When he got to sixteen I counted five groups of five and three lines.

"How do you know how much this is?" I asked, puzzled.

"I count by fives and then add the ones," he said.

"How do you count by fives?" I asked him.

"It's easy when you learn it! 5-10-15-20-25 and so on," he told me.

"Hey, fellows! Let's go. You're holding up the game," Stanyo said with mock annoyance.

"I want to put another two coins on Misha after that throw," the first boy said. "Loris just had a lucky shot. It can't happen again!"

Joko took out another coin and said, "Fine with me!"

Loris played again and this time the total came to ten.

"That makes twenty-nine," he said when he finished his tally. "One ahead of you, Misha!"

"Does anyone want to place a bet before I throw again; Loris?" Misha asked, looking around him.

No one replied. I guess the score was too close for anyone to risk another coin.

He threw the bones for the last time and let out an almighty howl when he looked down at where they had fallen.

"Four 'dogs'!" he yelled! 'What are the chances?"

"Whatever I throw will be higher that you!" Loris repeated back the words Misha had told him, with a derisive laugh. "Even if I get four 'dogs' I am one point ahead so I am the winner!"

He pocketed the fourteen coins with a smile. Joko collected his winnings, while the other boy looked dejected.

"I was supposed to use those coins to buy bread," he said. "I thought if I won I could buy some cheese, too. Oh well!"

"We can play again," Loris said, jingling his coins.

"You boys can play, but it's time I head back to the camp," I told the boys, brushing the dust off the seat of my trousers. "Thanks for showing me your game. Maybe I'll join in sometime."

"That would be great," Jelko said, giving my back a rather hard slap.

"It will be great taking his money," one of the boys murmured. The others sniggered until Jelko gave them a look that silenced them.

As I walked away, Jelko said quietly, "Thanks, Gogo, I appreciate what you did for me yesterday."

It seemed like I'd made a new friend.

Chapter 41 – Preparing for the Feast

The next days were spent in a flurry of preparation for the feast that would be held the following evening in the village square. Wreaths of multicolored wildflowers hung on every door and bright rugs were displayed on each balcony that overlooked the square.

The village church had pride of place on the east side. I had never been inside of it, but had seen the dark-robed priest hurrying in and out, sometimes pulling on the long rope that sounded the church bells to call the faithful to prayer.

All through the village cooking fires burned with heavy pots atop them full of bubbling stew or spits turning whole sheep, slowly browning to delicious perfection. People hurried to and fro, setting up and decorating the tables and bringing benches to place beside them. I spotted Misha and Stanyo crossing the square carrying a huge dry log between them. I ran over to see what it was for.

"Hey!" I said. "Where are you going with that? Do you need a hand?"

"We don't 'need' help, but it would be nice!" Misha answered.

"It's for the bonfire," Stanyo said, wiping his brow with his sleeve as I grabbed a hold of the log, taking some of the weight.

I looked the direction we were heading and saw that there was already a fairly large pile of wood ranging from logs like ours from the forest to old, broken furniture and barrels.

"It's for the feast," Misha said. "We know you gypsies like to dance by your fire."

"I'm not a gypsy" I snapped, before noticing the twinkle in his eye and realizing that he was only teasing me. "But I do know a lot of their tricks," I added, getting into the spirit of his joke.

"Do you know how to make a love potion?" Misha asked, joining the conversation.

"I wish I did!" I told him, really wishing I did! Then I could give some to Milada to make her feel about me the way I felt about her.

"Why?" he asked, "is there someone you want to fall in love with you?"

"Dunia, maybe," Stanyo said with a grin. "You don't need any magic potion. She is already in love with you!"

"What are you talking about?" I said, shocked at his words.

"Don't you see the way she looks at you?" Stanyo said.

I figured he was teasing me again and didn't want to rise to it.

"I wouldn't mind if she was in love with me!" he added. "Her father is the village blacksmith and I think there is some land from her mother's side. She'll have an excellent dowry."

"What's a 'dowry'?" I asked as we set down the log and headed back across the square.

"It's the money you get from a girl's family when you consent to marry her," he told me; "the 'bride price'."

"You get money when you get married?" I asked, puzzled.

"If you are lucky enough to marry a rich girl!" he said. "Not only money but land, maybe some animals, a house; it all depends."

"The girl has to like you," Misha chimed in, "but it's more important that her father does! In the end it is he who decides who she will wed and how much you get paid for it."

I must have still looked puzzled. Misha steered me to a seat in the outdoor tavern and ordered three ales.

"It's like this," he explained. "Once you get married you will be responsible for feeding and clothing your wife and your children. The father wants the best boy possible for a son-in-law; one who will take care of his needs when he gets older as well as his daughter's. There is much competition for the girls with big dowries like Dunia.

"Yes," Stanyo agreed. "We have all noticed how she looks at you. But you'll be travelling on with the gypsies so we aren't too concerned."

This was all news to me! Soon Jelko joined us, ordered himself a drink and we passed the time chatting together, anticipating the feast later that day.

"I like the look of some of your gypsy girls," Jelko said.

I wondered if he'd seen Milada.

"There's one with jet black hair and eyes," he went on. "I think she winked at me! I wanted to dance with her tonight, but I'm still limping a bit."

Misha raised his eyebrows and said, "Get her to work some of that gypsy magic on you!"

"Healed with a kiss!" Stanyo said.

"A kiss will make anyone feel better," Jelko said.

Maybe it was time for me to kiss Milada. Maybe then she would know what I felt for her.

As if reading my mind, Jelko said, "I bet this one has never even kissed a girl".

I felt my cheeks redden. "Of course I've kissed a girl," I lied. "I've kissed lots of them. I've kissed the one with the raven hair, the one you like. Melya is her name."

Jelko looked at me with admiration. I smiled smugly, continuing my pretense. In truth, I had hardly ever spoken to Melya. She was older than I was, and spent her time with the young men and women of Todor's age. She was very pretty, but she didn't charm me in the same way that Milada did.

I finished my ale and lay a few coins on the table. Jelko scooped them up and handed them back to me.

"No need, gypsy boy!" he said. "This one is on me. See you later."

This time I didn't rise to his comment. I simply thanked him and started off toward the camp to rest a little. I knew it would be a long night! I heard Jelko yelling after me, "And I expect an introduction to the lovely Melya tonight!"

I arrived back at my wagon and saw that Bora had washed out his clothes and mine, too.

"You're spending a lot of time in the village," he said when I thanked him.

"We need nice clean clothes for tonight,' he went on. "The girls are getting all dressed up. Maybe we can find something festive to wear as well."

"Where can we find festive clothes? I asked. The boys always noticed when I needed a bigger shirt or pair of trousers and provided them. I didn't know from where they had come."

"Dragan has a big trunk in his wagon," Bora said. "Let's go see what we can find."

"Doesn't Dragan mind if we take his clothes?" I asked, not sure if I wanted to wear anything of Dragan's anyway.

"They aren't his clothes," Bora said, "they just live in his wagon. They belong to all of us. He will have chosen what he will wear for the feast so we can pick from whatever we find there."

When we got to Dragan's wagon he was nowhere in sight but there were several other young men on the steps, including Nico, sporting a bright yellow vest, heavy with golden embroidery.

"Look what I found!" he said, wagging his shoulders back and forth. The shiny threads caught the light and reflected it into our eyes.

"That's pretty bright," I said, shading my eyes from the reflected glare, knowing that I would never want to wear any anything like it.

"Yes it is," he said. "The girls can't miss me in it!"

"Come on, Goran," Bora said giving me a push through the curtain at the wagon's entrance.

I had never been in the wagon that Dragon shared with his father, the Baron. Heavy purple velvet blocked out most of the light. When my eyes grew accustomed to the dim interior I noticed that the two bunks were covered with richly woven carpets. Narrow shelves set high on the polished wooden walls held fine china cups and saucers. I was surprised that such fine porcelain could survive the rigors of the harsh roads we travelled.

The others didn't seem to notice this richness; they were too busy rummaging around the brass bound chest at the back of the wagon.

Bora waved a green velvet waistcoat. "If this fits me I'm taking it!" he said.

I burrowed my way between other boys until I could look into the chest for myself. I didn't really want to wear the gypsies' clothes, but maybe Milada would like it if I made a bit of effort to fit in. I put my hand into the chest, choosing more by feel than by sight. My fingers found a very smooth fabric and I grasped it and gently pulled it to the top of the pile of clothes. I shook it free from the others to see what it was.

It was a deep blue color, almost black, like the sky when the moon is full. It was embroidered with silver threads around its edges. It was not too fancy; I thought that it would do. If it fit me, that is.

I moved to a less crowded place and put my arms through its openings. I flexed my shoulders and there was enough room to move. I stepped out of the wagon blinking in the bright sunlight and waved at Bora, who was still wearing the bright green vest, and looking good in it!

"What do you think of this one?" I asked him, noticing that the blue looked much brighter in the strong light of the sun.

'It's kind of plain," he said, "but is suits you."

"You mean I'm plain?" I asked.

"In a good way!" he replied. "Wholesome; not a show off like some!"

Was he thinking of Nico and his golden attire?

"Well, plain or not, I like it," I said. "Are you sure it's all right for me to take it?"

"We'll put them back tomorrow," he said. "Don't worry about it!"

Walking back to our wagon, I asked Bora, "Does it ever bother people that Dragan and his father have a much nicer wagon than the others?"

"It is one of the nicer ones," he said, "but there other fancy ones as well. It depends on what you want."

"But they have fine rugs and china," I said.

"Those things belong to us all," he said. "The Baron has more responsibility. Having beautiful things around him helps him to relax. Anytime we want to drink out of those fancy cups we can. But we don't really need or want to; maybe for a special occasion like a marriage or holiday.

The ale I drank with the village boys was making me sleepy. "I'm ready for a nap," I told Bora, pushing aside the curtain to our wagon.

"Good idea," he said, "me too.

Nico was already snoring gently on his upper bunk and soon we joined him in a relaxing afternoon nap, the yellow vest hanging beside him like a drop of sunlight.

Chapter 42 – The Feast

It seemed like I had just closed my eyes, but when I heard the boys moving about I saw that the sun was more than halfway down to the horizon.

"Wake up time!" Bora said, already looking very handsome in the green waistcoat. "There's some water outside to rinse the sleep out of your eyes."

I stretched in my bunk and then swung my feet to the wooden floorboards. Stifling a yawn I went outside to wash my face and rinse out my mouth, which tasted a bit woody after my beaker of ale. I realized how hungry I was and looked forward to all the delicacies that awaited us in the village square.

"Here," said Bora tossing me a clean shirt and a pair of sharp black trousers that I hadn't seen before. "Hurry up and get dressed so we can go and find the food!"

I pulled off my shirt, splashed water over my chest and under my arms, patted myself dry and pulled the clean shirt over my head. I was happy to see it was a newer one and the sleeves we long enough, then changed into the black trousers that narrowed perfectly to my ankles. I went back into the wagon to get the blue waistcoat and a pair of soft black leather boots. They had been big for me the last time I put them on a few months before when I needed them for warmth. Now, I put them on for looks and they fit perfectly.

I pushed aside the curtain and stepped out onto the wagon's step.

"Look at you!" cried Nico. "The village girls will go crazy!"

"It's only a change of clothes," I told him.

"It's not what you wear, but how you wear it," he said.

I looked at my friends and realized there was something in what Nico said. They both looked much more grown up; more like men than boys. In the dimming light I peered into the basin of water and could just make out my reflection. I pushed my hair out of my eyes and took a better look. My cheekbones and jaw had grown more prominent, and the hair on my upper lip looked thicker than it felt. I absentmindedly caressed it with my finger.

"You'll be needing a trip to the barber soon," Bora said.

Self-consciously, I dropped my hand and moved away from the basin.

"Let's go to the village and get some of that wonderful food before it's all gone," I told them, leading the way to the village gate.

"I wouldn't worry about that," Bora said. "I've never seen so much food being prepared for one meal, ever!"

I was looking forward to seeing Milada. I figured she and the other girls went ahead earlier to help with the preparations. As we passed through the gateway in the stone walls we were greeted by the headman of the village. He shook our hands and some village woman gave us each a flower and a small, fat wineskin on a cord.

Nico's eyebrows went up. As soon as we had passed the welcoming committee he popped the stopper out of the wineskin and brought it to his lips.

"Mmmm! This is a good vintage!" he said.

I followed his lead and took a sip. I found it a little bitter, not sweet like that blueberry wine. I liked it but I hadn't had any since the night I drank too much; the night of Layla's kidnapping; the night of her death.

"This isn't made from blueberries, is it," I asked, not wanting to dwell on the subject of Layla on such a festive night.

"No," Nico replied, "it's made from the black grapes of this region." He took another swig. "If you don't like it, give yours to me!"

I thought about it. I knew I didn't want to drink much. But if I was going to gather my courage and finally kiss my Milada I might need a bit of help from the wine.

"I'll hang on to it for now," I told him. "Come and ask me when you finish yours and I may give you some then."

We'd reached the tables heaving with food; all sorts of breads, fresh vegetables from the fields, trays and trays of grilled meat and sausages. Wooden plates were provided for us and we heaped food on them. Eating, sipping from the wineskins, licking our fingers, filling our plates again; soon the sun had set and the first stars appeared in the sky.

"Time for me to go," Bora said, picking up his viol and heading toward the fire.

Cakes and sweet preserved fruit had now appeared on the long tables. I thought I had eaten my fill but the unusual treats tempted me back to the table. I heard the band striking up in the distance and as soon as I sampled a good few of the sweets I went over to the fire. I hadn't seen Milada at all near the food. She must have finished early, or not eaten as much. I was sure I'd find her by the fire. She always loved to dance. And tonight she would be dancing with me.

I was standing near Bora, clapping my hands in time to the lively rhythm and thinking of Milada when I saw a beautiful girl in a bright red dress coming toward me, her hair making a halo around her head, a big smile lighting up her face. Then I realized who she was!

"Milada!" I exclaimed, "You look beautiful! Where did you get that dress?"

"Thanks," she said. "Zora gave it to me. It belonged to her mother".

"I wouldn't expect to see Zora in something so…red!" I laughed.

Milada twirled around and the skirt lifted to reveal her slim ankles and calves. "Zora said that it is too bright for her, but it's just right for me!" she said with a smile.

Before I could ask her, she held out her two hands and said, "Let's dance!"

Milada danced at every chance she had, often wanting to pull me in to join. I liked to sometimes, but I didn't always feel in the mood. Tonight, though, I had been looking forward to it. We moved together with the lively rhythm of the band, her red dress and long hair taking on a life of their own as she twirled and dipped. I felt handsome in my gypsy vest and jet black trousers and boots. The tempo of the music increased and I was feeling warm with all our activity coupled with the heat of the huge bonfire.

I was thankful when Milada said, "Let's go get a drink of water."

I'd seen big barrels of water near the trestle tables; the fountain was somewhere but the square had taken on a very different character that night with the tables, benches and bonfire. I saw Dunia and Yagoda sitting on a bench a little way off from the fire with some other young people from the village.

"Hello Dunia," I called. "Will you join the dance tonight?"

"I prefer to sit and watch," she said.

"Can I get you something to drink?" I asked her. "A cup of blackberry wine, maybe?"

"A cup of water would be nice," she said.

"I'll bring a cup for you, too, Milada," I said, finding some wooden beakers on a nearby table.

"Yes, please," she said, "the dancing has made me very thirsty."

I went in the direction I thought the fountain was and ran right into Jelko.

"Where are you going so fast?" he asked.

"I'm on a mission," I told him, "I have some thirsty girls waiting for me."

"Is one of them that black-haired girl?" he asked.

Oh! I had forgotten my promise to introduce him to Melya.

"No," I said, "I haven't seen her here."

"I have," Jelko said. "She was talking with a boy from the next village."

"Sorry, then," I said, relieved. "The gypsy girls decide for themselves who they will talk to."

I moved closer to the fountain and took a refreshing drink for myself and then filled up two beakers for the girls.

I hurried past Jelko, hoping he wouldn't bring up the subject of Melya again. When I neared the girls, Milada seemed angry! She was looking daggers at Dunia and I heard her say, "Well maybe if you were friendlier or would get up and dance and have some fun they would like to be with you!"

Without warning she stood up and I had to get out of the way so she wouldn't bump right into me.

"Slow down, Milada," I told her. "You nearly made me spill the water."

She glared at me and said, "I didn't make you do anything! Watch where you are going!"

She took one of the beakers and drank it all down. Handing me back the empty cup she said, a little more civilly, "Thank you. I'm going back to the music. Are you coming?"

What was that all about? I figured it was better to let her cool off a little and hopefully find her in a better mood later. "I'll sit this one out," I said.

I was surprised when I heard Yagoda say, "I'll come with you!"

"Stay where you are!" Dunia insisted.

"I am just going to watch the dancers," Yagoda said. She got up from the bench and followed Milada.

"Suit yourself," Dunia said, "but you may have to suffer the consequences if our father sees you."

Milada's look softened and she took Yagoda by the hand and led her away towards the music.

I took Yagoda's place beside Dunia. "Don't you like to dance?" I asked her.

"Sometimes I will join in with the village dances," she said, "but the way people are dancing tonight is crazy."

I had enjoyed my dance with Milada; enjoyed her enjoyment and also the nice feeling of being one with the rhythm of the music.

"Why do you think this dancing is crazy?" I asked her. "I think it's fun sometimes."

"It may be all right for you and the boys to throw yourselves around like wild things, but not for girls like me," she said.

"The gypsy girls like it," I told her.

"Maybe they do," she said, "but we girls in the villages know better. It may look like fun but when boys see us dancing like that the last thing they think about is marriage."

"Is marriage important to you?" I asked her.

"What a question!" she exclaimed. "It is the most important thing in a girl's life."

I wanted to ask her about the money her father would have to give away to whomever she wed, but I held my tongue.

"The gypsies don't seem to care so much about it," I said. "Sometimes they will celebrate a marriage, but often couples live with their friends rather than with their husbands and wives.

"Their ways are strange for us," she said. "When other gypsies come to our village we avoid contact with them. It is only this band that is welcome because of their healing skills."

"Other gypsies don't have those skills?" I asked.

"I don't really know," she said. "There is just something different about them. Maybe it's because we feel grateful to this particular band for having helped the village. Everybody might have died; it happened in other villages at the time."

After a while Milada and Yagoda returned, still hand in hand. Yagoda's face was flushed and she had a big smile on her face.

"Looks like you had fun," I said.

Dunia didn't say anything, but she did not look happy with her sister's antics. Milada went off to get some water. When she came back with it she was no longer smiling.

Chapter 43 – The Morning After

I wondered why Milada suddenly looked so serious. If I was going to kiss her tonight I'd have to get her in a better mood. I took a swig from my wineskin for courage at the thought.

"I guess you don't want to come?" I said to Dunia as I stood up and beckoned Milada to follow me to the fire and rejoin the dancing.

She shook her head, and looked down at her neat shoes.

"I'll come!" cried Yagoda, spilling her water as she jumped up and down.

"No, you won't," Dunia said, sternly. It's late and we needed to get home."

"I don't want to go home!" she moaned. "I want to stay and dance with the gypsies!"

"That's enough, Yagoda," Dunia insisted. "We are going home. Now!"

She grabbed Yagoda's hand and dragging the girl who would not budge of her own accord, headed for her home.

I felt a little sorry for them both; Dunia for not even trying to experience the dance and Yagoda for enjoying it but not being allowed to continue. But I was happy. Milada was by my side.

We joined the others, dancing and spinning around the fire. It did not seem to have burned down much; the boys must be feeding it with fresh wood. At this rate, it would burn until the morning!

For a while, Milada and I danced close together, but then the crowd separated us. I took a break, sitting near the musicians where I could keep an eye on things. Nico came and sat beside me.

"I've almost finished my wine!" he said. "Will you give me some of yours?"

I passed him my wineskin, but not before I took a long drink myself. We sat there for a while, passing the wineskin back and forth between us. When it was empty, Nico stood up and, with a loud whoop, went to join the dancers.

I stood up, too, but was unsteady on my legs. The ground seemed further away than I knew it was. Oh no! I knew this feeling!

I had too much to drink again. All of a sudden, the music seemed too loud and the dancers were making my head spin. I made my way to the water barrel and helped myself to a long drink. I put my head under the spigot and let some cool water run over my brow. It cleared my head a little, but I knew that tonight would not be the night that I kissed Milada. Mustering all my energy and concentration I walked back to the gypsy camp, managed to drag myself up the steps of my wagon, shrugged off the fancy vest and passed out on my bunk with my boots on.

I woke up the next morning in a sweat. The sun was high in the sky and light and heat poured through the open door of our wagon. I lay there, not wanting to move. I was thinking about how I'd kissed Milada in the moonlight. We were walking alone in the forest. In a clearing where the moon shone brightly I took her in my arms and she had willingly joined her lips with mine. I savored the feeling in my mind and in my groin. Milada had kissed me! Or had she?

As I sat up the inside of the wagon seemed to be spinning around. Focusing on a point on the wall opposite, my vision settled. I rubbed my eyes and sighed, realizing that I had kissed Milada only in my dreams. Slowly, I pulled off my boots, then changed into my everyday trousers.

I needed more than just a splash water on my face to bring me back to the present. I drank one beaker of water and then another from an earthenware jug outside the wagon. I was always amazed at how cool the water stayed when stored in clay jars like these. Then I made my way down to the stream that ran a short distance downhill from the camp. I knew that a little ways upstream there was a swimming hole.

Before I found it I heard voices. "I can jump further than you!" someone was yelling.

I didn't recognize the voice. When I reached the water I saw that it was Loris, one of the boys from the village. The others were either in the water or sitting on the bank of the stream. I saw Jelko there, soaking his feet; the wound in his thigh had healed well, with only a little bruising as a reminder of his encounter with the wild boar.

"Hey, Gogo!" he shouted when he saw me. "That was some party last night!"

I nodded, and patting the air with my hand as a sign that my head didn't need his shouting.

"Drink a little too much wine, did we?" he said more quietly as I pulled off my clothes and stowed them in the branches of a nearby tree.

I nodded again and eased myself into the coolness of the pond.

"Ahhhh, that's good," I said, before a splash of cold water hit my face.

"Ha, ha, gypsy boy!" said Misha, splashing me again.

Forgetting my wooziness, I splashed him back and the water fight was on. The others joined in, cool water flying everywhere. Some boys threw themselves into the pond from the rocks on the bank, making the biggest splashes of all.

When the activity subsided, we all settled in the shallow part of the pond to catch our breath. Stanyo reclined next to me, his toes sticking out of the water. He was looking down at our laps.

"That's quite a sausage you have there!" he commented.

Sausage? I thought of breakfast. What's he talking about? Then I realized what he meant. I looked at my "sausage" and then at his.

"Maybe when you grow up yours will get bigger!" I told him.

"Yeah," Jelko chimed in, "big like that horse we saw the other day getting ready to mount the bay mare."

The boys all chuckled at the thought.

"I wouldn't want to be that big!" Stanyo said. "It would scare away all the girls!"

"Maybe they would like it," Jelko said. "The mare didn't seem to mind. And speaking of mares," he said, turning to me, "I did speak to that girl, Melya, last night!"

"And what did you talk about?" I asked.

"I told her I thought she was pretty," he said.

"And?"

"She giggled and said I was cute."

"Cute?"

"Not exactly the response I was hoping for," he said with mock dejection. "I guess I'll stick with the village girls. There's one called Janka that I like the look of."

"You think you have a chance with her?" Misha said, splashing a little water in our direction.

"Why not?" Jelko said.

"She's too smart for you!" he answered, with a bigger splash.

"We'll see about that," he said, splashing back, and soon we were in the middle of another water fight!

When it died down I realized how hungry I was.

"I'm leaving," I told the boys. "I need to find something to eat."

"There was plenty of food left over from the feast," Misha said. "It's probably laid out in the square. Let's all go and eat."

We dried off in the sun then put our clothes on and headed to the village. The tables were there, but the food had all been put away. Dunia waved at me. She was putting the last of the left-over loaves into her basket.

"Good morning, Goran," she said. "You are a little late for breakfast! We just finished clearing everything up."

"I woke up late and then went for a swim with some of the boys from the village," I told her, my eyes more on the bread than on her flushed cheeks.

"Here," she said, noticing my hungry looks in the direction of her basket, "have a bit of bread. It's not the freshest anymore but when you are hungry the taste doesn't matter so much."

I took a chunk of bread and thanked her.

"We have plenty of food at our house," she said. "I made a big stew yesterday. Will you join my family later for the midday meal?"

I wasn't sure if anything would be prepared at the gypsy camp today. It felt very quiet there; everyone was relaxing after dancing into the wee hours of the morning.

"Yes," I told her, "I would like that."

I will see you in a little while then," she said and headed off across the square.

I saw some of the gypsies cooling themselves by the fountain and others sitting in the shade, chatting with the villagers. I recognized Mother Miriana's silver hair. Another of the older women was with her and some girls from the village, but Milada was not among them. I wondered where she was, but then spotted the boys and went over to join them at their usual spot in the square.

Chapter 44 - A Little Bird

After a while, Loris brought out a set of bones.

"Who's up for a game?" he asked.

"I'll play, Jelko said. "I have three coppers I can spare today.

"Only three?" Loris said. "I'd rather play for six! What did you do with the coins you won from me the other day?"

"I bought this," he said, pulling something small and shiny from his pack.

It was a hinged pocket knife. We all gathered around to see how smoothly he could open it.

"That must have cost more than ten coppers!" Stanyo said.

"It did," Jelko replied, "I've been saving up my winnings and the five I won from you, plus a special price in honor of the feast, meant I had enough to get it."

"Does anyone else want to play me for more than a measly three coins," Loris asked, itching to get on with the game.

No one spoke up.

"Get your three coppers over here," he said to Jelko, "and let's see who will go first."

I watched as they cast the bones. Loris won to start. The other boys had their hands in their pockets, rooting around for coins to bet on their favorite. When Jelko scored sixteen points on his first throw I considered betting a few coppers on him to win. That folding knife was great! If I won some more coins I could buy one, too. But before I could fish out my coppers, Loris scored eighteen points and most of the boys clapped and shouted. Betting on Jelko might not have been such a good idea, after all!

I was startled when I heard Milada's voice. She had come to stand beside me, watching the circle of boys.

"What are they doing?" she asked me.

"Good morning, Milada," I said, happy to see her. "Someone throws the bones and how they fall determines how many points the throw is worth. Whoever gets the most points in three throws wins."

"Wins what?"

"At each round the players put in a coin. If someone had a good score they might put in an extra coin or two. To keep playing the other player must match the coins. The player who has the best score after three rounds wins all the coins," I explained.

"Why are the other people all so excited?" she asked.

"We make bets on who will make the highest score," I told her, "so when one of the players wins, some of us win as well."

"And the ones who lose? What about them?" she commented.

"Maybe they will win next time," I said.

"And maybe they will lose all their money!"

"No one thinks they will lose," I said. "If they did, they wouldn't play." I could see by the expression on her face that she didn't like the idea of this game of chance.

"Look, here comes Dunia and some other girls," she said, looking over my shoulder. I turned to see the girls approaching us.

"Good day, ladies," I said, tipping my cap.

I liked making the girls giggle with my chivalrous little bow. Dunia smiled at me but then glanced at Milada standing close by my side and the smile faded from her lips. I was still amazed at how similar the girls looked; yet they were so very different from each other.

Milada's eyes were fixed on one of the young girls. Following her gaze I saw that she was holding something clasped in her two hands.

"What do you have there?" I asked her.

"It's little bird," she said. "I think it fell out of its nest".

"If you give it to my friend, Tanya," Milada said, "she will make sure it will be all right."

"I have a better idea," said one of the boys. I didn't know his name. He was a stocky lad about my age who hung around with Jelko's gang but didn't seem to really be a part of it.

"Give it to me," he ordered.

I thought Milada would step in and stop the girl from giving it over; there was fire in her eyes. I knew if she said anything there would be trouble. I felt these boys wouldn't take kindly to a girl telling them what to do.

"We can play a trick on the old witch," he said, roughly grabbing the fragile bird.

"The old witch?" Milada said. "What old witch?"

"The gypsy witch," the boy snapped. "I was having some fun with my mates yesterday, just teasing one of the mongrel dogs that hangs around the butcher shop."

"What do you mean 'having some 'fun'?" she asked.

"We were trying to see who could hit him with a stone using our sling shots," he said. "I was the best at it. It's just harmless fun. We get to practice our aim. We do it all the time".

"It's not harmless to the dog!" she said.

"It's a useless dog," he said, "good for nothing. So we are enjoying our sport when all of a sudden out of nowhere comes the witch swishing her broom at us and yelling to high heaven to stop and 'leave the poor beast alone'."

"Of course the dog was as startled as we were and ran off, so that was the end of our fun," he said. "Everyone says she is so wise. Now we'll see how wise she really is."

"What do you mean?" Milada asked him.

"We'll use this here little birdie," he said. "I will keep it like this in my hands so she can't see it. Then we say 'here is a bird - is it alive or dead'?"

"And what will that prove?" she asked, placing her hands on her hips as if squaring up for a fight.

"If she says it's dead I will open my hands and show her that it is alive," he said.

"And if she says it's alive?"

"Then I will squeeze my fist a split second before I open my hand and bye-bye little bird. Either way and she'll be wrong!" he said. "Come on, who's coming to watch?"

He took off across the square before she could say anything else. The boys forgot their game of bones and, scooping up their coins, followed him and the girls over to where the ladies were sitting in the shade.

"What a mean thing to do!" Milada said.

"It's a clever idea, though," I told her, "Let's go and see how Mother Miriana handles it."

Yagoda was close beside Milada. "I hope he won't kill the little bird," she said, putting her hand in Milada's and accompanying us.

"Over here, Goran," Dunia called to me as we approached.

"So, Grandmother," the boy was saying to Mother Miriana. "We have all heard about your wisdom. Here is a question for you".

He stood right in front of her, with his closed hands out in front of him. "I have a little bird in here," he said. "Is it alive or dead?"

For a moment, no one spoke. The children looked expectantly between the older woman and the smirking boy, waiting to see the outcome.

Mother Miriana looked coolly at the boy. "It is in your hands," she said and resuming her conversation, dismissed him.

The boy spat on the ground behind her back and made to squeeze his fist. But before he could do so, one of the village girls reached out and knocked the bird out of his hand. It fell on the cobblestones but seemed to still be moving. The girl knelt down and gently cradled the small bird in her palm.

Looking up at the boy, she said boldly, "Why are you always looking for trouble. Don't you have anything better to do?"

Jelko elbowed me in the ribs and whispered, "That's Janka. Spunky, isn't she? I like how she stands up to Viktor; he's such a pain; thinks he's so smart."

We watched as Viktor spat again, and trudged off without a word. Tanya knelt beside Janka and said, "Let me see."

"Here, take it," she said, carefully placing the bird into Tanya's open hands. "See if you can save this poor little creature."

"I'll see what I can do," Tanya said and set off back to the gypsy camp.

Jelko put out his hand to help Janka up. The two of them walked companionably toward the fountain.

"Have you had anything to eat yet?" I asked Milada.

"No," she said. "I ate so much last night but I am rather hungry again".

"Dunia has asked me to come to lunch," I told her, "Why don't you come, too, if it's all right with you." I smiled at Dunia, not thinking before I extended her invitation to Milada.

"I suppose we have enough food," Dunia said, ungraciously.

Before Milada had time to storm off back to camp I linked my arm with hers. I thought it was a good idea to bring her to her cousin's house. Maybe if she got to know and like her cousins and their parents she would consider making this village her home. Certainly she was entitled to some of her grandfather's land here, I thought, while we followed Dunia and Yagoda back to their house.

Chapter 45 - An Unpleasant Meal

On our way, Milada kept trying to pull away from me but I held on tight. We waited in front of the house while Dunia took a large iron key from her bag and unlocked the heavy oaken door.

It was very dark inside the house.

"Yagoda," Dunia said, "open the shutters so we can have some light. The day is bright enough. I will put the food on the fire to warm".

Yagoda climbed on a stool and pushed open the shutters to let in the midday sunshine.

"Where are your father and mother?" Milada asked.

"My father is the village blacksmith," Dunia said. "He is busy at his forge. He may come home in a while if there is not too much work to do."

"Our mother is probably still out in the fields," Yagoda said. "At this time of year there is much work to do tending to the crops as they ripen for the harvest. I would have gone with her but I did not wake up until the sun was high."

"I'm surprised that she let you sleep!" Dunia said, "The rest of us managed to do our jobs today".

"She is young and needs more rest," Milada said, in Yagoda's defense.

"She would have had enough rest if she hadn't used so much energy dancing like a mad cat last night" Dunia commented rudely. The conversation was getting out of hand. I felt I needed to step in and make peace between the girls.

"Ladies, ladies," I told them, "We are here to share a lovely meal that Dunia has prepared, let's not bicker."

Dunia sighed as she stirred the stew.

"Will you help me put this pot on the hook, Goran?" she asked me. "It is very heavy".

"Yes, of course," I replied. It was even heavier than it looked, but I managed to pick it up and fix it on the hook in the fireplace.

I stayed by the fire while Dunia brought out some cheese from the cooling cupboard and cut a loaf of bread into thick slices.

"Yagoda," she said, "fetch the plates and spoons and put them on the table".

I guess Milada was feeling a little bit awkward just sitting there while the rest of us had a job to do. She asked Dunia "Is there anything I can do to help?"

"No," Dunia replied, "today you are our guest. Just sit down and wait until the stew is warm."

From my station at the fireplace I watched the sisters bustle around the room, preparing our meal. The table was set for six. I saw Milada looking around, pensively. I wondered what she was thinking; if she remembered this place from when she was a very young child.

When Yagoda finished setting the table, she plopped herself down next to Milada.

"Look at this," she said, putting something into Milada's hand.

"Where did you find it?" Milada asked. I couldn't see what they were looking at.

"I found it in the field last year when we were preparing the ground," Yagoda said. "Isn't it strange?"

"I've seen one or two similar ones," Milada answered, "but they are rare".

"What kind of stone is it?"

"A stone like this is called a fossil," Milada told her. "A long time ago that snail-like creature lived and died. There was probably a sea here a long, long time ago. Over the years the sea dried and soil was compressed over it. Some of the creatures that lived and died there were preserved in the stone that formed."

I left the fire and went over to see the strange stone that Yagoda had found.

"Let me see," I said, taking the stone from Milada. It did look like a snail, but it was definitely a rock. "That's interesting!"

"Very pretty," said Dunia, "but it is still is a stone that needs to be cleared from the fields. The important thing is to have a good harvest".

I heard the front door creaking open and saw a tired looking woman standing in the threshold.

"I'm very hungry!" she said, "Dunia, did you prepare the meal?"

"Yes, mother," Dunia replied. "The stew is just warming up. I invited Goran and his friend to join us."

"Oh, hello," she said, a bit absently, looking at me and then at Milada. "Do we have enough food for guests?" I heard her whisper to Dunia.

"Yes, mother, we ate so much at the feast last night that we didn't touch the stew. I made enough for two meals. Shall we start now or wait and see if our father comes?"

"Let's eat now," her mother said. "I have been in the field since sun up and feel weak with hunger".

Everyone gathered around the table.

"Shall I bring the pot?" I asked.

"No, thank you, Goran," Dunia said, "I'll put some stew into a bowl for the table".

She ladled the stew into a large ceramic bowl and set it down on the table.

"Pass me your bowls," she said. "Help yourself to some bread and cheese".

Dunia gave me a large helping of stew. It was tasty and I was very hungry. I was just about to ask for seconds when the door burst open. A large man strode into the room.

"What is there to eat?" he asked in a booming voice, "I am very hungry."

"Dunia made a good, hearty stew today," their mother replied.

"Who are these young people?" he asked glancing at Milada and me while Dunia ladled out his stew. "Did you bring gypsies to eat at my table?"

Dunia said, "This is Goran and his friend, what was your name again?"

"Milada," she said, quietly.

"We are not gypsies," I told Dunia's father. "We have no parents and the gypsies let us travel with them for a time."

The man nodded in understanding but did not smile. He looked down at Milada and then at his own daughters. "Come closer, girl," he said to her. "Let me get a better look at you".

Milada stood up, not sure of herself at all and moved closer to the big man who had settled himself in his place at the head of the table.

"This girl looks like one of my own," he said, "but she cannot be my daughter."

Dunia's mother looked from one girl to the other. "She does look like our daughters," she said, "and they resemble your mother, God rest her soul".

"When did you go to live with the gypsies, girl?" he asked Milada.

"When I was very little," she replied. "I feel like I've always lived with them. They are my family now."

"She said she used to live in this house," Dunia said, "with her grandparents".

The man rested his hands on Milada's shoulders and looked into her eyes.

"This was my parents' house," he said. "You must be my brother's little girl. He will be shocked to find you so grown up."

"Little Anna," Dunia's mother said, "I remember her. She was always wandering off into the fields. How many times one or the other of us would fetch her home!"

The old man should have taken a strap to her," her father said. "She was lucky a bear didn't get her."

Milada tried to take a step back. She glanced at me as if asking for help, but I didn't know what I could do.

"Anna, you must stay here until my brother comes again," the man said, his grip tightening on her shoulders.

I saw her wince at his touch. "I couldn't do that," she said. "My place is with the gypsies now. I will travel with them."

"Come now, Anna," Dunia's mother said, "You are no longer a child. It is time for you to learn the ways of our women, to tend the house and plant the fields. It is time for you to start thinking about finding a good husband and raising a family of your own".

"My name is Milada," she said, her fear making her bold. "I am learning the ways of the gypsy women".

"I can't let my own flesh and blood abide with the heathen gypsies," the man insisted, his strong hands still clamped on Milada's delicate shoulders. "I say you will stay here!"

He might be her uncle, but he had no right to hold her against her will. Where was this family when she was little? Why didn't they take her in when her grandmother passed away?

Somehow, Milada twisted her body and managed to free herself from his grasp. She moved around behind my chair, gripping it to give her strength.

"These gypsies saved your village with their knowledge!" she said. "I am learning much more important things than how to keep a house clean!"

Before anyone could speak or react, Milada sprinted to the door, pulled it open and took off in the direction of the gypsies' camp.

I muttered a hasty thanks to Dunia and her family and ran to catch up with her.

Chapter 46 - A Proposal

I found Milada sitting with Tanya on the seat of the wagon they still shared with Zora. She was hunched over, her breathing strained, hardly able to speak.

"He grabbed me," I heard her telling Tanya, breathlessly. "He called me 'Anna' and said I must stay here in the village until his brother returned."

"Who grabbed you?" Tanya asked. "Who could insist you stay if it is not your desire?"

"I went with Goran to Dunia's house; the house I remembered. It was her father. He said his brother is my father," she explained, "but I never knew him. He is nothing to me."

Tanya laid her hand gently on Milada's back.

"He gave you the gift of life," I heard her say. "I'm sure he would be proud of the young woman you have become".

"I don't know about that; I don't know how to keep a house or work in a field," Milada said.

"You know what to do when someone has a fever or a sore tummy," Tanya reminded her.

"I might like to meet my father," Milada told her, "but I don't want to stay in the village."

"Why not?" I asked, interrupting their conversation. "Dunia's mother has a point. It's time to think about your future."

"My future is here with the gypsies," she said. "They are my friends, and my family."

"We love you and would miss you if you left us," Tanya reassured her, patting her hand. "I must go and check the horses now. You are safe here with Goran".

Tanya gave me a smile that said, 'take care of her, now" then disappeared in the direction of the pasture.

When Tanya was well out of earshot I looked up at Milada from the wagon's steps.

"You have found your real family now and they want you to stay here with them," I told her.

"I couldn't stay here," she said. "I would miss moving from place to place; the dancing, the singing by the campfire, the happiness of our people."

"I'm getting tired of moving from place to place all the time and of being an outsider," I said. "I think I would like to learn a trade, settle down and have a place and a family of my own."

"You are still young," she said.

"I've seen fifteen summers," I replied. "It will take time for me to make a start in the world."

"You know how to do many things," she said, "things you've learned from the gypsies."

"I know how to help out with many things," I told her, thoughtfully, "but not to do one thing well."

"The gypsies always work together," she said. "That's why things run so smoothly".

"In the villages people do one craft well and then exchange their work with others or else for money to buy things at the market," I said.

"How do you know so much about the ways of the village?" she asked.

"I lived in one for a long time before I travelled with the gypsies, remember?" I said, climbing up to join her on the cushioned seat of the wagon.

"Look, Milada," I said, taking both her hands in mine, "let's stay here together and make a new life for ourselves."

I held her gaze, looking deep into her beautiful eyes, loving her and willing, hoping that she loved me.

"What do you mean?" she said, without pulling away from me, but with a puzzled look on her face.

I took a deep breath and said, "Milada, I love you. I have loved you since the day we met and always dreamed that one day you would love me. I know you are still young, but not too young to be a wife. Marry me and let's start a new adventure together, here when you belong."

Milada was silent. I waited, hoping for a least an encouraging smile but there was nothing; no sign of an answer. I had to break the silence.

"Could you love me, do you think?" I asked her, uncertainly.

She remained silent for a moment longer then blinked and said, "Goran, dear Goran, of course I love you."

She loved me! That is what I had hoped to hear! I felt the corners of my mouth lifting into a wide smile; but then she went on.

"You and I have grown up together, travelled together, learned about life together. But I never thought about marriage. I love you like a dear friend, like a beloved brother."

No! My smile faded as I watched her face, her eyes, looking for any sign that would give me hope. "Can you consider my offer?" I asked.

"You know I want to travel with the gypsies. I really do not want the life of a villager," she said.

I knew I would rather settle in a village; settle in *this* village, but if the only way I could be with the girl I loved was to stay with the gypsy band I thought I could do so.

"If you could love me I would stay with you and the gypsies," I told her, looking down at our joined hands.

She knew me too well. "Could you be happy," she asked me, "if you stayed with our band?"

"I don't know," I answered her, truthfully. "You know I've always felt that I was different from them. I would rather have a more settled life, but I don't want to lose you."

I raised my eyes to hers; saw concern in them and maybe even love. I leaned over and kissed her tenderly; her lips were softer and sweeter that I could have imagined. I could not bear to stay any longer in case she told me off. I pulled back, let go of her hands and climbed down from the wagon.

"Think about it," I said, "please." I needed to be somewhere else; anywhere else to have some time to think about what she had said and about what I was feeling.

I ran toward the stream without a backwards glance. I didn't go near the swimming hole, but followed the brook downstream where it narrowed and I knew I could be alone. I sat in the shade of a weeping willow tree and felt like weeping myself.

She said she loved me, but like a brother! I wanted more from her than sisterly love. She had been my best friend since I came to live with the gypsies. It was true that these days she spent more time with the women than before and had less time for me, but the moments we spent together were pleasant and easy.

Maybe she hadn't forgiven me for not telling her it was Layla that those awful people were after; but that was all a long time ago; she must have understood why I didn't tell her.

Then there was the way she looked at Dragan. I couldn't deny that she was infatuated with him. But she must know that marriage between an outsider and the Baron's son would be out of the question. Maybe I had just taken her by surprise. After all, she was very upset by what Dunia's father said; how he had grabbed her and tried to hold her against her will. She had no experience with rough behavior with the gypsy band and it must have been very frightening for her.

Why did I have to say anything now? I asked myself. Why couldn't I have just sat quietly with her, helping her to calm down and feel safe? No! Stupid me, I had to suggest staying here just at the moment she most wanted to leave. Maybe it wasn't me that she was rejecting, but the idea of staying here. I have always talked about how we are not part of the gypsy band and how I want to settle down. Maybe she thinks I say I'll stay with the gypsies for her sake but will keep on trying to convince her to leave them.

Stupid, stupid me! I watched the water flowing by, sparking in the sunlight, its calming sound soothing me a little. I would wait a while, not give up all hope yet and maybe, in time, Milada would come to love me as more than a brother.

Chapter 47 – I Talk to a Horse

I must have dozed on the bank of the stream because before I realized it the sun was setting. I wandered back to the camp, ate a little bread and cheese then went to my wagon. I had no appetite for music or laughter that evening.

I spent the days that followed staying around the gypsy camp, making myself useful at the cooking wagon and hunting with the boys to provide meat for the communal table. Maybe if Milada saw that I was making an effort to be helpful she would see that I meant what I had said about staying with the gypsies if she would have me. But as the days passed I hardly saw Milada at all; not in the daytime at the cooking wagon or at the swimming hole for a refreshing dip; not in the evening by the fire enjoying the music and dancing that she loved. Once or twice I spotted her, but she always ducked out of sight before I could get near enough to speak with her.

When I saw the special tent being erected I knew that I wouldn't be running into her for the next few days. During this time when the women secluded themselves it was always quiet in the gypsy camp so took myself off to the village early in the day.

I smiled when I thought I saw Milada at the fountain with the girls but then realized, of course, that it was Dunia filling up her water jugs.

Good morning, Goran," she said, a little shyly. The last time we had met was the awkward meal at her home.

"Hello, Dunia," I said, tipping my cap and lowering my eyes. "Let me help you carry those jugs."

This time, she accepted my offer. As we walked toward her house she said quietly, "I haven't seen you in the village for days. Are you angry after what happened at our house?"

"It was not a pleasant experience," I admitted, "seeing your father so adamant."

"He was just doing his duty as he saw it," she said. "If Anna is his brother's child he has the right to keep her here."

"Even if she doesn't want to stay?" I asked.

"She is still a child," Dunia replied, "and children need to be protected."

"But her grandfather gave his blessings for her to go with the gypsies," I told her. "Where was her father to protect her then? Or her uncle, your father, for that matter?"

Before she could answer me I heard the sound of loud swearing coming from a workshop at the side of the road.

"Oh, no!" Dunia exclaimed. "That's my father's voice; and he doesn't sound very happy."

She moved closer to the half-door and peered inside of the blacksmith's workshop. I looked over her shoulder from a bit of a distance, not sure if her father would approve of my helping Dunia with her chores.

I saw the glow coming from the fire of the forge and the heavy black iron anvil and hammers. Dunia's father kept on with his litany of curses as a huge black horse danced around the confines of the workshop.

"Damn you!" he swore. "Get yourself over here! If M'lord gets back and I haven't got those shoes on you he will take his business elsewhere! And you're not the only horse in his stable! Just the nastiest!"

Dunia's father was swearing at a horse! Without thinking, I stepped up to the gate. Dunia's father saw me and yelled out, "You boy! What are you staring at? Away with you! And leave my daughters alone!"

I motioned Dunia to move away as I boldly opened the gate and quickly stepped in before the horse could bolt. I wasn't going to let this man scare me like he had scared Milada.

"What do you think you are doing?" he yelled. "This animal is dangerous. I don't need you here to rile it more!"

I looked at the horse and then at the man and saw fear in the eyes of both.

"I think I can help you, Sir," I said calmly, in contrast to his angry words.

"What can a weakling like you do that I cannot?" he shouted, his echoing voice making the horse even more jumpy.

"If you let me try, Sir, you will see," I told him. When he hesitated I said, "Stand away to the side of the room and stay quiet."

He looked at me with anger, but must have been worn out from fighting with the horse and moved aside with a grunt. The black stallion pawed the straw at its feet, its nostrils flaring. Using my mind, like I did when I went hunting with the gypsy boys, I sent a message to the horse.

"Be still," I told him, "be still; no one will hurt you."

At first the horse raised his neck and whinnied loudly. He wheeled around the back of the anvil and for a moment I was afraid that he would kick Dunia's father with his powerful hind legs.

"Easy there, now," I said, this time out loud but in a quiet voice. "Easy, boy; you are safe. No one will harm you."

I looked into the stallion's eyes. He seemed to understand what I was saying. Slowly I moved up closer, by his left side. When he didn't shy or move away from me I reached up and gently stroked the side of his neck, near the base of his raven mane. Out of the corner of my eye, I saw Dunia's father looking on in amazement.

"Come now, you beautiful creature," I told the horse. "It's time for some new shoes. It will not hurt you at all."

Gently I grasped the leather bridle then fastened the rein to a rail beside the anvil. I looked at the man in the corner and said, "I think he is ready now. Move slowly and be gentle with him and he shouldn't give you any more problems."

Dunia's father gazed at me with wonder and then, without a word, went on with his work, lifting up one of the horse's back feet and starting to pry off the old shoe. When I realized that an expression of gratitude would not be forthcoming, I caressed the horse one last time and quietly left the forge to join Dunia where she was waiting on the road outside.

I picked up the jugs and we continued toward her house.

"Well that was impressive," she said as we walked. "Where did you learn to talk to horses?"

"The gypsies do it all the time," I told her. "I thought it was pretty stupid at first; that is until I tried it and saw that it works!"

"You just saved my father a lot of money!" she said. "He was angry last night because he wasn't able to get near that stallion. It belongs to a nobleman who has more than twenty horses. He was not happy with his own blacksmith so he brought this black stallion, his most difficult horse, to my father saying that if he succeeded to shoe him he could have the job of taking care of all the other horses' shoes as well."

"He didn't seem to be managing very well when we were passing," I laughed.

"He must have been at his wit's end!" she said. "It's a good thing he didn't kill it, he was so angry."

"He seems to have a very bad temper," I said.

"He's not a bad man," Dunia replied, thoughtfully. "Yes, he is often harsh and angry, but there is always food on our table, money when we need to buy things and Yagoda and I will have good dowries when the time comes for us to wed."

"But, he doesn't seem very happy," I told her.

"He works hard," she said. "I think he is too tired to be happy. Once we are older and have families of our own, he will have time to relax and be happy."

By this time, we had reached her house.

"Would you like to come in?" she asked. "I baked a honey cake."

"Your parent's won't mind?" I asked, remembering that other times she insisted that I left before they returned to the house.

"They've met you now," she said. "And after what you just did for my father, how could he mind?"

I carried the jugs inside and placed them on the table while Dunia opened the shutters. She went inside the cool-room and brought out a plate with a golden colored cake on it. It made me think about how seldom I ate sweets with the gypsies. Maybe because when we were on the road we had no ovens to bake them in.

"What are you thinking?" Dunia said, handing me a slice of the cake.

"I'm thinking about how much I like cake!" I replied, taking a piece in my fingers and bringing it to my mouth. It was very tasty.

Dunia smiled at me and offered me a second piece.

Chapter 48 – Decisions

I was just finishing my second piece of cake when the door opened and Dunia father burst in.

"That was a hell of a job!" he exclaimed, sitting down heavily, his blackened arms resting on the table.

Dunia fluttered nervously, looking at me and her tired father sitting together unexpectedly at the table.

"Cake, Dunia," he bellowed, "and a mug of ale."

"Yes, Father," she said, "right away." She quickly set a plate with a large piece of her delicious cake in from of him and then disappeared into the cool-room, presumably to get the ale.

"And bring a mug for the boy" he called after her.

I was surprised! Dunia was soon back and placed a large mug of ale before her father and a slightly smaller one in front of me.

After stuffing the cake into his mouth and signaling for Dunia to bring him more, he turned his sharp eyes to me and said, "Impressive what you did with that horse."

I didn't know what to say.

"It saved my hide with the lord of the manor," he went on. "I was damned near ready to hit that horse on the head with a hammer to get it to settle down. But had I killed it, the lord would have killed me!"

"You know, Sir, that I am not one of the gypsies," I began, "but I have lived with them for several years and learned some unusual skills. They definitely have a way with horses!"

"I know," he said, "they have a way of making ours disappear with them when they leave!"

I knew that our band never stole horses but I kept my mouth shut.

"I was happy to be of service to you," I told him, changing the subject.

"It is a talent to be able to calm a wild horse. You're pretty scrawny, but a few weeks of lifting the hammer would put some muscle on those skinny bones. I can't very well train my girls in the business, but I could use and apprentice to give me a hand; especially one who can talk to horses."

That would be a great chance, I thought to myself. If Milada was sure that she could not love me I might stay here and learn the trade of a blacksmith. It would be hard work, but profitable; and my new found talent of calming horses could make the job easier.

"Sir, I would be honored to learn the trade from you if fate leads me to remain in this village," I told him. Dunia was at the fire behind her father and as I looked up at him, I saw a big smile spreading over her face. With that smile, she looked so much like Milada. We both looked down as our eyes met, her checks growing red, and probably mine as well.

"I should be going now," I murmured. "Thank you for the cake and ale."

"Be off with you, now, boy," Dunia's father said gruffly but with a hint of affection. "Come by my workshop some time and see if you can lift the hammer."

On my way back to the gypsies' camp I stopped at the market place to get some cheese to bring to the cooking wagon. The gypsy band had been camped at this village for neatly two turns of the moon, but the people were still very generous towards them.

Back at the camp there was much activity. I found Tanya at the cooking wagon. I handed her the cheese and asked her what was going on.

"The Baron announced that we would be moving on tomorrow so we need to pack up everything to be ready for the start of the journey," she told me. "We will meet the other bands of our tribe on midsummer's day and have a long distance to travel in a short time."

"Why didn't the Baron order the journey to begin earlier?" I asked.

"We needed to collect plenty of the rare herbs that grow in this place to share with the other bands. When we'd done that, it was time for the women's moon tent. That is not a time to travel so the Baron delayed our departure," Tanya explained.

"Here," she said, handing me back some of the cheese I'd brought and some bread and olives. "We won't be having a proper meal tonight. Eat this and then stow your things for the journey."

I thanked her and then looked around for Milada. I needed to speak with her. As if she knew what I was thinking, Tanya said, "I just left Milada in the moon tent. She said that she would go directly to her wagon to gather and pack her things."

This was it; the last chance to see if Milada would be mine. I didn't go directly to her wagon. I walked down by the brook to collect myself. I saw some wild roses growing near the stream and carefully picked a bunch, wrapping the thorny stems in soft green leaves and tying them together with a supple piece of long grass. Then, taking a deep breath, I headed to Milada's wagon hoping to find her alone there.

I approached it from behind. As I came around to the front I expected to see Milada there, busying herself with preparations for the journey I hoped she wouldn't want to make. But she wasn't there. I climbed up to see if she was inside, but there was no sign of her. I settled in a patch of shade beside the wagon and waited.

In a little while, I heard the sound of footsteps. Milada came from the woods into the clearing and saw me.

"Hello, Milada," I said, "I've been waiting for you".

"Hello, Goran," she said, sitting beside me. "Those are pretty."

"I picked them for you," I said, handing her the wild roses.

"Thanks," she said, blushing prettily.

I took a deep breath and asked, "Have you thought about what I said?" I looked down at the roses in her dainty hand, afraid of what I might see in her eyes.

"Dear Goran," she said, "you have been my best friend, my brother for many years. I love you dearly, but I cannot be your wife. We are too different; we want different things from our lives."

"Are you sure?" I asked, raising my eyes to hers.

"Yes, I am sure," she said, as tears started to trickle down her cheeks.

I could see that she loved me, even if she didn't realize it. Why else would she be crying? But how long could I keep waiting and hoping? I had an opportunity here in this village; it wasn't fair for me to give that up if she thought so little of me.

"I'm sorry that you feel that way," I told her. "In that case, if there is really no chance for you to be with me, I will stay here and make my life in this village. Dunia's father has offered to teach me the craft of the blacksmith."

"You will stay here?" she said quietly. "You'll be a blacksmith? That's hard work!"

"Yes, it is," I said, "But it is a good living. Horses always need new shoes." I smiled at the thought of how I'd managed to calm the stallion.

"Oh, Goran," she said, "I'll miss you so much!"

"Then say you'll marry me and I will stay," I told her, with a glimmer of hope.

"I wish I could," she said, "but it would not be true to my heart."

Something inside of me snapped. I would give up my dream of settling in this prosperous village and making something of myself to stay with her, but she thinks so little of me. 'True to her heart' she said. I knew what or *who* was in her heart instead of me and could not hold my tongue.

"You think that Dragan will marry you?" I spat.

She looked at me with wide eyes. I wanted to stop talking but I couldn't. "I see the way you look at him, all moon-eyed," I went on, "but he will never marry outside of the gypsy band".

I regretted my words as soon as they were out of my mouth. I felt angry with her and angry with myself. Before she could say anything I jumped up and ran as fast as I could back to the wagon that had been my home for so long. It was time to pack my things and start a new life; a life without Milada.

Chapter 49 – Letting Go

I'm climbing the steps to this wagon; for the last time, I thought to myself. I spread out a wide scarf on my bunk and lay my few possessions on it; one shirt, my bowl, knife and spoon, a leather jerkin and my cap. I wrapped the scarf around them and tied it in a knot at the top. I took my pouch full of coins from its place under my straw mattress and put it in my pack.

I saw the black boots I'd worn for the feast poking out from under my bunk. I liked those boots and they were very comfortable, but although I felt it that was acceptable to take my clothes and an extra shirt, boots were more precious and these belonged to the gypsy band. I looked around the wagon with a sigh. I was happy here with Bora and Nico but I knew that it was time to move on.

Pulling the curtain closed as I left, I went to find the boys and the Baron to tell them that I would be leaving.

As I approached the Baron's wagon I saw Milada walking away from it with Yagoda, carrying a bundle resembling mine, following behind her, scowling. I couldn't face Milada and ducked behind another wagon before she could see me.

"What a mean man!" I heard Yagoda say as she walked passed my hiding place. Was she talking about her father or about the Baron?

I couldn't make out Milada's reply. Once they had turned the corner toward the path to the village I made my way to the Baron's wagon. Dragan was there with him. The two were smiling and shaking their heads.

Dragan's smile widened when he saw me. Did he have any idea how Milada felt about him, I wondered, and the effect her feelings for him had on me?

"Goran!" he called, waving at me to approach. "Are you packed? We will be leaving soon."

"Dragon, Baron, Sir," I said, inclining my head as a sign of respect. "I've come to tell you that I will not be travelling on with you. I am very grateful for your generosity in taking me in and allowing me to travel with your band, but it is time for me to settle down and to make a life for myself."

The Baron smiled and said. "Goran, you have grown into a fine young man. I knew the day would come when you would decide to leave us. Thank you for gracing us with your company. I wish you well in the new phase of your life."

I was surprised when Dragan stepped close to me and engulfed me in his arms in a big, heartfelt bear hug. When he released me, he looked into my eyes and said, "I will miss you, my friend! We all will; especially Milada."

I felt my throat catch at the mention of her name and dropped my eyes.

"I will miss you all as well," I said, realizing that it was true.

"We will travel this way again someday," the Baron said. "Then we will see what a fine man you will have become."

He held out his hand. When I grasped it to shake, he pulled me into a manly hug.

"Go with the good, boy!" he said with a fatherly smile.

Tear prickled in my eyes but I resolved not to cry. I nodded my thanks then turned to go, before I changed my mind. I was moved by the kindness of these people; people I was now choosing to leave.

I headed to the village with the thought of passing by the blacksmith's workshop and asking if I could stay in the stable's loft. The hay would make a soft bed and the horses below would provide warmth during the coming chilly nights.

Passing through the village gate I saw Jelko sitting near the fountain with the girl he said he liked. He waved me to come over.

"Hey, Gogo!" he said, "Do you remember Janka?"

"Hey Jelko," I said. "Good day, Janka. You were the girl who saved the little bird. I've seen you at the gypsy camp."

She blushed at my words and looked down at her feet.

"You've been to the gypsy camp?" Jelko questioned. "You didn't say."

"I didn't think you'd care," she said, looking up at him. "Remember I told you that the silver haired lady and Milada cured my brother's earache? I wanted to learn more about their healing skills and they offered to teach me."

"Speaking of that girl, Milada," Jelko said, "We just saw her and the kid, Yagoda. Her father had them both by their wrists. He was dragging them along and they were both squirming and trying to get away from him."

"Why didn't you help them?" I said, in shock.

"It's none of my business," he said with a shrug.

"I'm going to see what's going on," I told them. "I'll see you later."

I ran down the cobblestone lane until I came to Dunia's house. The door was shut but I could hear screaming coming from within. What was happening?

I went around the side of the house in case I could see through the window. If that man was hurting Milada I would kill him. I stood on a stone and peaked into the window, careful not to be seen. I could see the man beating Yagoda with a leather belt. She let out a loud cry at every blow as the heavy belt reddened her pale flesh. Of Milada, there was no sign.

I wondered what transgression Yagoda had committed to merit such a beating. In all the time I travelled with the gypsy band no child was ever punished in this way, or even by harsh words, come to think of it. But I knew that in the villages it was thought important to 'teach a child a lesson' with punishment. I could remember the feeling of a belt on my backside, but not the offence that had let to my beating.

Where was Milada? Maybe she had managed to escape. Or maybe the blacksmith had locked her in the cool-room. I could see that the door was closed, with the key in the lock.

Suddenly, there was silence. The man was fixing his belt back around his waist. Without a word he took the key from the cool room door and dropped it in his pocket. He strode to the door, shaking his head, and left, slamming it behind him.

I heard Yagoda's sobs and watched as her mother came out of the shadows and tried to comfort her. She shook her mother off and ran to the cool-room.

"It's your fault," she yelled, banging her fists on the wooden door. "If you'd taken me with you this would not have happened!"

I heard a muffled voice coming from inside the cool room. I knew at once it was Milada's.

"It was not up to me!" she said, "Yagoda, open the door and let me out of here."

"He took the key," she said, "and even if he hadn't I wouldn't let you out. If I have to be stuck here, you can be stuck here, too."

Yagoda moved away from the door and hugged her mother, crying into her apron.

"Please let me out of here!" Milada called, "Dunia! Please!"

Was Dunia there? Sure enough, in the shadows near the fireplace I spotted her sitting with her head in her hands. I think that she was crying, too.

Milada was locked in the cool room. The gypsies were preparing to leave. If they left without her there would be no way for her to know which way they had gone. She would have to stay in the village; stay with me.

What a twist of fate! What luck! This was more than I could hope for. She would be upset for a while, but, over time, she would begin to forget the gypsies; forget Dragan. But as I looked at the cowering women in the dim light of the cottage I realized that this was no life for Milada. She was a free spirit and would wither and die if forced to live with these people. I ducked down and made my way to small incline at the back of the house.

There was a boarded-up window low to the ground. By its placement, I knew it had to be the window of the cool-room. I tapped on it lightly; I wanted Milada to hear, but no one else. At first there was no response. I kept tapping in an even rhythm so she would know it was a sign and not random noises.

When there was still no response I whispered, "Milada, Milada, can you hear me?"

"Yes, I can hear you," she said. "Who is there? Can you help me get out of here?"

"It's me, Goran!" I said very quietly.

"Can you get me out?" she whispered.

"I'll try to pry the boards loose," I told her, "but we have to hurry before they get back. Can you push from the inside on the board that I tap?"

I tapped on the lowest board. I could see it bending outward as she pushed on it. Slowly, she was able to push it out enough for me to pull it loose. I realized that the floor of the cool room was at a much lower level and that Milada was standing on something in order to reach the window. Her hand felt around in the air and I gave it a little squeeze of encouragement.

"That's my girl!" I said. "Push on the next one now".

She pushed and I pulled and the second board became loose enough for me to remove.

"Can you get out through the hole?" I asked.

"No," she said, "It's still too small. And it's very high".

"Let's get one more board off and then try," I told her.

With the third board out, the hole was large enough for Milada to squeeze through but, from her side, it was high in the wall and she couldn't reach it.

"Let me find something else to stand on," she whispered.

She disappeared for a moment, looking for something that would allow her to climb up high enough to get out.

I could hear voices coming from inside the house. Dunia's father had returned.

"Let's see if she has cooled down by now," I heard him say.

There were murmurs that I couldn't make out then I heard him say as if in answer, "Let her get hungrier. Maybe then she will be grateful for what we are offering her."

I knew Milada would have to hurry. Soon the top of her head appeared at the window, and then her frightened eyes.

As I helped pull her out she said, "He's back,"

"Quick, hand me those planks. I'll replace them so they won't guess how you got out!" I told her. "They'll think you learned a gypsy trick to disappear."

She handed me the planks and held them while I secured them back in place. For a moment, our eyes met. I saw the Milada I remembered from before I brought up the subject of love and marriage. Milada, my dearest friend; the girl I loved with all my heart. This would be my last gift to her.

"Go now," I said.

"You will not come?" she asked.

I was tempted to forget all my plans and go with her. I drew her into my arms and whispered into the hair, "You know I'll always love you".

Then, with a pain deep in my heart I did what I knew I must. I opened my arms and said, "Go. Live your life and be happy".

There were noises in the house and more yelling. Maybe they opened the cool room door and had seen that Milada had vanished.

"Go," I said. "Now!" I gently pushed her away. I ran down the lane that led, in a roundabout way, to the village square.

Chapter 50 –Taking Leave

I thought as I walked. The way Milada had looked at me gave me hope. I knew she couldn't stay in the oppressive house of the blacksmith and her cousins, but if I worked hard and saved the money I earned I could build her a sunny home on the edge of the village with a view of the forest. We could raise our family there; have some chickens for eggs and goats for milk. When the gypsies came she could spend time with them and we could enjoy their music and dance by their fire. I was heartened at the thought. The Baron said that the band would travel back here someday. And when they did, I would be ready to offer Milada a good life here with me.

I was lost in thought when I reached the village square and was startled when Jelko called me over.

"Hey Gogo!" he called, "Did you sort it out? I know I wouldn't want to cross the blacksmith. I've seen him knock a man across the square for looking at him the wrong way!"

I sat down on the edge of the fountain.

"The house was locked tight," I lied. "I don't know where they went."

"Look there," Jelko said, indicating the far side of the square nearest Dunia's cottage.

The blacksmith was storming from the lane, heading for the ale house, muttering loudly.

"There's the man," Jelko said, "but of the girls, no sign."

"I'm going to go and see," Jelko's girl said. "Dunia is a good friend. If there is trouble, maybe there is something I can do to help."

Jelko grabbed her wrist. "Don't go," he said. "Whatever it is doesn't concern you. Stay here with me a little longer."

"I will go and see Dunia now," if you are still around later I'll see you then," she said, shaking her wrist free and giving him a sweet smile.

"Hum," Jelko grumbled. "One of the things I like about Janka is her spunk; but sometimes it drives me crazy!"

I saw him looking at my bundle.

"What have you got there?" he asked me?

"My things," I told him. "I've decided to stay here in the village. Dunia's father offered to make me his apprentice. I think."

"You'd be brave to work for him!" Jelko said. "A few boys have tried it, but not many could stand his temper."

"Blacksmithing is a good skill to have," I said. "How bad can he be?"

"Don't say I didn't warn you!" Jelko said. "When he is in a temper he is mighty powerful!"

"And he seems to be in a temper today!" I said. "I was thinking that I could stay in his stable but now doesn't seem like the best time to ask."

"You can stay with me for now," Jelko said, giving me a slap on the back. "I don't know how the other boys will like it, with you likely to win Dunia's hand, especially if you get in with that father of hers, but, Gogo, you are all right with me!"

"Thanks Jelko!" I said, relieved that I had found a place to lay my head that night. Show me where you live."

We hopped off the edge of the fountain and I followed him down a winding route to the heart of the village. We arrived at a tall house in the middle of a narrow alley. He pushed open a heavy door and we were in a stable. In the dimness of the room it was hard to count the number of cows living there. There must have been at least three or four. Jelko showed me to a ladder on the left side of the door and I climbed up behind him.

The room on the first floor was very dark and warm and smelled of the animals below. Our footsteps caused the wooden floorboards to creak. I hoped that they would support our weight! Jelko went to the window and threw open the shutters to let some light into the room. Not much could penetrate from the narrow alley but the little light that filtered in allowed me to take a look around.

The far side of the room held a large fireplace with an iron hook for a cooking pot. There were shelves with a few bowls and cooking implements and a wide bench ran the length of the wall opposite the window covered with thin mattresses filled with straw. In the center of the room was a long table with a narrow bench on either side of it and one chair on the side near the fireplace.

"Welcome home!" Jelko said, turning back for the window. "You can sleep there," he indicated one end of the bench with the straw-filled mats.

I didn't think it looked very homey! "Where's your family?" I asked him. "Do they all sleep here?"

"We have a cottage at the edge of the village," he replied. "Sometimes I stay there, but most of the time I sleep here; I keep an eye on the cows. My sisters come and milk them in the morning and evening and bring food for me."

"And it's handy for me to be near the village square," he added. "Leave your things and let's go and have some ale."

I dropped my bundle on the mat but kept my pack and the pouch of coins it contained with me as I climbed down the ladder. I reminded myself to drink only one mug of ale; any more than that and I might not be able to make it back up again!

The sun was low when we emerged from the warren of narrow alleys into the open square. Misha and Stanyo were sitting outside the tavern, joking. They waved when they saw Jelko and me approaching.

I sat with them while Jelko went inside to get our drinks. Soon he returned, a mug in each hand.

"Gogo is staying in the village!" Jelko announced as way of a toast.

"Hey, that's great," Misha said, patting me on the back.

"Where're you going to live?" Stanyo asked, clinking his mug on mine.

"With this fellow for now," I said pointing my chin in Jelko's direction.

"With the cows?" Misha said.

"Above the cows, I hope!" I replied with a grin.

We passed a happy hour together. I was getting to like these boys and feel accepted by them. When the setting sun bathed the square in golden light I suddenly remembered that I had not said goodbye to my friends in the gypsy band.

"There's something I need to do," I told the boys. Will you be here for a while?" I knew I'd never find my way back to Jelko's place alone.

"We'll be here," Jelko said, "The others will be along in a while."

"Wait for me," I told them; "I'll be back soon."

I headed toward the village gate and the gypsy camp beyond. I knew that the band would leave early in the morning. Nico and Bora had been good friends. I wanted to thank them and wish them a good journey. Then I thought of the others; Tanya and Mother Miriana who scared me so at first, but I had come to like and respect. I hoped that I would not run into Milada. I said everything I needed to say to her. If I saw her I might change my mind again and go against everything I knew was right.

I reached the clearing where the gypsies' camp was, but I there was nothing there. Maybe I'd made a mistake; taken a wrong turn in the woods. I backtracked a bit, but after staying here for two turns of the moon, I was sure I knew where the gypsies were camped. They had already left! I wandered in the twilight to the place my wagon had been. Maybe the boys had held back in case I came to bid them farewell.

The oak tree that had given us shade still spread it branches majestically, but the space beneath it where our wagon had stood was empty. Or was it? I took a step closer. There, at the base of the oak tree, was a neat pile; the warm woolen blanket from my bed, the new black trousers and embroidered waistcoat I'd worn for the feast and, at the bottom of the pile, the pair of black boots, polished up to a reflective shine.

Mentally, I sent out my thanks to the boys who had been such good friends and to all the gypsies who had taken in a motherless boy and helped mold him into the independent young man he was today.

SUMMER

Chapter 51 - Endings and Beginnings

"So, grandfather," the little girl said, "is this the end of the story about you and Milada?"

The sound of her voice startled me. I had forgotten that I was telling her my story; that I was speaking at all.

When I did not answer, she asked me again.

"Is that the end? Milada left with the gypsy band and you stayed in the village?"

"Yes," I said, my voice hoarse and scratchy, whether from the length of my tale or the emotions I was feeling while recollecting those days I cannot say.

"Do you know what happened to her when she traveled with the gypsies? Did she ever come back to the village?" she asked, insatiable, just like Milada, whom she so resembled.

I didn't answer her; I couldn't. When I remained silent, the little girl hopped up, and gave my cheek a light kiss.

"Thank you, grandfather. Now I know Milada's story. I will tell the others if they ask," she said. "Shall I help you to your house?"

I shook my head. There was still some light in the sky. The story was not at its end. I had no reason or desire to share the rest of it with the child, but remembering those days brought back many feelings I had forgotten; feelings I had kept from myself for so many years. Now, for one last time, I wanted to go back to my youth; to feel what I once felt; to see if now, with the distance of time, I would understand the crossroads of my life differently.

I shuffled down on the bench to catch the last rays of the sun, closed my eyes and once again remembered myself as a young man, full of life and hope for the future.

*****

After the gypsies left I spent a few days exploring the village, getting to know my way around the alleys and the small squares within its walls. In the market place, people seemed surprised to see me.

The cheese seller called out, "Hey, boy! Are you still here? Did the gypsies forget to take you with them?"

"My name is Gogo," I told her. "This is such a nice village I decided to stay. From now on I will pay for my cheese!"

"It will seem odd to take money from you," the rosy cheeked lady replied.

"If you have some job for me to do, you could pay me with some of your delicious cheese!" I said.

"I could use a hand early the morning when I have to unload the wagon," she said. "Here; have a piece of cheese now on account."

"Thanks," I said "I'll be here at first light tomorrow to help you."

When others saw me the next morning, several asked me for help in exchange for their wares. I earned enough to fill my belly and to bring some food home to share with Jelko.

I saw Dunia at the fountain several times filling her jug, but I was still confused by what I had seen in her house and kept my distance.

After several days had passed I worked up enough courage to visit the blacksmith in his workshop. I stood outside the half door, watching him at his work before he saw me. He lifted the heavy hammer and brought it down again and again in a steady rhythm. He had to put it down to work the bellows to keep the forge fire steady.

I wasn't sure if I should walk in or call out to him. In the end, he saw me before I could do anything.

"Hey, there boy," he said, in his loud voice. "Are you still here?"

"Yes, Sir," I said with the hint of a smile.

"Why are you standing outside my gate? Don't you have anything better to do?"

"You said you could use an assistant, Sir," I said.

"I could use an assistant with some muscles on him," he said gruffly, "not a scrawny duck the likes of you."

"I could pump the bellows," I said, "and calm the horses so you can shoe them more easily."

"In with you then, and let's see what you can do," he said, pulling the bottom part of the gate open.

I was nervous but I didn't want him to know. I swaggered like I'd seen some of the village men do, my chest and chin high. I went over to the bellows but the blacksmith called me over to where he stood.

"Let's see what you are made of," he said, stepping away from the hammer and anvil. "Take up the hammer."

Oh, my! I moved close to the hammer, bent down and grasped it in my two hands. I managed to lift the wooden handle a little ways off the ground, but its iron head stayed firmly on the earthen floor.

The man let out a hardy laugh. "A lot of good you'll do around here," he smirked.

I took a deep breath, bent my knees, grasped the handle again a little closer to the hammer's head and, with an exhale, straightened my knees and managed to lift the hammer a little ways off the ground before letting it drop when I felt a twinge of pain in my back.

"Well, well, well." The blacksmith said, folding his hands over his chest. "Maybe you'll do. You've got determination, I'll give you that."

He showed me how to work the bellows and stoke the fire to keep its temperature steady and high. Perspiration dripped from my brow. When he finally put down his hammer for the day I was exhausted.

"That's enough for today, boy," he said. "Remind me; what's your name?"

"Goran, Sir," I said, "but they call me Gogo."

"Come and have some dinner, then, Gogo," he said. "If they didn't make enough the girls can go without."

I felt badly to think I'd take food away from Dunia and her sister, but truth be told, I was very, very hungry. I followed him back to the house, but as we went inside I'd remembered what I had seen there and felt less than comfortable.

The table was already set for the family meal. The blacksmith shut the heavy door behind him and called out to his wife, "I have brought this boy to eat. He has been working at the forge all day. Bring him some food."

Dunia looked up from the pot she was stirring on the hearth and her cheeks reddened. "Yagoda," she said, dropping her eyes, "set another place for Goran."

Their mother looked surprised to see me, but said nothing as she passed a bowl to her daughter. Dunia ladled the thick soup from the pot into the bowl. I was relieved to see that there was plenty for all of us. Dunia set the soup on the table as we took our places. He father muttered some words then crossed himself and began to eat. After he started, he girls picked up their spoons to eat and I did, too.

No one spoke at the table. It was so different from the cheerful meals with the gypsy band. I guess everyone was tired from their work; I knew I was. I looked forward to stretching out on my bench above the cows.

When we finished eating, the blacksmith pushed away from the table. Without a word to his wife and daughters he headed to the door.

"I'm going to the alehouse. Gogo, are you coming?" I muttered my thanks to Dunia and her mother and followed him out the door and down the lane to the square.

Jelko and the boys waved at me. I could see there was a game of bones going on. I waved back but indicated I was with the blacksmith. Jelko nodded in understanding as I followed the big man into the ale house.

When two mugs of ale were placed before us, he looked at me and said, "You did well today, boy. You did your job without questions or idle chatter. You aren't very strong, but I can see that you are willing."

"Yes, Sir," I am," I said, encouraged at his words.

"Believe it or not but once I was not so strong, either," he went on. "With time and practice, you will develop strength and skill. You are at a good age to begin this trade."

"I am willing to learn and do whatever you tell me, Sir," I said.

"I am a hard taskmaster," he said, "I do not tolerate laziness or sloth."

"No, Sir," I said, "I understand that."

"I can't pay you now, but you can sleep in the stable beside the forge and eat with my family."

I was hoping to be able to save some money toward a house of my own. My disappointment must have shown in my face.

"But," he continued, "I have no sons. If you work hard and please me, one day my business may be yours."

I was shocked by his words! A business like that would make me plenty of money. Horses always need shoes and there would also be work making farm tools and other implements of metal. But what if I spent years working for him and then he changed his mind, or found someone else to take over the business?

I did not want to question him now. It was my first day working with the blacksmith. I figured the best thing would be to let some time pass and then see. For now, he was offering a better place to stay and food to eat; it was enough.

"Thank you, Sir," I told him. "I won't let you down."

"You do and you're out!" he said, slapping me on the back a little harder than was comfortable. I didn't know if he was joking or not.

Chapter 52 – My Life in the Village

I bid the blacksmith farewell. He told me to be at the forge early the next morning. I was glad that the boys had dispersed for the night. They would have wanted me to join in their game, but I was much too tired. I made my way back to Jelko's place, let myself into the stable quietly so as not to set off the cows at this late hour and climbed up the rickety ladder.

Jelko lay on the bench. I settled myself in my place, thankful to lay down after a hard day's work. I appreciated that my friend had let me stay here with him, but I was looking forward to the deeper, softer straw of the blacksmith's barn. I thought Jelko would be fast asleep so when he spoke it started me.

"Good plan," he said.

"What?" I asked, sleepily.

"Getting in with the father," he said.

"What do you mean?" I asked him.

"Dunia," he said, as if that explained it all.

"What about her?" I asked. We hadn't spoken since Milada's disappearance. I couldn't let on that I knew anything about it and felt awkward whenever I saw her.

"Her dowry," he said.

"I don't want to marry the girl," I said, missing Milada.

"You could do worse," Jelko said. I couldn't see him but I knew that he was smiling. "You know she likes you."

"I just want to learn a good occupation," I said, "and make some money to give me a start in life."

"You'll be lucky of that old miser pays you," he muttered, "Better to marry the girl; then you'll have money for sure!"

Could I tell him I wanted the money to make a life for Milada and me? No. Milada had gone; it would just sound like a fantasy. Maybe it was a fantasy. Who could know if she would ever return? As I drifted off to sleep, I felt a lone tear trickle down my cheek.

In the morning, Jelko watched as I gathered my few possessions.

"Going somewhere?" he asked.

"It's not that I am not grateful for these sumptuous accommodations," I told him, "but part of my salary, a big part at that, is lodgings in the blacksmith's stable. It will be handier for work."

"And for midnight meetings with the daughter!" he laughed.

I felt myself blushing at the thought, but said nothing.

Jelko continued, "I like your company, but it's good you found somewhere else to sleep, I've been hoping to entice my Janka to pay a nighttime visit to my cows."

"Do you think she would?" I asked.

"No harm in trying," he replied. "Where are you off to so early?"

"Work!" I said, and with a wave, descended the ladder. I was surprised to see a girl not much younger than myself sitting beside the nearest cow. This must be one of Jelko's sisters. I wondered if she'd heard us talking.

"Good morning," I said to the girl. She looked up, her hands still grasping the cow's udder.

"Morning!" she replied. By the grin on her face, I figured that she had probably overheard our conversation.

When I arrived at the forge the blacksmith was sitting on a bench eating bread, cheese and olives. He beckoned me to join him.

"Here, sit. Eat," he ordered. "Men need fuel for a hard day's work."

Feeling no words were expected or necessary I joined him on the bench and ate. He looked at the bundle I'd set down at my feet and nodded. When the food was finished he grunted, and led me through the workshop and out a small door. We crossed a cobbled alley that backed on the forge and went in another door just opposite it. The smallness of the door belied the size of the stable beyond. On my right was a loft above a large area for storing dry hay. Ahead of me and stretching toward the left were a series of six stalls, four of which had horses in them. At the end of the row I could see high double doors that must open out to the wide street that linked the square with the market place.

The blacksmith indicated the loft. "You can sleep there," he said. "It's warm and it's dry and you can keep an eye on the horses in case thieves try to come in the night."

I climbed up the wide wooden ladder. I was expecting to see nothing but fresh straw and was very surprised to find a wide bed with a soft mattress stuffed with wool covered by a thick grey blanket. There was a bench and a small table with an oil lamp on it positioned under a high window shaded by a burlap curtain.

"The girls prettied it up for you," he admitted when I came down smiling.

"I will have to thank them," I said, "and I thank you for giving me this opportunity."

"Enough of that, now," he said gruffly as we went back to the forge.

He showed me how to stack the wood in a particular way and then light the fire from a small lamp that he always kept burning. I worked the bellows while he pounded the iron into the rough semicircular shape of horseshoes.

"Go and fetch one of the two horses in the furthest stalls," he told me.

"Does it matter which one?" I asked him.

He shook his head. I went out the back door, across the alley and into the stable. The horses whinnied when they saw me approach. I guessed he meant the stalls furthest from the small door. Neither was as big or as feisty as the black stallion. I smiled at them, looking into their deep brown eyes.

"Who wants to be first?" I asked aloud. I missed chatting but knew better than to try to engage the blacksmith in idle talk.

I stepped closer to one horse, reached out and pat its velvety nose.

"How about you, then?" I asked the dappled mare, as I untied the rope that bound her bridle to the stable post.

She nudged my head as I stopped to unbolt the large doors. The one from which I entered was too small to let a horse pass. I led her into the wide street and then around to the front of the blacksmith's workshop. I waited until the man stopped banging his hammer and then led the mare inside and tied her lead to a hitching post near the anvil, without a comment. I was pleased that I had brought one of the correct horses.

"Shall I go back and bolt the door, Sir?" I asked.

"You'd better," he said. "Those horses are not mine; I am responsible to their owners."

I hurried through the small doors and bolted the large one before returning the way I had come and resuming my position at the bellows. I watched the blacksmith as he pried the worn shoes off the mare. I could sense her discomfort and sent her reassuring words from my mind. I didn't think the man would like it if I spoke them aloud.

One by one, he replaced the old shoes and then told me to return the mare to the stall and bring the other horse. I did as I was told, making several trips to the stable to unbolt and bolt again the wide door.

When we had finished shoeing the second horse I watched the blacksmith douse the fire, glad to be finished for the day and ready for a meal and then a nap in my new room. I started to take off the heavy apron the blacksmith had given me to wear.

"Wait a minute," he said. "You aren't through yet."

I felt like I was indeed finished, but I left the apron on and waited.

"Come over here," he said. He stood by a strange contraption; an iron pole about the width and length of a broomstick balanced on two low blocks of wood.

"Watch how I lift this," he said, squatting down with the pole in front of him. He slipped his hands under the pole and wrapped his fingers around it from beneath. As he straightened his legs to stand, he bent his arms and raised the pole in front of him. Then he squatted again and returned the pole to the blocks. It did not look too difficult.

"You do it," he said, stepping away from the pole so I could take it.

I started to bend down to pick it up.

"No," he shouted. "Bend your knees first."

I squatted and grasped the pole from underneath. As I stood up, I bent my arms as he had done. The pole was heavy but I managed it. Then I set it down again and looked at the man for approval.

He just looked at me and said, "Now do that twenty more times," and went out the door.

Twenty times? I squatted down again and repeated the lifting exercise, once, twice, three times, five… By the time I reached twelve my arms were sore. I could stop now; he wouldn't know. But if I wanted to be able to wield the hammer I needed to build my strength. Thirteen, fourteen, fifteen. I stopped to rest; took some water from the jug and then did the last five. Sweat dripped from my forehead and my arms and shoulders ached but I felt proud of myself for managing all twenty times. I was starving and rushed to the door, nearly colliding with the blacksmith who was standing outside, watching me through a crack in the doorframe.

It was a good thing I hadn't given up! Did he praise me for managing all twenty lifts? Hardly! Without a word, he locked the door behind me and I followed him home anticipating the hardy stew that I knew would be waiting for us.

Chapter 53 – Settling In

After the meal, I could hardly keep my eyes open.

Dunia's mother noticed and said, "It looks like you worked hard today and could use a nap."

"Yes, ma'am," I said, slightly embarrassed that I was so worn out after my first day of work.

"Go on and take a rest, boy," the blacksmith said. "We've finished for the day."

I was glad to hear it, but couldn't help asking, "What about those other two horses in the stable?"

"Those two are mine," he said, "for ploughing or pulling the wagon if I need to deliver heavy goods."

I was relieved that the day's work was done.

"Do you need anything in your room?" Dunia asked shyly.

"Did you fix it up for me?" I asked.

"I helped!" Yagoda piped in.

"Thank you both," I told them. "It looks very comfortable." The girls smiled.

"Could I have a basin and a jug," I asked. I'd grown accustomed to washing my hands and face in the morning. The blacksmith gave me a strange look.

"What do you need them for?" he asked. "You can go to the fountain if you need a drink."

I thought it better no to try to explain. I knew it was not the custom for the people in the villages to wash so often.

"Yes, Sir; I can go to the fountain," I said. "Now, if I may be excused, I will go and rest."

I dragged my feet back to the stable, pulled myself up the ladder and immediately fell into a deep, dreamless sleep. When I opened my eyes, the sun was already low in the sky, casting a golden glow through the high window. I heard someone moving around the stable. The sound of footsteps must have been what woke me.

Thieves? I thought, in panic. What would I do? But before I could think of a plan I heard a girl's voice.

"Goran," it said, "Are you up there?"

I crawled out of bed, my arms and legs aching, and went to see who was there. I looked down and saw Dunia looking up at me.

"Hello, Dunia," I said with a smile.

"Hello," she replied. "I brought you the basin and jug you asked for".

"That was very thoughtful of you," I said, groaning a little as I bent over the railing.

"Shall I bring them up?" she asked.

"I would be very grateful if you did!" I said. "I don't think I could make it back up the ladder!"

I saw her white kerchief appearing at the edge of my loft and then those eyes that were so like Milada's in shape and color if not expression. She placed the basin on the floor and then disappeared. In a moment she was back and put a full jug of water next to it. Then she ascended the rest of the way up with a woven bag hanging from her shoulder.

"I didn't think you would want to come down for supper," she said, "so I brought you some food." She unpacked rolls, cheese and dried sausages and put them on my little table.

"That's very kind," I told her. "You didn't need to bring the jug full of water. It's heavy. I could have gone to the fountain myself." By this time I'd settled myself back down on the bed, with my feet up on the stool.

"It doesn't look like you are fit enough to go anywhere right now!" she said. "I remember other boys who have tried to work with my father. He wore them out!"

I smiled and nodded. "It's not easy work," I told her, "but I am determined to succeed."

"I know you will," she said, looking down at her neat shoes. Few of the village children wore shoes, but I had never seen Dunia without hers. I didn't know what to say.

"Funny you asking for a basin," she said eventually, breaking the awkward silence.

"The gypsies wash their faces morning and night and clean their hands many times during the day, especially before they eat." I told her. "I got used to it, too."

"What a strange custom," she said. "We wash well on Sunday before going to church or if we are planting in the fields and get mud on our hands, but certainly not every day."

"Zora, one of the gypsies who shared a wagon with Milada, told me it helped to keep them healthy." I noticed Dunia stiffen at the mention of Milada's name.

"Thanks for bringing me some food," I said, hastily changing the subject. "I'm too tired to eat now, but I'll have it in the morning."

"You're welcome, Goran," she said. "I'll leave you to get some rest."

She gave me a little smile, which I returned and then she disappeared down the ladder. I went over to the jug, drank some of the water then poured some into the basin to rinse my hands. The water immediately turned black! I dumped it over the railing to the stable floor below, refilled the basin and splashed some water onto my face. Black again, but a little less so. Seeing the dirty water reminded me of when I first stayed with the gypsies. Since then, with regular washing, I had never seen such dirty water again. It may be a strange habit, but I had a feeling that it was a good one.

And so the days of summer went by. I rose early, washed, and ate some food that I brought from the blacksmith's table. He worked me hard, but I felt my strength growing day by day. After a while, it was easy to lift the iron bar. The blacksmith tied a few pairs of worn out horseshoes on the either end of the pole, increasing its weigh; but he seemed pleased with my progress. Of course, he never said so, but with him, a lack of complaint was as good as a complement!

I was very pleased when one day, after a series of particularly restless horse that I helped to calm, he gruffly handed me a few coins.

"The Squire was pleased that we finished his horses early," he said. "He gave me some extra coins and I think you deserve a share of them."

"Thank you, Sir," I said, "I appreciate it."

"No need to thank me," he said. "You did good work; good work is rewarded."

I was happy that the man had paid me some actual money. I was grateful to have my room and board provided, but without money I could not make a home for Milada. When I got back to my room I added most of the coins to the pouch I had hidden inside my straw mattress. Pocketing a few, I headed off to see if I could find Jelko and the boys. I figured I could put some coins on the bone game and maybe win a few more.

Chapter 54 – A Sure Bet?

I found the boys at their usual spot on the far side of the square. As I had hoped, there was a game in progress.

"Hey, Gogo," Misha said looking up at me from where he sat on the cobblestones, cupping the four bones in his hands. "Long time no see!"

"Where've you been?" Stanyo asked, "Off courting, like our Jelko?"

"What?" I said. "I've been working and sleeping. What's Jelko been up to?"

"Not a lot of sleeping!" Misha chuckled, "if you believe what he says."

"I think he's just bragging," Stanyo said. "A girl like Janka will keep him at arm's length until after they go to church."

"I don't know about that," Misha commented. "She's pretty independent. If she likes him she will let him know, if you know what I mean."

"And what about you and that pretty Dunia?" he asked, turning to me.

"Hey, are we playing a game here or what?" Loris said, giving Misha's arm a smack.

"Sorry. I got distracted," he said. He cast the bones and whooped when he saw the score. I had to stop and think what sides scored how much, but eventually I realized that all the bones showed the same side up, the narrow side with an inward curve. That was six points; the maximum score for one throw.

"Ha! Beat that!" he said.

"You know I can't on my next throw," Loris said, "but it's only the first of three. Who wants to bet that I'll be the winner then?"

When no one spoke up, one of the other boys said, "I'll make it more interesting. If Loris wins I'll pay two to one".

I didn't know what he meant but several of the boys pulled coins out of their pockets including Stanyo.

Misha looked at him and said, "You're going to bet against me winning?"

"It's nothing personal," Stanyo said, "but if Rico is offering two to one I want to get in on it."

"How about you, Gogo," Stanyo asked me. "It's a good chance."

"Sorry, Misha," I said, taking out one coin. I had intended to make a bet, and judging from the behavior of the other boys, I thought this could be a good one.

I put the coin in front of Rico and he nodded as Loris cast the bones. A groan went up from the boys who had gathered close around to see the score.

"A measly nine points," Stanyo moaned. "Misha is fifteen points ahead!"

How did he figure that out so quickly, I wondered?

I wished that I had bet on Misha instead of that other boy. It looked like he would win. But then Misha threw the bones again and I saw two 'dogs' worth only one point each. The other bones added up to six making the total eight. I saw him tallying his score in the dust.

"Twenty-four and eight that's thirty-two," he said. "I'm still way ahead."

Loris scooped up the bones and quickly threw them down again. A cry went up when the boys saw the bones.

"Look at those sixes!" Stanyo shouted. "There are three of them!"

"And one 'dog'," Misha muttered.

Loris did the addition. "That's nineteen plus the nine from before; twenty-eight. Looks like I'm catching up!"

Misha took his final turn. The boys mumbled as they counted the score. It was only eight points.

"I'm up to forty points to your twenty-eight," he said. "I'm going to win!"

"I can get twelve points easily," he said.

Rico said, "Does anyone want to increase his bet?"

A couple of the boys added a coin or two to the piles on Loris side but I stayed with the one coin I had already bet.

Loris spat on the bones then shook them in his hands as the tension mounted. I liked Misha better, but I hoped that Loris would throw higher than twelve so my one coin would become three. I found myself holding my breath as he tossed the bones hard onto the cobblestones. Before I could calculate the total a big groan came from Loris and all the boys on his side. Only Misha and Rico were smiling. I counted up the points. Two 'dogs', a three and a four. Only nine points.

Rico pocketed all the coins we had bet on Loris to win. Misha collected his coins and that of his opponent.

"It's difficult to better a toss of all sixes!" he said with a grin.

I was thinking that I didn't like this game! I had a coin and now I didn't. Better to keep the rest in my pouch and not get greedy in games of chance.

"Ready to play again?" Loris said, putting three coins on the ground in front of him. In a moment one of the other boys had placed down three coins of his own and the next game was on.

Misha nudged me. "Look over there, by the fountain," he said. "It's the love birds!"

I looked where he was pointing and saw Jelko walking hand in hand with Janka. They were both smiling. I wished Milada were here. I'd rather be walking with her than losing money with these boys.

"He's spending all his time with her," Misha complained. "We used to have so much fun but now he says he's 'busy' all the time."

I just sighed as I watched the couple walking together. I'd had enough of the game and just wanted to go to my room and think about Milada and how we would be together one day.

"I'll see you around," I said to Misha and the others, stopping at the fountain to fill my jug on my way back to my comfy little room above the horses.

I was just turning down my lamp when I heard someone at the door. It creaked open and Dunia whispered, "Goran, are you awake?"

If I had been asleep I would not have heard her.

"Dunia, is that you?" I said, also in a whisper, though I didn't know why; maybe in case the horses were asleep!

"Yes," she said quietly, "I brought you some berry pie that I baked. Shall I bring it up to you?"

I was no longer sore or tired. I could go down and get it, but I said, "Yes, please."

I reached out my hand to help her off the top rung of the ladder. Her hand felt strong in mine; not as soft as Milada's but not at all unpleasant. She handed me a wooden plate with a big slice of pie, the berry filling oozing out of it.

"That looks delicious!" I said, placing it on the table. "Would you like to share it with me?"

"I had a piece before," she said, "This one is all for you."

I took my knife and cut off a bite sized piece and plopped it in my mouth. It was very tasty.

"This is great!" I said, for a moment thinking about picking berries with Milada long ago; and getting drunk on blackberry wine! Eating pie was better!

"I made it for *you*," Dunia said, blushing. She sat down on my bed and watched me eat another mouthful and then another. I thought I'd keep some for my breakfast but it was just too good. In the end I finished it all.

"That was so good!" I told her. "Do you have an oven at your house?" I hadn't noticed one.

"No," she said." We take things that need baking to the baker's shop. His big oven is lit all the time and for a small fee he will bake our food for us.

I had missed baked foods and especially pies when I was travelling with the gypsies. Sometimes, if they stayed in one place for a few weeks, they would construct an oven made out of mud, but they only used it to roast meat, not to make sweets like this.

A full moon was shining through the high window, making the room almost as bright day, but with the colors muted and cold. I turned down the lamp and sat on the bed beside Dunia.

"You seem to like your life in the village," I said.

"Yes, I do," she replied. "I like our neighbors; I like to cook and to keep house and when I have some spare time I enjoy working on my embroidery."

"Do you ever get restless here? Your father is not the easiest man."

"My father is doing what he thinks is right for our family," she said defensively. "He doesn't show his affection much, but if he didn't care for us he wouldn't stay and work so hard to put food on our table."

"It seems like he never talks to your mother, or to you girls."

"He is a man of few words," she said. I thought I sensed a touch of sadness in her voice. "His brother, our uncle, likes to talk and tell us stories about his travels."

"He doesn't live in the village," I wondered aloud.

"He left many years ago when his wife died giving birth to their child, Anna," she said. "I think it was ungrateful of her not to stay to meet him."

Milada's father.

"She never knew him," I said, not wanting to talk about Milada now and risk bringing up the subject of her disappearance.

"Still, he gave her life," she said.

"And then he left her," I replied. "I never knew my father, either."

"And your mother?" she asked.

"She died when I was little; but I can still remember her, the way she smelled like ale and meat pies. She worked in a tavern," I added, "so we always had something to eat and some clean straw for a bed."

"What happened to her?" she asked.

"One morning I woke up and she didn't," I said. I felt a tear escaping my eye. After so long, I was surprised at how much I missed her.

To my great embarrassment, Dunia noticed the tear. She reached over and dabbed it with her handkerchief. She took my hand in hers. It felt good to have contact with another warm, living person after so long.

"Dear Goran; Gogo," she said, "what a life you have had; growing up in taverns and with gypsies. I want you to be happy here."

We sat for a while in silence holding each other's hands. She felt like a lifeline for me. I hadn't realized how lonely I had been. The moon's light cast long shadows across the wooden floorboards; the sounds of the night birds punctuated the silence. Slowly, we were moving closer together, our arms touching and then our shoulders. I let go of Dunia's hand and put my arm around her, drawing her closer to me. She did not pull away, but lifted her face to mine. Without thinking I put my lips on hers and they joined in a kiss.

Her lips were soft and yielding as if she wanted this kiss as much as I did. It could have been Milada there in my arms, holding me, kissing me, wanting me. We stayed there, lost in each other's embrace until the moon moved past my window and the room was left in darkness.

"I had better go," Dunia whispered, making an effort to pull away from me.

"Stay," I muttered, wanting to sink down on the bed with her and keep on kissing her, and more.

"No," she said, pushing the bits of hair that had escaped back into her kerchief. "I must go; they will wonder where I am. I lost track of the time."

I couldn't see it in the dark, but I could feel her blushing. She left me there on the bed and hurriedly climbed down the ladder.

"I'll see you tomorrow. Good night for now, dear Gogo".

Chapter 55 – My Night Time Meetings

The next morning, it was business as usual in the blacksmith's forge. When we went to his house for lunch, Dunia's eyes never met mine. Yagoda, on the other hand, had the habit of greeting me with a hug when I followed her father into the house. It started with a simple 'hello' but day by day her welcome became bigger and more dramatic. This day, she practically threw herself at me.

"That's enough," Yagoda, her mother admonished her. "The boy is tired, let him eat in peace."

"But I am happy to see him!" the girl said. "You don't mind, do you, Gogo?"

I didn't know what to say. I wasn't very comfortable with her over enthusiastic greeting. I knew she was just looking for attention from her family, but I didn't like to be the focal point of her efforts.

Before I said anything, he father roughly grabbed her by her waist, pulled her away from me and pushed her onto the bench by the table.

"Your mother told you 'that's enough'," he said, taking his place at the head of the table. I sat down as far as I could from the younger girl and waited while Dunia and her mother finished bringing the food and took their places at the table.

We ate in silence. I noticed Yagoda pushing the food around on her plate and kicking the base of the table. Her family ignored her until the meal was over. Dunia stood up to clear the table, still not uttering a word to me.

"Yagoda, come and help me with the dishes," she said.

"Can I help?" I asked.

"Sit down!" the blacksmith bellowed. "Don't you know that's woman's work? Haven't you worked enough today? If you want to work, there are two more horses waiting to be shod."

I sat back down. "Shall we do them today, Sir?" I asked, "Or can it wait until tomorrow?" We had already taken care of three frisky horses and I was ready for a nap.

"Tomorrow morning will do," he said. "I will rest now; you may do the same."

"Thank you, Sir," I said, getting up and moving toward the door. I tried to catch Dunia's eye, to see how she felt after our intimacy the night before, but she was busily cleaning the plates, her back toward me. Yagoda looked over her shoulder and gave me a cheeky grin. I just shook my head and, bidding the family thanks and farewell, went to my room over the stable to lie down for a while.

When the sun had dropped I went to the square to fill my jug and see if I could find Jelko. We hadn't seen each other for a few days. I spotted him at the fountain, the only boy in a gaggle of giggling girls. When he saw me approaching he waved at me.

"Hey, Gogo! Where have you been?" he called.

"*I've* been around here," I said, happy to see him. "Where have *you* been?"

"He's been with Janka!" one of the girls said, giggling even more.

"You're just jealous," one of the other girls told her.

"Girls, girls," he said. "You have to understand how it is. There's only one of me and so many of you pretty girls."

The volume of the laughter increased.

"Why don't you find boys of your own?" He asked them. "How about Gogo here?"

"He's Dunia's!" one of the cheeky girls called out.

I felt myself blushing. "Look," the girl said, "here they come."

I watched as Dunia and Janka approached the fountain, deep in conversation. When they got near and noticed Jelko and me they stopped talking at once. Janka smiled at us, but Dunia just looked down at her shoes. The girls spread out a little to open a path to the fountain.

"Hello everyone!" Janka called. The girls smiled and muttered their greetings. Jelko stepped in front of her and, with a little bow, took her jug and held it under the fountain's spigot.

"Here you go!" he said. "But it's heavy now. I'll need to carry it home for you!"

"I've been carrying water for years before you decided to be so helpful," she said, "but if it would make you happy, you may carry it for me."

Jelko smiled and held out his elbow. Janka linked hers with his and the girls said "oooooww" as the couple headed back across the square toward Janka's house.

I made to approach Dunia to offer to fill her jug but from the look on her face knew that it would not be a good idea. I watched as she held the jug under the spigot until water splashed over the top. When she'd finished and stepped back, I filled my jug, but by that time she was already on her way back to her house.

"She really likes you," a girl said.

"That's why she didn't talk to you!" another added.

"Maria likes you, too!" the first one said.

"Be quiet!" said the other girl, who must have been Maria.

"Well you do!" the first one persisted.

I felt that a little diplomacy was needed and said; "Now girls, you are all so charming! You know I like each and every one of you!"

They all started madly giggling, the one called Maria having turned bright red. I tipped my hat, grasped my full water jug and took my leave. Girls!

After the sun went down, once again I heard someone entering the stable.

"Goran?" I heard Dunia whisper. "Are you there?"

"I'm here," I said.

"May I come up?"

"Sure," I said, a little surprised that she had come again. "Did you bring some pie?"

"Not this time," she said as her head popped over the edge of my loft." Just some jam and bread for your breakfast."

She handed me a parcel from her string bag and I placed it on the table. I wished that I had something to offer her. I thought about going to the market place the next day and buying something to have the next time she came; hoping there would be a next time.

She settled herself on the bed and I sat beside her. I didn't ask about her strange behavior. Instead I took her hand in mine and after a little conversation we were kissing in the moonlight.

All too soon she pulled back and whispered, "I have to go."

"Why?" I moaned, "Stay a little longer."

"My father is at the ale house. I must get home before he does or we will both be in trouble."

"Do you think he would mind?" I asked, hoping that she would stay.

"What do you think!" she said jumping up, smoothing her clothes and tucking loose curls back under her white kerchief.

"See you tomorrow then," I told her. "And thanks for breakfast!"

"Bye, Gogo," she said, giving me one little kiss that left me wanting more.

The next weeks followed the same pattern, with Dunia ignoring me by day, but showing up in my room every night. It felt a little strange; was she embarrassed that she liked me? For my part, I was still thinking about Milada. But Milada was not here; Dunia was. The two of them were alike in many ways. I had never kissed Milada the way I kissed Dunia but I could imagine it would be as nice. And, in the darkness of my room, it might as well have been Milada who was in my arms as she was in my mind and in my heart.

Chapter 56 – My "Little Love"

It was now high summer; the crops were ripe and ready for harvest. The forge would be open only early in the morning, keeping the working horses well shod and mending any tools that were needed to bring the crops in. The rest of the day the blacksmith used his horses and wagon to help carry baskets of grain from the field to the threshing floors on a windy spot just outside the village where the kernels of wheat would be separated from the chaff. The women of the village sang a rhythmic chant while they worked, tossing the grain in the air to let the breeze blow away the chaff. Their flat round baskets reminded me of the flat round drums the gypsy women played at their ceremonies. I observed the people in the village all working together to harvest, prepare and store the crops. I wondered how they would be divided. Did the villagers possess their own fields or were they just bringing in the crop for the Squire, I wondered.

Besides the crops that the villagers had planted, the wild foods of the forest were also ripening. The bramble bushes hung heavily with berries. One pleasant morning, the blacksmith had already left with this horse and wagon. I was just finishing up in the forge when I saw Dunia and Yagoda passing by, carrying a basket over each arm.

"Where are you off to?" I asked.

"We're going to pick berries in the woods!" Yagoda called out. "Will you come with us?"

Dunia cast down her eyes. She was still acting shy with me when we were in public; very differently to how she behaved when we were alone together in my room!

"Sure!" I said, closing the forge door behind me. "If you don't mind," I added to Dunia as I fell in step beside her.

She lowered her head. "Is that a 'yes' I can come, or a 'yes' you mind?" I asked.

She looked up at me through her thick eyelashes. "Yes, you can come," she said with a smile.

Yagoda skipped ahead, obviously pleased at the chance to get out of the village and go and explore the woods, even if it was

252

for the job of berry picking. We followed the cobblestone road through the village gate and then went down a path that led to the place where the gypsies had camped. Memories of Milada and of my other friends among the gypsies filled my head. Had they met with the other bands at midsummer, I wondered. Where was Milada now?

"What is it, Goran?" Dunia asked, noticing my preoccupation.

"I was just thinking about my time here with the gypsies." I told her.

"Do you miss being with them?" she asked.

"Not really," I said. Of course I missed Milada, but I wasn't about to admit it to Dunia. "I miss the music, sometimes; and the food. But yours is much nicer," I added when I saw her face fall at my words.

Her smile returned and, for a moment, I felt I was looking into Milada's eyes. How I longed to rip off that kerchief and let Dunia's hair flow around her shoulders. At the thought, I remembered the swimming hole that I used to visit with the gypsy boys.

We caught up with Yagoda who had found a large stand of bramble bushes and was busy picking berries. I noticed that as many as were going into her basket were also going into her mouth!

"Good girl, Yagoda!" I said, "You found a good spot! Stay here and keep picking. I think I remember another good bush a little further on. Stay here and we'll come back for you!"

"These are my bushes!" she said, happily, "I get to pick all these berries."

I took Dunia's hand a pulled her down a narrow path that led to the stream.

"Come with me," I told her. "I want to show you something."

"But, Yagoda?" she said, "I can't leave her there alone."

"She's busy picking berries," I said, "and eating them. She'll be there for a while. Look!"

We had arrived in the little clearing by the crystal clear pool. "Shall we go for a swim and cool off?" I asked.

"Oh, Gogo," she said, "what a beautiful place. But I cannot swim today. Let's just sit here in the shade."

She took off her simple, working apron, laid it on the leafy ground, settled herself upon it and patted the ground next to her. I sat down beside her and looked into her eyes. Softly, I raised my hand to her head and pulled off the kerchief. As I had hoped, her hair escaped into a soft brown halo around her face. She reached out and touched my lips with hers and soon we were in each other's arms enjoying the feeling of cuddling in the dappled shade. I slipped my hand into her blouse and my fingers found her budding breasts. She did not pull away when I caressed them, rather she moaned with pleasure. I wanted to touch more of her; it felt so good. I felt myself getting hard. I longed to couple with this girl, right here, right now. My hand wandered down between her legs and suddenly she pulled away.

"Dunia, what is it? What's the matter? Don't you like me?"

"Oh Goran," she said, "I like you too much."

"So, let me touch you there," I said, "You will like it".

"I want you so much," she said, "but we cannot do this now."

"Why not? Are you afraid of your father?" I asked, trying to be gentle, but getting a little annoyed at the delay.

"I wasn't even thinking of my father!" she said. "Of course he wouldn't like it."

"What then?"

"The same reason I cannot swim," she said looking down, her cheeks reddening.

"What do you mean?" I asked, confused.

"It is the time of the month when I bleed," she whispered.

Oh. She could have told me before, I thought. I gently rubbed her back. At least she said she wanted me. And looking at her sitting here in the forest, with her hair wild and free, I really wanted her. But I would have to wait.

"Let's go find Yagoda, then," I said, disappointed.

"Yagoda!" she exclaimed. "I forgot all about her! Where's my kerchief? I can't let her see me like this!"

The girl gathered her hair and covered it again; turning back from a wild creature of the forest into a village lass. We followed the path back to where we had left Yagoda picking berries but she was nowhere to be seen. There were still some berries on the bush. Where had she gone?

"She's not here!" Dunia exclaimed. "Do you think something happened to her? There are wild animals in these woods!"

"If she were in trouble she would have called for help," I said, "We weren't that far away."

"Yagoda! Yagoda! Where are you?" Dunia cried, but there was no answer.

"She probably went back home," I said, sensibly.

"Let's go!" she said and started back up the path then led back to the village.

I was wondering how we'd explain our empty baskets but Dunia was more concerned with finding her sister. I wasn't so worried; maybe because I was more familiar with the forest; for Dunia, it was a fearful place. When we reached her house, she quickly opened the door and called out to her sister. Again there was no reply. Where could she be?

Dunia looked like she was going to cry. I went over to her and put my arms around her, but instead of being comforted she pushed me away.

"Not here!" she whispered. "We have to find Yagoda!"

"Where might she have gone?" I asked.

"Maybe she tried to find us in the forest," Dunia said, her eyes widening. "What if she got lost there?"

Dunia was wringing her hands with worry. "What if an animal has eaten her? You know that there are boars in the woods and they can eat children!"

I was sure that we would have found Yagoda at home. Now I was beginning to get concerned as well.

"I will go and get my knife," I said, "in case we need to fight off any animals. I ran to the stable and climbed up the ladder to my room. I was shocked to see Yagoda sitting on my bed, idly swinging her legs back and forth.

"What are you doing here?" I asked her in shock. "Your sister and I were worried!"

"You didn't look very worried when you were kissing under that tree," she said.

"You saw us?"

"Kissing a lot," she said.

"I told you to stay and pick berries," I said.

"I wanted to go with you and Dunia, not stay by myself," she answered back. "You shouldn't be kissing my sister like that! When I tell my father he'll probably kill you," she added with a smirk.

"You are going to tell you father?" I said, with a sick feeling in the pit of my stomach.

"Unless you are nice to me, I'm going to tell," she said.

"I'm always nice to you," I said, knowing this was time to muster what charm I could for this little demon.

"You don't hug me anymore," she said, "and now I know why! You're too busy kissing Dunia!"

"I can hug you, too," I said opening my arms.

She ran to me and put her thin arms around my waist.

"Gogo! I love you!" she exclaimed.

"And you can be my little love," I told her, needed to find some way to keep her from telling about Dunia and me. "But you can only be my little love if you keep quiet about Dunia and me!"

She took a step back. "Do you love Dunia?" she asked, watching my face.

"If you can be my little love, she can be my bigger love," I said, hoping the answer would be acceptable.

"And when I get bigger?" she asked.

"Then we'll see," I told her, "but you must never tell anyone what you saw today, not even Dunia, or I will never hug you again."

She stood looking at me, thinking.

"Do you promise?" I asked her, hoping this threat would buy her silence.

"I promise," she said, throwing her arm around me again.

"Gogo, what's keeping you?" Dunia called from the stable door.

"I'm coming now!" I called back, and then whispered to Yagoda, "as soon as I leave, go back to house. Say you got lost but found your way back home."

She nodded and I hurried down the ladder, wondering what to say to Dunia. She was waiting for me outside of the stable, looking very worried.

"Let's go she said," the longer she is in the woods, the more dangerous it will be!"

We walked quickly toward the village gate. I saw the boys watching us walking together as we approached the fountain. I knew that they would be teasing me. For once Dunia didn't seem to care. I felt bad that she was so upset. Before we reached the village gate, I stopped. Dunia looked at me, puzzled.

"Let's go!" she said.

"Wait, a minute," I told her. "What if she found her way back home?" I looked up at the sky. "It won't be dark for some time. I think we should check the house once more before we go back into the woods."

"Wouldn't we have seen her if she went back to the house?" she asked.

"From where we were at the stable we could easily have missed her," I said. "She is a smart little girl. I bet we'll find her at home." I started back across the square. Dunia looked toward the village gate, but I knew she would not go into the forest alone. Quickly, she caught up with me and we made our way back to her house.

This time when she opened the door, there was Yagoda lying on the bed as if waking from a long nap.

"Where did you go?" Dunia exclaimed. "I was so worried about you!"

Yagoda looked past her sister at me and said, "Were you worried about me, too, Gogo?"

Before I could say anything, Dunia said, "We were both worried. We were going back to the forest to look for you but Goran thought you might have found your way home. Luckily, he was right."

"I told Dunia that you were a smart girl," I said to Yagoda, "and smart girls know what they have to do."

Chapter 57 - Jealousy

The next few days were filled with anticipation. I did my work as usual but my mind was on Dunia; the way she looked so like my Milada sitting by the stream with her hair loose around her shoulders. She hadn't visited my room since that afternoon and I missed having her there. I had to make an effort not to look at her when we were at her parents' house. I was afraid that we both would blush if our eyes met. It was a job to keep little Yagoda happy. I made a point to greet her with a smile before she came running to me, figuring it would attract less attention. If Dunia were concerned that I was paying more notice to her little sister she didn't let on. Probably, she realized that I was detracting attention from what was going on between the two of us.

Two nights after our afternoon in the forest, on my way out of the house I whispered to Dunia, "Will you come tonight?" She nodded, focusing on the plates she was washing.

I smiled in anticipation as I went to my room to collect my jug. When I went to the fountain to fill it, I saw the boys sitting in the shade. We'd all been busy with work so I was surprised to see them congregating in the square again. I wandered over to see if they were placing bones. Usually one of the boys would call out to me, but no one did. As I got closer I saw that Jelko and his good friends were not among the boys. Loris and Rico were there but I didn't recognize some of the others in the group.

"Hey!" I said, "No bones today?"

"Do you care?" asked Rico rudely. "You never bet, you only watch."

"That's not very sporting," Loris commented.

"When I have some money I can afford to lose, I may place a bet," I said. "But now I need to save my money."

"You'll have plenty if you marry Dunia," Rico muttered.

"That's not going to happen," said another.

I looked to see who had said that. It was the chubby boy who tried to play a trick on Mother Miriana.

"No boy from outside is going to pick our peach," he added.

I had no desire to get into a discussion, or a fight, with these boys.

"Suit yourself," I said and turned toward the fountain.

When I got back to my room I rinsed off my hands and face. That morning, I had rushed to the market when the blacksmith was taking a short break and bought some crunchy almonds lightly toasted and coated in sweet syrup made from honey. They were delicious but expensive. I had been given one to taste from time to time but this was the first time I bought any. I wanted something special to offer to Dunia, hoping that evening I would take her in my arms.

The sun was setting earlier now and before I knew it, it was dark in my room. I had the lamp on low and waited for Dunia's soft voice at the stable door. It seemed later than she usually came, but maybe it was because the days were getting shorter. I waited and waited, not wanting to doze off in case I could not hear her when she came. In the end, I must have fallen asleep because the next thing I knew, light was pouring through the high window and I was lying on my bed still in my shirt and trousers. She always came in quietly; I must not have heard her. She should have come up and awakened me!

I rinsed my face and hurried to the blacksmith, hoping he had brought something extra for breakfast. At the mid-day meal, we all ate in silence, but that was not unusual. I didn't get a chance to ask Dunia why she didn't come up and wake me. When we finished the meal, her father insisted I go with him to the ale house. We stayed there together until it got dark. He was telling stories about how he learned his trade from his father-in-law before him.

"He had two daughters like I do," he told me, "so he needed take a strong boy to help him. I was in love with his daughter, so I went to learn the trade."

I wondered if this was his way of suggesting I marry Dunia. I didn't say much. I just listened. It was unusual for him to talk at such length. Maybe he was getting used to having me around. I could see that he seemed satisfied with my work. I was now able to lift the hammer and do some of the preparation on the iron, but I had a long way to go before I could do the more precise work that is necessary to do the whole job well.

It was getting late and I wanted to get back to my room to be there when Dunia came, but I didn't want to be disrespectful. I was lucky that some of the blacksmith's friends entered the alehouse. When they came to join him, I bid them all a good night and took my leave.

I hurried back to my room, picking a few flowers from window boxes on my way. I put some water in my beaker and arranged the flowers as best I could. I still had the sweets, although I'd been tempted to eat them. And then I waited. And waited. And waited. But Dunia didn't come.

This time, I was sure, unless she had come very early while I was still at the alehouse with her father. But the next night and the one after that she did not appear at the stable door.

The following day, I arranged to get to the house a little before the blacksmith. Luckily, Dunia's mother was still in the fields. Yagoda must have gone with her because Dunia was preparing the meal alone as I had hoped.

She looked up from the stewpot when I walked in. He face reddened, and not from the heat of the fire.

"What's the matter, Dunia?" I asked coming up close behind her. She tried to move away, but the hearth was in front of her. I put my arms around her and nuzzled the back of her neck.

"Why haven't you come to my room?" I asked. "I've waited for you every night this week."

"I didn't think you would want me to," she said quietly, turning to loosen herself from my embrace and moving toward the door.

"Why would I not want you to?" I asked, confused.

"Now that you are seeing Maria," she said, a tear escaping her eye.

"What!" I exclaimed. "I don't know Maria. I've seen her at the fountain with the other girls, but that's all."

"That's not what I heard," she said, hastily wiping her eyes.

"Whatever you heard, it isn't true!" I said. "Who told you I was seeing another girl?"

"I heard the boys talking at the fountain," she said.

"What did they say?" I asked.

"The fat one was talking to Rico. He was saying how he saw you and Maria coming back from the forest hand in hand; how you both had leaves in your hair and you were grinning like a boy in love."

"The boys hardly ever wait by the fountain," I told her, taking her hand. "They must have wanted you to overhear them. I know they are jealous that you might like me, a stranger in the village".

"Please come tonight," I begged. "I've been thinking about you so much since that day in the forest."

At the same moment, we pulled apart, hearing the blacksmith's footsteps outside the door. Dunia looked up at me through damp lashes and nodded.

Chapter 58 – The First Time

"You got here fast!" the blacksmith said, looking at me and then across the room where his daughter stirred the iron pot on the hearth. Did he suspect that I'd come to speak with his daughter, I wondered.

"I am very hungry, Sir!" I said, tearing off a crust from the loaf of bread on the table, hoping that he believed me. In truth, I wasn't feeling hungry at all, I was too excited thinking about how I would be kissing Dunia that night, and also annoyed with the village boys for causing trouble between us.

Dunia's mother and Yagoda arrived as the blacksmith took his place at the head of the table.

"Hey, Gogo!" Yagoda exclaimed, running to sit close beside me on the bench.

"Hey, Yagoda," I responded with a grin. "Have you been in the fields with your mother?"

"Not in the fields," she said with a big smile, "on the threshing floor. I like the songs we sing while we work!"

She cleared her throat and broke into song with a surprisingly pretty voice, "Oh, how golden glows the wheat, as we cast it in the air; wind to sort it nice and neat, gently lifting up our hair…"

"Enough, girl," bellowed her father, drowning out the next line of the song, "You know it's not done to sing at the table!"

Yagoda looked crestfallen. She glanced at her mother for support, but the woman lowered her eyes to the table. For once, I felt sorry for the girl. She truly seemed happy when she came in with her mother, but her father shot down her enthusiasm and her happiness. Hidden by the table cover, I reached for her hand and gave it an encouraging squeeze. I saw the corners of her mouth raise just a little.

I could hardly wait to finish the meal. As soon as the blacksmith finished, I took it as my cue to get up and leave before he could suggest going to the ale house together.

"I'll be off then!" I said. "I'll see you at the forge tomorrow." And I'll see you tonight, Dunia, I thought to myself as I left her clearing the empty plates from the table.

The day was warm and I was feeling grubby from my work at the forge. I wandered out of the village toward the swimming hole. I left my clothes on the bank and jumped into the refreshing stream. Silvery fish tickled my ankles. I should have brought a fishing line and net! I climbed onto a fallen tree that lay across the stream, causing the water to pool up behind it. Floodwaters had polished its bark to a satin smooth surface. I lay there, enjoying the warmth of the late summer sun drying my skin. Looking down at my arms I could see that muscles had developed since I began my work at the forge. Gazing at my reflection in the calmer part of the pool, I saw that I had a beard coming! Of course I felt the downy hairs on my lip and on my chin, but I hadn't realized how think and dark they were becoming. I'd have to start visiting the barbershop! I wondered how much that would cost. Maybe it was time to ask the blacksmith for a regular wage, rather than only the occasional coins he gave me if a customer was pleased with our work.

When the sun had dipped below the trees, the air suddenly turned chilly. I walked over the log back to the bank where I'd left my clothes and hurriedly put them on. I didn't want to miss Dunia in case she came by the stable early.

On my way back I saw Jelko sitting in the square with Janka and Misha. He waved at me and I went over to say a quick hello.

"Been swimming?" Jelko asked, looking at my damp hair.

"Yes," I told him. "The water is warmer now than it was earlier in the summer. And you should have seen all the fish!"

"Maybe tomorrow we can go fishing," he said with a smile. "We could bring the girls".

"Maybe Dunia won't want to go!" Misha interrupted, "after what the boys were saying."

"You knew about that?" I asked him.

"Nasty business," he said. "But you know they're jealous of you. You always need to watch your back."

"Dunia was really upset when she heard you were seeing another girl," Janka said.

"But it's not true," I said.

"She didn't know that. I only found out now that it was a trick," she said. "Misha told me the boys were laughing about it."

"You knew about this, Misha?" I turned to him, my hand balling into a fist.

"Slow down, man," he said, "I had nothing to do with it. I just heard from some of the others. I didn't know if it was true or not. I think that girl likes you. Lots of the girls do. That's the problem."

"I told Dunia I didn't even know the girl, but I'm not sure if she believed me," I said. "Janka, would you tell her that it was all a lie? She'll believe *you*."

She nodded, gave Jelko's hand a squeeze and ran off toward Dunia's house. I just sighed and shook my head.

"I want to punch those boys!" I muttered.

"Don't bother," Jelko said. "They'll understand soon enough when they fall in love."

"I'm not in love with Dunia," I said. "I like her; she is very good to me, but I can't say that I'm in love."

"She's in love with you," Jelko said.

"How would you know?" I asked him.

"Janka told me," he said. "Be careful what you do."

I was silent at his words. I knew Dunia liked me, as I liked her; but love?

"I've got to go," I told the boys. "See you 'round."

"Beeee carefullll!" Jelko said as I made my way back across the square.

By the time I climbed the steps to my room the sun had set and the half-moon shone its light through my window. Would Dunia come? I fiddled with the flowers in the makeshift vase on the little table. The calico bag holding the sweet nuts was still beside it. I'd managed to refrain from tasting the delicious delicacies. I knew if I tried one I would eat the whole bagful!

I heard the stable door creak on its hinges then Dunia's voice.

"Goran? Are you there?" she whispered.

"I'm here! Come on up!" I said, lightly.

I held out my hand to help her at the top of the ladder. She carried a full basket over her other arm. I took it from her, placed it on the floor and then drew her into my embrace. She raised her chin and looked up into my eyes. I reached up behind her and pulled the kerchief off her lovely hair, then brought her head close to mine. Our lips found each other's and without a word we began to explore, lips, mouth, tongues; touching, kissing, gently at first but then with growing passion. We fell together on to my bed. My hands wandered down to her breasts as hers caressed my back sending shivers down my spine and throughout my groin. She pulled back when my fingers moved to part her legs.

"Gogo," she said, "should we be doing this?"

"Don't you want to?" I whispered, "Dunia, you know I want you."

"I want to," she panted, "but it isn't right."

"It's natural to want each other," I said. "All nature couples, why shouldn't we?"

She did not respond, but she did not pull away, either.

"You look so beautiful, here in the moonlight. Your body feels so good in my arms," I said, touching her gently, inviting her to open herself to me.

"Oh, Goran," she said, relaxing, "yes, yes."

There, in the soft moonlight, the air still holding the warmth of summer, we kissed and caressed and explored each other's depths. Gently I parted her legs and found my way to the softness inside of her. She moaned once as I pushed through her secret door then totally abandoned herself to the sensations that took over our bodies.

When we were spent, we lay in each other's arms, breathing hard, unable and unwilling to speak. The moon moved passed the window, casting the room into darker shadows.

"Goran," she whispered, "I didn't know it would be like that!"

"Neither did I," I told her, playfully licking the edge of her ear. Slowly we untangled our limbs. I got up and went over to the table, glad I had the candied nuts to offer as a little gift. I thought I'd pop one in her mouth as a sweet surprise. But when I opened the bag, the nuts were crawling with insects. Tossing them all out of the window, I couldn't help thinking that this was a bad sign.

Chapter 59 – One Hot Autumn Day

When I turned back I saw Dunia sitting up on the bed arranging her clothes.

"Where's my kerchief?" she asked, feeling around the dark bed.

I spotted it on the floor and went to pick it up and then handed it to her. She took it but she did not look up and meet my eyes. As she gathered back her hair and tied on the kerchief I wondered if she was regretting what we had done. Looking at her sitting in the shadows, her headscarf glowing eerily in the light, I was having second thoughts, myself. But it was too late. With her hair free, she was so like my Milada, the girl I still loved. Was it fair to be with Dunia in this way, when it was her cousin that I really desired? But she came to me willingly, I told myself; no need to feel guilty about it. I did like her, after all. Her kisses were sweet and her body responded to mine.

I shook those thoughts out of my mind as Dunia stood to go. Her head was down and I couldn't read her expression.

"Pleasant dreams," I whispered as she disappeared down the ladder. I didn't hear anything but the sound of the hinges creaking as the door swung open and then closed. I washed myself then lay down on my bed, but sleep did not come right away. I felt like I'd passed a milestone in my life; that I had gone from being a boy to being a man. Taking Dunia in this way gave me a feeling of power that I could not have imagined. Some force took over both of us as we moved together, carried by something that was greater than each of us as separate people.

What had Bora told me about coupling? I wished I'd paid more attention. I remembered the strange chant they practiced and something about breathing. In order for the girl not to conceive, the time of coupling in relation to the moon was important; but when was the right time? Hopefully, Dunia knew and would not offer herself when she might fall with child.

Eventually, I dozed off. When I awoke in the morning and looked into the basket that Dunia had brought. It was full of beautifully made tarts, some with cheese inside and others with fruit; berries and apples. Surprisingly hungry, I enjoyed one of each then hung the basket from a hook on the rafters, hoping no insects would find the rest of the tarts like they had found the candied nuts.

I went through my day in a bit of a daze, my mind going back to the pleasures of the night before. At the table, I kept trying to catch Dunia's eye, to smile my appreciation for our night together, but she kept her eyes cast down the entire meal.

Yagoda, on the other hand, was always looking at me. I could tell that she was afraid to talk; her father seemed in a foul mood, but when our eyes met she flashed me a quick smile.

That night, I waited for Dunia but she did not appear. I was disappointed, but also tired. I figured that she hadn't slept much the previous night either and was catching up on her rest.

The next evening she returned. Once again, we silently fell into each other's arms. As we kissed in the moonlight I pushed off the white kerchief and began to untie Dunia's blouse. I slipped it off her shoulders and saw her lovely rounded breasts reflecting the light of the moon. I slid down and began to kiss each one as she fell back onto the bed, softly moaning my name. She worked her fingers through my hair, letting herself enjoy my lips on her smooth skin. I pushed up her skirt and rubbed the soft spot between her legs. Her moans grew louder as I pushed myself against her, rubbing my groin against hers. Her arms encircled me, pulling me closer. I couldn't wait and plunged inside. All too soon it was over. I rolled off the girl with a sigh. She curled herself around me like a cat.

"Do you love me, Goran?" I heard her whisper.

I pretended to be asleep.

"Goran?" she whispered again. When I didn't answer, she slowly got up, collected her fallen kerchief, planted a light kiss on my forehead and then made her way down the ladder.

And so it continued, with Dunia ignoring me by day and quietly coming to my room at night. Sometimes we would talk about how we passed our day or joke about the way Yagoda tried to get attention.

The year was turning, with the nights nearly as long as the days but the weather was unusually warm. One very hot afternoon I had an idea. While Dunia was tidying up after the meal I whispered into her ear when no one was looking, "Come and meet me outside the village gate, near where the gypsies camped."

"I can't promise, but I'll try," she said. "It's so hot, probably everyone will lie down for a nap and then I can sneak away".

I smiled, took my leave and went to wait for Dunia outside the village. No one was in the square; the shutters of the houses surrounding it were all closed against the unseasonably hot afternoon.

I found a shady spot and, to my pleasant surprise, soon I saw Dunia coming through the village gate.

"Come on!" I said, taking her hand.

"Where are we going?" she asked.

"Remember that day we were picking berries?" I asked her.

"Yes," she said, a bit breathless with trying to keep up with my pace. "The berries have finished now."

"Remember where we went after we left Yagoda?"

"Oh, don't remind me of leaving my sister!" she exclaimed, "I was so worried!"

"But she was fine," I said, regretting that I'd brought it up. "Look!"

We'd arrived at the swimming hole. The bright sun was filtered through the leaves that were just beginning to turn into their golden autumn colors.

"It's so beautiful here!" she said.

"And today we are going for a swim!" I had already pulled my shirt over my head and was unbuttoning my trousers. "Come on! Off with your clothes!"

"What if someone comes?" she asked, looking at me without moving.

"We duck behind the rocks!" I told her. "Don't worry."

I took off my trousers, feeling free and so much cooler. I was pleased to see that she had taken off her kerchief and was stepping out of her dress. She took off her shoes and left her clothes in a neat pile on a high rock, well out of the way of the water.

I jumped into the pool.

"Ahhhhh! It's so nice and cool!" I yelled to her. Would she come? She stood on the bank in her light shift, looking at me uncertainly. But then a smile lit up her face and she ran to the edge and jumped in.

"Weeeee!" she yelled, her body splashing in the cool water. She came near and splashed me. I splashed her back and, for the first time, I saw Dunia having fun! We played in the water for a bit, splashing and laughing. She was standing shoulder deep near the log that acted as a dam for the pool, her lovely young body clearly viable under the thin fabric of her chemise. The dappled light brought out the golden highlights in her hair. I felt a stirring in my groin, seeing her alluring beauty. She looked so much like Milada, with her hair unbound, smiling and enjoying herself in the water.

"Look at all the fish!" she exclaimed leaning over the log into the stream that ran below. Coming up behind her I pressed myself into her back and nuzzled her neck, just below her ear.

"Where are the fish?" I murmured. "Are they here?" I reached down, caressing her waist and tickling her between her legs. "Is there a little fishy here?"

She moaned with pleasure.

"Goran, no!" she sighed, "No."

I let my other hand wander down her shapely buttocks, still tickling her sweet spot with my other hand. "What about here?" I said, "Are there little fishies swimming around here?"

"Goran, no," she moaned as I pushed her legs apart with my knee, moving closer to her soft body. "Goran!"

I pushed myself inside her body, luxuriating in her warmth surrounded by the coolness of the pool.

"Goran, yes," she cried, "yes!" as she yield her body to our building rhythm.

My face was buried in her wild hair as I embraced her, our passion rising moment by moment until I could not hold myself any longer and exploded. I was lost in the moment, the sensual feeling overriding any conscious thought. I heard someone yell "Milada!" then realized, to my horror and shame, that it had been me.

Dunia squirmed in my arms then pushed me away from her and pulled herself out of the pond.

"Dunia!" I pleaded, "Come back. I didn't mean it."

She quickly put her clothes on over her wet shift, in a hurry to get away. She slipped on her shoes and scrambled up the bank toward the path, but before she disappeared into the forest she gave me a look that said it all; the hurt, the embarrassment, the betrayal were all there in her pretty eyes. What had I done!

I knew I couldn't catch her so I just sunk down into the water, wishing I could wash away all I had done; to make it all go away. Dunia was a good girl. She deserved better, but I couldn't help it that I loved her cousin. I should have stayed away from her! But then I thought, it was she who came to my room at night. She didn't have to come if she didn't want to.

If she told her father he would fire me; no, he would probably kill me! But I didn't think she would tell him; she would be in big trouble, too, and he wouldn't hesitate to use his belt on her soft flesh. I could leave and try to start a new life somewhere else. But where would I go? I'd made friends here; I'd started to learn a trade. I needed to be here in case Milada changed her mind; if I went somewhere else she would never find me. Maybe Dunia would forget about my outburst. I would just have to wait and see.

Chapter 60 – A Horse Thief?

I can't say if I was disappointed or relieved when the hinges on the stable door remained silent that night. Maybe I felt a bit of both; disappointed that Dunia had not come to forgive me for my outburst and relieved that the blacksmith hadn't come with a knife to slit my throat.

When I went to the forge the next morning I found my employer in an unusually good mood.

"Hey, boy," he greeted me. "Have one of Dunia's tasty tarts before we start." He handed me a cheese tart from a covered basket. Had she made these for me, I wondered, but given them to her father instead after what I had said.

"Yum! These are delicious."

"My Dunia is a good cook. Better than her mother," he said, popping another tart in his mouth.

I didn't know what to say. He had never spoken to me like this before. I thought it best to change the subject.

"What work to we have today?" I asked.

"One plough horse needs new shoes," he answered. "Davko will be along with the beast any time now. It's the biggest horse in the village and needs the biggest shoes so I will charge him extra for them."

As he spoke, a shadow fell across the wide door of the forge. I looked over to see a huge horse blocking the early morning sunlight. It was the biggest horse I'd ever seen.

"Go get him and tie him to the post," the blacksmith instructed.

I greeted Davko then reached up and took the horse's bridle. Before leading him through the doorway I put my head close to his and said quietly, "There's nothing to fear here. We won't hurt you; we will just give you some nice new shoes."

The horse lowered his head as if to show he understood what I had said and docilely followed me into the forge. The blacksmith had already prepared four large semicircles of iron.

"Take the old one's off," he said, "and toss them over here."

I started to work and soon had pried the last one off. I realized that I was actually getting good at this job! I pat the horse's huge haunches and held him still while the blacksmith trimmed his hooves and fitted the new iron shoes. Before I knew it, we had finished and I realized that I was very hungry.

"Good work, boy," the blacksmith said, slapping me on the back. I didn't cringe when he did that anymore; my shoulder muscles were now strong enough to take it.

"Bring the horse to the stable and then come home for lunch. After, we'll go to the alehouse."

I led the plough horse around the corner to the stable. I had to pull his head down to get him through the door. There was plenty of height for a normal size horse, but this one was a giant. I led him into the first stall and tied him fast. He lowered his head and munched on some dry straw.

"I guess you were hungry, too," I said to him, then turned to go to Dunia house, a little nervous about how she would receive me.

But when I arrived and joined the others at the table, it was as if nothing had happened. Yagoda greeted me with a big smile, and Dunia kept her eyes down as usual. When we'd finished eating, the blacksmith told me to go back to the forge and wait for Davko to come and collect his horse.

I nodded and left without a word. Not long after, I saw the blacksmith passing by the forge. He popped his head in and said, "Come to the alehouse when you finish with Davko," then continued on his way.

I sat down on a bale of hay to wait. I didn't really like the taste of ale very much, but if the blacksmith wanted me to drink with him, then drink with him I must. I would rather rest in my room or go for a swim in the stream. My mind went to Dunia and what had happened the day before. I closed my eyes and could see her splashing and playing in the water.

"Goran," I heard her say. At first I thought it was my imagination but when I opened my eyes I saw that she was standing in the doorway of the forge.

"Dunia," I said, "What are you doing here?"

"Can I talk to you?" she asked.

I beckoned her to sit beside me on the hay. She did, but with a big space between us.

She looked down at her hands rubbing them together nervously. "Yesterday, in the pond," she began, as if reading my thoughts, "when you called out my cousin's name I was very upset."

I started to say something; to offer an explanation or an apology, but she put her finger to her lips and I remained silent.

"I always knew that you were in love with her," she said quietly, "but I had hoped that, over time, you would come to love me as I loved you."

Raising her eyes to mine, she continued, "But now I know that cannot be. I do not regret what we did together but it's time to stop. I love you, Gogo, but I know that you don't love me. You are working for my father, eating at our house; so it will be difficult for me, but for your sake I will try to let my feelings for you go."

"Dunia," I said, taking her hand in mine. She tried to pull it away but I held on to it tight. "What can I say except that I am sorry? My feelings for Milada are still strong. I hope she will come back one day and that we can be together. I like you, too, of course, but my feeling for her go back a long time, and even if I want them to go away I cannot make them. You were so like her there in the stream, I forgot myself."

"Maybe it's a good thing that you did," Dunia said, finally pulling away her hand. "Now I have stopped fooling myself that you love me."

I saw a tear roll down her cheek.

"I'm sorry, Dunia, I really am," I told her.

"I am, too, Goran," she said, "I am, too." I watched her get up and leave the forge, her head hanging low. She was right; it was better to face the truth.

"Where's my horse?" a booming voice roused me from my thoughts.

"Mr. Davko?" I asked? The man was oversized, like his horse.

"Yes," he bellowed, "where's the blacksmith and my horse?"

"I will get him now," I said squeezing past him out of the forge. "Wait here."

I ran around the stable but when I opened the door and looked inside the big horse was gone! I knew I'd tied it securely to the stall's bar but the horse was nowhere to be seen. Just in case, I ran along the other stalls, but only the blacksmith's two much smaller horses were there. Had the horse been stolen? What would I tell the man?

I returned to the forge. The big man was tapping his foot impatiently. "Where's my horse, boy?"

"The blacksmith took him out for a walk to make sure the shoes were all right," I lied, trying to buy some time.

"Out for a walk?" he exclaimed, "I've never heard of such a thing! Well, I'll go and have a jug of ale and wait for them to get back from their little stroll."

Before I could stop him he was heading out the door and down the road to the alehouse, where I knew the blacksmith was waiting. What had happened to the horse? It couldn't have just vanished? Someone must have taken it. But who? And why? And what would someone do with a horse so big? Everyone knew it was Davko's horse. I sat on the bale of hay, my head in my hands. What would I tell the blacksmith?

"Gogo," I heard a sing-song voice calling my name. I looked up and saw Yagoda standing in front of me swaying back and forth. "What's the matter, Gogo? Did you lose something?"

What was she talking about?

"Like a horse, maybe?" she said with a big smile.

"What do you know about a horse?" I asked her. Could she have taken it? It was so big and she was so small that I doubted it.

"The boys have it," she said. "I heard them talking."

"What did they say?" I asked, hoping she was telling me the truth.

"They say that you'll be in big trouble with my father for losing the horse and that he'll throw you out of the forge!"

"Did they say where they put the horse?" I asked.

"They said you would never find it in the stable with Jelko's cows!" she said.

"Was Jelko with them?" I hoped the answer would be no.

"No, of course not," she said, "he's always with his girlfriend, Janka. They just put it in his stable for now. They planned to let it walk free later on and find its own way home."

I grabbed Yagoda by her small waist and planted a kiss on the forehead. "Thanks!" I said, running out the door and heading towards Jelko's place as fast as I could. I ran down the dark alley and pushed open the door to the stable. Sure enough, the horse was there, its four new shoes standing deep in cow manure.

"Come now," I said to him as I grasped his bridle, "Let's get you out of here."

We got back to the forge a few moments before the blacksmith and Davko arrived at the door. I just had time to clean up the horses hooves.

"What's that you said about my taking Davko's horse for a walk?" the Blacksmith said.

"I wanted to polish up his shoes as a little extra for Mr. Davko," I said, thinking fast.

"Ha! Polished shoes for a horse; that's a new one," he chuckled. "Here, boy," he said, tossing me a coin. "Take that for your troubles."

"Thank you, sir," I said, tipping my cap to him, "my pleasure."

Davko lead the big horse away.

"I don't know what you are up to, lad," the blacksmith said, shaking his head, "but if the customer is happy, I am, too.

Chapter 61 - I Go to Church

Soon the days were shorter than the nights and the air was getting cooler. The harvest was finished and people were busy preparing provisions for the cold winter to come. I missed the warmth of Dunia's body and the sweet release I experienced with her. Some of the other girls flirted with me when I went to fill my jug at the fountain but I was not interested in starting something with any of them. All my thoughts were with Milada. More and more often, the clients at the forge would give me coins in recognition for my good work. My little pouch was bulging now; I would need to start a second one. I imagined saving enough to start a life with Milada; if she came back, that is. Something told me that she would.

When the first snow fell I felt happy to have a snug house to shelter me. I can't say that I was uncomfortable in the gypsy wagon, even in the cold of winter. The band camped in warmer, protected places, but there was always uncertainly. If there was a blizzard or a flood the camp would have been in danger. Dunia's mother provided me with a quilt stuffed with goose feathers and between that and the warmth coming for the horses below I felt safe and warm in my room above the stable. It had been a good harvest and there was plenty of food in the cold-room to see us through the snowy months.

The days passed quickly for me, working as usual in the forge, but the dark nights were long. Sometimes I went to the alehouse with the blacksmith or with Jelko and his friends. The other boys stopped bothering me so much once it was clear that Dunia and I were not courting. I could hear the rattle of bones as they gambled in the alehouse, but I had no desire to join them. Usually, I would take my leave and go back to my snug room and dream about that life I would have when Milada returned.

One Saturday, Yagoda said to me, "Gogo, are you coming to church with us tomorrow?"

I hadn't considered it before. I had vague memories of being in a church with my mother and seeing pictures of angels painted on the walls, but I didn't really remember much. Every

Sunday morning, when the bells of the village church were rung, Dunia, Yagoda and their mother went to a service there. Their father did not go with them. Instead, he met his friends in the tavern. I usually slept late; Sunday was the only day I was not expected to be in the forge at sun up.

"It's almost Christmas time," she said, "and their putting up the stable."

A stable in a church? This made me curious. "Would it be all right for me to come?" I asked.

"You are a Christian, aren't you?" Dunia's mother spoke.

"I remember my mother taking me to a church once in a while," I told her, "so I guess I am."

"Well then it is all right for you to come to a service," she said, "Do you have clean clothes to wear? We always wear our best clothes when we go to the house of God."

"That's woman's business," the blacksmith grumbled.

I knew that most people in the village went to church, men and women, and wondered why the blacksmith did not. I figured that if I wanted to make a home here it would be good to follow the customs of the people. I hadn't thought about going with them to church, but now that it was suggested it seemed a good idea. I had some clean clothes to wear, even though they were not very new. I didn't want to spend any of my hard earned coins on buying clothes for myself, but I would soon have to. My trousers were getting much too short! It's a good thing that the boots the gypsies gave me were big enough to grow into and high enough to cover my bare ankles.

I told them that I would go with them and was up and dressed in clean clothes the next morning when the bells began to ring. I saw the boys watching me as we approached the entrance to the church. I walked with Yagoda, not with Dunia so they wouldn't think that we were back together. They hadn't played any more tricks on me since the day they took Davko's horse and I didn't want to give them cause to start again.

When we went into the church I smelled an unusual fragrance perfuming the air. It was much more pleasant that the smell of the people! I saw that the women were all standing on the left and the men on the right. The left side was much more crowded! I spotted Jelko and went over to stand near him as the others joined the women.

"Hey, Gogo," he said, "I haven't seen you here before."

"I never thought to come," I said. "I was curious."

I looked around at the paintings on the walls, hoping to see one of the angel that I remembered. There was one holding a sword, but it wasn't the same. In the front of the church was a carved wooden screen that blocked off the space in the very back under a small dome. On it hung many more pictures, some covered with cloth so I couldn't see the painting beneath. On the left side, in front of where the women stood, was a picture of a sad looking lady holding a child. On our side was a painting of a man, I guess it was meant to be Christ, the founder of Christianity. Off to one side I saw a small model of a stable with a carved wooden cow and a donkey looking over the shoulders of a kneeling man and woman. I wondered what it meant.

Just then a man in a long, richly decorated robe and high hat came out from behind the painted screen at the front of the congregation. There was a murmur in the crowd as the service began. People started moving their hands around, touching their foreheads, shoulders and belly.

"What are they doing?" I whispered to Jelko.

"It's the sign of the cross," he said. "We do it to remember how Christ died on a cross for our sins."

I didn't know what he was talking about. While the priest droned on in a language I could not understand, my eyes ran over the paintings on the walls that told the story of Christ. In one painting, I could see a pretty angel handing a flower to a young woman. The next one showed a fat woman riding on a donkey, led by an old man with a beard. Then there was a scene in a stable, like the model in the church, complete with cow and donkey. But in this picture there was a baby lying in the straw and a big star shining its rays down on the scene. This must depict the birth of Christ, but what was he doing in a stable?

There were other pictures of serious looking men with golden circles painted around their heads and some of naked people screaming in a fiery pit, prodded by dark creatures with iron tools. When I spotted those, I nudged Jelko.

"What does that picture mean?" I whispered, pointing at the strange scene.

"Those are the bad people, burning in hell for all eternity," he said.

I looked at the scene. The people looked like they were in pain, their mouths open in silent screams. But as I looked at the women's naked bodies, their breasts lifted with their arms in supplication, their rounded buttocks as they bent over to gaze at the waiting flames, I was embarrassed to feel a hardening in my groin. What were pictures like those doing in the 'house of God' I wondered.

I saw Jelko looking down at my trousers and smiling.

"I'm used to them now," he whispered, "but before, that happened to me, too."

The priest continued to chant for a long time. I was getting tired standing there and noticed that several of the men had already left.

"How long do we have to stay?" I whispered.

"We can go now, if you want," Jelko whispered back. "The most important thing is that we came and were seen here. Let's go."

He looked over at the women's side, caught Janka's eye and give her a little wink as we made our way outside, where a light dusting of snow had covered the path to the church. The alehouse across the square looked warm and inviting.

"Let's go and have a drink." Jelko said. For the winter, a hot spicy wine was served that made me feel warm inside and out. I liked it much better than the bitter ale that the blacksmith insisted I drink with him.

We could see our breath as we quickly walked across the square. Inside the alehouse the air was warm from the blazing fire and the crowd of men. I saw the blacksmith sitting in his usual table, but I did not recognize the man who was with him, although there was something familiar about him.

Jelko and I joined Misha and Stanyo at their table. From there I watched as the blacksmith, looking none too happy, as he and his companion got up and left the alehouse together.

Chapter 62 - Music in the Afternoon

By the time I returned to the house to eat, the women had already set the table. The meal was always bigger on a Sunday. I guess the women had more time to prepare it since the only chore they did on that say was to take care of the animals. In the villages, Sunday was considered a day of rest, although, for the women who needed to prepare a special meal and clean up afterwards maybe it wasn't! With the gypsies, one day was much like the other, with a balance of activity and rest. There were special festivals to celebrate the days of full moons and the longest and shortest days of the year and those when day and night were of equal length, but even those times didn't present the contrast of a village Sunday to the other days of the week.

I was surprised to see the man from the alehouse sitting beside the hearth with Yagoda on his lap. He looked up at me and smiled when I walked in the door.

"You must be Goran," he said. "I'd get up and shake your hand, but Little Miss here would be angry with me."

"Yagoda," the blacksmith bellowed when he noticed she was on the man's lap, "Get off of him, now. You are far too old to be sitting on your uncle's lap."

Her uncle? Yagoda's face dropped as she slid down and came over to greet me.

"Gogo, come and meet my uncle," she said, taking my hand and pulling me toward the man. "He's Milada's father," she said pointedly.

I felt my face flush. Milada's father. The man who had left her as a baby. I had felt such anger when I heard her story, thinking of my own father who I had never known. How could a father leave his child? But seeing the warmth in the man's eyes, such a contrast to the cold stare of the blacksmith, his brother, I didn't feel hostile towards him.

He stood up and reached out his hand. "Pleased to meet you, Goran," he said. "I am Milan. My brother told me that you are friends with my daughter."

"Yes, Sir," I said, shaking his hand, then glancing over to where Dunia busied herself with the food. I knew she would be upset if I talked about Milada. She'd been acting a little differently the past few weeks. I caught her watching me and felt that she wanted to speak with me, but stopped herself. Of course, I liked her, but after what had happened I thought it better to keep my distance.

"I want to hear all about my little girl," he said.

Before I could answer, Yagoda blurted out, "She was here! My father locked her in the cold-room, to keep her here for you. But she disappeared right into thin air! It must have been a trick she learned from those gypsies."

I took a deep breath and kept my eyes down.

"I would love to meet her," Milan said, "but not if she were kept here against her will. Maybe, one day, when the time is right we will meet. For now, I am pleased to hear that she is alive and happy."

"The meal is on the table," Dunia's mother said. "Please come and sit down."

I hardly tasted the meal, so lost in thought I was. Milada's father was here. Maybe if he stayed in the village it would be all the more reason for her to stay as well. When we'd finished eating, the blacksmith got up and left without a word. His brother watched him go, with a slight shake of his head. When the table was cleared, he took a strange shaped bundle from this pack.

Dunia and Yagoda smiled. "Will you play for us, Uncle?" Dunia asked.

"It's not proper to play music on Sunday," their mother commented. But then she smiled, too, "But you do play so well and it's been such a long time since we heard you."

"Think of my music as a prayer," he said, "after all, it is what saved me in my time of despair."

He took his instrument and moved to sit closer to the hearth fire. I had never seen such a thing in my time with the gypsies. It had a round, gourd-like body with a long neck with a kink in it and five strings. He took a moment to tune each string while we pulled the mat off the bench that served as Yagoda's bed and put it at Milan's feet so we could sit close to the music and to the fire. Then he started to play a cheerful tune. It was as if the cottage became brighter as the happy music chased the heaviness out of the dark corners.

We passed a pleasant afternoon listening to one piece after the other. The girls' mother stopped her incessant work to sit on the bench and enjoy the music. Yagoda was on the mat on one side of me and soon Dunia came and settled herself on my other side as we lost ourselves in the tunes.

Finally, Milan laid his instrument down. "Enough for now," he said. "I could do with a rest."

Dunia's mother spoke. "Goran," she said, "the place where you sleep is usually kept for my brother-in-law. You will need to share it with him."

"Are you sure you don't want me to find somewhere else to sleep while you are here?" I asked Milan.

"No, please don't. I don't mind sharing if it is all right with you," he said.

"It would be my pleasure, Sir," I told him.

"Here is a warm quilt for you, Uncle," Dunia said, handing him the thick coverlet. "You two can carry that mat by the fire. Yagoda and I will share a bed while you are here."

"Many thanks to you all," Milan said as we shouldered the heavy mat together. It would be tricky getting it up the ladder, I thought.

Dunia held out a covered basket. "Here's some food for you and my uncle," she said, her eyes downcast.

"I'll come back for it," I told her.

"I'll bring it," said Yagoda.

"Wrap yourself up warmly if you are going out there," her mother said. "It's snowing hard now."

We made our way to the stable, Yagoda between us, sheltering under the straw mat. She laughed as we pulled and pushed it up to the loft, but we managed, warming ourselves well in the process. I lit the small brazier that provided heat for my room and a way to warm water for washing. I didn't have go to the fountain for water now. I just scraped some snow though the window and melted it.

Yagoda had made herself at home on my bed and I felt a little badly telling her it was time she went home. She always seemed happier when she was somewhere else. She whined a little but Milan produced a pretty doll from his pack.

"Here you go, Niece!" he said, "this little doll reminded me of you. Take her home to show your sister."

"Oh thank you, Uncle!" she cried, throwing her arms around him. "I love it. And I love you! I wish you were my father!"

"Don't say that, child," he told her, smoothing down her wild hair. "You have a father who loves you very much. He just doesn't know how to show it."

"He never gives me presents," she moaned, "and he beats me sometimes with his belt."

"He thinks it's for your own good, Yagoda; he doesn't know a better way," he told her gently.

"I hate him!" she spat, "and as soon as I get big enough I'm going to join Milada and the gypsies!"

"When you are older, you may do whatever you think will make you happy," he told her, "but it may not turn out to be what you were expecting."

He was sounding like the gypsies, I thought as he kissed the top of Yagoda's head and sent her on her way.

"See you tomorrow!" she said as the door creaked open and the shut behind her, leaving me alone with Milada's father.

Chapter 63 - Revelations

We settled down on our mats, he on the bench and I on the floor. It was very dark in the room so I could not see his face when Milan said, "Goran, will you tell me about her?" I knew he meant Milada.

"She is full of life," I said, seeing her in my mind's eye. "When I met her she looked a lot like Yagoda does now; but her smile is different. Yagoda smiles with her mouth, but her eyes are cold. Milada's eyes were always shining."

"Was she happy, do you think?" he asked.

"Most of the time, yes, I think she was," I said. "And if something happened that made her feel sad she was able to talk about it and release the bad feelings so she could feel happy again soon."

"That's a good thing to be able to do," Milan said. "So many people keep their sadness and hurt bottled up inside. Women often are full of bottled up anger. It's easier for us men to express that feeling, it's the tears that we hold inside."

"Did you hold your tears inside when you wife passed away?" I asked, feeling he wouldn't mind my question. "Milada told me that you went away."

"Someone must have told her," he said, "she was a new born babe when I left. At first I kept my tears inside. All I felt was anger; anger for the women who tried to help with the birth, anger for the baby who didn't come out easily, anger at God for letting my Anna die and even anger at Anna herself for leaving me."

"They called the child 'Anna' after her mother, but I knew her by the name Milada," I told him.

"It's a pretty name," he said.

"It's a bit like yours," I commented. I wondered if he was smiling at the coincidence.

"When my Anna died I think I went crazy with grief. I stayed a few days but everything around me reminded me of her. I had to leave the village," he said, continuing his story.

"Where did you go?" I asked.

"I just saddled my horse and rode. I rode all day until I was exhausted then stopped at the first village I found and drank ale until I passed out, anything to keep my mind off what had happened. I don't remember how long it was, but eventually I came to the sea. There was no more road on which to run. I thought about catching a boat and traveling on to unknown lands, but something happened on the coast to bring me back to my senses."

"I was drinking in a tavern on the docks, looking at the vastness of the sea and wishing it could wash away all the hurt and the pain. A man about my age came and sat beside me. I turned my back to him, not wanting or needing to talk to anyone, or so I thought."

"I was startled when he lay his hand on my shoulder. "Friend", he said gently, I can see that you are troubled.' It was the first time anyone had touched me since Anna's death; and, hard to believe, this stranger's touch somehow unlocked all the tears that I'd been holding inside of me."

"'Come with me," he said, taking me by the arm and leading me up a narrow staircase me to a small room. It was nearly empty, just two narrow bunks separated by a low, chipped table. What made the room remarkable was the unusually large window that directly overlooked the churning sea."

"He sat me down on the bed and held me like a child while my tears flowed unstemmed. Finally they abated, leaving me breathless and exhausted. The man gently moved off the bed and lifted my feet onto it. I curled into a ball and fell into a deep, dreamless sleep. When I awoke, the man was there, holding a bowl of soup.

"'It would be good for you to eat', he said. I nodded and took the bowl and wooden spoon from his hand. When I'd finished I set the bowl down on the table. 'Who are you?' I asked him, 'and why are you being so kind to me?'"

"'When I saw you downstairs you reminded me so much of myself a few years back', he said. 'What do you mean?' I asked him."

"'I knew that look of sorrow and desperation. It takes a long, long time to get over tragedy. Nothing cures like time, but a helping hand and a kind word can ease the process.'"

"'My wife died giving birth to our baby', I heard myself telling him. 'I loved her so much; she was my life and my joy.'"

"'I lost my beloved wife, also', the man told me, 'and my two young children'. For the first time I realized that I was not the only man who had suffered loss. 'What happened to them?' I asked, 'was it sickness?'"

"'No', he said quietly. 'We lived in a village a little way down the coast from here. One day I was in the city, just visiting with my friends like I did most afternoons. We saw the sky darken at the far side of the bay, where my village was. People were gathering on the dock and murmuring, wondering what was going on. We could see an orange glow along the coast and then actual flames. Pirates!'"

"'I ran to find my horse to hurry back home. Some people told me not to go because it would be too dangerous but I had to get to my family. I pushed the horse to gallop as fast as it could but when I reached the village all that was left were piles of smoking rocks. I followed the remnants of the road to where my house had stood. The roof has caught on fire and caved in. I could only hope that my wife had taken the children and hidden somewhere. But then I realized that there was nowhere to hide. When the stones cooled off enough for me to look inside I saw three charred bodies huddled together at the back of the house.'"

"His voice faded away and, as tears came to his eyes, it was my turn to offer him comfort. I suggested that we go downstairs for a drink but he shook his head. 'At first, I, too, drank to forget. But over time I realized that I will never forget. Drinking kept me from moving on, from realizing that though I lost my loved ones, I am still living. I owe it to them to carry on so they can live in my memory.'"

"His wise words struck a chord in me and from that moment I began to heal. I will never forget my beloved wife, but for the first time I realized that I'd left our child without a thought. I decided then and there that I would find a way back and make it up to her."

"I stayed on the coast for a while, spending time with the kind man and learning how he made a living traveling from village to village buying and selling various goods along the way. With the little money I had left I bought some hard to come by items in the port town and sold them in villages on my way back here. Besides goods, I also brought news and stories from other places. I guess I am a good story teller because over the years people got to know me and liked it when I passed through their villages."

"It took a while, but I returned to the village of my birth to look for my child and to beg the pardon of the family I'd left. But the years had taken their toll. The grandparents who had raised me had both passed away and my child had gone."

"Why didn't the blacksmith, your brother, take her in and raise her with his girls?" I asked, thinking that if he had done so I would never had met Milada and what a different girl she would have been.

"That's another story," he said with a sigh.

Chapter 64 - Further Revelations

I looked forward to the next night to learn more about Milan. As we settled ourselves and blew out the candle he spoke first.

"They say that my daughter just disappeared!" he said. "I know the ways of the gypsies. Some are strange but I don't believe that they can make themselves invisible or that Anna could have learned that trick."

I didn't know what to say. When I remained silent, Milan spoke again.

"Were you in love with my daughter?" he asked quietly. "My young niece seems to think so."

"That girl talks too much," I muttered, then heard Milan chuckle.

"If you loved her, why didn't you stay with her and the gypsy band?"

"She was in love with another," I said, barely above a whisper. "I would have stayed if she would have me, but she refused. Although they welcomed me and provided for my every need, I never really felt like I was a part of their group and longed for a more steady life settled in a village."

"Will you stay here?" he asked.

"I like it here," I said. "The blacksmith is teaching me his trade. The gypsy band may pass through here again and maybe by that time Milada will have changed her mind about me and about settling down here with me and her family. Are you going to stay and wait for her return?"

"I will not stay but I will return more often and hope that she will be here when I do," he said.

"Why do you keep traveling and not stay here close to your brother?" I asked.

"When we were growing up my brother and I were very close," he began. "He is just a little older than I am and I followed him around everywhere, wanting to do what he did. He was very patient with me, showing me how to make traps for wild birds, taking me fishing with him, not minding if the other boys teased him that I was always tagging along."

"You don't seem very close now," I said, seeing how the two men seldom spoke to one another. Milan seemed more comfortable in the company of Dunia's mother and the girls.

"The trouble came when we got older and started noticing girls. He saw Anna first and fell madly in love with her. He was going to ask for her hand, but before he got around to it, she and I had fallen in love. She told her father that it was me that she wanted to marry, and not my brother. When her father consented to our match and suggested that my brother wed her sister instead he was very angry with me. He tried to persuade Anna that she would be better off marrying him. He was already learning the blacksmith's trade from her father, whereas I was more interested in wandering in the forest looking for wild fruit and small animals to catch. I was a dreamer, he said. And he was probably right, but, right or wrong, Anna preferred to be with me."

"My parents had died in the great sickness and I was living with my grandparents. When Anna and I wed she came to live with me. My brother went to the house of her sister, Gahla, and their father, the blacksmith. But from that day, he didn't speak to me. I am happy that my little girl was able to stay with my grandparents and then found a home with the gypsies. I think that my brother would have been very cruel to her to get back at me for, as he saw it, stealing away his love."

"If Milada comes back I will take good care of her, Sir," I said. "I've already saved up one pouch full of coins and a second one is halfway full."

"What if she doesn't come back this way?" he asked me. "How long will you wait for her?"

"As long as it takes," I said.

"You really do love her," he said.

I remained silent, feeling a little sad that she was so far away.

"Did you help her to escape from my brother?" he asked, quietly.

I didn't know if I should answer. I thought I could trust him, but if he said anything to his brother my job, if not my life, would be in jeopardy. But I guess my hesitation was enough of an answer for him.

"Now I know you love her," he said. "She was trapped and would have had to stay here in the village with you, but you let her go. I'm impressed and happy that my girl could inspire such a love."

I felt tears coming into my eyes when he continued.

"I hope that she will come back and find you here waiting for her," he said as I drifted off to sleep.

The next day, I was alone in the loft resting after the midday meal. I heard the stable door opening and figured it was Milan, also coming for a rest. I called out to him, but instead of his low voice I heard a high one.

"Goran, can I come up?" Dunia said, "We have to talk."

"Yes," I called, "come on up." This was strange. She hadn't come up to my room for months. Seeing her in the brighter loft, where the snow reflected sunlight through the high window, she looked different. Although I saw her every day at our meal, it was dark in the cottage and more often than not she had her back toward me as she busied herself with the food. Her skin looked brighter and her cheeks pinker in spite of the winter cold. I couldn't help letting my eyes wander down to her breasts. They seemed larger, pushing at the fabric of her blouse.

I motioned her to sit beside me on the bed. Shyly, she sat as far away from me as she could. She looked down at her hands and then up at me through her thick brown lashes.

"I don't know how to say this?" she said quietly.

"What's the matter, Dunia?" I asked, reaching out for her hand and surprised that she let me take it. "You know we are friends; you can tell me anything."

She took a deep breath, than looked up at me and said, "Goran, I am with child."

My breathing stopped. This couldn't be happening.

"It's not what I wanted but it just happened," she said, tears starting to flow down her cheeks. I dropped her hand and went to look out of the window, needing to put some distance between us.

"Gogo," she said, coming up behind me and putting her arms around my waist, "what are we going to do?"

I felt confused and angry. Had she done this on purpose to keep me from Milada? I did not want to be with her. I did not want to father her child! I tried to dismiss a small voice in my head that was saying 'then why did you couple with her?'

My head was pounding. I couldn't speak now. I needed to be alone. I pushed pass Dunia, grabbing my jacket as I went and bounded down the ladder two rungs at a time. All I knew is that I needed some air and some time to be alone. It was freezing outside, with snow falling thickly. I couldn't go to the forest. I remembered Jelko's place and headed in the direction of the alley.

I pushed open the wooden door and was happy to find no one there, only the cows. I went upstairs and lit a candle. It was very cold, but between my jacket and the warmth coming from the cows it was not unbearable.

I needed to think. What was I going to do? I had to realize that I couldn't know if Milada would ever come back and if she did travel this way with the gypsies would she want to stay with me. I was making a life here, learning a good trade. I didn't want to spend more years on the road. I was going to be a father! I didn't feel ready to take that step, but there would be no going back now. I could leave; go to another village and start again far from here; but then I would be abandoning my child like Milan had, and like my father. No.

I would have to make the best of things. Dunia said she loved me. She is a good girl; she cooks and sews and would keep our house tidy and clean. Her father likes me and would pass on his business to me for sure if I wed his daughter. And, with her hair free and out of her restraining clothes, I could fool myself once again that I have my beloved Milada in my arms.

I sighed, my decision was made. I would ask Dunia to be my wife and stay and raise our child together. Maybe, over time, I would learn to care for her as she did for me.

Chapter 65 - Another Proposal

By the time I returned to the house, the evening meal was steaming on the hearth. Dunia looked at me as I entered the room, shivering slightly, whether at the blast of cold air that blew in with me or in anticipation of further rejection, I couldn't say. Rather than directly taking my place at the table as I usually would do, I went over to where she stood by the great iron pot hanging over the cooking fire, ladling the thick vegetable stew into our bowls. I stood behind her and whispered into her ear, "Everything will be all right," as I took a bowl from her hand and placed it on the table.

She looked up at me, uncertainly; but when I smiled at her, she smiled back, her eyes brightening. We finished our meal in silence then the blacksmith left for the ale house. I was glad that he didn't suggest that I go with him. While the girls cleared the table, Milan took out his instrument and began tuning the strings. While he played, I drew Dunia to the far side of the room.

"Your news came as a shock to me, "I told her. "I did not expect it."

"I knew that you would not be happy," Dunia whispered, "but I had to tell you."

"Does anyone else know?" I asked her.

"I think my mother suspects something," she said, "but I haven't said anything to her."

"I will speak to your father," I told her.

"So you will marry me?" she asked. "You don't have to, you know."

"It's the right thing to do," I said, knowing that is was, yet wishing that there was another way out of the situation.

I settled near the hearth and let my mind drift while Milan played. I was going to be a father! What did that mean? How would I know what to do; I'd never known my own father. I didn't want to be like the blacksmith. Milan seemed a good man, but he had left his child as my father had left me. At least he returned, though. But what did he know about being a father? I guess I would just have to figure it out as I went along. One thing I did know; I would not leave my child to grow up without his father.

The days went by and the feast of Christmas was approaching. The villagers were busy with their preparations, baking special breads and cakes and looking forward to the end of the long fast, when they refrained from eating meat. I had wondered about that custom. The gypsies had no such prohibition of eating meat before feasts. Maybe it was because their feasts were different to those celebrated in the villages. I had to admit sneaking a sausage or two when I was very hungry after a hard day's work. I knew the blacksmith did the same but his wife and the girls felt it was an obligation to abstain from eating meat until they would break their fast with a rich meat soup after the midnight Christmas service.

I knew I must speak with the blacksmith and ask for Dunia's hand in marriage, but I kept putting it off. I had trouble meeting Dunia's eyes when I came for my meals. I could feel her watching me. I knew that she was anxious to announce our engagement. Soon her pregnancy would become obvious and she would need protection from village gossip. It would be bad enough that such a prized girl would wed an outsider, but it would be better than giving birth to a child without the acknowledgement of its father.

Finally, on Christmas Eve, the blacksmith and I were in the forge, tidying up after the last job of the day. He took off his heavy apron, wiped his blackened hands on it then sat down on the bench by the door where the customers waited.

"Boy," he said, "Is there something you want to ask me?"

I took a deep breath. I knew that I should have been to one to bring up the subject. Dunia's mother must have said something to him.

"Yes, Sir," I said, standing by the anvil, looking down at my shoes. "I would like to ask for your daughter's hand in marriage."

Before I knew what was happening, the blacksmith was up and holding me by the collar. I had grown in the months that I'd been working with him, but he was still half a head taller. I was up on my toes feeling his hot breath on my face as he shouted.

"You little ingrate! I took you in as an apprentice and you couldn't wait to stick my daughter! I should kill you like vermin, you little fox!"

I could hardly breathe, let alone answer him. Part of me agreed with him. It was not the right thing to do and I knew it.

"It's lucky for you that Dunia wants you," he said, abruptly releasing his hold on my shirt.

I nearly lost my balance but steadied myself on the anvil.

"And I have already invested time in training you," he said more gently. "You are coming along well as a blacksmith. I suppose my daughter could do worse with one of these lazy village boys."

"I'm sorry for the way it happened, Sir," I said, still unable to meet his eyes, "but I will be good to Dunia and the child. You have taught me a trade and with it I will be able to provide for them."

"Don't expect any other dowry," he growled.

"No, Sir," I said, beginning to feel relieved, "I won't."

"Let's go to the ale house then and drink to your engagement. We can get something to eat. There won't be anything at the house tonight."

"Yes, Sir," I said, "Thank you, Sir."

He slapped me hard on the back. I wasn't sure if it was a punishment or an endearment. I was totally confused by our exchange. Was he angry or was he pleased? I guessed that only time would tell.

Later that night, wrapped in our warmest blankets, I accompanied the blacksmith and his family to the village church. There was no moon and our lanterns could hardly cut through the blackness of the night. Just before we reached the church, I took Dunia's arm and held her back from the others.

"You father has given his consent," I told her.

"Are you sure this is what you want to do?" she asked me.

"Yes, Dunia," I said. "I will not abandon my child the way my father abandoned me. We can announce our engagement tomorrow at the Christmas meal."

She just nodded, then ran to catch up with her mother and sister as they took their places on the left side of the church. That was it. I knew that from that moment on my life would never be the same.

After the service, we returned home to a warm house and soup boiling in the iron pot hanging over the fire. The blacksmith was in an unusually good mood. I think he may have slipped out to the alehouse before the end of the service because, despite the cold, his cheeks and nose were shiny and red.

He disappeared into the storeroom and brought out a jug of plum brandy.

"Gahla, bring the cups," he called to his wife.

I couldn't recall the blacksmith ever offering brandy to his family before.

"Come over here boy," he said, "and you, too," nodding his head in Dunia's direction.

We joined him at the table and watched as he poured some plum brandy into each of the cups.

"Bring one more cup, woman!" he yelled.

His wife took the last cup from the dresser and the blacksmith put a drop of brandy in it.

"Here, Yagoda," he bellowed, "you are old enough to have a sip to congratulate your sister on her engagement."

I looked around to see that only Milada's father seemed surprised by the announcement.

"Drink to the happy couple!" the blacksmith ordered.

They all raised their glasses and nodded at us, but only the blacksmith was smiling. Dunia looked like she was about to cry. I didn't know what to do. I took a step closer to her and held up my cup. She took hers and gently touched it to mine, her eyes downcast.

Milan broke the silence and said, "I know it's late and it's Christmas but this occasion calls for music."

He took up his instrument and began to play a cheerful tune. The Blacksmith refilled our cups and the brandy and the warmth of the fire soon had us in a happier mood. I sat beside Dunia and whispered, "Don't worry. Everything will be all right."

I took her hand in mine and we sat together in silence while the others chatted or sang along with Milan until the fire had died down and the effect of the brandy was sending us to sleep. Milan and I bundled up and silently made our way through the drifting snow back to our room above the horses. I was thankful for the warm quilt since there had been no time to light the small brazier that night.

In the darkness I heard Milan's voice.

"So you will marry Milada's cousin then?" he said. "You told me you loved my daughter and would wait for her to return."

"This is not what I had planned or hoped for," I said, quietly. "Dunia is with child; my child. I will not leave him as my father left me;" and as you left Milada, I thought, but left unsaid.

Silence and sleep overtook us. That night I dreamt that Milada had returned, and I had to let her go.

Chapter 66 - Spring Comes

Christmas day came and went. I don't remember enjoying all the special foods of the day. Soon after the Twelfth-night feast Milan left on his travels. The weather was still very harsh but he said that he must reach the coast in good time to purchase goods to sell in the spring. He would come back then, he told me, in the hope of seeing his daughter if the gypsies made their way to the village again as they had the previous year.

When he left, Dunia took his place in my room over the stable. Once the announcement had been made that we would wed we were treated as man and wife. At first it was awkward between us. I knew that Dunia didn't trust me and could sense that I was only marrying her because of the child growing in her womb. But as the weeks went by and the child grew I began to feel protective of Dunia. I'll never forget the first time I saw the child moving in her belly. It was early in the evening. The room was bathed in a pinkish glow from the setting sun. Dunia was sitting on the bed, resting her back on a large pillow when all of a sudden she gasped.

"What is it?" I asked her.

"It's the baby" she said, her eyes wide open. "He moved!"

Just then I could see a movement under the apron she had tied just below her expanded breasts.

"There," he moved again!" she exclaimed.

"May I feel it?" I asked, a little shyly. I hadn't touched Dunia since that day in the river. It seemed like years before. Gently, I placed my hand on her rounded belly and before long I felt something hard moving inside.

There was a life in there; a life that I had helped to make! For the first time I believed that I was really going to be a father. This girl was carrying my child. I felt tears filling my eyes. Dunia noticed them and, without a word, caressed my hair.

After that day, I was more attentive to Dunia. At night, I crawled into bed bedside her and cradled her expanding body in my arms. Sometimes I felt myself harden with her warmth, but I never pressed myself on her. It didn't feel right.

As the days became warmer, Dunia seemed to blossom. After my work I would often see her sitting in a sunny spot in the square chatting with Janka and the other girls. Once our engagement was announced the boys teased me less. I guess they knew that they would have to answer to the blacksmith if they insulted his son-in-law. He finally paid me a regular wage. I guess he figured that the money would go toward caring for his daughter and grandchild.

The boys still gambled on the shady side of the square but I had no interest in joining them. I liked spending time with Jelko, when he could spare a moment from courting Janka, who seemed set on resisting his charms.

"You are so lucky, man!" he told me one day. "Dunia let you lie with her. Janka loves kissing but if I try and get any farther – smack!"

I didn't feel very lucky, under the circumstances. It seemed so long since Dunia and I had even kissed with any feeling of passion, but I didn't share those thoughts with Jelko!

By the time the days grew longer than nights, Dunia began to feel uncomfortable. The women said that it was still at least two moons until the child would come. Dunia's narrow ankles were swollen and she complained that her back hurt her most of the day. Yagoda took over her job of stirring the food on the hearth and anything else that needed to be done while standing. Dunia continued with her sewing, weaving and fine embroidery; things she could do sitting down.

One afternoon I ran into Yagoda when we were both at the fountain filling our jugs.

"I think Dunia just likes to complain!" she said. "She likes sitting and sewing all day and leaving the hard work for me."

"That's not a nice thing to say about your sister," I said. "One day, you will be with child, too, and then see how you feel."

"I don't want to have a child!" she exclaimed; "unless it's yours," she added, quietly.

Had I heard right? My jug was almost full. I didn't wait until it overflowed as I usually did. I needed to get away from this strange girl.

When I got back to the house, I found Dunia in tears. Her mother was trying to comfort her. I put the water jug on the table and tried to leave before they saw me, but Dunia's mother called out, "Goran, please give the pot a stir so the food cooks evenly."

When I went to the hearth and did as she asked, I couldn't help overhearing Dunia's words.

"I'm so frightened," she said, through her tears. "I know it's going to hurt when the baby comes. And what if it dies? What if I die?"

"There, there," her mother whispered, "women have babies every day. It's what we are made for."

"But lots of times they die!" Dunia cried.

"Sometimes they do," he mother agreed, "but it won't happen to you."

"How do you know that?" Dunia asked.

"I pray to Mother Mary every day for you to have a safe delivery."

Who was 'Mother Mary' I wondered. Maybe she was a lady who helped women give birth like Mother Miriana in the gypsy band.

"Don't worry, Dunia," I said, going over to the two women. "I'm sure Mother Mary will help you give birth safely. I have plenty of coins saved up and can pay her well for your care."

Dunia and her mother looked up at me, with puzzled expressions on their faces.

"We don't need to pay Mother Mary," Dunia said. Just then Yagoda arrived back with her water jug, followed by the blacksmith demanding his dinner. They left me to wonder at this woman who helped girls give birth free of charge.

Chapter 67 - The Traveler's Homecoming

That evening, we had finished our evening meal shortly after the sun had set. The blacksmith had already gone to the ale house and I was getting ready to go and find Jelko for a chat when I heard a loud knocking on the oaken door. It swung open and there stood Milan with a full pack of goods on his back.

Yagoda jumped up and down in excitement at seeing him and his bundle.

"Uncle, Uncle!" she exclaimed, "Did you bring me a present from your travels?"

"Yagoda," her mother said, "let your uncle come in first before demanding gifts."

"Welcome, Uncle Milan," Dunia said without getting up from her cushioned seat.

"Good to see you, Milan," I said. "Let me help you with your bundles". I could see that there were other bags just outside the door.

"Greeting to you all," he said, shrugging his pack off into my arms. It was very heavy.

"What have you got in here?" I asked, setting the pack down on the flagstone floor.

"Things people will want to buy, I hope!" he said with a chuckle. "I have copper pots, sharp knives, silver jewelry, some rare spices and soft silks from the East."

"And something for your little niece, right?" Yagoda asked, flirtatiously.

"Of course I have something for my little niece!" he said with a grin; "and something for my bigger niece and her husband-to-be and for my sister-in-law and even something for the baby!"

Yagoda clapped her hands. "Show us, Uncle! Show us what you brought for us!"

"Milan, there was no need to bring us gifts," her mother said. "Let me get you something to eat. You must be hungry and tired from your journey."

"Thank you, Gahla," he said. "And you, Little Miss, will have to wait until tomorrow for me to unpack my bags and find your present."

"I wasn't sure where I'd be staying this time. Goran, I suppose that Dunia is staying with you now?"

"She was, but now the narrow ladder is too difficult for her to climb so she is staying here. You are welcome to your old bed," I told him.

"I will store my wares in the barn below the loft while I'm here," he said. "We can pile the last of the hay in front of them to keep them hidden. I already tethered my horse in the barn."

"Do you want me to come and help you now, or would you like to eat something first?" I asked him.

"Let's get the hard work over with and then we can relax with some food and drink," he said.

He shouldered his heavy pack and I held open the door. Taking a bundle in each hand we made our way to the barn. I cleared a space under the loft while Milan unloaded the wagon that he had left outside. It was smaller than the gypsies' wagons; big enough to transport goods but not to live in as they did.

When most of the goods were stowed at the back of the barn we piled up the hay to hide them from view. Milan carried two smaller bundles up to the loft. He removed his dusty cloak and then climbed back down the ladder where I was waiting.

"The room look's different now," he said with a smile. "It has a woman's touch."

I just nodded, still feeling awkward about my situation with Dunia.

We walked back to the house in silence. Later that night, when we were both settled in our beds and the small lamp had been put out Milan said quietly, "How are things with you and Dunia? She seemed nervous to me, not a glowing happy mother-to-be."

I knew he was right. I'd observed the same thing myself and thought of the conversation I'd overheard.

"I think she is afraid of giving birth," I told him.

"Are you helping her?" he asked.

"As much as I can," I answered, truthfully. "She knows I was in love with your daughter, but I will try to be a good father to the child."

"And a good husband to Dunia?"

"As much as I can," I said, quietly. Milan's presence was a painful reminder of my love for Milada. I tried to put her out of my mind, knowing that we could not be together, but often I found myself wondering what if things were different; what if Milada wanted to be with me…

"Dunia is a good girl, Goran," he whispered, "try not to hurt her."

I nodded and then dropped off into a dreamless sleep until the early morning sunlight woke me. Milan's bed was empty. I rinsed my face in the basin then climbed down the ladder, anxious to get to the house and have some breakfast before going to the forge for the day's work.

I greeted the family as I entered, but they hardly noticed me. I saw that the blacksmith was already gone as Dunia's mother looked up from shining a copper pan she held.

"Goran, good morning!" she said, putting the pan on the table and fetching me a bowl of porridge from the pot on the hearth.

"Look what Uncle Milan brought me!" Yagoda exclaimed. She held out her slim arm to show me a narrow, finely worked silver bracelet. "Isn't it sweet?"

"It's very pretty," I told her.

"Just like me!" she said, tossing her hair.

"Yagoda!" he mother said. "Be more modest. And put your headscarf on; you look like a gypsy."

A look passed between Milan and me. Yes, I was thinking that Yagoda resembled Milada; in looks but not in personality!

"Good morning, Dunia," I said, gently touching her shoulder. "What did Milan bring for you?"

She looked up at me with a shy smile. "He brought me this piece of silk and some beautiful thread for embroidery," she said, gently fingering a square of nearly white cloth. "I'm thinking about the pattern I will work. And he brought us this," she said holding out a fluffy grey mass. "It's for the baby."

I took the item from her, not sure what it was. It felt very soft in my work- hardened hands. I shook it out and saw that it was a small blanket.

"That is made from the hair from a type of very rare goat that live high in the mountains," Milan said.

"I've never felt anything as soft as that," Dunia said. "Our child will be kept nice and warm in it."

"I have something for you, Goran," Milan said, holding out a long leather pouch.

"Thank you, Sir," I said, "but it wasn't necessary to bring a gift for me."

"I know," he replied, "but when I saw it, I thought of you. It is my pleasure to present it to you."

I untied the thong, opened the pouch and pulled out a knife, the likes of which I'd never seen before. Its sharp blade glistened in the morning sunlight. The hilt was made of something white with carvings and patterns inlaid with dark wood.

"Milan," I said, "this is wonderful! I've never seen anything like it."

"It comes from across the sea, "he told me. "I was told that the handle is made from the tooth of a great beast, but I can't say that it's true."

"Whatever it is made of, it is truly beautiful," I said, "and useful, too! This blade is very sharp!"

"Keep it in its sheath," Milan said, "and well away from the baby when it arrives."

"Thank you, Milan," I said. "Do you have others to sell? My friends will be very jealous when they see it!"

"I have, but not to sell here," he said seriously.

"Why not here, Uncle?" Dunia asked.

"Because I am known here; I am kin. Men here expect me to lower my prices since I am 'one of them'. The goods I bring from the coast are rare and have great value. It is my livelihood to make as much profit as I can from them so it is better for me to keep them for markets where I can ask for and get a higher price."

"But, why have you given me a gift of such value?" I asked, now that I realized what it meant.

"I like you, boy!" he said with a smile. "You share your room with me, and now you are part of my family. There is no price to be put on affection."

I nodded my thanks and made for the door. I felt hot tears welling up in my eyes. Maybe that's what it felt like to have a father.

Chapter 68 - The Gypsies Return

Milan's presence lightened the spirit in the house. Each day he traveled to nearby villages with a selection of his wares. Sometimes he would bring his instrument with him and stay overnight. He told me that the people liked it when he played and sang in the tavern in the evening. He shared stories of his travels and they, in turn, informed him about the local goings on; the success or failure of crops and livestock, the whims of the local lords, predictions about the weather and the like.

When he returned he shared his stories with us. It was good to see Dunia laughing when he related tales of reluctant mules or jokes that villagers played on one another. But, one night in our room, after the lamp was extinguished he told me some news that was not funny at all.

"Goran," he said, "I heard some worrying reports from the villages east of here."

"What did you hear?" I asked.

"Some men spoke of horsemen raiding nearby villages," he said. "They were concerned about arming themselves in case the horsemen came their way."

"Do you think there is danger?" I asked. "Our village has a wall around it; surely we would be safe if we keep the gates barred."

"It has been many years since this village was threatened. I have no memory of it. There were stories, but men of my generation were never taught to fight," he told me.

"The village guards knows how to fight," I said, "Don't they?"

"Without a real threat, we have no way of knowing if our fortifications will hold or if the guards are strong enough to ward off an attack. I will speak with the village elders. It is well to take precautions."

That night I dreamt of fighting wild horsemen, threatening them with my new knife. It grew to the size of a sword and I loped off heads and arms as Milada looked on from her wagon. I woke in a cold sweat, glad that it was only a dream, yet happy to have had a glimpse of the girl I loved.

Little did I know that I would soon see her in the flesh!

After breakfast, I went to the forge as usual, but that day, the village felt very different. Women were scurrying around and there was excitement in the air. After a while, the blacksmith and I took a break and went together to the tavern in the village square. I saw Jelko there with Janka, setting up the long trestle tables used for village feasts.

"What's going on?" I asked them. "It's not a holiday today!"

"The gypsies are back," Janka said with a smile. "I saw them setting up their camp. I will go soon and see if they will teach me some more of their healing skills. I've been able to help my family so much since I spent time with them last spring."

"Of course we are offering them a meal tonight," Jelko said.

"And they will play music for us and tell us stories from their travels," Janka added.

I thought about the news I'd heard from Milan and wondered if I should tell them but just then a group of village women came to lay the table and my friends were caught up in the hustle and bustle.

I joined the blacksmith in the tavern. He was grumbling to the owner, "Those gypsies have come back and here we go again with all the fuss and bother. No one will want any horses shod while they are here."

"They do bring us news," the tavern owner commented; "and since it feels like a holiday while they are here, my business improves!"

"Well, good for you, then," the blacksmith said, taking a swig of plum brandy.

When the tavern man had left us I turned to the blacksmith and said, "Did Milan tell you what he heard in the village to the east of here?"

"No," he said, "we don't talk much to each other. What did he tell you?"

"He said that he heard that a horde of horsemen were attacking villages; burning them to the ground," I told him.

"Sounds like a tall tale to me," he said. "If any of those horsemen come here I'll show them. I still have my sword, and I keep it sharp. It may be good for business to spread the word. People will come to the forge to get their swords sharpened or to make new ones. Good boy! Yes, we will tell people that they need to be ready; to protect themselves from these horsemen. The more gruesome the story, the better our business will be."

With that, he got up and went to speak with the tavern owner. I could see that he was telling him about the threat by the way the color drained from the other man's face. Oh, no. Frightening the villagers was not my intention.

When we left the tavern the smell of roasting meat tickled my nostrils. The thought of the delicious meal, and the possibility of seeing Milada, made the work day pass quickly. When we finished for the day, I went up to my room and washed myself well. I put on a clean shirt and dusted off the boots the gypsies had left me which just about still fit. I knew I'd changed in the year since I'd seen Milada; I supposed that she had changed as well. I hopped down the ladder in anxious anticipation.

In the alley I saw Yagoda and Dunia's mother hurrying toward the square. I joined them, taking the basket laden with nuts and dried fruit from Dunia's mother's arm.

"Where's Dunia?" I asked as me walked.

"She isn't feeling well enough to come," her mother told me. "She said she wanted to stay home and rest. I know the baby is not due for a while yet, but she seems very tired all the time."

"She just likes doing nothing," Yagoda smirked.

"That's enough, Yagoda," he mother admonished.

"Will you stay with her this evening, Goran?" her mother asked.

"If she is tired, it's better to let her rest," I said, dismayed at the thought of not seeing Milada.

Dunia's mother pressed her lips together and said nothing as we approached the square, already bustling with villagers and gypsies alike.

A bonfire had been lit on the far side of the square. I knew that where music was playing would be the place to find Milada.

I set the basket down on a long table then set off to see if I could find her. Before I could reach the fire I saw some young men waving and me and whooping.

"Goran! Look at you!" one of them exclaimed

I knew the voice as Bora's but hardly recognized the man he had become. I'm sure he was thinking the same thing about me.

He engulfed me in a one armed bear hug; the other hand holding onto his viol by its neck. "Nico, look! It's Goran all grown up!"

Nico had grown into a very handsome young man. I could see some of the village girls watching us, and watching him in particular, giggling behind their hands.

"It's great to see you again!" I told them, meaning it.

"Looks like this village life suits you!" Bora said, smiling. "How did you get all those muscles?"

"I'm working at a forge," I told them. "I make tools and give horses new shoes. And the horses really like me! I learned to talk to them from you!"

"Let's have some of this good village food," Nico said, "and then it will be time for music and maybe dancing with some of these pretty girls."

"Nico, Nico," Bora tutted, "you know how it is with these village girls. Look but don't touch!'"

"I bet Goran has touched one or two. Look at him! The girls must be all over him!" Nico said, playfully slapping my back.

I felt color rising to my face and wished I had some way of stopping it.

"Let's go get something to drink," I said, turning toward the barrel of ale to hide my blush."

We sat together, reminiscing about the times we spent together and the fun we had.

"Do you regret leaving the band?" Bora asked.

"No," I told him. "I am grateful for the time I spent with you, but have made a life for myself here."

"There must be a girlfriend," Nico muttered under his breath.

I wasn't ready to tell them about Dunia and the baby. Not before I spoke with Milada. I excused myself from the boys and headed toward the fire, looking for Milada's wild locks.

Chapter 69 - A Love That Could Not Be

A knot of people waited near the fire. I saw someone moving that reminded me of Milada, but when I looked closer I saw a girl in a drab brown dress with a none-too-clean kerchief pulled tightly around her head. As I drew nearer I saw that this girl looked a lot like Milada.

I moved close behind her and said, "Milada, is that you?"

"Goran! It's so good to see you!" she replied, t turning to me and throwing herself into my arms.

Last year she was almost as tall as I was but now the top of her head rested snugly on my chest. Oh how I longed to keep her here in my arms! She did not seem to be in any hurry to pull away. She looked up at me with her playful eyes and ran a smooth finger over my moustache.

"Where'd you get this little brown mouse?" she asked. I could see she was trying to look serious, but the sparkle in her eyes gave her away.

"Look who's talking about a little brown mouse!" I told. "What happened to *you*?" She looked odd in such a dull dress rather than the brightly colored ones I remembered that she loved.

"I'm hiding from that man!" she said. "Don't worry, I'm still the same girl who likes bright colours and wild hair."

"I've missed that girl," I said, realizing just how much I had.

"Oh, Goran," she said, "and I've missed you! A lot more than I thought I would!"

"You sit here and hide," he said, patting the awful kerchief that hid her lovely locks, "I'll get us something to eat and we can catch up on all our news."

I hurried off to the tables laden with all sorts of mouth-watering food and filled two plates. Even in that tight kerchief the sight of Milada stirred my heart; and my groin. I took a deep breath to calm myself then returned to where she sat on a bench near the bonfire.

I handed her one of the full plates and asked, "So, how do I look?" knowing that most girls found me rather handsome.

"Well, except for the brown mouse," she said wiggling her nose, "you look just fine!"

"I feel good," I told her. "I've found my way here in the village."

"But isn't it boring to stay in one place all the time?" she asked, toying with the sausage on her plate.

"I haven't been bored at all," I said. "It was difficult at first to learn the blacksmith's trade. I could hardly pick up the hammer! But little by little I got stronger and learned the right way to handle the tools."

"You are working for that man; the one who locked me in the storeroom?" she asked, the color draining from her face.

"Dunia's father isn't as bad as he seems, once you get to know him," I told her. "And I have big news for you".

Putting my plate on the ground, I took her face in both my hands so she could not look away and I could watch her expression. "Your father is back!"

I was shocked by her reaction. She pushed away my hands and jumped up, her plate clattering noisily to the ground.

"Let me go!" she yelled, "I have no interest in these people. The gypsies are my family! No one can keep me here."

"Wait, Milada," I said, locking my arms around her waist.

She struggled hard to get free. This time last year she probably would have been able to, by now my arms were so strong I could hold on to her with ease. Like calming a wild horse, I held her with one arm and used the other hand to gently stroke her neck until she began to calm down.

I needed to see her hair and to touch it. "This is no good," I muttered as I pulled off the silly kerchief. I freed her wild hair and caressed it. "Milada," I whispered, "it's all right, it's all right."

"Oh, Goran!" she said turning to rest her head on my shoulder, sending shivers down my spine, "I've missed you so. So many times I wanted to share my thoughts with you; or a funny thing that happened during the day".

"I've missed you, too," I told her, "especially at the beginning".

"And then you forgot about me?" she questioned.

"It's not that I forgot you. How could I ever forget you? It's just that you had made your choice and I had to get on with my life," I said quietly, feeling the pain of knowing that we could never be together.

"Maybe I made the wrong choice," she said.

I couldn't believe my ears! It was the hope I had carried in my heart the months that we were apart. The hope I forced myself to extinguish when I learned that Dunia was with child.

"Milada," I murmured, holding her close.

"Goran, I love you," she whispered.

I held her so tightly I could feel her heart beating next to mine. I knew it was wrong but just for a moment I allowed myself to feel the love between us; a love that could no longer be. I felt tears trickling down my cheeks. I wanted this so much and could hardly believe it was happening; but why did it have to be now when it was too late?

"Milada, why didn't you tell me before," I said, through the tears I hoped she wouldn't see.

I don't know how long we stood there in each other's arms, feeling each other's warmth, each other's desire. I never wanted her to leave my embrace, but my revelry was disturbed by a woman's voice behind me.

"Goran! Is that you?"

I let go of Milada and quickly wiped my eyes to erase the tell-tale tears. I turned and saw Tanya standing there with a huge smile on her face and a decidedly rounded belly.

"Tanya!" I exclaimed in surprise, "Well look at you!"

"I am called 'Radha' now," she said. "Since Dragan and I were wed!"

"You and Dragan married?"

"Yes, didn't Milada tell you?" she asked, looking over at Milada, who stood by, looking down at her feet.

I shook my head in dismay, beginning to understand what was happening.

"It was at the Summer Solstice gathering," she said. "Come and say 'hello' to Iovan and the others."

"Iovan?" I wondered.

"My husband!" she replied.

"I'll come in a moment," I told her, "I have something to say to Milada".

"Don't be too long," she said, "we've all missed you".

As Tanya walked away, I turned to Milada and said, "So now you love me; now that your precious Dragan is wed."

"Is that what you think?" she answered. "I have always loved you".

"That is not what you said last year when I was ready to go against my better judgment and stay with the gypsies to be with you," I said, trying very hard to control my anger. I felt like striking the face the moments ago I was longing to cover with kisses.

"You can come now!" she said. "We can be together."

"It is too late, Milada; much too late".

"What do you mean?" she asked. Before I could tell her about Dunia and me I heard that pest Yagoda calling, "Goran! Where have you been? We've been looking for you everywhere."

Her eyes widened when she saw who was beside me.

"Goran is that Milada?"

Before I could answer she was off. I figured she would run and tell Dunia, just to make trouble for us both.

Milada stiffened. "I have to go," she said. "She will tell her father!"

I reached out and grasped her wrist so she could not run. "Many things have changed. I have to tell you something," I said.

"Let me go! That hurts!" she yelled, struggling to get out of my grip. "You are just as bad as they are!"

"Calm down, Milada. I won't hurt you and I won't let anyone else hurt you," I told her. "Please, just sit down for a moment and listen."

She sat down on the bench, with her head in her hands, her hair hiding her face. I was still angry, but I could see that she was frightened and, I guess, my long standing love for her was stronger than my newly found anger. I stroked her back while I told her my story.

"When you left, I was very sad," I began. "I had lost my best friend, and the girl I loved. I thought the two of us had a special bond since we were not of the band. I could see you thought you loved Dragan. I hoped that you would realize that you could never be together."

"I do now," she said softly.

"Now it is too late," I said, sadly.

"You don't love me now?" she asked.

"I'll always love you," I told her.

"So it's not too late," she said, looking up at me through her long lashes.

"You told me that you could never love me," I went on, "so I decided to make my life here. Dunia was very good to me. She prepared special food. She kept my clothes clean and always had a kind word for me when I returned from the forge."

"Dunia?" she whispered.

"And she does look like you," I said. "I thought if I can't be with Milada, at least I could be with someone like her".

"You can be with me now," she said, clasping my hand in both of hers.

"It is not that easy," I said.

"Goran!" I heard Dunia call my name and shuddered at what I knew would be a difficult encounter.

"Dunia and I are going to be married." I said as Dunia and Yagoda approached the bench where we were sitting.

Milada dropped my hand and stared at Dunia rounded belly. I didn't need to say anymore. Milada's face was ashen as she jumped up and ran toward the village gate.

Chapter 70 – My Decision

Milada! This was not the sweet reunion I had so often pictured in my mind. It could have been, if I hadn't been such a fool. But Milada said that she loved me as a brother, I recalled, and it broke my heart. I was afraid to hope that she would change her mind. And she probably hadn't until she finally realized that she could never be with that Dragan. All these thoughts rushed through my head as I stood there, watching the girl I had loved for so long running away from me in tears and the girl who was carrying my child standing there looking at me with contempt.

Dunia turned away and walked back towards her house. Yagoda lagged behind, watching me and waiting for my reaction. I felt anger bubbling up inside of me; anger with Milada and at Dunia's sister who, by bringing her here brought sorrow on all three of us.

"You little brat!" I yelled, grabbing Yagoda hard by her wrist. "Why did you bring Dunia here to see this?" I was very close to slapping the girl, barely able to control my rage.

"Let me go!" she sputtered, "You're hurting me!"

"You hurt me, and Milada and your sister," I said, keeping my hold on her. I knew she would run off if I let go.

"You shouldn't have been talking to her," she hissed. "You're going to marry my sister, aren't you? Or are you going back to that girl and your life of fun with the gypsies?"

"It's none of your business," I said, "but I wanted to tell her about Dunia and me before she heard it from someone else."

"When I saw you, you weren't talking!" she spat like an angry cat.

"Yagoda, you are a very nasty girl. You must have known that your sister would be hurt to see me with Milada and still you brought her here. Why?"

"Because no one pays any attention to me!" she said, suddenly bursting into tears. "Dunia has always been the 'good girl' the favorite. I'm the left over one. 'Stop it, Yagoda; don't do that, Yagoda; be quiet Yagoda'. It just makes me angry!"

I let go of her wrist and the next thing I knew she had her arms around me.

"Gogo, I'm sorry," she murmured through her tears. "I didn't mean to make you angry. Please forgive me."

I looked down at her hair, the same wild brown locks as Milada's and couldn't help feeling sorry for the girl. It was true that no one really gave her a chance. She was not a docile village girl; she had a wild spirit that did not fit in with the life she was expected to lead.

I stroked that wild hair and, feeling my anger draining away, tried to comfort her.

"I think you need to apologize to your sister and reassure her that I was only telling Milada our news," I said.

"If that's what you want me to do, dear Gogo, I will," she whispered, looking up at me through her teary eyelashes and so resembling my Milada that it took my breath away. I nodded and stepped back, momentary lost in confusion.

Gazing over Yagoda's head I saw Bora had taken his place with the musicians and was looking at me and smiling. He was probably thinking that Yagoda was my girlfriend. I shuddered at the thought! It must look like I found a replacement for Milada; but then again, wasn't that exactly what I had done?

"Go now and speak with your sister," I told Yagoda.

"I want to stay and listen to the music!" she said, back to her willful self. "If I go home they won't let me out again!"

"From the look on her face, I don't think Dunia will talk to me," I told her. "Please, go and speak with her. She has to walk slowly; maybe she is still in the village square. Please go and tell her I will be along soon."

"All right," she said, "I'll go. But she probably thinks you ran into the woods after that girl."

"You tell her that I did not!" I said, beginning to get angry again. "Just go!"

"Yes, Gogo," she said. "If it will make you happy, I will."

She took a step closer to me and planted a little kiss on my cheek, then ran off toward the village square.

I could see Bora laughing. I shook my head and sat down on the bench to collect my thoughts while the musicians played their familiar old tunes. Am I really happier now that I was when I was with the gypsies? With them, my needs were all met, there was food on the table, a warm bed at night. I didn't have to work all day with a strict taskmaster. I was surrounded by friends and close to the girl I loved. If she had loved me back, could I have made a life with the gypsy band?

But being here, I had proven myself in a way. I developed my body and was on my way to mastering a profitable trade. I was confident that I could make my way in the world now through my strength and skills at the forge. I had made some new friends in the village; I knew I could count on Jelko in times of trouble. I thought that Dunia loved me, even though at this moment I wasn't so sure. And now I had a child coming; it would be a new chapter in my life.

I had made the right decision, I thought, as I watched people gathering around the fire and beginning to dance. I enjoyed an evening like this once in a while, but I didn't need it all the time. I didn't need the uncertainty of moving camp at every turn of the moon; of not knowing what would happen in case of trouble; of the way the gypsies let their children travel with other bands and stay far away from them. I wanted to be close to my son; to be the father that I never had. I would make it up to Dunia. I had to. It was my duty to the child.

Feeling resolved, I stood up, waved Bora 'good night' and headed back to the house. I found Dunia there, crying in her mother's arms.

When her mother saw me come in she whispered to her daughter. "He's here. I will leave you two alone."

I could see that Dunia didn't want to let her go, but her mother stood up, took her shawl from the peg by the door and left without another word.

I took her place on the low bed by the fire. Dunia's swollen body was propped up by pillows, her eyes red and puffy from tears.

"Did Yagoda speak with you?" I asked, trying to take her hand. She pulled it away from me and probably would have pulled herself away if she could.

"She told me what you told her to say," she murmured.

"I told her the truth. I didn't want Milada to hear about our betrothal from anyone else," I said.

"If you didn't still love her, what difference would it make?" she asked, her voice full of bitterness.

I had no answer to that, but I took a deep breath and spoke form my heart.

"Dunia, I've been thinking. I decided to make my life here in this village; here with you and our child. Seeing Milada again, seeing the gypsies and remembering the life I led with them made me feel more certain that my decision was the right one."

"Things did not start well with you and me. I know that. We were not ready for a child, but soon we will be blessed with one. Believe me when I tell you that I want to be here for the child, to be here for you. Be patient with me" I begged, "please."

Dunia sat there, tears rolling down her cheeks. "Oh, Goran," she said, "I'm just so scared. I'm frightened of the birth; I'm afraid you will leave us or stay just because you feel you have to."

"Let's take things one step at a time," I said. I couldn't pretend to know how I would cope. I was staying because I felt it was my duty, but I couldn't admit to it now. I thought it would hurt her too much.

"For now, tonight, just rest here in my arms and know that, somehow, everything will be all right," I said, moving closer and gently threading my arm between the pillow and her neck.

We sat in the glow of the hearth fire with no sound but the crackling of the dying embers. I felt more at peace than I had in a long time and hoped that Dunia did, too.

When Yagoda and her mother came back and saw us, they moved quietly not to disturb Dunia who had nodded off into a peaceful sleep. Gently I moved my arm, got up from the bed and made my way out of the house.

I went to my room above the stable and found Milan already there getting ready for bed.

"Did you see her he asked?" when he saw my head pop up at the top of the ladder?

"Dunia?" I asked, still lost in my own thoughts.

"No," he said, "Milada, my daughter."

"Yes, I did," I said, "I told her you were here."

"And?"

"And she was ready to run and hide in the forest," I reported. The last thing I wanted to think about now was Milada.

"Did you tell her about Dunia and the child?" he went on.

"Yes," I murmured, extinguishing the lamp. This conversation would be easier without light.

"And?"

"And, what do you think! She was overjoyed?" My anger was back! I knew I shouldn't vent it on Milan, but his questioning brought back my pain and confusion.

"She wanted me back," I said, once I calmed myself.

"Will you go with her?" he asked quietly. "Will you go back to your life with the gypsies?"

"No," I told him, "it is my decision to stay here, follow my trade and be a good father to my child."

I didn't know if he would take the last comment personally, as a judgment on him for leaving Milada, but, frankly, at that moment I didn't care.

The room lay in silence for a while and then I thought I heard the sound of Milan crying.

"Milan," I whispered.

"I know it was wrong to leave my child," I heard him say; it seemed as if he was talking more to himself than to me. "If there were a way to make it up to her I surely would. I need to meet her; to see my child and hold her in my arms."

"Too much happened tonight," I told him. "It was a shock for her to learn that you were here and another shock that I would be father to her cousin's child. Let's go to the gypsy camp together, tomorrow. In the light of day things might be easier for us all.

Chapter 71 - A Reunion

"Goran, wake up', Milan said, rousing me from my from my dreamless slumber. "Let's go and find my daughter!"

The blacksmith had been up until late, drinking in the alehouse. With the holiday atmosphere at the gypsy's arrival I would not be expected at the forge early that day.

I wiped the sleep from my eyes, poured some cool water over my head to help me wake up and then accompanied Milan down the ladder and out into the ally.

"Do you know where the gypsies are camped?" he asked, taking long strides in the direction of the village square.

"I know where they camped last year," I told him. "They will probably be there again now. Let's go and see."

As we passed through the village gate I noticed Milan looking at its construction and shaking his head.

"What is it? " I asked him, matching his wide stride with my own.

"These fortifications will never stand up against an enemy attack," he said. "If those horsemen ever come this way your best chance it to hide yourselves in the forest."

"Run away, you mean?" I questioned. "What about our houses, our horses and our goods?"

"Bring the horses and livestock with you," he said. "It wouldn't be a bad idea to build some pens in the forest now, just in case."

"But what about our houses? Wouldn't it be better to stay and fight to protect them?"

"Believe me when I say that the horsemen are brutal," he said, seriously. "A house can be rebuilt but a life once taken is over forever."

By now I could see the smoke of the gypsies' cooking fires ahead of us.

"Look, over there. It's the camp". I told him, relieved to change the subject. Milan had caught me off guard this morning. I didn't have the chance to think how it would be to see Milada again after what transpired the previous night. Oh well, I would just play it by ear. I knew it was good that she and her father would meet. He was a good man; a kind man, unlike his rough brother. Once she met him, things would be fine. Of that I was convinced!

As I approached Milada's familiar wagon I felt a pulling in my heart. How many mornings I'd sat outside it, having brought a jug of warm water for the girls to wash their faces; waiting to see Milada as she emerged from the wagon to start her day.

We sat under an overhanging tree and waited. I remembered well that Milada was not an early riser so was pretty sure that she was still in the wagon. I hoped the wait would not be too long, since I had to make an appearance at the forge before the sun rose too high in the sky. I thought it better for me to make the introduction than to let her come across her long lost father alone.

Luckily, we didn't have long to wait. Pretty soon a sleepy-eyed Milada stepped out of the wagon, both her hands cradling a cup of morning tea. I called to her in the most cheerful tone I could muster.

"Good morning, Milada. Why did you run off like that last night! You missed all the dancing. That's not like you at all."

"Goran, it's you," she said looking over to where I was sitting. "I was not in the mood for dancing."

She looked at me and then, questioningly, at her father. We both stood up and walked toward her wagon.

I could see tears building up in Milan's eyes.

"Milada," I said gently, "come down and meet your father".

At my words, she nearly dropped the cup she held. She set it down on the wagon's seat and steadied herself, looking confused and afraid.

Milan took a tentative step toward her. He had such love in his eyes. I could tell that he wanted to rush to Milada an take her in his arms, but he sensed her fear and held himself back.

"Milada," he said, "I can't believe it's really you".

I hopped up on the wagon's bench and put my arm around Milada to give her courage, like the friend I always was, and always would be, if she let me.

"Don't be afraid, Milada," I told her. "Milan won't hurt you or try to make you stay. I've told him all about you and he just wanted to meet you."

Milada grasped my hand in hers and squeezed it tightly, taking courage from having me close by.

"You are my father?" she asked Milan, he voice trembling.

"Yes," he said, "I am."

"Why did you leave me," she asked.

Tears streamed down Milan's face as he answered her.

"I am so sorry, Milada," he said. "When your mother passed away my heart broke and I lost my reason. I loved your mother very much; everybody did. My brother had wanted to marry her, but she chose me even though I was the younger of the two of us. If my parents had lived, they would have insisted that he be wed first".

"What happened to your parents?" she asked, never having known anything about her family's history.

"They both perished in the sickness that came to the village when my brother and I were very young; the sickness that your gypsies helped us survive. I can remember one beautiful lady. She impressed me, even at my young age with her knowledge and her beauty. I even remember her name."

"What was it?" she asked. I felt her loosen her grip on my as she began to relax.

"Miriana," he replied. "Is she still among you?"

"She left us last summer," she said.

"Mother Miriana is gone?" I was shocked at that news. "I always liked the old thing, even if she didn't always approve of me!"

Milada turned to look at me," She thought you were fine," she said.

"How did she die? She couldn't have been all that old," I asked.

"She decided that it was time and just died," she said. "The gypsies say 'she died of death'".

"I think that the gypsies are very wise," Milan said. Milada smiled a little at his comment. I began to feel that things would be all right between them.

"Who took care of you and your brother? Did you live with the gypsies?" She now was sounding like the Milada I remembered; always full of questions!

"The gypsies came in time to save my grandparents. My brother and I went to live with them, in the house where you lived and where Goran lives now," he said.

"So my Grandma and Grandpa were your grandparents?" she asked.

"Yes," he replied, "they were very old, too old to care for a child like you".

"Tell her why you didn't leave her with your brother," I said. "Since he and his wife had Dunia who is not much older than Milada".

"My brother and I had never spoken after I married Anna, your mother. I was afraid he would mistreat my child out of anger and resentment towards me," he said.

"My mother was called 'Anna'?" Milada asked.

"Yes," my father replied, "that's why they called you Anna. But I think 'Milada' suits you better".

Now Milada's smile was real. She dropped my hand and took a step toward her father.

"Do I look like my mother?" she asked.

"You have her beautiful, wild hair," he said, "but your features resemble my mother".

"So do Dunia's. That's why you are so alike," I said without thinking. I could sense Milada's tension returning.

"Milada is much prettier that Dunia," her father said. "Sorry, Goran. I know you and she will wed, but just look at this girl!"

Thanks to Milan for saying just the right thing. Milada was beaming at his words and I felt this was the right time to take my leave and let the two of them have some time alone together.

"Are you all right with your father, Milada?" I asked, gently patting Milada's hand.

She looked at her father then back at me.

"Yes," she said, "I think I am".

"Then I will leave you," I told them, "I have work to do".

Milan winked at me as I hopped off the wagon. Somehow my feelings for Milada had mellowed over the course of the night. The rage I had felt the night before had shifted into a gentle sadness at our situation. I knew that I would always love Milada and want the best for her but, at least for now, I would have to put my thoughts of her aside.

Chapter 72 – A Child is Born

The blacksmith scowled at me when I entered the forge.

"Kind of you to come in today," he muttered. "Get over to the bellows; the fire needs to be hotter."

I hurried to the rear of the forge and started pumping the bellows with all my strength, hoping the blacksmith would not question my whereabouts, but I had no such luck.

"Off with those gypsies, were you?" he asked.

I pretended not her hear him and continued to pump the bellows until the roar of the fire covered the sound of his voice.

We worked in silence; sharpening the edges of hoes, shovels and ploughs; tools that had been dulled from preparing the earth for the spring planting. When the last piece was done, I raked the coals to cool the fire, wiped the sweat and dust off my face and hands and then followed the blacksmith back to the house for our midday meal.

"Did you take him to her?" the blacksmith growled as we made our way through the cobbled lanes to the house.

"Who?" I asked. My mind was focused on the coming meal. I hadn't had any breakfast and my stomach was rumbling in hunger.

"My brother; that girl," he muttered.

I could lie and pretend to know nothing about the meeting, but I figured he'd find out the truth soon enough.

"Yes," I told him, keeping my eyes on the stones in front of me. "I took him to meet her."

He did not respond. We had reached the house. I pushed open the door and was happy to see that the food was already on the table. Yagoda was stirring the stew pot and didn't greet us when we entered. At first I could not see the girls' mother.

As my eyes adjusted from the sunny street to the dimness inside the house I spotted her sitting on a low stool beside Dunia's cot. I went over to them and heard Dunia moaning. There were tears in her mother's eyes.

"What's the matter?" I asked her. "Is there something wrong?"

"Dunia is in pain," her mother whispered. I could see great sadness in her eyes.

I looked at Dunia and almost didn't recognize her. Her skin was very pale, her forehead pinched, her narrow shoulders writhing in pain. I saw a pool of water on the floor beside the bed. Some rags had been placed there to soak it up but not enough to do the job.

Dunia's mother followed my gaze.

"Her waters broke; it means the baby is coming," she said.

"But isn't it too soon?" I asked, "She said it would be at least another moon before her time."

"Sometimes a baby comes too soon," the woman whispered. "The midwife was here earlier, she said the baby was not in the birthing position. She didn't know what to do to help. She told us that she will be back, but I think she is afraid. If Dunia or the baby die, God forbid, she knows my husband will blame her and want vengeance.

"So she will leave them to die on their own?" I asked. "Isn't that the same thing?"

"No one taught us what to do when there is a problem with a birth. The midwife can help when all happens in its time, but the woman who held the knowledge of healing for this village was taken many years ago in the great sickness before she could pass down her skills."

"The gypsies have those skills!" I have heard many a story about them assisting at difficult births," I told her. "We are lucky that they are her. I will go and bring Zora, now."

Dunia mother looked down at her stricken daughter and then over at the blacksmith who was already eating the stew.

"I will not have gypsies in my house," he said.

"Dunia cannot be moved," his wife said, with tears in her eyes. "Please don't let our child die."

"How do we know this gypsy can help?" he grumbled.

"It is the best chance we have," she said.

There was no time for discussion. "I'm going to get Zora. The life of my child as well as yours is at stake."

I ran out of the house, to the village gate and the gypsies' camp beyond. As I ran, thoughts ran through my head. If Dunia and the baby were to die, I would be free to be with Milada. Yet, I hated myself for thinking that. Seeing Dunia in pain, imagining that our child might never be born, I realized how much I wanted to do this; to be a father to that child and try to make a life with its mother, here in this village.

I kept running, pushing aside low bushes that blocked my path. I reached the clearing where Milada's wagon stood and was relieved to see that she and her father were still there. There was a little girl I didn't remember and a huge black dog. I hoped that Zora would be close by.

They all turned to look at me, but when I tried to speak I couldn't. I needed to catch my breath after my long sprint, my heart pounding.

"What is it Goran? Milada asked. "What is the matter?"

"It's Dunia," I sputtered, "The baby is coming!"

"But it is not her time for some weeks," she said.

"Yes, that is what I was told. But she is in great pain and her waters have broken," I told her. "Is there someone here who can help her; Zora? The village midwife said that the baby is not in its correct position and she doesn't know what to do to help Dunia."

"Adela," Milada said to the girl with the dark curls, "do you know where Zora is?"

"I saw her this morning going out of the camp with the boy from the Band of the North. They had a big basket with them. They probably went for a picnic," she said.

I was beginning to panic.

"You don't have time to look for them," I said. "Can someone else help? Can you help us, Milada?"

"I have helped with birthing," she said, "I will come and do whatever I can".

She disappeared into her wagon. I was surprised at her offer to come herself. The night before, she was hiding from the blacksmith. Now she would come to his house. The night before she was hurt by the thought that I betrayed my love for her by lying with Dunia, yet she was prepared to come and help give birth to our child.

She emerged from her wagon, carrying some bags and bundles of dried herbs. Her father's voice interrupted my thoughts.

"Goran, run back to be with Dunia and tell her that we are coming," he said.

I nodded and took my leave, hoping that Milada would not be too long behind me.

On my way back to the house I saw the blacksmith entering the alehouse. I didn't stop to ask him how his daughter was, I just kept running.

Before I even opened the door I heard Dunia's screams. The sound wrenched my heart.

I went over to her and tried to take her hand as she thrashed on the bed but she pushed me away. After a moment, she calmed down.

"That pain has passed now," her mother said, "but it won't be long before another one comes. Is someone coming to help her?"

"Milada is coming," I said, quietly.

"Anna?" Dunia's mother asked.

"There was no one else," I told her.

Before I could say anything else, Dunia's body shuddered and she started to scream again.

I saw Yagoda go to the door. When she opened it, Milada came in, followed by her father and the little girl. Milada gave the herbs to the girls and whispered some instructions, indicating the kettle by the hearth and then joined me at Dunia's side. Her pain had subsided once again; she lay catching her breath.

"Hello, Dunia," Milada said, gently taking her limp hand.

"Milada," she said, "you are back."

"Lucky for us that the gypsies are here now," I told her, trying to sound positive. "They will know what to do".

"So why didn't they come? Why send Milada?" Dunia asked, turning away from Milada.

Milan came over and placed his hand on his daughter's shoulder.

"Milada knows what to do," he said. "Rest now while you can and be thankful for her help."

"When was the baby expected?" Milada asked.

"Not for another turn of the moon," I said.

"And when did the pains start?"

"About an hour ago," I told her.

Dunia convulsed and screamed in pain.

"Get this out of me. I want to die!" she yelled.

Milada called to the young girl to bring a cloth soaked in cool water. She placed it on Dunia's brow, resting her hand on her forehead.

"Don't say such things, Dunia," Milada said softly, when the pain had passed. "The child will hear you. Welcome this child, yours and Goran's child, with love".

"But it hurts so much," Dunia moaned.

The girl brought over a mug of the warm herbal tea and handed it to Milada while Yagoda watched from her place at the table.

"Have a sip of this," she told Dunia, "It will help you to relax. Try to flow with the spasms in your body rather than fight them. Giving birth is a natural process, let it happen".

Dunia sipped the tea than looked Milada in the eye. "You are doing this for Goran," she said, "I know you love him".

Milada took a deep breath then said, "I am here because Goran asked me to help you. If you would like me to go, I will."

"No, Milada," I said. "You must help us".

"Be quiet now," I couldn't help adding to Dunia. "Milada is here to help. We need her."

Dunia opened her mouth to speak but before she could another burst of pain came over her, her face contorting in pain and terror.

Milada took something out of her pocket and pressed it into Dunia's hand.

"Hold this," she her, "and keep breathing."

I watched as Dunia took deep and even breaths; she calmed down and looked less frightened. When Milada changed the cloth on her forehead, she opened her eyes and smiled until the next pain came.

Milada had her hand on Dunia's belly. I saw a shadow pass across her face. She took a deep breath then, using both hands, pressed down and forward. Dunia cried out as I saw the bulge in her belly shudder.

"Breathe, Dunia," Milada murmured. "Your baby is moving into place. Let's do that one more time. Inhale and now exhale."

When Dunia breathed out, Milada, pushed again, then lightly rested both her palms on Dunia's belly and kept them there, her eyes closed. Her breathing, deep and steady, had a calming effect on us all.

After the next strong pain had passed, Milada put her hand behind Dunia's back and helped her sit on the edge of the cot and, from there, onto a low stool. She instructed Dunia to put both feet flat on the floor and had me push the straw-filled mat down to cushion her back.

Milada rocked slowly back and forth, and told Dunia, "Let mother earth call the baby to herself. Push with your feet on the earth, breathe and let the baby come".

"Put your hands on your knees and when the pain starts again, push!" she said.

Dunia's mother and I moved away in silence. We watched as Dunia pushed at Milada's suggestion and listened to her deep, rhythmic breathing. Milada moved closed to Dunia and all I could see was the top of her head and familiar wild curls. Lost in thought, I was brought back to the present by the sound of the new-born's cry.

Dunia relaxed back onto the mat as Milada cradled the tiny child. I watched as she gently wiped our baby and then passed it over to its mother.

"Hold her close to your breast," Milada said, "and tell her how much you love her".

'Her'! My baby was a girl! Somehow I always pictured the child as a boy; as my son!

"Is she alright?" Dunia asked as she reached out her arms to take the baby.

"She looks beautiful," Milada said. She and the girl busied themselves cleaning up the mess from the birth. I put the mat back on the cot and helped Dunia settle onto it. Soon she was fast asleep with the child curled on her breast. My child.

Dunia's mother thanked Milada for her help, but Yagoda just glared at her, without saying a word.

I went over to Milada and took her hand. "I don't know how to thank you," I said. "Let me walk you back to your wagon."

"No, she said. "Your place is here with Dunia and your child. Be here when she awakens. I will return later to see how they are doing."

As I watched her leave, the little girl with dark curls trailing behind her, I couldn't help thinking that, in spite of her wild ways, she was a knowledgeable young woman, capable of alleviating pain and even saving lives. Milada. My Milada.

Chapter 73 – Celebrations!

"I think we could all use a drink," Milan said, rousing me from my reverie. I saw him take a flask from his pack. "The finest plum brandy for this very special occasion," he said, patting me on the back, a big smile on his face.

"We'll make it a quiet celebration, not to wake the new mother and babe," he said as he poured the clear liquor into the beakers that Dunia's mother had placed on the table. She did not speak, but I could see both joy and relief on her face.

I hadn't noticed that Dunia's father had returned from the alehouse. He picked up his beaker, glanced over to where his daughter slept, looked at me and shook his head. I heard him mutter to himself, "I guess, she could have done worse."

"Let's drink to the health of the new baby" Milan said, "and to my own little girl, newly found, who helped her into this world."

The strong spirit burned my throat as it slid down. I thought of how lucky we were that Milada had come to help, with no thought of her own safety. I saw with my own eyes how she pushed the baby into place and shuddered to think of Dunia's peril.

Before I knew it, Milan had filled my glass again. I did not want to go back to the forge with the blacksmith, who was already on his feet, moving toward the door. There was nothing I could do for Dunia, but I wanted to stay near her and our child. I felt very comfortable with Milan; I enjoyed his company and we drank companionably together as the spring afternoon light faded to the golden glow of evening.

I heard a cat mewing by the fire, then realized that it was the baby! Dunia opened her sleepy eyes and, very naturally, opened her blouse to let the baby suckle at her breast. I couldn't help smiling, seeing the contentment on her face; so changed from the morning when it had been drawn in pain and fear.

Soon it grew dark. I watched as Milan lit a small candle and placed it on the stone windowsill.

"What are you doing?" I asked him.

"It's for Milada," he said. "She told me that her grandfather promised to leave a candle burning in the window to guide her home."

"I wonder if she will come back" Dunia said.

"She said that she would," I told her, "and she will."

I heard someone at the door and thought that it would be Milada. My heart dropped when I saw that it was the blacksmith. He came in unsteadily; he must have been in the tavern celebrating on his own.

"Where's my food?" he demanded.

Yagoda was at the hearth. She lifted the lid off the iron pot and the room filled with the aroma of a savory stew.

"Take your seat," Dunia's mother said. "The food is ready."

As she was ladling the stew into our wooden bowls, there was a knock at the door.

"Get the door, Yagoda," her mother said.

Yagoda, dragged herself up from the table, taking her time to get to the oaken door. When she pulled it open, I could see Milada standing outside.

"Oh, you are back. I wasn't sure you would come again," Yagoda said. "My father is home now".

"Good evening, Yagoda," Milada said, ignoring her rudeness. "How are Dunia and the baby?"

"See for yourself," she said, letting the door swing closed. Milada caught it before it could hit her and tentatively set foot into the room. When her eyes met Milan's, I saw her relax. He got up and wrapped his arms around her.

"Milada, my girl, welcome," he said. "Come and join us for supper".

"Thank you," she said with a smile. "Let me check on Dunia and the baby and then I will join you. I haven't eaten at all today."

Dunia's mother brought another wooden bowl and spoon.

"You are welcome, Milada," she said quietly. "Thank you for your help today".

Milada went over to look at Dunia and the baby.

"Isn't she beautiful?" Dunia said, with a shy smile.

"Yes, she is," Milada replied. "What will you call her?"

"It is the custom to call the first born girl after the father's mother," she said.

Without thinking I interrupted their conversation. "I don't want to call her after my mother! She had a hard life, and a short one. I want a better life for our girl," I told them.

"You can call her 'Milada' since Milada helped her get born," Yagoda sneered.

I felt like slapping the girl, but before I could react, Milada made a suggestion.

"What about calling her after your mother?" she said to Dunia.

"Gahla," said Dunia, looking at her daughter. "Do you like that name?"

The baby opened her eyes and looked at her as if to say yes.

"We'll call her Gahla then, after you, mother; if that is all right with you, dear," she added, looking at me for the first time since the baby's birth. And she called me "dear"!

I liked the idea of called the baby after Dunia's mother. "'Gahla' it is!" I exclaimed, "Let's drink a toast to Gahla!"

One more toast couldn't hurt, I thought, as I splashed another shot of plum brandy into my beaker, then raised it for a toast.

"To my daughter, Gahla, my father-in-law who has taught me his trade, to my mother-in-law who feeds me and to Dunia who will soon be my wife!"

Milan offered Milada a drink. My cheeks reddened when I realized that I didn't think to do so.

She accepted, telling him, "Yes, a small one, please, to toast the health and happiness of this family and to celebrate meeting you!"

Milan said, "This toast is for Milada. I am so happy to have met you at last. Thank you for your help today and may you be happy always!"

As we drank again I noticed that Milada was avoiding the blacksmith eyes. I could see her relief when he pushed his empty plate away.

"I'm going to the tavern," he said. "This place smells like a baby. It is not place for a man. Goran, are you coming?"

I did not want to go with him. I wanted to stay here with Milada and her father, with Dunia and our child, but I could see anger brewing in the blacksmith eyes. Milada was looking at me, as if waiting to see what I would do.

"Well, are you coming with me or staying with the women?" he growled.

I felt I had no choice. "I'm coming," I said, putting on my cloak and following the man out the door.

It was not cold outside, but I felt a chill leaving the warmth of the family table. I did not look forward to spending the next few hours listening to the blacksmith's rantings. Luckily, when we got to the tavern I saw Jelko and Misha sitting in the corner. The blacksmith settled in his usual place and began a grumbled conversation with the owner of the tavern and I went to join my friends.

"Hey, Goran!" Jelko said, "We figured you'd be off with the gypsies tonight; sitting by the fire with your old girlfriend!"

"My 'old girlfriend' is at home with my almost wife!" I told them, "and with my new baby girl! Let me buy you a drink to celebrate!"

They both whooped and clapped me on the back.

"Goran's a daddy now!" Jelko said.

"You have a girl? Too bad," Misha added.

"What do you mean, 'too bad'?" Jelko said. "A girl is the best. When she grows up a little she will learn how to cook! And Daddy will always be well-fed."

"But you can teach a boy to hunt and fish with you," Misha said.

"I'll teach my Gahla to fish!" I said, "Why not!"

"And to play bones and to spend time with the little boys," Jelko interjected, "And pretty soon you will be a grandfather! Mark my words, my boy!"

"Maybe your baby will be a girl, too!" Misha said, elbowing Jelko.

"Your baby?" I said in surprise. "Is Janka with child?"

"I thought you knew!" he said. "Didn't Dunia tell you?"

"We don't speak much these days," I said, wondering if the fault were mine.

"And you won't now, with the baby come. That's all she will think about!" Misha said.

"To babies," Jelko said, raising his beaker, "and their mothers!"

I spent a pleasant evening with my friends and somehow found my way back to the stable. I woke up the next morning lying in the straw with a drum playing in my head; and then remembered. I was a father!

Chapter 74 - Milan's News

I didn't see much of Milada in the days that followed. She came to the house every morning to check on Dunia and the baby, but I was busy then with my work at the forge. By the time I came home she had gone. I was amazed at how quickly baby Gahla grew. Day by day, her cheeks rounded and took on a rosy glow. Dunia seemed to blossom, too. Her mother and Yagoda performed her usual tasks, allowing her time to sleep when the baby did.

Often Jelko's girl, Janka, was there, keeping Dunia company. She told me that she was learning some of the gypsies' healing secrets. I thought of Milada being here in the house with them and couldn't help wondering how our life together might have been. I quickly banished such thoughts as useless and instead focused my attention on my darling baby.

Sometimes when I arrived for the mid-day meal I found Dunia sitting by the window concentrating on the intricate needlework that she enjoyed and prided herself on, humming softly with a relaxed and contented expression on her face. But when I approached her, her eyes hardened and her voice fell silent. I wanted to bridge the space between us, but I didn't know how. I figured that when she was ready she would let me know.

She and the child still slept in the house. It was warmer there and easier to care for the baby than having to climb up and down the ladder to the room over the stable. Milan had left to make a circuit of the neighboring villages to trade some of the goods he'd brought from the coast. I felt a little lonely, missing his company. Often our conversations had lasted late into the night. I liked listening to the tales of his travels, but I had no desire to leave the village I'd decided to make my home.

One morning while on my way to the forge, I heard some men in front of the tavern yelling in heated argument. Approaching them to see what was going on I noticed that Milan was back and deep into the fray. I had never heard him raise his voice before. It seemed as if he was trying to convince the men of something.

"Believe me," he said. "I've seen it with my own eyes."

"It cannot be as you say!" one man yelled. "I won't leave my house and land."

"If you don't leave you may lose more than your possessions!" Milan exclaimed.

"We will stay and fight; not run off like cowards," a third man said. "You have no house, no roots here anymore. So how can you know how it feels to lose them?"

"What's going on?" I asked.

The man who spoke turned to me and said, "This man says we may be in danger, but, me, I don't believe it."

"Milan, it's good to see you're back!" I said, slapping his back fondly. "Why do you think we are in danger?"

"I don't *think* we are in danger," he said, "I *know* we are."

"What kind of danger?" I asked him.

"I hate to say what I saw in villages not three days ride from here," he said, dropping his voice as some young girls scurried toward the fountain in the center of the square.

"Tell us," one of the men insisted.

"I'll tell you this," Milan continued, "You don't want to be here when the horsemen come! Many armed men ride into a village demanding food and money. If they don't get what they want they kill the people, take whatever they find of value and burn the rest."

"We can fight them off, I tell you!" a man exclaimed.

"You can try, but untrained farmers with hoes and shovels are no match for their experience and their weapons."

Just then I felt a strong hand clap my back.

"What are you doing dawdling here, boy?" It was the blacksmith.

"Come on," he said, "There's plenty of work to be done."

I glanced questioningly at Milan then followed the blacksmith to the forge.

"You should have had the fire glowing by now," he growled, "instead of wasting your time gossiping like a woman in the square.

"Yes, sir," I muttered as I stoked the fire.

Once he had calmed down I said, "Milan's returned."

"So I saw," he grunted.

"He was telling those men that he thinks the village might be in danger," I told him.

"Danger? How?"

"He said that armed men on horseback raided some villages not far from here," I reported.

"We'll fight them off," the blacksmith said as he hammered a slab of red hot iron.

"It will be good for business," he added. "Good, let the men talk. I'll bring it up later in the tavern. Everyone will want swords and knives. We can start making them today."

"I don't know how to use a sword or a knife," I said.

"What's to know? Just stick it in wherever you can," he said. "No one can get through our city walls, anyway," he said, "but we don't want people to remember that; then they'll think they won't need swords."

We spent the rest of the day working in silence; making long and short blades that we wouldn't know how to use in case of an attack. I couldn't help imagining an army on horseback storming the village defences and breaking down the door of our house. How could I protect Dunia and the baby? I saw myself wielding a bright new sword, lopping of arms and heads of the enemy to keep my family safe. But then, as the day wore on, I realized that I did not know how to fight. Yes, my arms were strong from my work at the forge but I had no skill with any kind of weapon.

I planned to ask Milan about what he had seen when I returned home at the end of the day, but as soon as I walked in the door Yagoda exclaimed, "The gypsies are gone!"

"The gypsies left?" I asked. I had planned to go again to their camp and see my old friends but somehow, I had never made the time.

"Yes," she said, "and Milada went with them."

"She told me to say "goodbye" to you," Dunia said quietly.

"Will you and the baby be all right without her help?" I asked.

"Yes," she said. "We are fine. Gahla is growing well and Janka has learned so many things about herbs that can help us if we start to feel unwell. You know, I came to like Milada and can see now why you were good friends."

Her words came as a surprise.

"She told me that you belong here with us now," she added.

"Yes," I replied. It's my responsibility to keep you both safe and sound."

"What about me?" piped Yagoda. "Will you keep my safe and sound, too?"

I sighed and said, "Yes, Yagoda. I'll keep you safe and sound, too."

I looked around to see if Milan was there. I saw him sitting and staring pensively into the fire. The blacksmith burst through the door demanding his evening meal and I decided that it would be better to wait and speak with him later in the privacy of the room above the stable.

Chapter 75 - Preparing for Trouble

The blacksmith was in an unusually good mood as he sat down to eat.

"What did I tell you, boy," he said between mouthfuls of sausage.

I must have looked puzzled. He continued.

"About the swords and knives! The few men who have swords want them sharpened and many others have asked me to make them some. We will be busy tomorrow, boy. Be at the forge at daybreak."

I nodded, and then glanced at Milan, wondering if he would speak. He kept his eyes lowered to his food and remained silent. As soon as the blacksmith finished eating he got up and put on his coat.

"I'm going back to the tavern," he said. "To remind people of the danger and pick up a few more orders. Milan said the horsemen were near so there won't be much time. The people who pay the most will get their swords first. Some men have even offered me gold!"

As he pulled the door shut he looked at me and said, "Tomorrow morning. Don't be late!"

"What did he mean about 'swords and knives'? Dunia asked as she picked Gahla up and held her to her breast.

I looked at Milan wondering how much we should say.

"What is it?" Dunia said, looking up at me through her long lashes.

"I don't want to alarm you," I said, "but we may be in danger."

"What kind of danger?" Yagoda asked. "Are people going to fight each other with swords?"

"It was something Milan saw on his travels," I said.

"Tell us, Brother," Dunia's mother said. "We need to know so that we can prepare."

"I saw some villages after," Milan said with a sigh.

"After what?" Yagoda demanded to know, "After what?"

"After an attack by a band of armed men," Milan said.

The girls and their mother gasped.

"What happened in the villages?" Dunia asked quietly.

"I did not see the horsemen," Milan continued, "but I saw walls demolished; houses burnt to the ground fields scorched; people lying dead with no one to bury them."

"Many men in our village, including your father, think that we can fight off any invaders," I told them.

"I know that we cannot," Milan said, his head in his hands.

"What can we do?" Yagoda asked, "Just sit and let them come and get us? We need to fight!"

"If we stay and fight we will die," Milan said. "I told them we should flee. We could find safely in the forest but your father wouldn't hear of it."

"Thank you for telling us," Dunia's mother said. "I will prepare some supplies in case we need to leave. Hopefully, it will not come to that, but it's better to be ready in case."

"Better not mention it to the blacksmith," I said knowing that he would be angry.

I went over to where Dunia and baby sat. I kissed little Gahla's forehead and then, without thinking, kissed Dunia's as well. She didn't flinch or pull away.

"I'll do all I can to protect you," I whispered then followed Milan out the door and up to the room we shared.

"I heard that the gypsies left today. Some of them men think that they are cowards; running away from a possible threat. Do you think that's why they left?" I asked him when we were both settled in our beds, then added, "Did you get to say goodbye to Milada?"

"I think they were planning to leave anyway," he said. "I saw Milada and bade her farewell. I hope that our paths will cross again someday."

"Is there anything we can do to prepare for a possible attack?" I asked him. "We can't just hide in the forest and wait."

"I spoke with the gypsies' Baron," Milan said.

"You met the Baron?" I asked.

"Yes," Milan replied, "and his son and the son's lovely wife."

Dragan and Tanya; my old friends. The days with the gypsies seemed a lifetime away.

"I told him about Tonsho's birds."

"You mean those smart pigeons that always return to his loft from where ever he takes them?" I asked.

"Yes," Milan replied. "We gave some to the Baron. If the gypsy band comes across any sign of the invaders they will send us a diagram tied to the bird's leg showing where they were."

"How will we understand it?" I wondered aloud.

"The Baron came up with a brilliant idea. He will make a circle to represent our village and add a mark to show the place - north, south, east or west and the distance from the village."

"So one of those birds may give us a warning," I said, thinking that old Tonsho's attention to his birds was not so fanciful after all.

After several minutes of silence I asked Milan, "Will you stay and fight?"

"No, my boy" he replied. "I am not a fighter. I will also take some of Tonsho's birds and travel south. I can easily hide myself if I see danger and send a message back here.

"I don't know how to fight," I said, "but I need to protect Dunia and the baby. Our village walls are very thick. We won't have to fight if the walls hold," I told him.

"Gogo, I've seen villages with walls twice as strong as ours laid to waste. The best thing you can do is to find somewhere safe in the forest to hide," Milan advised. "It seems the invaders are passing through the area, taking whatever they can and then moving on."

"But what if they destroy our village?" I asked.

"If they destroy the village you can rebuild it. If they take your life it won't matter if the village is there or not."

I could see the sense in his words, but the idea of running away was not appealing. Surely we could hold off an enemy, protect our homes and not hide in the forest like cowards.

The next morning I woke as the first rays of light were coming through my window. No time for breakfast! I splashed my face with water and hurried to the forge to start the fire so it would be good and hot before the blacksmith arrived. Luckily, all was ready when he did. He was in an unusually good mood.

"Here, boy," he said, tossing me a chunk of bread and some cheese. "I see the fire is ready. Have a bite and let's get started; we have a full day's work ahead of us."

We toiled all day, not even taking a break for the midday meal. While I worked I thought about places I knew in the forest that might provide safety for Dunia and the baby. When the sun was low in the sky, turning the dust particles in air into a thousand tiny points of golden light I heard the door of the forge groan open.

It was Milan. I could see his cart piled high with trading goods and, strapped on the back of it, a wicker cage holding several cooing pigeons.

"What do you want," the blacksmith growled. "We have work to finish before we lose the light."

"I've come to tell you that I am going," Milan said, looking at me rather than his brother.

"So you're running away," the blacksmith said. "I am not surprised. I've always known you are a coward. Off with you, then."

I waved at Milan and he nodded at me; leaving without another word. I would miss this man I'd come to love as the father I never knew. I hoped that fate would allow us to meet again.

Chapter 76 - Danger is Upon Us

The next day I was back at the forge at the crack of dawn, pondering Milan's words as I kept the fire red hot. I thought about Tonsho's pigeons, wondering if we would get a message soon enough to hide. Should we run away or should we stay and fight? I wondered what Jelko would do. Janka was with child; surely it would be safer for the women to go to the forest. But if there was no threat, if the horsemen were going in a different direction, why should they have to suffer in the woods instead of being comfortable in their homes?

I knew better that to speak with the blacksmith. He would not consider sending the women away. He was confident that we would be able to fight off any threat. It had been a long time since anyone had attacked the village or any of the villages in the area. From the very old men I had heard tales of wars and pillage, but they always seemed more like bygone legends than true history. The people of the countryside had lived in peace and prosperity for so long that our men had never learned how to defend themselves. There was the occasional brawl bred of jealousy or insult but nothing more serious than that for as long as most people could remember.

I was jarred out of my thoughts by a clatter on the cobbled street outside the forge. The door burst open and, breathlessly, Jelko exclaimed, "They are coming! They are coming!"

Before I could ask what he meant or what we should do he had disappeared down the road. I heard other doors being pushed open and his excited cries of warning. I looked expectantly at the blacksmith. He threw down his hammer and went to the back of the forge. From under a pile of straw he drew two long swords.

"Here, boy," he said, handing me the shorter of the two. "I saved the best ones for us. No one will get into our house or threaten our women. Come on!"

I felt the weight of the sword in my two hands. Could I use it? Could I kill another person with this piece of iron? If my life was threatened, or Dunia's or our baby's, I thought I could. The blacksmith was already out the door. He held a large brass key.

"Come on, boy," he shouted. "What are you waiting for? Douse the fire and let's get out of here."

I lay down the sword then quickly put out the fire. Taking up the weapon I rushed to the door. I'd never known the blacksmith to lock the forge before. I watched as he turned the big key in its lock.

In the street, people were running this way and that. Women rushed about carrying baskets and bundles while men armed which whatever they could find: swords, picks, axes, shovels and knives headed toward the village square. I followed the blacksmith in that direction even though my instinct was telling me to go home and get the women and my baby into the forest and out of harm's way. Once the village gate was secured I knew that it would be difficult for them to leave.

It was chaos in the square. There was no one in charge; no leader to direct the men and their makeshift weapons. Our village headman was an old man with no experience of directing a battle. Finally, one of the younger men climbed up the side of the fountain and commanded everyone's attention. I saw that it was Boban. He was known and respected for his skill and bravery in hunting wild boar.

"Hear me! Hear me, men!" he shouted. The noise of the crowd quieted to a rumble as the men gathered around the fountain. "The horsemen have been spotted on the other side of the hill, less than half a day's ride from here."

"Are they coming this way?" someone shouted.

"We don't know yet, but Misha and Stanyo are observing their movements from the top of the hill. If the horsemen start to come this way they will rush back and let us know."

"So what do we do now?" another man called out.

"We ready ourselves!" Boban said. "Go home and hide your women and your valuables. Provide yourself with a weapon and come back here as soon as you can."

I saw men mobbing the blacksmith; offering him coins of gold and silver, offing their best horses for a good knife or sword. I made my way back to the house, determined to get my child and her mother out of the village, just in case the horsemen came.

When I reached the house I saw that the women were busy packing baskets with food and with the items that they valued most.

Dunia was at the cedar wood trunk taking out her embroidered bedclothes, aprons and vests. I looked around for baby Gahla and saw her wrapped in a warm rabbit skin, fast asleep in a basket.

"Gogo!" Dunia exclaimed when she saw that I was home. "What's happening?"

"The horsemen have been spotted nearby," I told her. "We don't know yet if they will come this way."

"What should we do?" she asked, "shall we hide in the pantry? I think we can lock the door from the inside."

"If the men come it won't be safe anywhere in the house," I told her. "I think it's best to hide in the forest, there where the gypsies had their camp."

The door banged open and the blacksmith bellowed. "They are coming this way! Where is Goran? "

"I'm here," I said.

"Come and fight!" he yelled. "You women get in the pantry and wait for us there."

"No!" I yelled defiantly. I am taking them to the forest. It is not safe for them to stay here."

"You will do as I say," the blacksmith bellowed.

"Here, take this sword," I yelled, thrusting its hilt into his hands. I don't know how to use it! There are plenty of men who will pay you well for it."

I knew his greed would prevail. He took the sword and said "Go then with the women, you coward."

On his way out he pushed Dunia away from the trunk. "Don't waste your energy carrying useless things. Better take the keg of ale than these rags. If you are going, go now. I will lock the door."

He stood aside as Dunia grabbed some blankets and went out the door, looking back at her beautiful work with tears in her eyes. Her mother followed carrying a basket of food. I took up my sleeping baby and Yagoda followed.

"Go; go with the women, I always knew you had no guts," the blacksmith muttered to me, as he locked the heavy oaken door. From what Milan had told me I knew that a locked door would not stop the invaders. "At least I'll get a very good price for this sword," he muttered.

345

I just shook my head and hurried down the road with my precious bundle. I knew in my heart that my course of action was right.

Chapter 77 - In Hiding

I hurried the women through the village square. Men were collecting there in small groups.

"Hey, Gogo!" Someone called.

I looked around and saw that it was Jelko. With him were his sister, Janka, her younger brother and two older women who probably were their mothers.

"Are you bringing the women to the woods?" he asked, coming up beside me.

"Yes," I said. "It's not safe for them here."

"Can Janka and the others go with you?" he asked.

"Of course," I told him. "Will you stay and fight?"

"I feel I must," he said. I wondered if he thought, like the blacksmith, that I was a coward.

"I will come back once I know the women are safe," I said.

"I would feel better if you stayed with them," he said, "just in case the horsemen come across them in the forest."

I didn't know what I would be able to in that case, one unarmed man trying to protect a group of women and children.

"They'll feel more confident with you there," Jelko added when he saw my hesitation. "Go now, before the gate is secured."

I nodded at him and led my growing flock toward the village walls. The number of women and children increased as we left the square. I guess they saw us and figured that it was a chance to be out of harm's way.

Jelko came with us as far as the gate, then kissed Janka tenderly and said, "Don't be afraid! The danger will pass and we will be together by nightfall."

When the last of the women had gone through the gate, Jelko and some other men pushed it shut. I heard the heavy iron bar bolted into place and felt a pang of doubt. What if the walls held? Maybe the horsemen would comb the forest looking for outlying homes or farms to raid. What if it would be safer for Dunia and baby at home behind stone walls? And now I felt responsible for Jelko's girl, their family and the others who had joined us in our flight.

But this was not the time for doubts. I knew where I wanted to go. I remembered the place deep in the forest, near the rock pool where I swam; first with the gypsy boys and later with Dunia. The path there was narrow and the new spring growth would make it difficult to spot for anyone who didn't know its location. As soon as we reached the cover of the woods I gathered the women around me. Some looked very frightened, clutching baskets, bundles and the hands of their children. I saw Janka, her pregnancy now obvious, comforting some of the others. Dunia reached out for baby Gahla while I addressed the group.

"Don't worry!" I assured them, with more confidence in my voice than I actually felt. "We will be safe here in the woods. As we go, step lightly. We don't want to leave a trail for anyone to find. Keep as quiet as you can and follow me!"

They did as I directed and before long we were at the place of the gypsy's camp. Visions of my days spent there with Milada and the gypsy band flashed before my eyes. I hoped that they were all safe and sound somewhere beyond the reach of the marauding invaders.

I looked around, trying to remember the way to the pool. Everything looked different than it had in the autumn, with new thick growth of grass and nettles.

"Is this where we will stop?" one of the women asked.

"No," I said, "I'd like to take you deeper into the woods."

"But we've never been in this far!" Jelko's sister whimpered. It isn't safe in the wood!"

"It's safer here than in the village," Dunia said. "Goran knows what he is doing. Follow him."

Just then one of the small children began to wail. "It hurts! It itches!" he moaned.

I looked over at the child and saw a rash on his arms. Immediately, Janka went to him.

"Did you touch those tall plants over there?" she asked, squatting down beside him to have a better look at the developing rash.

He just nodded, tears running down his cheeks.

Janka stood up and picked a plant with flat roundish leaves. She went back to the boy and gently rubbed his arm with them. Immediately, the rash began to disappear.

Some of the women started mumbling about "the gypsy's magic". Janka picked some more of the leaves and said to the women, "Look here! When someone is stung by those nettles," she indicated the tall bright green plants on the side of the clearing, "use these dock leaves to counteract the rash. There is no magic here, just nature offering us a remedy. Wherever you find the nettles you will find dock leaves nearby."

I grabbed a thick stick and used it to push aside the nettles that blocked the way to the pool and then led the group down the narrow path. Once they were assembled near the stream I went back and swept the ground with an oak branch erasing our footprints from the soil of the clearing. When I returned, the women had settled themselves and their children along the top of the riverbank a little ways back into the forest. It would be difficult to see them there if they kept still.

I sat beside Dunia. Gahla was suckling greedily at her breast. Her mother sat beside her, looking dazed and her sister was off with her friends, treating the situation more like a picnic than a life and death crisis.

"How long do you think we will have to stay here?" Dunia asked quietly.

Not too long, I hope," I replied. "I will go back to the edge of the forest where I can see the village walls. I'll keep watch from there and let you know when it is safe to return. Will you and the baby be all right here?"

"I think so," she replied. "It seems that we have all brought some food; at least enough for today. The weather is mild; the other women are worried, though, about their men."

"Their men are happier knowing that they are safe in the forest," I told her. "Stay safe. I'll be back when I can."

I got up and ran back to the clearing by a different path. When I got there something felt wrong. Then I realized. It was the smell of a fire; it was so familiar there in the clearing, bringing back memories of feasting with the gypsies; memories of evenings sitting with Milada, looking at the stars and talking for hours. Tears came to my eyes remembering how much I missed her; hoping she was safe; wishing we could have made a life together. But this was no gypsy campfire!

Carefully, moving from tree to tree I came to a place where I could see the village walls. A dense cloud of dark gray smoke rose from beyond the open gate. The walls had been breached! I waited and watched in horror as villagers, women and men alike, ran from the gate, ducking into the thick woods on the opposite hillside. I hoped that none would come this way and lead the invaders toward the place where the women hid. The smell worsened and as the sun set an eerie red glow appeared in the sky above the village. Should I go back to the women? What could I tell them? But if I did not return they might panic.

I turned my face from the tragic scene, wondering if the blacksmith still lived. As I made my way back to the stream I thought of my friend Jelko and the other boys, Misha and Stanyo who had been keeping watch. What of the brave Boban? Did they stay and fight or had they escaped into the woods? I found the women huddled together for warmth, Dunia and the baby among them.

"They wanted to make a fire to cook on and to keep us warm," Janka said, coming up to us, "but I stopped them. If the horsemen were around they might see the smoke."

"You were right," I told her. "We need to keep our location a secret."

I felt someone pull on my shirtsleeve. I looked down and saw a head of unruly curls. Milada?

"Can we go home yet?" Yagoda whined, bringing me back to reality.

"No, Yagoda," I said. "Not yet."

"Here, Goran," Dunia said, handing me a piece of bread and some cheese. "You must be hungry."

With all the danger and excitement, I hadn't thought about eating but at the smell of the cheese, my stomach growled and I realized that I was very hungry indeed.

"Thanks," I said quickly swallowing the proffered food. "Is there any sausage?"

"I think so," Dunia said, rummaging through her basket. "Here," she said, passing me a sausage and another piece of bread.

"Could you see anything?" she asked.

I didn't know what to tell her, but my hesitation was enough. Tears streamed from her eyes. Some of the other women had been watching us, hoping for news, I guess. At the sight of Dunia's tears some of them began to wail.

"Shhhh! Shhh!" Janka said, "Keep calm. We don't know what's happened."

She came and sat beside us. "Goran," she asked, "What did you see?"

Her steady gaze gave me the strength to tell the truth. "The village is on fire," I said.

Dunia gasped.

"The gate was open," I continued. "People were running out and going into the woods on the other side of the village.

"So some people got away?" Janka asked.

"Yes," I told her. "Many people were running out."

"We need to wait here," Janka said.

"Hopefully the invaders will take what they want and move on like Milan said," I told her.

"My Jelko is all right. I can feel it," she said.

"And father?" Dunia murmured. "I will pray for his safety."

Chapter 78 - Ashes to Ashes

All through that night we stayed hidden in the forest. I went back and forth to check on the situation in the village from the cover of the edge of the woods. I was exhausted but there was no way to catch any sleep. I was glad that Dunia and the baby seemed comfortable enough to get some rest but I noticed Janka kept awake, reassuring the others when the stress of the unknown fate of their men and their homes overwhelmed them.

The smell of fire persisted throughout the long night. Just as the first light of dawn illuminated the sky, slowly bringing color back to the sleeping valley, I heard the rumble of hooves. I looked toward the village and saw men on horses galloping through the gate and down the hill. I tried to count their number, but they kept coming and coming, raising a cloud of dust as they went.

Behind the men on horses came wagons. These moved more slowly and I could see that they were *our* wagons! They were being pulled by *our* horses with *our* cows and goats and sheep tied behind them. More horsemen brought up the rear of the moving line that now stretched down the entire hillside between our village and the main road in the valley below. I waited and watched as the dust settled and the last men disappeared beyond the hills in the distance. Then I went back to where the women and children were hiding.

When Janka saw me she cried out, "Have they gone?"

I guess she could see from my face that they had.

"Yes," I told her and the other women who had gathered around her in the hope of good news. "I will go back to the village to make sure that it is safe. You stay here for now and I will be back soon."

"Can I come with you?" Yagoda said? "I want to see what happened."

"No, Yagoda," her mother admonished.

She looked down and restlessly kicked the ground, raising a puff of dust.

"Yagoda, come with me and help me prepare some breakfast for us all," Janka said, defusing the tension. "Ask the women what food they have left and let's see what we can make. By the time we've eaten hopefully Goran will have returned with the news that it's safe to go back to our homes."

If there are any homes to return to, I thought; but I keep my fears to myself. Maybe it wasn't as bad as it looked. I thanked Janka with my eyes and ran back to the edge of the woods. I saw villagers approaching from the other direction, making their way up the hill towards the open gate.

As I got closer I recognized Jelko on the road a little ahead of me.

"Jelko!" I yelled, "Jelko!"

He turned toward me slowly, as if in a daze; reacting to his name but he didn't seem to recognize me.

"Jelko, what's the matter? It's me, Goran!"

"Goran," he said, slowly coming around. "Gogo! Is my Janka safe? My mother? My sister?"

"Yes, yes, they are fine," I told him.

"Thank God!" he said. I saw that there were tears his eyes.

I stood beside him and said, "Jelko, what is it? What happened in the village? I saw people running out. Did everyone escape?"

Jelko broke down. He fell into my arms and cried. I held him there in the middle of the road and waited, wondering how bad the situation was; wondering what he had seen.

After a few moments he pulled himself back from me, quickly wiped his eyes with the back of his hand and shuddered.

"Gogo," he said, "It was terrible. Thank God you took the women away. We thought that the gates would hold, and were ready to fight if they didn't. But nothing could prepare us for what happened."

He looked down at his feet, picking up the courage to continue.

"It took them no time at all to break through the gate. Then they poured in, slashing people with their long swords. Boban tried to fight back. We were massed behind him, but they were on horseback and had the advantage. Boban fell and they were upon us."

"Was Boban killed?" I asked in horror.

"I don't know," Jelko said, we all ran, trying to save ourselves."

More tears came to Jelko's eyes. "Gogo, it was terrible! I could feel people beneath my feet as I ran but I didn't stop to see if they were alive or dead. People were running behind me and I was afraid that if I stopped I would be crushed. I heard women screaming and the sound of wood and stone being smashed. All I could think about was getting out of the village to the safety of the forest."

"They didn't follow you?" I asked.

"No," he said, "I guess not. They were more interested in taking what we have than in pursuing us."

"I saw them leaving this morning," I told him, "and taking our wagons and our livestock."

By this time we had reached the village gate. We stepped through it and what I saw took my breath away. The square was littered with broken crockery, shards of brown water pots and bowls. Here and there I saw what looked like bundles of rags strewn on the ground. Then I realized that there rags were my townsmen, felled by the invaders.

I saw the color drain from Jelko's face and knew that it mirrored mine as we looked around the devastated square. I took a deep breath and said, "We need to see who is here."

One by one we joined the other dazed men and approached the lifeless bodies to identify them. Some I recognized from the tavern; one had been a regular customer at the forge. Here was Davko, the man with the biggest horse I'd ever seen. I wondered where that horse was now. Thinking of horses, I left the sad scene of the square and ran to check on our home and stable. Some of the houses on the square looked untouched except that their doors were all wide open but others showed signs of destruction, their roofs caved in, collapsed into blackened rubble.

First I came to the forge. I saw that the door was open but the heavy anvil and hammer were where we'd left them. The unfinished swords that we were working on were nowhere to be seen. I ran out the back toward to the ally that led to the stable. The small door was ajar. I pushed it open and blinked in the bright light. The big door opening to the road that we always kept shut was gaping wide. Our horses were gone. I climbed the ladder to my simple room and to my surprise, it was untouched.

Then I made my way to the house. In some places I had to climb over fallen timber. I saw that most of the houses had been ransacked and burnt. The stone walls were standing but fire had caused the roof beams to collapse. I saw with relief that the blacksmith's house was still standing. Maybe the invaders missed it, I thought hopefully. Peering into the open door, my hoped were dashed. The house stood but everything in it was either missing or destroyed. The oaken dresser stood bare of the bowls and cutlery. Bedding lay on the floor and the bedsteads overturned as if someone had searched for items of value that might have been hidden within. The trunk that protected Dunia's fine embroideries lay in pieces on the floor. The storeroom door lock had held but the door itself was splintered by an ax; the shelves were empty, all of our provisions gone.

As I gazed at the destruction I heard a noise behind me. Afraid that the invaders had returned I grabbed a heavy board that had been part of the storeroom door for protection and turned to see who was there.

It was the blacksmith, covered in soot. He looked frightened. I saw his relief when he recognized that it was me.

"Well, boy," he said, "The house and forge still stand."

"The women are safe," I told him, shocked that his first thought was not for his family. "Let's clean the house up as much as we can before they return."

"They took the horses," he said, as if he had not heard what I said as I began to pick up the overturned chairs.

"Help me with this table," I said.

Without thinking he came over and together we righted the heavy piece.

"I'm going to the tavern," he said, "and see if they left us any ale."

He pushed past me, and I watched him go, not caring to know if he fought or if he ran. I fixed the beds as best as I could. It would take time to repair everything that has been damaged but for now I just wanted to lessen the shock for the women when they returned. I knew I needed to get back to them soon. They were waiting for me. Satisfied that I'd done all I could for the moment I headed back to the square, closing the door behind me.

The rag piles that had been our friends and neighbors had been moved to the open space beside the church. I saw Jelko by the fountain and went over to tell him that I would go and bring the women.

"Stanyo's dead," he said, "and Boban's father".

"What about Boban?" I asked after the only man who had the courage to lead the attempted resistance.

"He is gravely injured," Jelko said. "It isn't known if he will live."

"How many have fallen?" I asked, looking over at the bundles lined up in front of the church.

"More than twenty," Jelko said, "so far. Until everyone returns from the forest we won't know for sure. Many of the houses have collapsed. There might have been people hiding inside of them. Oh. Gogo! You were so smart to get the women out in time. I don't know how I can ever thank you, my friend."

"I wasn't sure that it was with right thing to do," I told him, "but with your encouragement I did it. There is no need to thank me."

I left him with that thought and hurried back to the forest. Dunia looked at me, hopefully, as I came upon them.

"Is it safe to go back?" she asked.

I nodded.

A cheer went up among the women.

"The horsemen came and left," one woman stood up and shouted. "Our brave men protected the village!"

Everyone was stirring; gathering up their bundles and preparing for the walk back to their homes.

"Before we go," I said, trying to focus their attention, "Before we go I have to tell you something."

Some of the women had already started down the path, but at my words they stopped and turned to listen.

I said, "The horsemen have gone, it's true, but not before destroying our village."

The women gasped. Dunia, who stood beside me cradling our baby said, "Is everything gone?"

I figured that it would be better to prepare them for the worst; then they would be relieved to see that some houses had been preserved.

"The gate was breached," I told them. "Our houses have been robbed and many have been burnt. Some of our friends have fallen."

"My husband?" one woman yelled. "My son!" shouted another. "Who has died?" they demanded to know.

"I cannot say," I told them. "I saw bodies but I don't know whose. It seems that most people escaped so keep up your hopes until we know for sure. Let's back go now and put our lives back together as best we can."

I saw tears in Janka's eyes as she moved with the others down the narrow path.

"Your father lives," I whispered to Dunia then went over to Janka. "I saw Jelko," I told her. "He is shaken but fine, and very happy to know that you and his family are safe."

"Thank you, thank you, Gogo!" I was so worried about him!"

"You were wonderful with the women," I told her, "putting aside your own worries to help the others."

"It was one of the things I learned from Milada," she said. "She told me that a person's happiness depends on how much she can help others. And she was right. When I was tending to the women and children I had no time to think about my own fears."

"Your skills will be needed now," I told her. "Boban was gravely wounded and I'm sure that others were, too."

"Be sure to take care of yourself and my friend Jelko's child!" I added.

"Yes, I will," she said. "I felt it move for the first time last night. Now is the time to celebrate new life as well as grieving for the loved ones we have lost".

Chapter 79 - Aftermath of Disaster

I led the anxious group out of the forest and up the road to the village. Some of the children ran ahead but stopped in their tracks when they reached the open gate. When their mothers caught up and gazed at what had become of their village some of them began to wail.

I stood beside Dunia as she looked around the square. "Let's go home," she said, "if we have a home to go to. Did you see it, Gogo? Does the house still stand?"

I tried to block her view of the rows of the dead lined up next to the church. I told her, "The house is there but there's not much of use left inside it."

Yagoda, still carrying a large bundle, and her mother followed us through the devastated streets. The young girl's eyes darted here and there, taking in the destruction around us. Dunia held baby Gahla tightly to herself, both giving and receiving comfort from her soft little body. Overhead, the sun shone brightly, the mild summer morning belying the sorry scene on the ground.

When we reached the house, Dunia's mother pushed open the damaged door then took a step back and gasped. I couldn't image what she would have done had she seen it before I tidied up what I could. Taking a deep breath, she stepped over the threshold with Dunia and Yagoda close behind.

"Look what those evil men did!" exclaimed Yagoda.

"We can be thankful that they did no worse," her mother said quietly.

"Yes," I told them, "many houses were burnt and collapsed entirely. This isn't so bad, really."

Dunia looked over at the remains of the trunk that had held her precious embroideries. I could see her thinking of the years she had spent working the fine stitches into delicate patterns. We all stood in silence, lost in our own thoughts, overwhelmed by the situation.

I shook myself out of my stupor and said to Dunia, "I will make you a new trunk better than the last".

"It's not loss of the trunk that makes me sad, but what was it in," she said.

The door was pushed open and almost came off its hinges as the blacksmith strode in. "You're back," he said, "we were luckier than our neighbors."

He eyed the large bundle at Yagoda's feet.

"That's my girl," he said lifting the bundle from the mud-caked floor, "leave it to you to rescue our goods. I hope it's the last of the sausages from the pig I slaughtered before winter!"

He opened the bundle then threw it to the ground in disgust. "I told you not to waste your energy on those silly things!" he bellowed.

"You told Dunia, not me!" Yagoda snapped back.

With one step he was upon her and the back of his hand cracked across her face. "Don't you dare talk back to me," he spat, kicking the contents of the bundle across the floor.

When Dunia saw her treasured needlework her eyes lit up. I was surprised that Yagoda had risked her father's wrath to save them. No one said a word as the blacksmith grunted then stormed out of the house muttering about his useless daughters.

As soon as the door swung shut behind him Dunia handed me our child and ran to pick up the brightly embroidered pillow slips, vests and aprons.

"Yagoda!" she exclaimed as she picked up each piece and held it loving to her breast, "Sister, thank you! Thank you!"

Yagoda had sunk down to the bed, touching her cheek where her father had slapped it. "I hate that man!" she said.

Her mother sat beside her, "Hate is a very strong word, my girl. He is the man who gave you life."

"He might have given me life, but he has never given me love," she said, "or you either, for that matter!"

"Yagoda!" Dunia said, looking over at her sister, "what a thing to say."

"It's true, though!" she retorted. "I bet he'll be happier to see his horses that he was to see us."

"The horses are gone," I said.

"Let's give thanks that we are all alive," the girls' mother said. "Dunia, put those things down now and let's go to church and offer prayers of thanksgiving."

I thought of the bodies lying outside the church as the women silently left. I followed them, trying to shut out the cries of people returning to the little that was left of their homes and their lives.

I found Jelko outside of the church. "How did you fare?" I asked him. "Does your house still stand?"

"Barely," he replied. "There's not much left inside. All the provisions are gone. We will need to begin again and build up our stores before winter sets in."

"Working together we can do it," I said. It is still summer. We will harvest the fruit and then the nuts from the forest."

"The cows are gone," he said gloomily, "so no milk for the children or for making cheese and butter."

"I saw the horsemen taking the livestock," I told him. "I wondered if any were left behind."

"I know Stanyo, God rest his soul, had some sheep in the high pasture," Jelko told me, "but maybe the invaders went that way and rounded them up."

"Someone will have to go and see," I said, remembering our fallen friend. "How did Stanyo die?"

"After you left," Jelko began, "we barred the gate shut. Boban had us all line up with our makeshift weapons. The men with hoes and shovels were in the first line and then came the men who had swords."

"Why not put the men with swords in front?" I asked.

"I guess he thought the first line could weaken the enemy then the men with swords could strike the final blows," he said. "Of course your father-in-law insisted to be in the front line with his sword."

"I didn't think he was that brave," I said.

"Well he wasn't! Once the invaders smashed through the gate I saw him fall back behind the other men," he said.

"Did our men fight well?" I asked.

"We didn't stand a chance! The invaders rode in on their horses and had the advantage of height and of superior weapons. Those who stood their ground, like our Stanyo, were cut down like stalks of wheat. We could only watch in horror and try to get out of the way."

"Luckily for us they seemed more interested in getting to our stores and animals than in wasting time fighting us," he continued. "Anyone putting up resistance was struck down. You know that old lady, Evriki, who sells that good cheese in the market place?"

"Yes," I said, "she always has the best cheeses and was generous with letting us taste them."

"Well, she didn't want to give her stock to the horsemen."

"What did she do?" I asked with a sinking feeling in the pit of my stomach.

"I saw her standing in front of her stall with a broomstick as if she could bar the men from taking her cheeses," Jelko said.

"And then what happened," I asked, dreading his answer.

"She yelled at them to 'be off'," he said. "Calmly, without a sound, the horseman drew his sword and slashed off her head."

I felt bile rising in my throat. I wretched and vomited on the side of the road. Jelko came up and put his arm around my shoulder.

I wiped my mouth and looked up to see that he was crying.

"You saw this with your own eyes?" I asked him.

He just nodded. We fell into each other's arms, finding some comfort and relief that we and our families had survived.

I don't remember which one of us pulled away first. It was not becoming for two men to show such weakness, even in these dire circumstances. Jelko punched my arm and said, "Enough now. Our families are safe and we have full sleeves and full trousers. We can rebuild our lives. Let's go see what we can do to help those less fortunate."

By the time we reached the churchyard several graves had already been dug. In the warmth of summer it would not do to have bodies lying in the street. I could hear chanting coming from the church but I had no desire to go inside. Jelko and I took up shovels and joined the other men at their grim task. We would see to disposing of their bodies; those in church could see to soothing their souls.

Chapter 80 - Rebuilding

The following days were spent rebuilding our shattered lives. The people of the village put aside their usual occupations and worked together to salvage what they could from the piles of rubble that had once been homes, warehouses and stables. All in all, forty-two people had lost their lives in the invasion; twenty-six men, seven women and nine children. The women and children had been hiding in houses that had collapsed around them.

Jelko's barn still stood but the sad-eyed cows had vanished. Most of the livestock and provisions on which we depended for our winter's food were gone, but we shared the meager supplies that remained. The invaders took most of the cooking pots so the people who were lucky enough to still have them loaned them to their neighbors or prepared enough stew to share.

Jelko and I made the long trek to the high pasture and were relieved to find Stanyo's sheep fat and content. We herded them down the steep slope and people actually cheered when we followed the fleecy flock into the village. The butcher immediately chose the two plumpest ewes and we all ate spit-roasted mutton that evening. It was the first hardy meal any of us had eaten since the raiders came, but in spite of the good food there was no joy in the square that day. The fresh meat fed our hungry bodies, giving us much needed strength to continue the work of rebuilding our devastated village, but a pall of sadness and loss hung over us.

The next morning Jelko had a pleasant surprise. One of his cows had returned! He found her standing by the barn door, wanting to get to her familiar hay! She must have stayed behind, hidden in a narrow lane, unseen by the invaders. At least there would be some nutritious milk for Janka, to support the new life that was growing within her womb.

By the time the days were growing shorter, life was beginning to feel more settled. The market place started up again. There were fewer stalls than before and the ones there were had fewer items but at least the pace of life was returning. Once they had harvested what remained of the crops in the fields, the men had time to gather again in the tavern. We had been busy in the forge;

not making swords but melting down the few that were left to cast new cooking pots and tools to replace those that had been stolen from the villagers.

In spite of the hardships, I took delight in my little daughter. When I finished my day at the forge, instead of going to the tavern I went home to see my bonny girl. Still feeding from Dunia's breast, she had not suffered deprivation during the crisis and was growing day by day. Her mother was back to doing her usual chores and was relieved that I enjoyed spending time with baby Gahla. She took the opportunity to run errands in the village and to go and visit Janka who was expecting a baby of her own very soon.

One chilly night in autumn I heard the door to the barn creak and then footsteps on the straw below.

"Who's there?" I called, thinking maybe Jelko had come for a chat, but there was no reply.

I could hear someone coming up the ladder. By the faint moonlight seeping through the thinly woven burlap curtain on the high window, I saw something white appearing at the loft. One more step up and I saw a face. It was Dunia.

Without a word she sat beside me on my bed. "Dunia!" I whispered.

She held her finger to her lips, indicating silence. I reached up and gathered her in my arms. She came willingly. It had been so long since I held her warm, soft body next to mine. By the way she moved I could feel that she also missed the comfort of our togetherness. Wordlessly, our bodies intertwined. Her lips willingly met mine and we dissolved together into waves of rhythmic pleasure.

We lay there, spent, in each other's arms until Dunia roused herself, gathered her clothes and disappeared as silently as she had come. When I awoke the next morning I thought of Dunia's nocturnal visit and wondered if it had only been a dream.

Before going to the forge I went to the house to get some breakfast. Dunia greeted me as usual, with no indication that anything had passed between us in the night. I quickly ate some fresh porridge, kissed my daughter and went to work. I thought about kissing Dunia, too, but when I moved toward her she averted her eyes so I just waved and left as I always did. Last night I must have been dreaming, I thought. But, in the days and weeks that followed the dream repeated itself several more times!

I did not enjoy spending all day at the forge with the blacksmith. He constantly grumbled about his stolen horses and the fact that he had lost business shoeing those of the other villagers. Never mind that the strongest men in the village had to hitch themselves to ploughs and makeshift wagons to do the work of the missing horses.

One day I became so annoyed with his complaining that I asked him, without thinking, "What did you do with all that money you made selling swords? Buy yourself some new horses, why don't you."

His rhythmic hammering grew suddenly silent and I regretted my outburst.

"What I do with my money is my business, boy," he snapped. "If I had horses now, the others would want to borrow them all the time. Let someone else find some and pay for them to eat while others profit from their labor."

I knew better to than to say anything else and kept my mouth shut. I thought of the coins I had saved when I hoped to build a home for Milada and me. I could use that money to buy some horses and rent them out to people until they could afford to replace the ones that they had lost. Come spring, there would be many fields to plough and a pair of strong horses would be in high demand.

That evening I went to find Jelko in the tavern and tell him my idea.

"Where are you going to find horses to buy?" he asked. "The invaders probably took all that were anywhere near here."

"There must be some to be had somewhere," I told him.

"And you are going to be the one to find them?"

"If I am the first to look!" I replied.

"I don't know," he said. "If you can get some it's a good idea. But the price will be high. Do you have any money?"

"I have some savings," I told him.

"And with your skills as a blacksmith you can make more," Jelko said. "That is, if the old man lets you."

"And if he doesn't it will be good to have another way to earn a living," I said with a grin. "Shall we have another drink?"

He nodded his agreement but before I could call for another round Janka's brother pushed his way to our table and breathlessly announced, "Janka had the baby! Come quickly, she's asking for you!"

"Jelko's face went white for a moment at the boy's news, then his mouth widened into a beaming smile.

"Drinks for everyone!" he called out running toward the door. I followed him, figuring that Dunia was probably with Janka to help with the birth.

We rushed to Jelko's house and before we even crossed the threshold we heard the hearty cries of his new born baby. Just as I thought, Dunia was there beside Janka, holding the wriggling child.

"He wants his mother," Dunia said, passing the child to her friend who lay, propped up on cushions in the bed beside the hearth.

"*His* mother!" Jelko exclaimed. "I have a boy!" He rushed over to Janka and the baby, smiling down on the mother and child.

My eyes met Dunia's. For the first time in a long, long time, she met my gaze and smiled.

Chapter 81 - A Strange Visitor

We spent the night celebrating the birth of our friends' baby. It felt good to have something positive happen after the difficult period the village had experienced. There were many toasts so by the time I decided to go home I found it hard to climb the narrow ladder to my room. I was ready to bed down in the straw but the night was cold and I longed for the warm quilt on my bed. With effort, I carefully made my way up the ladder and found a nice surprise. Underneath my warm quilt was a warm body! Dunia was there waiting for me.

"Isn't Janka's baby beautiful?" she whispered when I joined her in my bed.

"Not as beautiful as our Gahla," I said, drawing the girl close.

"Wouldn't you like to have a son?" she asked.

"Yes," I said. "Let's make one tonight!"

We dissolved into each other, and this time, when the light of dawn pierced the thin curtain, Dunia was still in my arms. I heard her sigh as she stretched away from me.

"I must go," she said.

I was not ready to leave the warmth of my bed and didn't want her to go. I tightened my arms around her. "No; stay awhile longer," I pleaded.

"Our Gahla will want her morning feed," she said. I loosened my grip and she slid out of my arms, dressed quickly to fend off the morning chill and, with one last smile, disappeared down the ladder.

I remained in bed, savoring its warmth and the afterglow of my closeness with a woman. I felt a passing shadow and looked up. At the window there was a bird silhouetted by the early morning light. At first I thought nothing of it but then I noticed that there was something tied to one of its legs. I remembered what Milan had said; about birds that can carry messages. It must have been one of Tonsho's! By the time I realized what it was, the bird had flown off.

When I finally dragged myself out of bed the sun was high in the sky. The blacksmith would be furious, but, frankly, I didn't care! When I eventually got to the forge, Jelko was outside waiting for me.

"We got a message" he said, "from a bird."

"I know," I told him. "I saw it this morning."

"The message?" he asked, puzzled, "how?"

"Not the message, the bird!" I said. "What's the news?"

"It seems that the horsemen were spotted a long ways off north-east of here," he said.

"A long way off, you say? That's good!" But who saw them? Could Milada and her friends be in danger, I wondered.

"The note came from Milan," he said, as if reading my thoughts.

"How do you know," I asked him.

Tonsho recognized the bird as one that went with Milan," he said with a grin. "You know how Tonsho loves those birds of his! I think he has a name for each and everyone one of them."

"In that case, I'm surprised he let them go," I said.

"He is a good man and knew that it would be helpful for the village," he said. "And, sooner or later, his birds will return."

"Unless someone makes a meal of them," I couldn't help adding.

"Anyway," he went on, "it's good news that they are far away."

"Too bad that Milan is far as well," I said. "I was hoping he would come back soon. Maybe he would know where I could find some horses."

"Are you still thinking about that crazy idea!" he exclaimed.

"It's not crazy!" I countered. "I have a family to consider and so, now, do you! How is the baby this morning?"

"Well rested, unlike his Dad!" he laughed.

"That was quite a celebration last night!" I said.

"Indeed it was! I want to go back to bed, but instead I'm off to the forest to collect some wood for the fire. It's getting colder day, by day and mother and baby need to keep nice and warm!"

"And I'd better get into the forge before the blacksmith kills me," I said, pushing open the heavy door. I wasn't looking forward to spending a day with the gruff man. How lucky I was to have a good friend like Jelko.

~

Soon the first snows arrived and with them came some people I'd never seen before. It was in the evening, just before sunset. I was sitting in the tavern chatting with Jelko and a group of our friends when I felt a blast of cold air as the tavern door swung open and shut. I looked to see who had arrived and met the eyes of a very strange character.

He was a man of short stature. At first I thought him very young, but the more I watched him, the older he seemed. His doffed his dusty grey cape. When it fell onto the bench I saw that it was lined in thick, dark fur. Under the cape he wore a bright red jacket spangled with shiny silver sequins. It was then I realized. He was a gypsy!

But he was very different from the members of the band that I knew. I noticed a sharp look in his eye when he called the tavern owner over and demanded a tankard of ale.

"Do you have money to pay for your drink?" asked the tavern keeper sharply. He was usually very friendly and loved to banter with his customers, but I could see that he thought that this man was trouble.

"I can give ye money," was the strange man's reply, "or I can play ye for the drink, like. If I be losin', I'll be buyin' a round for everyone, like. But if the winner be me, me drinks is on the house."

I could see that the tavern keeper wanted none of this wager but the other customers were excited about the chance of getting a free drink if the strange man lost his bet.

"Go on," one man said to the tavern keeper. "Let him play you for it!"

"If he loses" chimed in another, "think of how much you will make."

"And we'll all drink for free," another added.

"What is this game, then," the tavern keeper asked, doubtfully.

"Simple," the man replied, taking three small silver cups from one pocket of this colorful jacket and a shiny brown hazelnut from another.

We all gathered around as he set the three cups on the oaken table, worn smooth by generations of elbows.

"Watch ye careful like," he said as he placed the hazelnut in front of the middle cup. One by one, he turned the cups upside down, placing the central cup over the nut.

"Which cup covers the nut?" he asked us.

We all pointed to the one in the center. He lifted it and showed us that the nut was there.

"Right," he said, "now comes the fun part. Watch ye careful, mind."

We followed the stranger's horny hands, nails black with grime, slowly and deliberately sliding the cups around on the table. I followed the central one with my eyes and was sure that I knew which one concealed the nut. I'd seen this trick before and was not easily fooled.

"Now, me dear sir, where's that nut?" the strange man said, looking at the tavern keeper with a smile. "Remember, if you find that there nut there'll be drinks from me all 'round!"

A cheer went up from the men. Some of them were making suggestions to the tavern keeper as to which cup he should choose. Most of them were pointing to the cup closest to the visitor. That's where I thought the nut was as well.

"That one there," the tavern keeper said, indicating that cup.

With a flourish, the man lifted it to reveal – nothing! The men groaned in unison, myself included. I was sure that the nut was under that cup! Before we had a chance to see which cup concealed the nut the man had slipped the three of them back into his jacket pocket.

"So me drink is on the house!" the stranger sniggered. "Make it a large one."

The tavern man brought the ale and set it down hard, sloshing foam over the rim of the beaker.

"Our friend the tavern master seems none too pleased," Jelko murmured as we went back to our conversation.

"Who is that man?" I asked, "Where did he come from."

"He's a gypsy," Rieko replied.

"The gypsies don't come in the winter, do they?" I asked. "And besides, he doesn't resemble any of the gypsies that I knew so well. They kept their hands spotless, not at all like his."

"He is from another tribe," Jelko explained. "Our village does not welcome them like it does your pals."

"Why do they come here then," I asked. "I've never seen them before."

"They, and others like them, pass through now and again but they don't visit regularly," he said.

"Where do they camp?" I wondered aloud.

"They stay nearby, just outside the village gate," he said.

"Not in the forest?"

"No," he said. "If they stayed in the forest, the villagers wouldn't come to them."

"You're kidding me!" I exclaimed. "Why would they want people to come and bother them?"

"That's how they get money," he said.

"How?" I asked, remembering that my gypsy friends seemed to have no need or desire for coins.

"There are games of chance like this one," he said, "They tell stories and bring news from far and wide. There's lively music and friendly women to dance with, if you know what I mean."

I must have looked confused because he laughed and said, "Tomorrow we will go and you can see for yourself!"

Chapter 82 - New Acquisitions

The next evening, true to his word, Jelko met me at the forge at sundown.

"Are you ready to go to the gypsies' camp?" He asked.

"I thought I'd go home and have a bite to eat," I said, not sure that I wanted to spend time with strange people.

"For a few coins we can get some good food at the camp," he said. "Come on, let's go."

The blacksmith had already left for the tavern. I rinsed my hands and face with some water I'd warmed before dousing the fire for the night and then followed Jelko out into the dusk, pulling the forge door shut behind us.

"I'll just pass by the house and tell Dunia I won't be home to eat," I said.

"Never mind that," Jelko said. "She and the babe were at our place with Janka. I told her I was taking you with me to the gypsy camp."

"I guess it's all right then," I said, with more enthusiasm than I felt.

By the time we left the village, night had fallen. I saw the glow of fires from the gypsies' camp not far from the village gate and heard strains of cheerful music getting louder as we approached. It reminded me of the evenings spent watching Milada and the others dancing by the fire, spinning and laughing with joy. But when we got near enough to see, I had a very strange feeling. The music, the fire, the smell of herbs and roasting meat were so familiar, but the people were very different. When they saw us, a group of girls came up to us, fingering our clothes and smiling with their lips but not with their eyes.

"Welcome, boys," one said. "Come with me!" Her gaze cut through me. I didn't feel any warmth in her eyes.

I looked over at Jelko. He was smiling, but looked nervous. "Can we buy something to eat?" he asked.

"Oh, if it's food you want, go over there," the girl said, cocking her head in the direction of the cooking fire. "Eat your fill, then if you want to have some fun come find me by the fire." She ran her grubby finger along Jelko's cheek, gave him another cold smile then ran off to greet some other village men who were approaching.

Jelko and I hurried over to where a man was cutting slices off the succulent lamb, sizzling as it rotated on a spit above glowing coals.

"Would you some?" the man asked us and said. "Two florins for as much as you can eat."

Jelko opened his pouch and took out four small coins. "Here," he said to the man, handing over the coins, "these are for me and my friend."

We were handed a metal plate each and waited for the meat. "You can get some pickled cabbage from the pot over there, too, if you want."

We took our food then moved closer to the warmth of the fire to eat it. A group of young people were laughing loudly. I turned to look at them and my heart stopped. I thought I saw Milada, laughing with the boys. What was she doing with this band of gypsies? But as I kept looking, the girl's eyes met mine and I realized that it was not Milada at all; it was Yagoda. She stopped laughing and the whole group went quiet. She left them and approached Jelko and me.

"What are you doing here?" she asked.

"What are *you* doing here?" I said, "If you father finds out you'll be sorry."

"I like to dance like I did with Milada and her friends," she said. "You won't tell him, Gogo, please!"

I felt sorry for the girl. "I won't tell him," I said, "But it's late. Go home now so you'll be there when he gets back from the tavern."

"Thank you, Gogo," she said, giving me an unexpected kiss on the cheek. "I won't tell Dunia that you are here, either."

She waved at the boys then ran off in the direction of the village.

"That girl will get herself in trouble one of these days," Jelko said.

"Unfortunately, I think you are right," I agreed, taking a bite of the tender meat.

As we ate, we couldn't help watching some girls dancing by the fire. I noticed that none of the men were dancing and that the movements of the girls were very provocative. I was trying to focus on my food, which was delicious, but distracted by a hardening in my groin.

I looked over at Jelko to see if he was having the same reaction.

He was!

His eyes followed where I was looking. He snorted and said, "Lucky you to have had this kind of entertainment every night!"

"Jelko!" I said, shocked by his words, "I've never seen anything like this in my life!"

"But you lived with gypsies for years!" he said.

"They did not behave like this," I told him. "The men and women, old and young, all danced by the fire when the mood took them."

"Did you dance, too?" he asked.

"Once in a while," I said, "when Milada dragged me into it."

"You really liked Milada, didn't you?"

I had no answer for him. I didn't want to think about her and how strong my feelings had been, and might still be if I allowed myself to remember our years together. Instead, I focused on a group of horses tethered beyond the fire.

"Look, Jelko," I said, pointing in that direction.

"Yes, the redhead is a looker!"

I looked to see what he was talking about. "I was pointing at the horses over there, not at that girl!" I told him.

"Horses!"

"I'm going to have a closer look," I told him, handing over my empty plate. "Hang on to this for me; I think I'll get some more meat later. After all, we paid for 'all we could eat'".

I went over to the horses. There were a couple of dozen of them standing close together against the cold. Several of them were large, better for pulling than for riding one, just the type that I was hoping to find. As I approached one of the larger ones, I heard a voice behind me.

"He, he; boy! What'cha doing here? Not planning on stealin' one of them gypsy's horses, now, are ye?"

I turned to see the strange little man from the tavern. He looked even smaller next to the tall horse.

"No, of course not!" I told the man. "I was thinking of buying one or two if anyone was interested in selling them."

"If the price is right, everything is for sale," the man said with a sly grin, "even me own daughter!"

"How much would I need to pay for this horse and this one here?" I asked, indicating two of the biggest horses.

"Them's the strongest of the lot! Why not take this one here?" he said patting a swayback old mare.

"I need a horse that can pull a plough, not one that can barely stand up," I told him. "If you are not interested in making a deal, I am not going to waste any more of my time." I really wanted those horses, but turned to walk back to the fire, remembering all the tricks I'd learned as a lad in the market place.

"Wait a minute, sonny," the man said, calling me back as I knew he would. "Maybe we could let ye have the big 'uns."

"I'm not sure I want them now," I said, keeping my face as blank as could. "How much would you want?"

"For a pair of pullin' horses like then there," he said, scratching his head, "five silver coins."

"Ha, ha!" I exclaimed. "That's a good joke!"

"I'm not a-jokin' ", the little man said, "You won't find finer horses than these."

I knew that it was a difficult to find any at all horses. I could pay the five silver coins that he asked, but I knew I could get them for a better price!

"The horses are fine," I said, giving one a pat on its haunches, "but I've seen much better!" I started to walk away again.

"Wait a minute, young man!" the strange man called to me. "Ye can have them for four coins."

I turned back, "Take three and it's a deal."

"Three coins for these fine beasts!" he exclaimed. "You'll be a-robbin' me!"

"Take it or leave it!" I told him.

"Have ye the money now," he asked.

"Come with me to the village and I will give it to you," I said, pleased that he seemed to agree to the deal.

"Let's go then" he said, stepping up beside me.

"Well, get the horses!" I told him.

"Oh, you'll be takin' them now?" he asked.

"Of course!"

I watched him as he untied two horses. One of them was the large one I'd first seen, but the second was much smaller and, from what I could see by the light of the fire, much older.

"Not that one!" I said. "I want two strong horses! That one there!"

"You're a-robbin' me!" he exclaimed, as he untied a second tall horse.

We walked back through the camp together. I waved at Jelko and he ran to me.

"Horses!" he laughed.

"That's what I came for," I whispered so the little man wouldn't hear. "Are you staying here or coming back to the village?"

"I'll come with you," he said, "I used to enjoy coming down to the gypsy camp, but now all I can think of is getting home to Janka and the babe! I'm getting old, man! I'm getting old!"

"Not older," I laughed, "just wiser!

"Do you want to get some more meat before we go?" he asked.

"I would have liked to but I don't want this little man to change his mind or switch horses on me if I get distracted by food!"

I led the way to the stables. Once the horses were settled in the empty stalls I handed the man three coins.

"Where's the other three!" he exclaimed, sputtering and swearing under his breath. "Ye agreed to three coins for each!"

"We agreed on three for the pair," I said calmly, not surprised that he was trying to trick me. "If that's not enough, give me back my silver, take your old horses and be gone!" I held out my hand as if I expected him to give me back the coins. He spat on the ground and, head down, stormed out of the barn as fast as his short legs could carry him!

I turned up the lantern to get a better look at my new horses. I was pleased by what I saw. They looked strong and their eyes were clear. I locked up the wide stable door before climbing up the ladder to my waiting bed just in case the man decided to keep the silver *and* the horses.

Chapter 83 - Nesting

I was very pleased with my horses! Their first job was to pull carts full of wood from the forest up the steep hill to the village. I took no fee for this service, just a share of the firewood for our house and for the forge. The blacksmith said nothing about the horses. Having our firewood provided for us allowed us much more time to work.

Dunia was coming to my little room almost every night. I asked if she want to bring our child and come and stay there with me. She agreed and I set about making the little room more comfortable for my family. From scrap of metal I found in a collapsed house I fashioned a stove that could quickly heat the small space. I built a proper wooden staircase with a gate at the top to keep Gahla safe and sound. They still spent most of the day in their old home but every night my family was together in our own little nest above the stable.

The feast of Christmas was again approaching. This year I had a better idea of what it was all about. I accompanied Dunia and her family to the church most Sundays, but I didn't stay there long. I left early with Jelko to enjoy a morning away from the forge and the blacksmith's perpetual bad humor.

On the Sunday before the feast of Christmas, Jelko and I sat companionably in the tavern, sipping spiced wine as fine snow dusted the village.

"It's warmer here than in the church," I commented lazily.

"It'll be hot in there by now, too," Jelko said. "We always leave before the warmth of the people can crack through the morning chill."

"Maybe," I said, "but I get bored in there. I don't understand what it's all about."

"Never mind," he said, "the women like it. Speaking of which; Janka and I will marry in the spring. Why don't you and Dunia do so at the same time? Then we can celebrate together."

"Do we need to go to the church?" I asked. "Dunia, the baby and I stay together; isn't it the same as being married?"

"Not in the 'eyes of God'" as the girls would say," Jelko replied. "Hasn't Dunia mentioned it?"

"No," I said taking another warming sip of wine, "I don't think so. Oh, wait. When Yagoda saved her needlework she did say something about a special skirt and bodice she had embroidered for her marriage."

"There! You see! They all think about it," he said, slapping me on the back. "So, what do you say? Shall we do it together?"

"If I have to do it, it would be better to do it together," I said, "Will the girls go for the idea?"

"They are good friends," he said. "I'm sure they will like it".

We kept an eye on the church from the warmth of the tavern. When the first people started to come out, we bundled up and headed toward them. Dunia and Janka came out together, each with a well wrapped baby in their arms. They smiled when the saw us waiting.

"Come with us to the tavern," I said.

"I need to get home and put our meal on the table," Dunia said.

"Yagoda and your mother can do it today," Jelko and I have an idea we want to share with you."

"Now?" said Dunia.

"Come on, Dunia," Janka said, "A cup of hot spiced wine would do us both some good. We'll warm up and the babes will, too. Let's go!"

Janka's prodding was enough for Dunia and the four of us hurried into the warm tavern. It was very crowded as others had the same idea. We found a relatively quiet place to sit in the corner and soon Jelko was back with four cups of steaming hot wine.

He place one down in front of Dunia and said, "How would you like to get married with me?"

Dunia looked shocked. "Aren't you marrying Janka? She said you were!"

I rolled my eyes at Jelko. Dunia never knew how to take a joke.

"I didn't ask you to 'marry me'," he said with a grin, "I asked if you wanted to get married 'with' me!" Dunia still looked confused.

"With me and Janka!" Jelko clarified. "You and Gogo; me and Janka. Together. The same time."

Dunia's eyes widened. She looked at me, shocked and then returned my smile.

"You want to marry me, Gogo," she asked, "at the church?"

"If that is what you want," I replied.

"Oh, Dunia," Janka said reaching our and taking her hand, "it would be wonderful if we all wed together!"

"We'll wait until springtime," Jelko said. "Then we can have the feast in the village square."

"It will need to be before the Lenten fast," Dunia said softly.

"We could wait until after Easter," Janka commented.

"No, we must do it before," Dunia insisted.

"Why is that," I asked her.

"I may not be able to fit into my beautiful wedding clothes if we wait," she said with a shy smile.

Janka's face broke into a huge grin.

"Are you planning to eat a lot at Easter feast?" I asked her, confused.

"No, silly!" Janka said with a smile.

Dunia looked at me and said, "Gogo, we're going to have another child".

I looked at her and the Janka; they were both nodding and smiling. I let out a whoop of joy!

"Good for you, old man!" Jelko clapped me on the back. "We will go and talk to the priest after the Christmas festivities and tell him to get ready for two weddings!"

Dunia smiled all the way back to the house. The blacksmith muttered, "shut that door, you're letting in the snow." He'd already eaten and was getting ready to spend the afternoon at the tavern with his friends.

"Father, Mother, Yagoda," Dunia said after she settled baby Gahla in her cradle by the hearth, "Gogo and I are going to be wed!"

Her mother moved closer and embraced her first born. The blacksmith grumbled. "I thought you already were married."

"Not in the church, father," she said.

"Well, if makes you happy, good for you then," he said then turned to leave.

Yagoda said nothing but she looked at me strangely.

"Aren't you happy for your sister and Goran?" her mother asked, inviting Yagoda into the embrace.

"Yes, of course," she said, but her eyes did not meet theirs.

"Let me show you our wedding clothes!" Dunia said excitedly. She skipped over to the newly fashioned trunk and drew out several pieces of heavily embroidered fabric.

"Look," she said, lovingly spreading the clothes out on the bed.

The work was exquisite. There was a bodice and matching skirt heavy with intricate designs of vines, flowers and birds.

"Here is the apron," she said, holding out a piece worked with gold thread. "Milan brought me this thread from far off lands," she said. "There is nothing like it here; and without you, Yagoda, it would be gone."

"And this is for you, Gogo," she said. "Would you like to try it on?"

Dunia handed me a waistcoat of dark blue velvet also embroidered with the precious golden thread.

"This is very grand!" I said, carefully taking the vest in my hands.

"I made a fine linen shirt to go underneath," she said, "You will look like a prince!"

"And you will be the princess," Yagoda said. From where she was standing, Dunia could not see the hard look that accompanied her words.

"Yes! For my wedding day I will look like a princess, thanks to you!" Dunia said.

I wondered again why Yagoda risked her father's anger to save her sister's precious possessions. She was not known for her thoughtful nature.

Later that day, while I was tending to my horses in the barn, I got my answer. I was just finishing with them when the small door opened and Yagoda, wrapped in several shawls for warmth, came in and stood beside me.

"So you are going to marry my sister?" she said.

"Yes," I told her, "it could hardly have come as a surprise. I am the father of her child, after all."

"But you love our cousin, Milada," she said, "and you said you loved me. That's why I saved my sister's stupid embroideries. I thought it would make you love me more."

"Yagoda," I said, surprised at what she said and not wanting to hurt the girl's feelings, "I am proud of you for the kindness you showed towards your sister; you know I am very fond of both you and Dunia."

"Fond of us, yes; but you're in love with our cousin," she said. "Why don't you go and find her?"

"Yagoda, you must get used to the idea that Dunia and I will wed," I explained.

"But you said you loved me, that I would always be your 'little love'!"

When I marry Dunia, you will be my sister and I will I love you like one," I told her, echoing the words Milada had once spoken to me; how she loved me, but as a brother.

"A sister's love is not the kind I want from you," she said, then turned on her heel and stomped out of the barn.

All I could do was sigh. I knew how it felt to be in love with someone who could not love you in return.

Chapter 84 - Learning About God

The girls were getting anxious for us to go and speak with the priest and set a date for our marriages. I thought we'd be able to speak to the priest right after the feast of the birth of Christ, but then learned that there was another holiday; something about kings bringing him presents. I still didn't understand about this holy child who ended up as the naked man hanging on the cross. One night, while we were cozy in bed, I asked Dunia to tell me the story of the Christ child.

"Don't you know the story of Our Lord?" she murmured sleepily.

"No," I told her. "You know my mother died when I was very young and I pretty much grew up on my own. I had no one to tell me stories."

"They aren't 'stories'," Dunia said, "They are the Holy Truth."

"Well, tell me, then," I said.

"Long ago in a far off land," she began, "the people were sinful. They had lost their way. They were unhappy and selfish. They were waiting for God to come to earth and show them the way to salvation."

"So a baby was born?" I asked.

"It wasn't just any baby!" she said, "It was the son of the Lord God himself, made flesh."

"So, if God had a son," I wondered aloud, "now there were two Gods?"

"No, no!" she exclaimed. "There is only one God, but he has three aspects: God the Father, God the Son and God the Holy Ghost."

"A ghost; like a dead person come to life?" I asked, confused.

"No, no!" she said, getting flustered, "try and understand. God is eternal, everlasting and can never die."

"But, the man on the cross; isn't he supposed to be God? Didn't he die?" I said, beginning to regret I started this conversation.

"Jesus Christ died as a man," she said, "but he rose again as the son of God!"

"So that's why there's a 'holy' ghost!" finally I was beginning to understand, or at least I thought I was.

"No, no!" she said with a sigh. "The Holy Ghost is the third person in the Holy Trinity, besides the God the Father and God the Son."

"What about 'God the Mother'?" I asked.

"Gogo!" That's enough. Now you're just being silly," she said. "Go to sleep!"

But sleep did not find me. I lay awake trying to make sense of her words. How could there be only one God if he had a son? And how could he have a son without a mother? And if God did have a son, why would he let him die on a cross? It just didn't make any sense!

A few days later, Jelko and I went together to the church to see the priest to arrange our marriage ceremonies. The priest's assistant was busy and asked us to wait a while a while. We took off our hats and entered the church; it was a little bit warmer there than it was outside.

Looking up at the paintings on the walls, I asked Jelko, "Can you tell me what the story is here? I asked Dunia, but I couldn't understand what she said. Maybe, the pictures will help the story make sense."

"I don't remember all the details," Jelko said, "but I think it starts with this one."

He pointed at an illustration of a tree with a snake on it. A naked man and woman stood on either side of the tree.

"Why is there a snake?" I asked. "Any why aren't those people wearing clothes?"

"The story goes like this," he began. "God was all alone living in emptiness. So he created everything; day and night, the earth, the rivers and lakes, the animals and the birds and lastly the people; us. He made the man first, from some wet clay, but then the man was lonely so God took one of his ribs and stuck some more clay on it and made a woman."

"Do women have more ribs than men?" I asked, feeling mine.

"I don't know," Jelko said, "I never really thought about it. It doesn't matter. Shall I go on?"

"Yes. Tell me about the snake".

"Well," he continued, "God put these people; Adam and Eva were their names, in a beautiful garden. He told them they could help themselves to anything in the garden except the fruit of this one tree."

"This tree in the picture?" I asked.

"That's the one," he replied, "And what do you think happened."

"They ate the fruit?"

"You got it!"

"And then the snake bit them?" I still didn't get the point of that snake!

"No!" he said. "The snake told the woman, Eva, to taste of the fruit. He said it must be pretty special if God saved it for himself."

"It was a talking snake?" I asked, thinking this was a pretty strange story.

"In those days people could talk with animals!" he said.

I thought of how Tanya seemed to communicate with the creatures under her care so maybe this wasn't so farfetched after all.

"Shall I go on?"

"Please!"

"So the snake convinced Eva to take a bite of the fruit. It must have been good because she talked Adam into having some, against his better judgment. So the next time God came to visit they were feeling guilty for disobeying him. Eva told Adam that God wouldn't even notice that one of the fruits from the tree was missing but Adam thought that they'd better hide in case God got mad."

"And did he?"

"Did he what?"

"Get mad?"

"Of course he did! He'd given those people everything and they disobeyed him!"

"What did God do?"

"He threw them out of the garden!" Jelko said, "that's why we all have to work hard now for our food and shelter. It's all that Eva's fault. That's why girls can't be priests!"

"Really? Wasn't it the snake's fault?" I asked, not taking his story too seriously.

"The snake was the devil in disguise!" he said. "The devil always wants to come between you and God. That's why we have the Church – to save us from the devil!"

"Do you believe all of this?" I asked him.

"I'm not sure," he said. "This is what we were told, but really, I don't know."

"What about Christ?" I asked. "Where do his pictures begin?"

"Here," Jelko said, pointing to a pleasing picture of the angel giving a lily to a pretty girl.

"This is the Angel Gabriel announcing that this girl, Mary, will be the mother of God," he explained.

"This angel is a boy?" I exclaimed, "It looks like a girl to me!"

"Angels aren't girls or boys," he said. "They don't have bodies at all."

More ghosts, I thought, but this was taking longer than I thought and the priest might come at any moment so I decided to keep my thoughts to myself and let Jelko get on with the story.

"In this next picture," he continued, "the one with the ass, Mary and her husband, Joseph, are going to Bethlehem so the baby will be born there like it said in the old prophesies."

"Here they are in the stable," he said, moving on to the next picture. "There was no room for them at the inn but the innkeeper let them stay in the barn".

So that's why we have a stable in the church at Christmastime, I thought.

"See that star in the sky?" Jelko asked, pointing at the picture.

"Yes," I said, "is it important?"

"Yes. It leads to the next picture of these three kings coming to bring presents to the baby."

"We celebrate that as a holiday," I commented.

"Yes, it showed that this baby was really God," he said.

"How did the kings know?" I asked.

"God told them to follow a star and they would find the newborn king," Jelko said.

"Was he a king or was he God?" I asked.

"Just let me tell the story!" he replied.

"Let's skip these in the middle for now," I said. "Tell me the part about dying on the cross."

"Here you see Christ and his twelve disciples," he said.

I looked up and saw what looked like a delicious banquet. My eyes had gone this picture on many a Sunday morning. It made me hungry!

"Looks like a good meal they're having!" I said.

"It was a good one, but it was their final one with Christ! It's called 'The Last Supper'. Later that night one of his friends betrayed him for thirty pieces of silver. You can see him over there." Jelko pointed at a small insert of a man dangling by a rope from the branch of a tree.

"He regretted it, I guess," I said.

"Right, he did!" Jelko said. "See here; the Roman soldiers found Christ praying in a garden later that night. They took him to Pontius Pilot and then whipped him and nailed him to the cross between two common thieves to die."

"Where were his other friends?" I asked. "Why didn't they do something to help him?"

"They were cowards! They hid away and even pretended that they didn't know him!" Jelko said.

"Then what happened?" I asked.

"He was laid in a tomb. The next day was a holiday so no one could do anything but the day after that some women went to the tomb to put some oil on the body as was their custom but the body was gone."

"Did someone steal it?" I asked.

"No," Jelko said, "look over here! It's the risen Christ. He comes back and shows his friends that he is alive again. Then they believe that he really is God."

"Why did he have to die?" I asked, beginning to understand the story of the pictures but not their meaning.

"In the old time the people believed that a savior would come and die so that their sins would be forgiven," Jelko explained.

"And so he did, so he did!" The voice of the portly priest who had come up behind us startled me. "I hear you two young men would like me to solemnize your marriages".

Chapter 85 - Meeting the Clergy

We followed the priest into the sacristy behind the main alter. We sat beside a small brazier there for warmth and were offered a cup of the thick sweet wine that was used during church rituals.

"Is it alright to drink this?" I whispered to Jelko? "I know it's supposed to be special."

The priest must have heard me. He said with a smile, "This wine is only special when I consecrate it during the Holy Mass. Then, as you know, it is transformed into the blood of our Lord Jesus."

Jelko hadn't told me anything about drinking blood! Oh, but it wasn't blood; it was wine. I was getting more and more confused.

"You are Goran, are you not?" the prelate looked at me and asked. "I have seen you coming to church with the blacksmith's family."

"Yes, sir; I mean Father," I said, stumbling over my words. "I'm going to marry his daughter, Dunia."

"She's a good girl," the priest said. "She is very skillful with a needle and thread. Even though she is young she has already contributed a lovely altar cloth to my church."

"And you, my boy," he said, turning to Jelko, "You will wed Momir's daughter, Janka?"

"Yes, Father," he replied.

I was stunned by what the priest said next. "You need to keep an eye on that one. I hear she is practicing the magic arts of the gypsies."

"She is not practicing any magic!" I said, unable to hold my tongue. "She is helping people to get better when they are sick; Helping girls have a safer, easier time when they give birth!"

"Surely God has given us pain and suffering for a reason, my boy," the priest said to me. "It is not for us to us to question His will or mitigate the trials He gives us to face."

Jelko stabbed me in the ribs with his elbow and I took his cue to be quiet and let the priest get on with the discussion of our weddings.

With a look I could not fathom, the priest stood up and opened a huge leather- bound book set on a tall wooden stand. "Let me see now," he said, turning some pages.

I wondered what it would be like to know how to interpret the strange symbols in books. I knew that only the priests could do it.

I whispered to Jelko, "Why can't we learn how to read?"

"What good would it do us?" he whispered back.

"We can see what it says in those books," I indicated a shelf lined with many volumes.

"We wouldn't understand what's in them. The priests interpret them for us," he said.

"Ahem, we can consecrate your unions on the Sunday after the feast of Saint Juliana," the priest said, looking darkly at me and then at his bookshelf.

How long from now is the feast of Saint Juliana?" I asked, never hearing about such a person before.

"Less than two moons from today," was his response.

"Most likely it will still be cold then," I said.

The priest consulted his big book once again and then said, "After that, the next possible date is the Sunday after Easter; no marriage may be celebrated during the days of the Lenten fast".

"What do you think, Gogo?" Jelko asked.

"You know Dunia's concerns," I reminded him. If we don't do it soon she will want to wait until well after the baby comes. Let's take the first date and hope for good weather."

"We could always have the celebration in the tavern," Jelko said.

"Boys!" the priest exclaimed. "This is about the Holy sacrament of Matrimony, not about frivolous festivities!"

"Can we baptize our children on the same day?" Jelko asked.

"The church will require an additional contribution to do so," he replied.

"How much is this all going to cost?" I asked, not realizing that I would have to pay for the priest's services.

"There is no fixed price, young man," the priest replied, sounding a little put out. "However a donation to the church is customary."

"How much of a 'donation'?" I asked, not sure that I liked this man in a dress.

"At least one silver coin for each service," was his reply.

"Even if we do them together?" I asked.

"It's all right, Gogo," Jelko said to shut me up. "It's the custom."

"So, is it arranged then?" the priest said, obviously ready to end this meeting and get home to his supper; "The Sunday after Saint Juliana's feast; two weddings and two baptisms."

"Yes, that's right," Jelko said. "Here is one silver coin for you to keep the date for us. We'll give you the rest later."

"You are a fine young man," the priest told Jelko as he pocketed the coin. "Do continue to teach your friend about the ways of our Lord. And keep an eye on your future wife. Keep her busy with bringing up your children so she won't have time to meddle with the work of God."

We left the warmth of the sanctuary and hurried through the chilly nave. Just before I pulled open the heavy church door I noticed a very thin old man with a long grey beard standing under the picture of the snake in the tree. Our eyes met. I had never seen such eyes! They were a piercing blue and seemed to shine from within. After a moment, he smiled at me as if we were old friends.

"Come on!" Jelko said. "The girls are waiting to hear the news.

I wanted to go with him but somehow I was rooted to the spot. I felt I had to approach the old man.

"You go and tell them," I said. "I'll be along in a while."

"Suit yourself!" he said. The blast of freezing air when he pulled open the door made the chilly interior of the church feel mild as a summer's day.

The old man continued to smile as I walked toward him. I couldn't help smiling back.

"Good'ay, my boy," he said, holding out his hand.

The stick-like fingers of his outstretched hand reminded me of a chicken's claw. On the fourth finger he wore an extraordinary gold ring. Sometimes, another priest, one with a high hat and a grandly embroidered garment, came to the village. I'd seen some of the people kissing that priest's ring. Was I supposed to kiss this man's ring or shake his hand? I didn't know what to do!

His bright eyes studied me and then, to my surprise, he began to laugh. His laughter was contagious and soon I began to laugh as well. He reached for my uncertain hand and then covered it with his other one, still holding my gaze.

"I like the looks of you, my boy," the old man said, "but if old Father Polikarpos catches us laughing in his church he will have strong words for us both.

"Who are you," I asked, looking down at his dirty black robe. "Are you a priest, too? I've never seen you in the village before."

"I am Brother Louka," he replied, "I am a monk."

"What's a 'monk'?" I asked, puzzled.

"It's like a priest," he told me, not bothered at all by my ignorance. "Priests take care of people in the community but monks live all together in monasteries. We spend our days in study and prayer."

"So you must know all these stories," I said, pointing at the painted walls of the church. "My friend was trying to explain then to me."

"Did they not teach you when you were a child?" he asked.

"No, Brother," I said, remembering to call him the correct title of respect. "I was on my own from an early age and then went to live with a band of gypsies."

"So, these pictures mean nothing to you?" he asked.

"I'm trying to understand them but they don't make a lot of sense," I told him truthfully.

"Ah, my boy," he said, "That's why the stories are taught to the young who will not question them. The little ones are told to have faith and believe and they do not know enough of the world to make them think otherwise. They grow up thinking that everyone believes the same stories; that the stories are the truth."

"And they aren't?" I asked, surprised both by his words and by my boldness.

"They contain the truth," he said, "but not in the way most people think."

Somehow I knew that this peculiar old man was very wise. In a way, he reminded me of the gypsy woman they called Mother Miriana; the one everybody went to when they needed good advice.

"Could you tell me about the stories?" I asked him. "I would really like to know."

"Knowledge can be a dangerous thing, my boy," he said. "Are you sure you would like to know?"

"Yes, sir," I said; "I mean Brother. The gypsies I lived with had much knowledge and they were happier than the people I've come to know here. With more knowledge, I think I would be more happy."

"Maybe so, maybe not," he said enigmatically. "But I can tell from your aura that you are destined to lead. And a good leader needs knowledge."

I wondered what an 'aura' could be. Was it something I was wearing called by a different name?

"I am staying in the priest's stable behind the church," he said. "I was sorry to hear that all the horses had been taken, but it makes a cozy place for my old bones. Meet me there tomorrow at sundown and I will tell you some stories; mine and God's.

Chapter 86 - Conversation with the Monk

The girls were happy that the day of our marriage would be coming soon. Dunia was busy embroidering a wedding apron for Janka. I wasn't very happy about having to wear the vest that she had prepared. I could see that it was a fine piece but I felt it was too good for the likes of me. If any of the shiny thread remained, maybe she could embroider one for Jelko, too; then at least I wouldn't stand out!

I didn't really want to have a ceremony at all but I knew it was important to Dunia. I figured it was better to go through with it with Jelko; at least we would have a laugh between us. But throughout that day my mind was not on the wedding. Rather I couldn't get that old man's shining eyes out of my head. As soon as we finished our day's work I cleaned myself up and headed for the stable behind the priest's house and knocked on the door.

"Come in, come in!" the old monk said, "I've been expecting you. Come, sit; let me offer you a drink."

"Thank you, Brother, "I said, settling myself on a bench near the glowing brazier.

He handed me a small glass cup containing a pale green liquid. I'd never seen the likes of the cup or the liquid before.

The old man saw my wonder and laughed.

"The cup is made of glass," he said. "I brought it with me from Egypt, a land far from here."

"I can see right through it!" I exclaimed. "Is it magic?"

"Not at all!" the monk replied with a smile. "It's the knowledge and skill of the glassmaker. It's actually made out of sand and fire."

"I've never seen anything like it," I told him.

"There are many things in the wide world that you have never seen and cannot begin to imagine!" he said.

I brought the delicate cup up to my mouth. It was cool and hard, yet so light and thin that I could hardly feel it touching my lips. As I lifted it, the green liquid hit my tongue. Another new sensation! I could describe the taste as a spring morning in the woods, cool, earthy and full of herbs. But when the liquor hit the back my throat it was anything but cool! It felt like fire sliding down to my tummy. Beads of sweat came out on my forehead!

"What is this?" I exclaimed, hoping that it wasn't some kind of poison!

"Something we distill in the monastery," he said. "It feels like ice and fire and it will open your mind, loosen your lips and heal all manner of ills."

"From where have you come and what brings you here?" I asked, feeling my lips loosened already.

"That is a long story of a long journey," he said. "In brief, I started life not far from here. My mother was very devout and brought me to church with her every day. I loved looking at the paintings that covered the walls and asked her over and over again to tell me their stories. "God loves little children like you" she told me, many times each day."

"I loved listening to the priest chanting, his voice echoing off the stone walls. I felt the love of God in my heart when I was in His sacred house. I told my mother that I wanted to be a priest when I grew up and it made her happy."

"When I was a little older, she took me to our village priest to ask him how I could follow in his footsteps. That same day he took me to a seminary in a big town a long way from my village and left me there. I did not understand that I would not be going home! I didn't have a chance to bid farewell to my dear mother and father or my little sisters."

"I hated my life in the seminary. We had classes with a strict task master every morning. He seemed to enjoy beating us if we made even a small mistake. I no longer felt the wonder and joy that I felt in my village church with my mother, although I could still feel God's love for me deep in my heart."

"Every night I prayed to Him for guidance. Our master said we must suffer and offer our pain as a sacrifice for the love of God; after all, 'He gave his only Son so that we might live', we were told."

"Maybe it was true, but it didn't feel right to me," he continued.

"We were not allowed out of the monastery walls except on high feast days such as Christmas and Easter. Then we were marched in file to sing in a huge church in the center of the town.

Singing was the one thing I enjoyed. When we were singing I felt close to God."

"I'd been at that accursed place for over a year when, after a high Mass on Easter Sunday, I saw a chance to escape!"

"How did you get away?"

"The monks herded all us young boys up to the choir loft at the back part of the church. While we were singing I noticed a small alcove, a little niche in the wall. When we'd finished and it was time to go back, I ducked into the niche and hid until they had all gone."

"Didn't anyone notice you were missing?" I wondered aloud.

"We boys were not allowed to speak," he said, "so if any of them noticed they would not have said anything! Luckily for me, none of the monks missed me."

"I waited in the shadows, giving the others time to leave the church then took off my robe and left it in the niche. Keeping in the shadows, I made my way out into the crowded square where, in my shirt and trousers, I blended in with the townsfolk."

"This city was near the sea. I went to the harbor and, since by now I had learned to read and write, it was easy to find a captain to take me on, exchanging my services for a passage East. I knew I wanted to go to the birthplace of Christ; to find God for myself."

"The ship docked at the great city of Alexandra. I had never seen anything like it! The wide streets were lined with exquisite buildings. Covered markets were full of fine goods, strange beasts, colorful fruits, all sorts of fragrant spices and incense. The sound of haunting music was everywhere as was the smell of cooking at any hour, day or night. Where I came from, the people all look more or less alike, but in Alexandra I saw all sorts; some were tall and as black as night, others pale with slanted eyes and shiny black hair. And the knowledge that these people had, I cannot begin to tell you! We know how to add and subtract enough to trade our goods, and simple skills so the houses and churches we build will not fall down. These people practice advanced calculations that enable them to build up into the sky and foresee the movement of the stars and planets."

"I was shocked to learn that most of the people there held a different system of beliefs. They knew the Christ stories but they were not taught that Christ is God. They followed the teachings of a prophet called Mohammed and celebrated different feasts than we do."

"But isn't God, God?" I asked, taking another sip of the fiery green liquor.

"Yes, of course God is God," he said, "but I learned that there are many ways to reach Him; or Her."

"Her?" I asked in shock.

"Yes," said the monk, "I learned that many people worshiped God in a female form. Both the male and female are aspects of life are sacred so why should we not worship a Divine female?"

"But you are a monk. Doesn't that mean that you have to believe in Christ?" I asked.

"I was brought up with the stories that you see painted on the church walls," he told me. "So, Christ was my starting point. Imagine God is at the top of a mountain; a mountain like the one to the north of here. Do you know which one I mean?"

"Yes," I told him, "Jelko and I climbed up to the high pasture there to fetch back some sheep."

"Did you notice that there was more than one path leading to the top?" He asked.

I nodded.

"You can start on this side of the mountain and go straight up the steep path or you can take the one that zigzags back and forth. Or you can start from the other side of the mountain all together. There are countless ways to reach the top, as there are countless ways to come to know God."

"Which one is the best?" I asked.

"It all depends on where you start and how you like to travel!" he said with a chuckle. "No one path is better than any other."

"So how did you come to be in a monastery?"

"I was hungry for knowledge and set about finding a way to get it. One day as I walked through the market place I heard a man speaking my language. I had not heard it since leaving the ship and could hardly control myself when I had the chance to talk to someone who could understand what I was saying."

"It turned out that he was from the monastery of Santa Katarina deep in the desert. I sensed that I could learn what I wanted to know at the monastery and asked him if I could go there with him".

"What's a 'desert'?" I asked.

The old monk raised his eyebrows, poured more of the green liquid into my cup and said, "Oh, my boy, you have a lot to learn!"

I nodded in agreement and waited for his answer.

"A desert," he explained, "is a place where it almost never rains. Without rain no plants can grow, few animals can live. "

"What is there?"

"Sand and stone and the blazing sun by day," he said; "and the most amazingly clear view of the stars at night. In the monastery, we watched the stars and studied the ancient books".

"What did you learn there?"

"Many, many wonderful things," he replied. "I was young, and I guess I was bright, or else just so anxious to learn that I applied myself! I had learned how to read Latin, the language of the Western church. At the monastery most of the book were written in Greek, a very ancient language, so I had to learn that language as well as learning to read and then to write it."

"And when I was able to decipher the old books by myself, I realized that everything that I had been taught as a child was wrong."

Chapter 87 - Stories and the Stars

"What was wrong with what you were taught?" I asked him, fascinated.

"I was told that the stories were about real people, doing real things in this word ", he said.

"And they are not?"

"My boy," he said, "you told me yourself that you had trouble understanding the pictures in the church".

"I wondered about the talking snake!" I told him, emboldened by the effect of green liquor.

"What about kings traveling from afar to finding a baby in a manger?" he asked, "not to mention people coming back from the dead!"

"So," I wondered aloud, "if these stories aren't true, why are they painted on church walls? Why do people believe them?"

"In my studies," the old man said, "I learned many things. I learned that Christ is one of many Gods said to have died and then came back to life again."

I must have looked puzzled because he continued, "As I told you before, there is one God, with many names and many aspects. It's not surprising, because God is all there is!"

"Ah, but I am getting ahead of myself," he laughed, taking another sip of his drink.

"I was shocked when I learned about the ancient Egyptian God, called Osiris. He, too, was slain. His sister and consort, the Goddess Isis, brought him back to life. Then there was the Greek story of Adonis. He was a man, not a god, but he died and was brought back to life by the Goddess Aphrodite."

"What these stories are telling us is that all life is reborn. Think of the plants and the trees in the forest. In winter they seem to be dead, but come springtime all life is reborn. The feast of Easter, when we celebrate Christ rising from the dead, is always in the spring," he said.

"What does that mean to us?" I asked.

"It means that a part of us, like all of nature, will continue to live after the death of our physical body."

"How is that?" I asked.

"We will live on as spirits, or if we choose we can come back to this earth in a new body," he said.

"No one talks about that," I said. "They say that when we die, if we led a good life we will go to heaven and if we've been bad we will burn in hell; and from the church pictures, that looks awful!"

He sighed. "That's what they are teaching the people," he said, "but it's not what's in the old books. The men at the head of the church think that they need to scare people into behaving themselves instead of inspiring them with the truth".

"Why is that, Brother?" I asked.

If people knew that they could connect with God, the sacred life force that permeating all things, including each and every one of us, then they wouldn't need the church."

"Maybe people wouldn't behave themselves if they weren't afraid of ending up in the fires of hell," I said.

"If people came to know that we are all one," he said, "and anything hurtful that they did to anyone else was actually harming themselves, they would follow the beautiful saying attributed to Jesus Christ, without needing the threat of hell."

"What is the saying" I asked.

"Do unto others as you would have them do unto you," he said.

"That's it?" I asked, "It seems too simple."

"In my years of learning and experience," the old monk replied, "I've found that the more simple something is, the better!"

"Tell me more about the stories!"

"The reason there are so many similar stories from different places and traditions is because they are all based on truths that are universal, like the rebirth of spring after the darkness of winter."

"Have you ever considered why it is colder and darker in winter than it is in summer?" he asked.

"No," I said, "it's just the way it is."

Shall I tell you why?" he asked with a twinkle in his eye. "You may not believe me, but what I will say is the truth."

"Yes, I want to know!"

"It's because of the movement of the earth."

"Not the movement of the sun?" I asked. "It seems to move closer and farther from us."

"It is our earth that it moving closer and farther from the sun," he explained. "Our earth is a sphere. It circles around the sun; a journey that takes one year. Because the earth tilts a bit around its central axis, for some part of the circle we face the sun more directly. This is summer. The days are warmer and longer. At two places in the circle, the earth faces the sun straight on and days and nights are the same length. This moment is called the 'equinox', because day and night are of equal lengths."

"On the two days of equinox, the sun seems to rise directly in the east and set directly in the west. This is how we know how to align our important buildings and crossroads. In Alexandria, I saw sundials that divide the day into hours based on knowing the directions from the observation of the apparent movement of the sun."

"This is all very interesting," I said, trying to be courteous but actually getting a little bored, "but what does it have to do with the stories?"

"I'm getting to that!' he said. " Each day after the autumn equinox the sun seems to rise a little bit further south. When the days are the shortest in the middle of winter, the sun is in its most southerly position. It stays there for two or three days and then starts to move north east again. It is that movement that we celebrate as the birth of Christ; the one who brings light back to the darkened world."

"People from many places and many cultures observed this movement and created different stories about the same celestial event".

"What about that story with the tree and the snake?" I asked.

The tree is the symbol of the central axis of the world," he explained. "Each time the earth spins fully on its axis we experience a day and a night. It was known as 'the Tree of Life' "

"And the snake?"

"Remember, I told you how, in the desert, we had a very clear view of the stars," he said.

"Yes."

"I could observe, as so many people from many countries had seen and written about, thousands of individual stars and constellations."

"What's a constellation?"

"It's a group of stars in the sky," he replied. "By watching how they seem to move around the night sky we can learn many things."

"Why is it so important that people would want to make up stories about it?" I asked.

"It's important for people to realize their connection to all creation," he said; "that they are a part of everlasting life."

"The serpent in the story is actually a constellation known as 'Dracos', the dragon. The dragon was the guardian and protector of the Tree of Life."

"And Adam and Eva?" I asked. "Who are they?"

"They represent the sacred union of the male and female principles, through which new life is born."

"But then God throws them out of the garden," I said, "Why?"

"This is part of the story that was added by the church fathers," he said. "In most of the very old practices it was the women who led the rituals as mothers and givers of life. For the new priesthoods to establish their power they had to suppress the important role of women."

"Is that why there is no God the Mother?" I asked.

He laughed. "Yes," he said. "The men in the later establishment created God in their own likeness, as an authoritarian male. But they could not totally repress people's deep knowing that there must also be the Divine feminine principle and, over time, Mary, the so-called 'mother of God', was given a place in the church."

"You know that when a woman's body is prepared, the seed of a man planted into her womb will create a new life," the old monk continued.

I felt myself blushing at his mention of intimacy between men and women. We never spoke about such things.

"My boy!" he said noticing the color that had risen in my cheeks, "the love between a man and a woman is sacred! It is to be celebrated. It is how all things come into being. The feminine principal waits in readiness, calling all things to itself while the masculine principle is active, enlivening and creating through the feminine. Both principles exist in men and women alike, as they do in all creation. The stories, in their true form, remind us about this; how if we observe ourselves and strive for balance we will live in accordance with the laws of nature and bring happiness to ourselves and others."

Chapter 88 - Forgiveness

"Brother, will you tell me more about the laws of nature?" I asked. Maybe they would be easier to understand than the strange stories of the paintings.

"By observing nature," the old monk said, "we can learn many important truths; we can figure things out for ourselves and not rely on anybody else or books to tell us".

"But didn't you learn from the old books?" I said, now becoming confused anew by his words.

"I learned what I am telling you now," he said, "not facts themselves but a way of paying attention to everything around me in a new way; knowing that everything is sacred and everything can help me in my life and in my dealings with other people."

"One of our greatest teachers is our own body," he said. "Stand up, my boy!"

I looked at him for a moment without moving. He nodded at me, and waved his hand up and down indicating that I should do as he bid. I put the cup down gently and got on my feet.

"Go over there," he said; "where you have some space".

I followed his instructions and stood in the center of the small room. I saw his bright eyes moving up and down my body.

"Take a step or two forward," he instructed.

I did as I was told.

"Now take a few steps back".

I started to turn around to go back to where I started but he called out, "No! Stay facing me and step backwards."

This was hard! I felt very uncomfortable and reached out to touch the wall to steady myself.

"Ah, ha!" said the old monk, nodding and smiling. "Come back and sit here."

"You had a rough time in the past, didn't you, my boy," he said; "but don't worry, you are ready to face the future with strength and confidence; but you need to develop your emotions if you want to be truly happy in your life."

"How do you know these things," I asked, "just from looking at me?"

"I'll explain; as I said before, your body is one of your greatest teachers. It is written in the ancient books 'as above, so below'. This means that by observing and contemplating things close to you, you can learn and understand everything in the cosmos."

"Your backbone is the axis of your body, and, like the axis of the world it holds you in balance. I can see that your left shoulder is a little lower than your right one and that you put more weight on your right foot. This shows me that your male, thinking side is stronger than your female, feeling side."

"I'm a man," I said, "isn't that the way I should be?"

"You are a person," he said, "in a male body; is important for you to balance both principles. Imagine if it were always summer. There would be no rain to make the plants grow. Heat and dryness are male principles, but without times of cool and wetness all of nature would be out of balance."

"Aren't hot and cold very different; aren't they opposites?" I asked.

"Opposites are always aspects of the same thing. One could not exist without the other," he replied.

"Watching you walk forwards I could see that you are confident. You held you head high and stepped firmly with both your right and your left foot. But I could see that moving backwards made you uncomfortable; this shows that you are holding on to old fears from difficulties that you experienced in the past. The things we carry from the past can burden us and stop us from being happy in the present."

"How can I change that?" I asked. "I don't want to carry around old fears".

"The fastest way to lighten you load is forgiveness," he told me.

"Forgiveness?" I didn't understand what he meant by that.

"Every morning when you wake up and last thing at night before you sleep, repeat to yourself these words: 'I forgive myself and anyone who has ever hurt me'," he said. "You will see, over time that you will begin to feel free. Think now, for a moment, about whom you will need to forgive."

I thought about the people in my past. Should I forgive my father for disappearing? Forgive my mother for dying and leaving me alone? Forgive the shepherd for forgetting to feed me? Forgive the blacksmith for making my days a misery? Forgive Milada for not loving me back?

As if reading my thoughts, the monk said, "Think now about the good things these people have done for you; the gifts you received from your experience of knowing them".

My father gave me life. My mother worked hard to provide food and keep me alive. The shepherd gave me shelter when no one else would. The blacksmith taught me a profitable trade. And Milada? Milada gave me happy hours of friendship.

Breaking into my thoughts, the monk spoke up again. "Gratitude is another powerful force. When you are grateful for all the experiences in your life, when you acknowledge that even the things that seem bad at the time are serving a purpose, teaching you a valuable lesson, you will begin to feel happier and most positive here and now."

"Use what I am telling you now, my boy," he said. "Never judge a person by what he says. Words are a very small part of expression and many people are skillful in their use. Rather observe a person's body; how he stands, how he moves. Look into his eyes and you will be able to read his intentions."

"Thank you for your wise advice," I said, still lost in thoughts of my past, and of Milada.

"You never lose by loving," the old monk said, once again seeming to read my mind. "At the end of the day, God is love."

"God is love?" I asked. Again, it seemed too simple.

"I can see from your eyes that you know the feeling of love," he said.

I nodded.

"You are young, still," he went on, "it was probably love for some pretty young girl."

I nodded again.

"The love we feel for an individual is like a drop of water compared to the sea. It gives us an idea of what love is. As we learn to grow and expand that love to *all* people, *all* creation, we become like God."

"How can we love people who are mean to us?" I asked, thinking of the bad-tempered blacksmith and, much worse, the horsemen that raided our village.

"All people are here on this earth to serve a purpose," he said. "Sometimes we are not able to understand what it is and it may seem 'bad' to us."

"The teachings of Jesus Christ say to 'love you enemies'," he continued. "It's easy, after all, to love your friends, but by loving your perceived enemies you become like the sun that shines down on all without distinction; this is the love that is God."

"The gypsies never fought," I murmured. "Maybe they understood this idea."

"What else did you learn from your time with them?" the monk inquired.

"I wasn't that interested in what they believed," I admitted. "Some of what they said sounded so odd. They, too, thought that the world was a ball, but I didn't believe it!"

"They often gazed up at the night sky and, once, they even told me that their people came from the stars!" I went on.

"I would love to know these gypsies," the old man said. "In my studies there were many stories about beings that came from the stars in the distant past to help the people here on earth to evolve in consciousness."

I didn't understand what he meant and before I could ask I heard the door squeaking open behind me. I turned to see the village priest stepping into to our cozy nest.

"What are you telling this lad?" he asked the monk. "Filling his head with your foolish ideas, are you?"

The monk said nothing; a little smile lifted the corners of his lips.

"You, boy," the village priest said to me, "run along home now. And don't believe anything this wild old man has been telling you!"

I didn't like the tone of the priest's voice and would rather stay and listen to the monk.

"I said 'go now", the priest repeated.

"It's all right, my boy," the old monk said. "It's time for me to rest these weary old bones."

"Good night, Brother!" I said, "Thank you. You have given me a lot to think about!"

As I was leaving I heard the priest say to him, "You have overstayed your welcome, old man. Come morning, be on your way. You have no business poisoning this boy's mind with your crazy ideas."

I hurried back to the warmth of my room. Dunia was already in bed. I crawled in beside her and, remembering the old monk's instructions, whispered to myself, "I forgive myself and anyone who has ever hurt me," before falling into a dreamless sleep.

Chapter 89 - A Marrying Man

When I awoke the next morning, once again I repeated the phrase that the old monk had taught me, "I forgive myself and anyone who has ever hurt me."

Dunia, still by my side, asked, "What did you say?"

"Oh, just something I learned from a wise old man," I said.

That day in the forge, my mind went over the monk's words. I observed the blacksmith as he moved in the course of his work. I could see that his shoulders slumped forwards as if to protect his chest. He favored his right side in all his movements, with his left arm often hanging limp at his side. I already knew that he had difficulty expressing any emotion except anger and watching how he moved his body seemed to confirm what the old man had told me.

I finished my work for the day I went to the stable next to the church looking for the monk but the stable was empty. I guess the old monk had moved on. In my mind, I wished him well on his journey and wondered if he, in his wanderings, would cross path with the gypsies; and Milada.

His words whispered in the back of my mind as the day of my wedding drew near. I observed the people around me and even asked Jelko to take some steps backward and was surprised when he did so with ease.

"Have you always been happy?" I asked him.

He looked at me in surprise. "Yes, of course!" he said with a laugh. "But not as happy as I am now with Janka and the baby!"

On the day before the wedding ceremony I came home for the midday meal. The house seemed empty. I knew the blacksmith had gone directly to the tavern, but there was no sign of the girls or their mother. I could smell something cooking, though, and went over and lifted the top of the iron cooking pot hanging from a hook over the hearth.

A blast of cool air hit me as the door opened and shut.

"It's just the two of us today, it seems," Dunia's mother said, hanging her heavy cloak on the peg beside the door.

"Are the girls with Janka?" I asked. They'd been spending quite a bit of time fussing over the wedding preparations. Luckily for me, it was mostly at Janka's and Jelko house, a recent addition to the side of her family home. If they'd been here, there would have been no end of complaining from the blacksmith.

Dunia's mother filled two bowls with some fragrant soup and set them on the table side, by side.

"Goran," she said, "I'm glad we have this moment alone. I'd like to talk to you".

I realized that all the time I'd been living with the blacksmith's family I'd never really spoken with Dunia's mother.

"Yes, certainly," I said. "Do you want to talk about the wedding?"

"I want to talk about the life you and my daughter will share," she said.

I nodded and looked down at my soup, feeling a little uncomfortable at her words and the sadness I could see in her eyes.

"I think that you know that her father never loved me," she began.

I remained silent and let her continue, sensing that this conversation was difficult for her.

"He was in love with my sister, Anna," she continued. "When Anna wed Milan, he was furious. He refused to speak with his brother and kept trying to tempt Anna away but she always refused him. When he realized that she would never be his, he courted me. I guess he thought I was the next best thing. We did resemble each other, in looks if not in personality."

"If you knew he wanted your sister and not you, why did you marry him?" I asked.

"It might be hard for you to believe, seeing him now, but the girls' father was a very handsome man. He had a temper, yes, but there were not many boys in the village after the great sickness and I hated the idea of moving from my home. I married him in the hope that one day he would come to love me. Maybe one day he will," she finished in a whisper.

"Why are you telling me this story now?" I asked, fearing her answer.

"I want something better than that for my girls," she said. "It is known that you were in love with my sister's girl, Anna, whom you called 'Milada'," she said, looking over at me to gauge my reaction.

"I cannot deny that I was," I said softly; once again remembering the pain I felt when I learned that she did not return my love. "But Dunia will be a good wife and is a fine mother".

"Yes, she is well prepared to fill those roles, as was I," her mother said with a sigh. "Her father is a good husband in that he provides well for us. We are never without a meal or a roof over our heads."

"But that's not enough, is it?" I asked, our eyes meeting, maybe for the first time.

She just shook her head. "All girls dream of love," she said.

"I will try to love your daughter as she deserves," I said.

"You know that she loved you from the first time you met," she said, dropping her eyes. "But don't tell her that I told you so!"

"I know that she loved me enough to have my child," I said, smiling thinking of my beautiful daughter.

Just then I heard someone at the door. As it opened, Dunia's mother said quietly, "Don't hurt her, Goran. Please."

"I gently patted her work worn hand and said, "I won't, Mother; I won't".

"Did you leave any soup for us?" Yagoda exclaimed, dropping her cloak on the bench. "I'm famished!"

"Didn't you eat at Janka's," I asked.

"No!" she said, filling a bowl for herself and sitting down beside us. "There was plenty of food but it's all for the feast tomorrow."

"Even though we lost so much to the invaders," Dunia's mother said, "there is still enough for a fine celebration."

~

Dunia spent the night before our wedding in her parents' house as was the custom. My wedding day dawned with a cloudless blue sky. Barely out of bed, I heard Jelko at the stable door below.

"Aren't you dressed yet!" he hollered up to me.

"It's early! I just woke up!" I yelled back.

"Well put on your wedding duds and get down here to hitch up the horses. Then we'll go and fetch our blushing brides!" I could hear the happy anticipation in his voice.

That night I'd been thinking about what Dunia's mother had said. Was it fair to marry her daughter? I knew that Milada still held my heart. Yet I loved my little Gahla and, for her sake, I would wed her mother and make us a family. There had been moments when I felt love growing for Dunia; I liked her and respected her but had to admit that I didn't feel toward her the way I did to my first love, Milada.

I rinsed my face in cold water and put on my fancy wedding clothes. As I pulled on my boots, highly polished for this special occasion, I couldn't help thinking about Dragan and his father; how their boots always shone even on the dustiest journeys. I thought how excited I would be if I were preparing for a wedding with Milada. Then I remembered the monk's words and realized that my thoughts of the past were taking away any joy I might find in the present.

"I forgive myself for these thoughts and anyone who has hurt me," I whispered to myself as I hurried down the steps to find Jelko putting the finishing touches on my horses.

I burst out laughing. "What have you done to them?" I exclaimed.

"I just made them fancy for our pretty new wives!" he said. He had draped each horse with a white sheet and over the horse's rumps he'd positioned two heavily embroidered aprons.

"Are those Dunia's?" I asked, fingering the fine needlework on one of them.

Jelko nodded; a big smile on his face.

"Does she know you put them on the horses?" I asked, not certain is Dunia would appreciate it.

"Of course not!" he said, "It's supposed to be a surprise!"

"You know they look silly!" I said.

"The aprons are lovely," he called back; "Everybody says Dunia's work is the best in these parts."

"I don't mean the aprons," I said, "I mean the horses! Maybe on a smaller horse all this fanciness would look all right, but on these two monsters it just looks silly!"

"Wait until you see the cart!" Jelko said with a chuckle. "We made it so fancy that the horses will look plain by comparison!"

I just sighed, taking one of the horses by the bridle and followed Jelko and my other overdressed horse out the wide stable door.

Chapter 90 - We Are Wed

We entered the village square riding on a cart loaded with bunting, boughs and bows pulled by the equally decorated plough horses. Jelko and I sat in our resplendent waistcoats, the late winter sunlight reflecting off the golden thread in the designs that Dunia had worked so beautifully. First we went to Janka's home. She looked lovely in her finest clothes, her long hair braided with brightly colored ribbons and her eyes lit up with joy.

Jelko hopped down from the cart and lifted her to the seat behind me. He settled himself next to her while I guided the horses to the blacksmith's house.

When I turned the corner I saw a man standing at the door. At first I wasn't sure it was the blacksmith at all! He wore a waistcoat almost as beautiful as mine. His unruly hair was combed back, he was clean shaven for once and his face, always covered with a fine layer of soot from the forge, was scrubbed clean.

"They're here, they're here!" I head Yagoda shouting and soon she and her mother accompanied my bride to the waiting cart. Following Jelko's lead I descended to help Dunia climb up to the front seat. She looked very pretty in her embroidered bodice and skirt but her eyes were guarded. The neighbors who had gathered around our festive cart didn't seem to notice, or maybe they just didn't care. This was a special occasion; the first wedding feast since the invaders had disrupted all our lives and people were ready to celebrate and forget their troubles for a little while.

"You look nice," I whispered to Dunia as I clicked to the horses to get them moving toward the church.

"Are you sure you want to do this?" she asked.

"Dunia!" I said, maybe a little too loudly. Her eyes told me to keep my voice down. "Yes, Dunia," I whispered. "Yes, I want you to be my wife."

At my words, the start of a smile appeared on her lips.

As we neared the church, more and more people were gathering and waving at us to wish us well. "Where are the babies?" I asked Dunia as we arrived in the church.

"They are with their grandmothers," Dunia said. "Our mothers are bringing them to the church. See; over there."

Looking where she indicated I saw my little Gahla in her grandmother's arms.

The priest was waiting for us on the church porch. Jelko and Janka went first. The priest asked each of them if they agreed to wed the other. When they said that did, he gave them his blessing and they proceeded into the church, smiling into each other's eyes.

Then in was our turn. I offered Dunia my hand and led her to the waiting priest. I felt her hand trembling in mine. "It will be fine", I told her. "Relax."

I couldn't fathom the look she gave me. I thought she might bolt! We'd come this far; we had to go through with the wedding now.

Smiling at her in a way that I hoped was reassuring I said, "Come now, my bride. Don't you know how beautiful you look today; just like a princess. All you need now is a smile."

At my words, her eyes softened and by the time we reached the church door she was beaming. The priest asked us the same questions and we gave the same, affirmative answers. I felt a little tightening in my stomach as I committed myself to be Dunia's husband in front of the priest and the whole assembled village but I knew that, for the love of my baby at least, it was the right thing to do.

"Are you happy?" I whispered to Dunia as we entered the church together.

"Yes, dear Gogo," she said, with tears in her shining eyes. "Yes, I am."

We took our places beside our friends at the front of the church. This was one Sunday service that Jelko and I couldn't leave early and make for the tavern!

For a while, I listened to the priest droning on in a language I did not understand. My mind began to wander to the paintings on the walls and the strange words of the old monk. In truth, his stories sounded as unbelievable to me as the ones Jelko and Dunia had told me. I felt restless, standing there, waiting for the service to be over. I really wanted to leave, but I knew that I couldn't.

Then a strange thing happened. Although I could not understand the meaning of the words, the rhythmic chanting was somehow getting to me. I looked over to see Dunia, smiling. Beyond her was my best friend, Jelko and the girl he loved. I felt the villagers standing behind us, celebrating our union. And for the first time in my life I felt I belonged. A feeling of warmth spread from the center of my body up toward my heart and I knew that I was smiling; that I was feeling the love that the old monk had said was God. At this moment, I didn't care about the stories, whether they were true or not; what mattered was to be here, together with others, sharing this moment of peace.

I reached out for Dunia's hand. It felt small and cold in mine. She looked over at me and smiled. After the service we all stayed in the church for the babies' christening. Both my Gahla and Jelko's Ivan looked like little angels and hardly cried at all as they were dipped into the baptismal font.

Dressed in fresh clothes, they were placed in their mother's arms and our two little families led the way to the tavern for the wedding feast. One of poor Stanyo's sheep provided a welcome change from the monotonous diet left to us by the invaders. Without their visit we would have had plenty of dried meat and sausages to last us through the winter, but since they took all our pigs we subsisted on dried fish, beans, shriveled apples, prunes and a little cheese made from the scant milk of Stanyo's flock.

The autumn fruit crop provided us with wine, at least, and we drank many a friendly toast until the sun was low in the west. Our brides had already left to settle the babes in their cribs and most of the villagers had returned to their homes when Jelko and I heard excited voices at the tavern's door.

A little unsteady on our feet after so many toasts, Jelko and I made our way over to see what the commotion was all about. I saw that it was Tonsho. In his hand he held a bird.

"What is it?" Jelko asked.

"I bet that bird brought another note," I said. "Let's get closer and see."

I saw Tonsho gently untie the string that held the small piece of cloth to the bird's leg. Cradling the cooing pigeon to his chest, he passed the note to another man to decipher.

I saw that it was Boban, now fully recovered from his injuries, thanks in part to Janka's ministrations.

"Eh, Bobo," Jelko yelled, "What's it say?"

"It seems like the horsemen are now south east of here," he replied.

"Are the close by?" I asked, my heart tightening. Just when we were beginning to feel settled a new threat might be upon us.

"No, thank God!" Boban reported. "The mark is far from our village."

There was a collective sigh of relief at his words, and then a cheer rose up among the men.

"This calls for a toast!" cried Jelko; "One more round for everyone!"

Chapter 91 - Looking for a Bull

In the weeks following the wedding, I noticed that each day was a little longer than the previous one and that light coming through my little window was at slightly different angle as winter loosened its grip on the world. This must have happened every year, but I never paid attention to the subtle, daily changes of the passing seasons.

My idea to procure horses had been a good one. Now that the ground had thawed, each day the pair was loaned out to pull the plough through the greening fields to prepare them for the spring planting. In return I received gifts of food, tooled leather, needlework or coins. One of the empty stalls was filling up with these gifts. There were too many for me and my family to use. I figured I would ask Milan then next time he came through the village if he would be interested in taking some to trade. These things would fetch a good price in other villages where they would be harder to come by.

But, before Milan returned to the village Jelko came up with an idea.

"I need a bull!" he said to me one afternoon in the tavern.

"A bull?" I asked.

"I have a cow, right?" he said.

"Yes," I replied. "You were very lucky that she found her way back to you!"

"Well," he said, "if I introduce my cow to a strong and handsome bull, she will make me a second cow and then I'll have more milk."

"Unless she makes you a bull!" I said, with a grin.

"In which case I'll let him get fat on the plentiful grass and then we can roast him and have a delicious meal," he said. "Either way, I will profit."

"Where will you find a bull?" I asked. There are none here in the village."

"There are other villages hereabouts," he said.

I figured there must be. When I was living with the gypsy band, we came usually came to a different village after a day's journey; but I never considered visiting any other village since I'd decided to settle in this one.

"What I was thinking," Jelko continued, moving his chair closer to mine so other patrons of the tavern could not overhear what he was saying, "is for you and me to take one of your big horses and the cart and find us a bull. You can bring the goods that you collected in exchange for the use of your horses to sell. They'll bring a good price."

As the goods piled up, I was thinking that if I could sell them for coins I could add them to the ones I had already saved and maybe have enough money to buy a piece of land of my own. I liked the idea of building a new house for my family and being able to grow the food we needed ourselves.

"I like your idea!" I told Jelko. "I will ask the blacksmith for some time off. We have repaired or replaced most of the villagers' tools now and since there are no horses to shoe but my own there is not much work at the forge."

The next morning we set out early, the cart loaded with a selection of handiwork, from embroidered pillow slips made by the village women to a pair of sturdy boots and bags made of tanned leather. I figured the needlework would fetch a good price since the women of our village were well known for their skill.

We headed northwest; away from the place the invaders had last been spotted. As we passed through the village gate I wondered if we would be safe traveling alone like this with a cartful of goods. Milan did it, but he knew the routes and how far it was from village to village.

"Do you know where we are going?" I asked Jelko, thinking that since he grew up here, he might be familiar with the nearby villages.

"Yes," he said, "We will be in the Havida, the nearest village to ours, well before the sun is high in the sky. There is another one not far beyond that."

We passed the journey pleasantly, joking and enjoying the spring sunshine. But when we reached the village the smiles faded from our lips. The invaders had been here. The village gate was gone altogether and many homes still lay in ruin.

"I don't think we'll find a bull here," I said to Jelko, surveying the village square in dismay, "or anyone who will want to buy my goods."

"Let's keep going," Jelko said, "Maybe the next village had stronger walls."

We made our way back to the main track and followed it around the village where it led through a narrow gorge onto a wide plain. Perched on the side of the hill overlooking the valley, I saw some stone walls.

"Look up there!" I said, "Is that a village?"

"Looks like it could be," Jelko said. "Shall we go up and see?"

I guided the horse up a winding cobbled road that led to a tall wooden gate. Even though it was well after sunrise the gate was firmly closed. A rope hung down next to the gate. I could see that it was attached to a large brass bell.

"Pull the rope!" Jelko said. "Let them know that we are here!"

I did so and soon a small window in the gate opened.

"Who goes there?" said a man wearing a tight leather helmet

"We have goods to sell!" I said. "May we enter?"

The man looked out at Jelko and the cart.

"Fine big horse you have there," he said. "It is for sale?"

"The horse? No!" I replied, but I have some first-rate needlework and leather goods."

The little window slammed shut; then I heard the hinges on the gate groan as it slowly opened.

I hopped back up on the cart and we rolled into a village square that seemed untouched by the invaders. The man in the leather helmet welcomed us and said that we could set up our goods near the market place.

I did so while Jelko went in search of a suitable bull. People flocked around my cart and before I knew it I'd sold everything that I had brought! I used some of the coins to buy sausages, cheese and some big bags of flour to bring back to our village.

My work done, I went to the tavern and introduced myself to the people there. I asked them how they managed to keep the invaders out of their village.

"Our village is well hidden on the hillside," a man said. "Unless you are looking for it, it's hard to see."

I thought about how we had nearly passed it by. "So you think they just didn't see it?" I asked.

"We spotted a cloud of dust moving along the plain and knew trouble was coming," another man told me. "So we sent out the word for everyone to extinguish their fires so there would be no tell-tale smoke rising from the village."

"It was dusk when the cloud of dust was near enough for us to see that it was indeed a band of horsemen. Night fell as they passed through the gorge beneath us, unaware that our village was here. The next morning we could smell the smoke from the village on the other side of the hill. The folks there did not fare as well as we did."

"Neither did we," I told them. "Only now is our village beginning to recover."

I saw Jelko walking past the tavern and called out to him through the open window. Instead of coming in, be beckoned me to join him.

I bid the men farewell, paid for my drink and found Jelko at the cart.

"Let's get out of here," he grumbled.

"What," I said, "no bulls?"

"There are bulls alright!" he said, "but these people are asking too much money for the privilege of letting my cow mate with one."

As we approached the village gate the man with the helmet waved us down.

"You've sold you stock, I see," he said, eyeing the nearly empty cart.

"Yes," I said.

"You will need to pay tax then," he told me.

"Tax?"

"Yes. How much money did you make?" he asked me.

I opened my pouch and counted the coins inside. There were six silver coins and about twenty Florins. I had spent another twenty Florins on the supplies.

When I told him he said, "We take one part in ten of what visitors make here. Give me one silver coin and I will give you forty Florins back."

I didn't know that I would have to pay to sell my goods in this village. Milan never mentioned a 'tax', but then again, I had never asked him about it!

Chapter 92 - An Encounter by the Stream

"Did you know that I would have to pay tax?" I asked Jelko as we clattered down the hillside.

"No," he said, "and I didn't think that anyone would want money to let a bull have a good time with my cow."

"The sun is halfway down already," he continued, "We'd better get back to our village before nightfall. Can we try a different direction tomorrow?"

"Yes we can!" I said. I was enjoying being out on the road, exploring with my friend, yet knowing that I would be back in my own bed that night. I thought of the money that I had made. It was a substantial amount, even if I did have to pay tax on it.

I put aside what I needed for my family from the provisions that I bought and sold the rest at the same price as I had paid for them. It didn't feel right to profit from my neighbors' suffering. When the blacksmith heard that I hadn't made a profit he called me a fool.

Over the next few days Jelko and I traveled to villages all around our own. We didn't come to any other that had totally escaped the invaders. At each place we stopped we heard stories of death and destruction. I sold some goods here and there, but nothing like I had in the village on the mountainside. Jelko, on the other hand, was luckier. Although a price was asked to mate his cow, it was a fraction of what was requested at the prosperous village.

Having finally located a willing bull and willing owner we returned to a village due east of ours, with Jelko's cow in tow. This village was also on the edge of a cliff, but not so well hidden.

But the time the cow was mated I had sold most of my goods. Most of the ploughing has been done, but there were always odd jobs for my horses. The feast of Easter came and with it came the longer and warmer days of springtime.

I thought of the monk's words as I watched the fields and forest coming back to life. The sheep were giving birth to their lambs and I could now see another child growing in Dunia's belly as Gahla began to take her first steps.

One warm spring day I decide to let my horses have a day of rest. I led them out of the village to the clearing full of succulent young grass where the gypsies had made their camp. I left the horses to graze and wandered along the stream to the place we had sheltered from the invaders. I lay down on the mossy bank, enjoying the warmth of the sun on my body, listening to the sound of the rushing stream, and let my thoughts wander where they may.

I my mind, I could see Milada, smiling in the sunshine. I thought I could hear her voice calling me, "Goran, it's me, Milada."

My mind must have been playing tricks on me, I thought, letting myself drift away in happy memories. In my dream, Milada was lying on the grass behind me, her soft arms caressing my side. I felt her lips gently kissing my ear, then my neck; her wild hair tickling my face.

I turned to face her and our lips met, my arms reaching over to caress her back.

"Ahh, Gogo! How long I've waiting for this moment!"

I opened my eyes and knew that this was no dream; and neither was this my Milada!"

I pushed the girl away.

"Yagoda! What are you doing?" I exclaimed, shocked by the realization of what I had done.

"You can call me 'Milada'; I don't mind," she said, moving closer to me again.

Had her sister told her what I had said, right here in the swimming hole; how I had called out Milada's name when I was with Dunia?

"Yagoda, you must stop this!" I said shoving her away.

"You know you like it, Gogo. And Dunia is so fat now; you don't want to lay with her," she said. "Please, Gogo, come to me now. I'm just like Milada; you know I am."

At that moment her resemblance to Milada ended with her shining, wild hair. Her cold eyes and pouting mouth were nothing like those of the girl I had loved so deeply.

I stood up to go.

"Not now, Yagoda. Not ever," I said, leaving her there on the grass.

"I'll tell them you kissed me!" she yelled at my back. "I'll tell Dunia you made me lie with you because I am like Milada!"

Would she do that, I wondered? Sometimes I thought that girl was evil, but would she go so far as tell a lie that would hurt her sister so deeply and upset the happy family that I was trying to create?

I knew if I went back she would be all over me. Quickly I took the horses' halters and led them back to the stable. I needed to speak with Dunia before she did! Luckily, I found her alone with a sleeping Gahla in our room, sitting in the light of the small high window, working on a piece of intricate needlework.

"Dunia," I said gently putting my hand on her shoulder.

"Yes, Gogo, what is it?" she asked

"It's that pesky sister of yours again," I said, not sure of how to express what I needed to say.

"What did she do now?" Dunia asked. "Did she hide a horse again?"

"No," I said, "I think it's worse than that."

Dunia put down her work and looked up at me. I sat beside her on the bench and took both her hands in mine.

"I was down by the stream enjoying the sun while the horses grazed and must have fallen asleep. When I awoke, Yagoda was beside me, holding me."

I watched as the color drained from Dunia's cheeks.

"What happened then," she asked softly.

"Before I was awake," I said, hoping that she would believe me, "she kissed me."

"On your lips?" she asked.

I just nodded. I didn't tell her that Yagoda said to call her 'Milada'.

"Did you kiss her back?"

"I'm not sure," I said truthfully. "I think I thought I was still dreaming."

"Dreaming of Milada," Dunia murmured.

"Or dreaming of you!" I said, hoping to save her feelings. "As soon as I realized what was happening I pushed her away and told her never, never to do anything like that again."

"What did she say?"

"She said that she would tell you that I tried to kiss *her*," I said.

Dunia looked deeply into my eyes. "Can you tell me in all honesty that you didn't want to kiss her?" she asked.

"Dunia, dear Dunia; truly what I said is what happened. I feel nothing for your sister, nothing at all."

As I spoke those words I heard a gasp from the bottom of the stairs. I got up and looked over the railing to see Yagoda there, her hand clasped in front of her mouth, a hurt look in her eyes. I suppose she had come to tell Dunia her lies. Instead she heard me telling Dunia the truth about my lack of feelings for her.

"Who's there?" Dunia asked, rising.

"It was just one of the horses," I said, meeting Yagoda's glaze, and letting her know with my eyes that she held no place in my heart.

Chapter 93 - The Gypsies Return

I was dreading seeing Yagoda as Dunia and I made our way to the house for the evening meal. But when I got there, instead of a sulky girl I was greeted warmly by a cheerful man. Milan had finally returned!

"Milan!" I exclaimed with pleasant surprise; "It's good to see you!"

He drew me into his warm embrace.

"It's good to see you, too," he said. "I hear you are a happily married man now!"

"Yes," I told him. "Dunia and I were wed at the end of the winter. We have another child on the way!"

"Good for you!" he said, clapping me on the back. He turned to Dunia and smiled.

"Motherhood suits you, niece!" he said.

Dunia blushed at his words. I looked around for her sister but she was nowhere in sight. I felt relieved and sat down at the table, looking forward to talking to Milan about my new ventures.

"I've been doing a little trading myself," I told him.

"Have you now?" he said.

I explained to him about the horses and the goods their work was earning me.

"I didn't know I would have to pay tax when I sold things, though!" I told him.

"Ah, yes. Tax!" he said, shaking his head. "Some villages require we pay it and others do not. It's good to know which ones do so you can increase your prices to cover it."

I hadn't thought of that!

"Most of the villages around here are still recovering from the raid last summer," I told him.

"I saw that," he said. "I traded more in stories than in goods in these parts. That's why I was away for so long. I had to go far away to find villages that still had money and goods to trade. I only came back now in the hope of seeing my daughter. It is the time of year when the gypsies sometime pass this way."

I thought back at all that had passed since Milada left with the gypsy band. I wondered if, indeed, the band would return; and if so, how would I feel now that I was making a new life here.

After the meal and the blacksmith left for the tavern Dunia asked her uncle if he would play some music for us.

He said that it would be his pleasure, took up his instrument and played. The music soothed Gahla to sleep and, after a while Dunia silently took her in her arms and left to put her to bed in our little room over the stable. Her mother had already fallen asleep on the divan near the hearth.

When they had gone, Milan put away his instrument and sighed.

"What is it?" I asked him, quietly.

"Seeing my niece with her child; seeing you with them as a happy father reminds me of what I missed when I left," he whispered.

"You could marry again," I said. "Have you never met a woman on your travels that you could love?"

"Some women would like me to," he said, "but my heart still pines for my Anna."

"Even though she had been gone for so many years?" I asked.

As he nodded sadly, I thought of my feelings for Milada. As much as I tried to put them out of my head, to convince myself that I was over her, in truth, deep down I still wished that we could be together somehow.

"If only there were some magic potion to heal us from these impossible longings," I murmured.

"Do you still think about my daughter?" Milan whispered.

"I wish that I could say 'no'," I told him. "I want to make my life here, I really do and I am trying to do right by Dunia and my child."

"You are an honorable young man," Milan said as the front door opened and the blacksmith walked in, ending our conversation.

He looked around the room and then said, in a voice loud enough to wake his sleeping wife, "Where's that daughter of yours?"

"Dunia went to our room with the baby," I said, annoyed at his rudeness.

"Not Dunia," he bellowed, "the younger one. They said in the tavern that those gypsies are back. If she's gone to them again I will tan her hide!"

Milan and I looked at each other. The gypsies had returned. His eyes lit up at the thought of seeing his daughter. I wasn't so sure I wanted anything to disrupt my life now.

Just then, the door opened a crack. I could see Yagoda peeking in the door, most likely checking to see if her father was home. Their eyes met and before she could shut the door and get out of the way of his anger he pulled it open and grabbed her by the hair.

"You were with those people again, weren't you!" he yelled in her face.

Yagoda looked at him defiantly, foolishly fearless. "I can do whatever I please," she spat.

The blacksmith slapped her hard. "Not while you are living under my roof!" he yelled.

Milan went over to his brother. "Leave her," he said, "she is just a girl."

"Get out of my way or I'll beat you, too," he said. Still holding on to the girl's hair he used his other hand to push his brother to the ground.

I didn't know what to do. Part of me wanted to help the girl, yet part of me was still angry with her for what she had done to me. But, before I had the chance to act, the blacksmith had already stripped off his belt and was using it to beat his struggling daughter.

He mother looked on in silence. I knew that this was not the first time Yagoda had been beaten by her father.

"Stop it! That's enough!" Milan called but the blacksmith was caught in a frenzy of anger and kept striking his daughter over and over.

"This'll teach you not to defy me," he spat; "You bring shame on me and our family, you wanton slut!"

Finally, he dropped his arm and let go of the girl. She slumped to the ground, her face mottled, tears running down her cheeks.

The blacksmith looked down at her. "You disgust me!" he said then marched out the door, probably back to the tavern for yet another drink.

Yagoda's mother went over to the girl and helped her to the divan. It was hard for her to walk after the beating that she had received. There was nothing I could do, so, without a word, I left.

Back in our room I told Dunia what had happened.

"That girl is trouble," she said.

"Still, it was not right what your father did," I said.

"But how will she learn if she is not punished?" Dunia asked.

"I will never beat our Gahla!" I said. "The gypsies never beat their children to make them behave."

"The gypsies, again," Dunia sighed. "We are not gypsies."

"No, we're not," I agreed, "but there are some things that we can learn from them."

The next morning I did not want to see the blacksmith. Instead of going to the forge I went to find Jelko. I figured he'd be checking on his cow as she was due to give birth any day. I followed the narrow lanes to the barn where I stayed when I first came to live in the village and found Jelko there with his cow and a newborn calf.

"Congratulations, my man!" I said patting him on the back. "Are we going to have milk or roast beef?"

"Milk, I'm happy to say" he replied with a smile; "and the possibility of more cattle!"

"Are they all right?" I asked.

"They seem fine to me!" he said.

"This special occasion calls for a drink!" I said, "Shall we go to the tavern?"

Jelko looked down at the cow and her calf. "They look contented to me," he said, "Let's go!"

I sat down at a table on the square in the sunshine while Jelko went inside the tavern to get our drinks.

Soon he was back. He placed the beakers on the well-worn table and said, "You'd better go and lock you stable door!"

"Why should I do that?" I asked him, puzzled.

"That strange old gypsy man is back with his tricks," he replied. "He knows you have some fine horses because he was the one who sold them to you!"

So it wasn't Milada's gypsies that were back, I though. I was surprised to realize that I felt relieved rather than disappointed.

Chapter 94 - New Beginnings

I avoided the forge for the next few days. Instead I spent time with Milan, showing him my wares and learning some tricks of his trade. He paid me several silver coins for the finest of the embroideries and other goods that I had received in exchange for the services of my horses.

"I think I have enough money to buy a piece of land," I told him one afternoon as we sat together on the sunny side of the village square enjoying the warmth of early summer.

"Here in the village?" Milan asked.

"Yes," I told him. "It suits me here. And I don't think Dunia would want to move away from her family and friends."

"You seem happy," he told me. I heard sadness beneath his words.

"Isn't it time for you to settle down, too?" I asked. "There are several young widows living here who would be happy to share their homes with a pleasant man such as yourself."

"Would that I could," Milan said with a sigh. "But I know that after a season I would get restless and want to be on the road again."

"Yes," I said, "but at least you would have you own home to come back to and not need to rely on your brother's hospitality".

"If you build a new home of your own," he said, "I'll give you a gold coin to build on an extra room for 'old uncle Milan'!"

We both started to laugh. "I'll be happy to have you in my home!" I said, "And you don't need to give me any coins for the privilege," I added.

"I wouldn't have it any other way!" he exclaimed, taking a shiny gold coin from his money pouch. "Here, take this now. Consider it a wedding present for you and my niece."

I had never held a gold coin. "This is too much!" I said, hesitating.

"Take it!" he said. "It would please me."

With this coin I could put my plan in to action immediately. Hard work and some help from my friends would have a new house ready for my family in time for winter.

"Thank you, Milan, "I said, pocketing the heavy coin and shaking his hand. But a handshake was not enough to express my feeling for this man. I pulled him toward me in a warm embrace. "Thank you, my friend. You will always be welcome in my home and in my heart!"

At least he would have a place with me and my family when his legs were no longer strong enough to carry him down the long, dusty roads through villages and towns, I thought, but I said nothing; I'm sure he knew what I was thinking.

I saw Jelko coming across the square and waved at him to come over. When he approached I saw that he carried a long bow and had a quiver of arrows slung over his shoulder.

"Enjoying the sun, you two lazy bones?" he asked.

"We aren't so lazy," I said, "Milan and I have been discussing business".

"Well, I've been out hunting venison!" he said.

"Did you shoot any deer?" I asked.

"I shot at plenty," he said. "Pity I didn't hit any!"

"I don't remember you every using a bow and arrow', I said, "That is Boban's specialty."

"Boban made some bows and is showing me and some of the others how to use them," he told me. "Until we can build up our livestock we need to get better at hunting."

"Why didn't you tell me?" I asked. "I would like to try my hand as well."

"You've been busy with your 'businesses'," he replied with a laugh, "but if you want me to I'll ask Boban to make you a bow. I'm sure you can afford the best he can make."

"A simple one will be fine," I said. "Let's see if I have any aptitude for shooting first. If I do, then I'll invest in a finer one."

"You are a prudent young man," Milan said as Jelko swaggered back across the square to find Boban and pass on my request. "Many would insist on getting the best that they could afford to show off their wealth and stature."

"First let me get some land and build my house!" I said. "Once, many years ago when I traveled with the gypsies, I worked for a lady who lived in a grand house with many beautiful and unusual things. Since then, I've wanted to have a fine home of my own. After that, we can see about fancy toys like bows and arrows!"

"And now, I am hungry," I said. "Let's go to the house and see what the women have prepared for us."

We made our way back to the house, my mind distracted by the possibility of procuring a piece of land. Which side of the village would be the best? Should I buy an existing house, one of the damaged ones in a good position in the village and fix it up, or build a new one on the land. I was certain that Dunia would prefer to be in the village. I could build a small shelter on the land and have our main home in the village; maybe even on the village square if I could find someone who wanted to sell me one there.

I could smell the stew even before I opened the front door of the house. The day was warm and the windows were open to let in the last rays of the evening sun. Yagoda had not left the house since the blacksmith's beating so I was surprised to see that she was not at the table with Dunia and her mother. The blacksmith was probably at the tavern, as usual.

I was hungry and glad when Dunia went over to the hearth and ladled out bowls of stew for me and Milan.

"Where's your sister?" I asked, after polishing off my first bowl of stew and asking for some more.

"She said she was feeling better today and offered to go to the market to buy a loaf of bread to accompany the stew," Dunia said, "but she hasn't returned yet."

"She's probably chatting with her friends," I said, "since she hasn't seen them for a few days".

"Did you see them by the fountain?" Dunia asked. "That's where they usually meet."

"Milan and I were in the square," I said, "but, in truth, I didn't notice what was going on at the fountain. I'm sure that she will be back soon."

"She'd better be," Dunia said. "If our father gets home first she will be in trouble again."

But as the evening wore on, Yagoda did not return. When the blacksmith arrived worse for drink, as usual these days, he was furious.

"This time I will kill that girl!" he stormed. "No one defies me! She must be with those gypsies. I am going to find her, and when I do, she will never disobey me again!"

The blacksmith stormed out of the house. The girls' mother looked terrified.

"He will do it," she said. "Please, please stop him if you can!"

Milan and I jumped to our feet and ran after the angry blacksmith as he headed toward the gypsy camp. We were close behind him at the village gate; it was just about to be closed for the night.

"Keep it open!" the blacksmith bellowed. "I have business outside."

We followed him through the gate and turned in the direction of the gypsies' camp. But all we saw was an empty field. The gypsies had gone, and Yagoda with them.

The blacksmith spat on the ground.

He saw us standing there, speechless. Would he go after her, I wondered?

He scanned the horizon but the gypsies must have left some time before; there was no sign of dust in the air from their horses and carts; no way of knowing which direction they took.

The blacksmith spat on the ground. "Damn that girl," he grumbled. "She's been nothing but trouble to me. Let her go with them. And God help them to have her!"

He turned and made his way back into the village with us trailing behind. At the village gate, I gazed out onto the plain. As much as the girl had caused me trouble, I silently wished her luck on her onward journey.

Autumn

Chapter 95 - A Home of My Own

As spring warmed to summer I scouted for a piece of land to buy. Several of the villagers expressed interest in selling and it wasn't long before I secured a large field southeast of the village. It would provide good land for grazing sheep and goats and the soil was rich enough to plant vegetables and some hardy wheat. A stream ran through the land so I would have plenty of water. I planned to build a small house on a low rise that overlooked the valley beyond.

When I told Dunia about the land her face dropped.

"It's far from my mother's house and from my friends!" she said.

"This land is to work," I told her. "I will go there in the afternoon hours when I finish my work at the forge. It is not far to go if I take one of the horses."

"So we will still stay here in the room above the stable?" she asked. She looked down at her very large belly and added, "We will need more space when this baby comes."

"I was thinking of buying old Nikolas' house," I told her.

Her eyes widened. "Old Nikolas who has that big house right on the square?" she asked. 'Didn't his grandson die in the raid? That house was badly damaged, but once it was one of the best in the village."

"Yes," I said, "That's the one. It's sad that his grandson was killed. He has no other heirs and no means or desire to repair the house. If you think that you would like to live there, I will make him a fair offer and see how he responds."

"Gogo!" she exclaimed, "I never imagined living in such a fine house! Could you really afford to buy it?"

"That will depend on how much he asks," I told her.

"But you already bought a piece of land," she said. "Do you have enough left for the house? And we'll need some money to repair it, as well."

"Don't worry about the money," I told her. "Your Uncle Milan gave us a very generous wedding present."

I took out my pouch and drew out the gold coin.

"Oh, my!" Dunia said with a gasp. "That was a very, very generous wedding gift! I'm surprised that you accepted it."

"I didn't want to, at first," I told her, "but I told him that we will always have a special room for him in our house, in case he ever decides to settle down."

"Yes," she said, "It would be a pleasure to have him stay with us."

"I will go and speak with Mr. Nikolas now," I told her. "If he agrees I'll talk to the boys and get them to help me make all the repairs we need. Hopefully, we will be able to have it ready before winter sets in. By then the baby will be big enough so you won't have to stay with your mother."

"I'll say a prayer that he says 'yes'," she said, clapping her hands together.

I kissed her forehead and went to the square to find old Nikolas. I knew he'd be sitting in the sun with the other old men. Sometimes they chatted, but often they just sat, lost in their own thoughts and memories.

Sure enough, he was there. I asked him if he would be interested in selling me his damaged house. He inclined his head. I took that to mean 'yes'. I asked him how much he wanted for it. There was no response so I offered him what I thought would be a fair price and once again he inclined his head! This time he held out his hand as well. I took it in mine and sealed our bargain with a handshake.

The next day, in the presence of the priest and the headman of the village I handed the precious gold coin and five silver ones over to Mr. Nikolas. I didn't know what he would do with the money. I suppose it would pay the rent for the room in which he stayed on the upper floor of the tavern until the end of his life.

That summer my days were full. I rose early and rode out to my land. I'd managed to plant a late crop of vegetables. It pleased me to tend to it while the sun was still low in the sky. I returned to the village and had a bite of breakfast with Dunia and Gahla, delighting in watching my growing girl explore the world on her pudgy little legs.

Then it was time to go to the forge and help the blacksmith. Business was picking up. Several other villagers had been able to procure some horses as well as tools that needed to be sharpened before the autumn harvest.

After the mid-day meal and a little rest I worked on the house. Once we'd finished clearing the rubble, the damage wasn't as bad as I had originally thought. We would have had to change the roof anyway since I wanted to build a second story. There was a large yard behind the house. Next year I would plant some vegetable there, as well; a little garden to be handy for the kitchen. With the help of my friends I cut several trees from the forest and hew new beams for the roof. Despite the limited time I had to work on it, the house was coming along at a good pace.

I didn't have much free time but, when I could, I joined Jelko for target practice with Boban. Sometime we actually went hunting, but using a bow and arrow with swiftness and accuracy was not as easy as Boban made it look!

Late that summer, Dunia, with Janka in attendance, gave birth to our son. Everyone said that he looked just like me. I don't know if I would agree, but I liked it that other people said so! I wanted to call him 'Milan" after his generous uncle, but Dunia thought that her father would be offended. I didn't want to call him after the blacksmith, but since I couldn't remember the name of my own father, if ever I knew it to begin with, Dunia persuaded me to call him Viktor, after hers.

Once the baby was born, I redoubled my efforts on the house and, as I hoped, when the cooler weather and shorter days came we were ready to move into our new home. Dunia had used the time before the baby's birth to embroider decorative covers for the tables, beds and cushions. Although we still would need time to fully furnish our new home, it had a warm feeling from the start. During my time traveling and trading goods, I had collected a few special pieces; some delicate chinaware and silver. These, I did not trade on, but kept to furnish my own home. It was nowhere near as grand as the one I remembered from my former travels, but the first steps had been taken.

Janka was at our home every day, helping Dunia settle in and keeping an eye on Gahla but Jelko had not come by since the building work was completed. I wanted to stay out of the girls' way and so was spending more time with the boys, working on my shooting skills.

With more consistent practice my aim improved quickly. My arms were already very strong from hoisting the blacksmith's hammer so I could draw the bowstring back with ease. What took more time and effort was releasing the arrow at the right time and aiming at the right place to bring down my prey.

Soon, I could hit a target from a distance of thirty paces, but hitting a moving animal is very different than hitting a static target. Boban said that the trick was to find a static animal, but that took patience and stealth. Several times I took my bow into the forest hoping to bag a deer but every time I spotted one it sensed me first and ran away before I had time to draw my bow.

Jelko was more accomplished. One autumn day I saw him striding through the square with a deer slung over this shoulder.

"Venison roast tomorrow!" he called to me. "I'll bring a piece around to your house. I want to see what our girls have been up to."

True to his word, that evening he knocked on our door. I opened it and laughed.

"You don't have to knock!" I said. "You are like a brother to me!"

"Yes," he said, formally doffing his cap, "but you now have such a grand house it doesn't seem proper to just walk on in."

Before he stepped over the threshold he spat on the ground outside.

"What did you do that for?" I asked at his strange behavior.

"To ward off the evil eye, of course," he replied. "With such a fine house as this, people will be jealous. You need some protection, my friend."

I had never thought about people being jealous! I just wanted the best for my family, as did we all. Maybe I was luckier than most; or maybe I just worked harder. Never mind what other people thought; I loved the new home that I provided for my growing family.

Chapter 96 - Shattered Peace

We passed that winter snug in our new nest. Although Dunia still spent most days at her mother's house we enjoyed the evenings by our own fire. Gahla loved her baby brother, treating him like a living doll. My fields had produced a good harvest and food was plentiful as I settled into a new rhythm of life as the provider of my own growing family. In the spring, Dunia announced that, once again, she was with child and late the following autumn a second son was born.

I insisted that we call the child 'Milan' after the man I had come to love as a father. He was staying in the room we prepared for him at the time of the baby's birth. He passed through our village more often now that the surrounding areas were recovering from the invaders' raids, always hoping for a chance to see his daughter, but the gypsy band had not returned.

One season followed another; the dark and cozy days of winter quickly passing to the warmth of spring and summer; the busy times of planting and harvest. The blacksmith left most of the work in the forge to me, spending more and more of his time in the tavern drinking and gossiping with his friends. Then one evening I came home to find Dunia in tears.

"What's the matter?" I asked. "Is there something wrong with one of the children?"

"No," she replied, "it's my mother."

"Is she ill?" I asked. "Maybe Janka can help her."

"No. She isn't ill," Dunia said, hesitating.

"What is it then?"

"It's my father," she said, her voice barely a whisper.

"Is he ill?" I wondered aloud. "He seems well enough to spend most of his time in the tavern downing ale and plum brandy."

"That's the problem," Dunia said. "You know his temper..."

"Yes," I said, "I know it very well."

"With Yagoda gone, he is taking his anger out on my mother."

"What do you mean?" I asked, shocked at her words.

"When he comes home worse for drinking at the tavern, he always finds something to complain about. Mother tries to stay out of his way but he picks a fight and then he strikes her."

"Why didn't she say anything?" I asked, feeling my own anger rising at the thought of the blacksmith's cruelty.

"She made excuses; blamed herself," Dunia said. "She told me that she hoped it would pass, but it's been getting more and more frequent and more and more violent. Oh, Goran! I'm afraid he will really hurt her the next time!"

"She must come and stay here with us!" I said, feeling sorry for the gentle woman.

"I suggested that she come here but she said her place is there with him," Dunia said, with tears in her eyes. "She said that it was her duty to stay with him."

"I will go to her tomorrow and insist that she come," I told her. "It's for her own safety. We can say that we need her here to help you with her grandchildren."

"I don't know if she will come," Dunia said, looking a bit more hopeful, "but if *you* ask her, maybe she will say 'yes'".

When I spoke with Dunia's mother the next day, at first she denied that her husband had hit her. But, now that I was aware, I could see the signs; a bruise on her wrist and discoloration beneath her eye. I insisted that she come and live with us.

"But my husband needs me!" she said. "He has been a good provider for me. It is my duty to keep his house, prepare his food."

"Mother Gahla," I reasoned, "one of these days he will hit you so hard that you will not be able to care for him at all."

"He doesn't mean it," she said. "It's the drink that makes him do it."

"Well, then," I reasoned, "come to us and when he stops drinking you can return to your home."

I could see that she was considering it so I persisted.

"You can prepare food for him and leave in on the hearth," I said. "That way he can have his meals but you will be safe from his temper. And, besides, we need you at our place to help Dunia with the children."

"I do love being with the children," she said.

"And they love you having you near," I said, "we all do. We don't want to see you hurt. Please, take what you need and come home with me now. Dunia has prepared a place for you to sleep."

So, from that day, Dunia's mother joined us at our house on the square. At first the blacksmith was angry and took his frustration out on me at the forge. But now I felt confident to stand up to him. He had come to depend on me to keep the forge going and he knew it. After a while, I felt he was content to spend most of his time in the tavern, knowing that there was food at home when he wanted it.

As soon as my son Viktor could handle it, I brought him with me to the forge to learn to pump the bellows. It was a big help to me and also the beginning of his apprenticeship in the trade. His little brother, Milan, wanted to come, too, and it is wasn't long before the two of them spent some time with me each day, taking turns on the bellows.

Now Gahla had two younger sisters and loved helping Dunia with their care. Since my hands were full, I employed two village boys to tend to my crops and the small flock of sheep that grazed on my land. I remembered the 'magic dust' that the old gypsy woman had exchanged for a golden ring. I didn't have any dust, but I made a point of riding out to the fields every day to check on the work being done and give a few words of encouragement to the lads.

Some evenings I would meet Jelko and my other friends in the tavern and catch up on their news. Jelko's family had also grown. He was now the father of three healthy boys and one little girl who was the apple of his eye. Janka was known and respected in the village for her knowledge and skills at childbirth and tending to the sick and injured.

Even though we now had a plentiful supply of livestock, Jelko and I liked to go hunting. I was getting better with my bow and arrow and Jelko was an expert.

I hardly ever thought of Milada now; once in a while something would jog my memory, the sight of a young girl running through the square with the hair unbound, the smell of a particular herb the gypsies favored or the taste of fresh honey. I could not say that I was unhappy with Dunia. She kept our home clean and tidy and always had a meal prepared when I came home hungry, yet sometimes I felt that there could be more warmth between us; more laughter.

One day merged into the next; I noticed time passing by the church holidays coming and going and my children growing taller. Every Sunday we went to the church together. I had come to enjoy the gentle singing and the sense of belonging. I didn't really follow the service but let my mind wander where it would; to the paintings on the walls, to the old monk's words, to distant memories of things the gypsies had said. It gave me a feeling of peace to be there, without any work to do, resting myself and feeling at one with the others.

But this peaceful existence was too good to last. One hot summer's day, Milan arrived in the village baring frightening news.

"The horsemen have returned" he told me as he unhitched his horse and led it to a free stall in the old stable beside the blacksmith's house.

"Are they coming this way?" I asked him, concerned that all I'd worked so hard to build would be lost.

"It is probable that they are," he said.

"We need to make a plan!" I exclaimed.

"They are even stronger than before," Milan said sadly.

"Did you see them?" I asked.

"I saw where they had been," he said. "This time they left nothing standing."

"Did the people manage to get out before they came?"

"Some did," Milan said. "I met some hiding in the forest. They said there were a thousand or more horsemen."

"How could they count them?" I asked. "Surely they exaggerate."

"Maybe they did," Milan said, "but even if there were not a thousand there must have been more than the last time."

Although I was very happy to see Milan, my mind was full of heavy thoughts. That evening, as we sat in the yard behind the house Milan's playing delighted Dunia and the children, who, one by one, drifted off to sleep in the warmth of the summer's night. I looked up at the thousands of stars that shone brightly overhead. If each of them was a horseman, how could we keep them from sacking our village once again?

But as I gazed to the heavens I got an idea. Individually, there was no way we could fight them off. But if we banded together with people of the nearby villages we would have a chance.

I remembered the village that was passed over by the invading hordes. It sat on the edge of a deep gorge. If we could keep the invaders from passing through it, they would not be able to attack our village. That is, if the invaders were coming from the west. It would be difficult for them to attack from the north because of the high mountains or from the south where a wide river flowed the length of the valley. If they came from the east, we could defend the narrow valley that separated the plain, where our village and several others were located, and the lowlands beyond.

But, for my idea to work, we would need to visit the other villages and make a plan together. I didn't want to say anything in front of Dunia. The longer she could enjoy her peace and happiness the better. It wouldn't be long before the village would be buzzing with the terrible news.

Chapter 97 - Preparing to Fight

The next day I went to find Jelko and tell him my idea.

"It could work," he said after a moment's consideration. "Go get Milan and we'll tell Boban and see what he thinks."

We found Boban in the tavern with a group of young men. They had already heard the news that the horsemen had returned.

"We can fight them off with our bows and arrows," one man said.

"This time we will be prepared!" another exclaimed.

Boban was shaking his head. "If the reports are correct, there are too many of them to fight off," he told them.

"Gogo has an idea," Jelko said and we joined the group.

"What's that?" Boban asked.

"We need to join forces with men from the other villages in our valley," I told them. "Individually our villages are impossible to protect, but if we all work together to defend the passes into the valley we may be able to stop them."

The men looked at me in silence, considering my words. They looked up when Boban spoke.

"You know," he said, "that just might work."

"I don't think there's a better option," Milan said, "unless we take everything we can carry and run in the other direction!"

"Do we know where they are now?" I asked.

"They were spotted to the east of here," Milan said.

"We need to send some scouts on the fastest horses we have to find out," Boban said.

"In the meantime, we must visit the other villages and see if the people there agree with our strategy," I said.

"I know the roads well," Milan said. "Sasha, you have a fine horse; you and I can be the scouts."

"Gogo and I are known in the villages 'round here. We will go and propose his idea. Boban, you are the finest shot. You organize and train our men. Make them a force to be reckoned with!"

The men agreed that the plan could work. No one wanted to run away; but then again, no one wanted to die at the hands of the invading horsemen, either.

That very afternoon Jelko and I rode to Paramitha, the nearest village to the east of ours. We arrived late in the day and found most of the men sitting in the square on the benches outside of their tavern. They, like the men of our village, were deeply concerned about the impending threat of invasion.

Jelko and I were welcomed into the group and the men listened attentively while we explained our plan. Just as our men had, they considered my idea in silence. One by one, they began to nod.

The headman of the village was the first to speak.

"Fighting together is our best chance to preserve our villages, our families, our homes, our livestock and our fields," he said, "but we will need support from all the villages hereabouts in order to have a chance."

"It will give us the advantage if we can choose where to fight," I said. "Each of our villages is protected by a wall, but the walls can be approached easily and even if the horsemen don't breach them, which is unlikely, we can still be trapped inside until our food runs out."

"Goran's idea to stop them at the narrow passes is brilliant!" Jelko said. "If you agree, start practicing with your bows and arrows, sling shots and spears!"

"We will send men to the villages north and south of here to recruit fighters to our cause. You can go in the other direction from your village. It seems that the threat is coming from the east, but we need as many men as we can get. If they come into the valley none of the villages will be safe!" the headman agreed.

I looked at the men gathered respectfully around him and the words of the old monk came to mind. I could see by the way he held his shoulders that the headman would keep his word. His calm confidence would inspire the men around him. With no time to lose, I grasped his hand as a bond to our agreement of mutual support then Jelko and I mounted our steeds and made it back to our own village with the encouraging news before nightfall.

Over the next three days we visited six more villages. Most of the men we encountered were for the plan. The one place we met resistance was the village on the mountainside that had been overlooked by the invaders. I guess they thought that their luck would hold again and were not prepared to risk sacrificing any of their men to help the rest of us.

The headman of Havita was hard to convince even though the village had suffered terribly in the last raid. Because of the proximity of this village, I had done business with many of the men there. I felt that they trusted me. But when I met the headman I did not have a good feeling. He would not look me directly in the eye; rather he gazed past my right shoulder when he spoke.

"You say the horsemen will approach from the east," he said, "so why should we risk the lives of our men to help people so far from here?"

"To prevent them from entering the valley that we all share," I tried to explain, "we need as large a force as we can muster. Otherwise, they will push through and sack all the villages one by one including Havita."

"It is a sound plan, father," a young man said. "Remember how we suffered the last time the horsemen came?"

"Be quiet, Yion," the headman spat, "this time we have more warning. If we are going to fight, is it not better to stay here and protect our own village?"

"But alone, we will not be strong enough," the younger man persisted.

There was mumbling and grumbling among the gathered men.

"We must return to preparations in our own village," I said, realizing that there was disagreement here. "When the time comes to travel east to defend the pass, church bells will be rung throughout the valley. If you will join forces with the rest of us, ride east. We will come together at Paramitha, the closest village to the eastern pass."

"And please," I added, "even if you decide not to come, ring your own church bells to carry the message on."

"I will make sure that the bells are rung!" the headman's son said, glaring at his father. "I, for one, will fight with you to protect our valley."

"Thank you, my friend," I said, clapping the youth on the back. "If, by some chance, the horsemen instead approach from the west, your village would be the first to fall. In that case, the men from the villages in the valley would come to defend the gorge. In these difficult times we must put aside our rivalry and selfish thoughts and work together for the common good."

Most of the men nodded in agreement, but the headman looked away. Jelko and I took our leave and hurried home by the light of the nearly full moon. The next afternoon, Milan and Sasha returned, their horses panting and drenched in sweat.

"There isn't much time to prepare," Milan said.

"Did you see the horsemen?" I asked.

"Yes," he replied, "we spied their camp in the distance. There are several hundred of them, that's for sure."

"How close are they?"

"We spotted them yesterday morning and rode as fast as we could to bring the news," he said. "We only stopped briefly to let the horses rest."

"So if they come this way they could be at the pass soon!" I exclaimed. "We need to mass the men!"

"I'll go ring the church bells!" Jelko said, taking off at a trot to alert the men to take up their weapons, saddle their horses and be ready to go and fight.

Soon I could hear the distant sound of bells echoing throughout the valley as the other villages picked up the signal.

Before I could go, there was something I had to do. I ran to my house to find Dunia and the children huddled in the front room by the hearth. Everyone knew the terrible news that the sound of the bells signified.

"Take the children, your mother, some blankets and food and go to the place in the forest near the pond," I told Dunia.

"You will go and fight?" she asked quietly.

"Yes," I said, "I must go with the men and do what I can to prevent another invasion. But just in case we cannot stop them, it's better for you and the little ones to stay in the forest."

She nodded as she and her mother gathered up some blankets, using them to wrap up earthenware jars of preserves and cheese. I saw Dunia looking over to the chest where her finest embroideries were stored.

"Take one of the horses," I told her. "You can load it with supplies and let the children ride. But be quick, there isn't much time."

I heard a noise behind me and saw that the blacksmith had staggered through the threshold. He looked at the activity around him.

"Where is my wife?" he bellowed. "I went to the house and the hearth was cold!"

"We have more important things to worry about than your dinner!" I said, crossly.

"Where do you think you are going?" he snarled.

"I am going to fight with the village men; the women and children are going to wait in the forest. Go ahead; go with them," I said.

"I? Go with the women?" he scoffed. "I still have my sword and I'm ready to use it! You are the coward. You were the one who hid in the forest the last time the horsemen came. What gives you the right to tell me what to do?"

He took a swipe at me, but I easily dodged his heavy hand.

"Well," I said making for the door, "if you are going to fight, get your sword and let's go!"

"Gogo," Dunia cried reaching her hand out to me, "Stay safe and come back to us soon!"

I turned to see the sadness and concern in her eyes and something in me changed. When I looked at her I realized that I truly loved her; loved Dunia, not just as the mother of my beautiful children but as a woman who cared about me and loved me.

I ran to her and took her in my arms. "Dunia, my Dunia!" I murmured into her hair, tears coming to my eyes.

I felt her arms tighten around me; felt her heart beating next to mine. I *would* come back to her, I vowed.

Chapter 98 - Going to Battle

Before long all the able-bodied men and even some strong young women were mounted and gathering in the village square. My horse pawed the ground, restless to be among so many others. We all turned toward the village gate as it creaked open.

"I'm coming with you!"

I looked over and saw my eldest son, mounted on one of our plough horses.

"Viktor," I said, "you are a brave lad and I would be honored to have you by my side..."

"But, Father? I know you are going to say 'but'!"

I had to smile at how well my son knew my thoughts.

"But I need you to stay and protect your mother and your brothers and sisters," I said.

"Milan will protect them!" he said, referring to his younger brother.

"Milan is too young," I said, "I need you to do this for me; so I go and fight our enemies knowing that my family is safe in your keeping."

By now, the horses were jostling toward the gate.

"Please go home," I told my son. "I am very proud of you for wanting to come, but if you truly want to be of service, stay here and help those who will remain. I hope to be back soon with news of our victory."

"Yes, father," he said, "I understand the wisdom of your words. I will keep our family safe until you return."

He pulled his horse close to mine and we embraced, then parted with a shared look of love and respect.

As he turned the horse toward the stable, the blacksmith came running up to him, brandishing his sword.

"Damn you, boy! I was looking for that horse!" he yelled. "Get off it. Now!"

The boy looked at me, then slid off the horse and ran off as fast as his legs would carry him. The blacksmith slid his sword into a leather sheath and clumsily mounted the tall horse.

I had nothing to say to him, so, without a word, I guided my horse through the village gate. When the track widened I trotted along the column of men until I spotted my friend Jelko near the head of the line. I pulled up beside him and sighed.

"What's the matter?" he asked. "Aren't you ready to fight?"

"I was hoping that we wouldn't have to," I told him honestly; "that the horsemen would turn away from the valley."

"At least this time we stand a chance," he said.

"If the other men turn up as promised we just might," I said.

We rode along in silence, the sun hot on our backs casting long shadows on the road before us.

I was beginning to have doubts about our success. What could a bunch of untrained men with a few bows and arrows and farm tools do against a hoard of experienced marauders?

But, that evening when we arrived in Paramitha I began to have renewed hope.

"Look at all the men!" Jelko exclaimed when we approached the village walls. I could see that the gate was open and that the square was so full of men and horses that the rest were massed outside. As he had several years before when the horsemen had come to our village, Boban assumed a position of leadership.

Leaving us to wait by the walls, he rode into Paramitha and was soon back with news.

"I met with the leaders of the men from the other villages," he told us. "The men from Paramitha have identified the best places for us to hide and wait for the horsemen. He has assigned a place for each village."

"Do we know if the horsemen at coming this way?" I asked.

"Yes," Boban replied. "They can be seen from the watchtower."

"They're that close?" exclaimed Jelko. "Will they come through the pass tonight?"

"They seem to be setting up their camp," Boban said. "That gives us time to get into place. They will probably move through the pass early in the morning, but by then we will be ready".

"Tell the men to let the horses graze in that field," he said, indicating a nearby meadow and gather the men to hear our instructions."

Jelko and I passed the message on and soon Boban was ready to address us.

"Men," he began, "we have the advantage of numbers and of surprise. We can do this! The men of Paramitha are already in place at the head of the pass. But you won't see them there! They are well hidden in the forested slopes. We must hide ourselves as well. Once the horsemen are deep into the valley a signal will be given and we will attack!"

"Do we attack at the same time?" one man asked.

"No," Boban replied. "At the first signal, one blast of the horn, the men with bows and arrows will shoot down on the horsemen from the cover of the forest. They have the longest range and can take out many men before the invaders realize what's happening. That may be enough to send them running."

"If there is a second blast of the horn it is the signal to attack on foot using swords, knives, hoes and spears. Try to stay on the slope of the hill and knock the men off their horses. As long as they are mounted they have the advantage over those of us on foot."

"Can't we fight from our horses?" another man inquired.

"If you can do so, yes," Boban replied, "but you will need to stay well back at the beginning. Horses are harder to conceal than men."

"How many men have come to fight?" I asked.

"More than a thousand," Boban answered with a smile. "Those horsemen won't be expecting such resistance!

I was feeling much more confident now that I saw that we had so many fighters on our side. When night fell we began to take our positions on each side of the narrow pass. Jelko and I left our horses tethered in the meadow. We were confident about our skills with a bow but not from horseback. I hadn't seen the blacksmith. I figured he would be with his friends from the tavern. I could hear their raucous laughter at the edge of our group. Someone yelled at them to be quiet as we moved out toward the pass.

Quietly taking our places I saw other men moving around between the trees, but at the first light of dawn we were all concealed, waiting in silence for whatever might come. Before long, I heard the sound of hoofs in the distance. They grew louder as the rays of the sun began to pierce the valley. I could smell the dust shaken loose by galloping hooves. Slowly, I peeked out from behind my sheltering tree and glimpsed the horsemen moving through the valley below us. I readied my bow and waited.

The horn sounded. I stepped out from behind the tree, aimed as well as I could at the moving target and shot. My aim was true and I watched the man drop off his horse as I positioned my next arrow.

It took the horsemen some moments to realize what was happening. Some kept riding forward, while others spun around in confusion, shocked at the sight of their fallen brothers. Some looked up toward the hillside to see from whence the arrows had come.

These men made easier targets and I picked off several in rapid succession. Would this be enough? I looked at the bloody scene below and hoped that the horsemen who still stood would turn tail and leave the valley. But, no. They were standing their ground. I'm sure that they had no idea of our numbers.

Just then, there was a loud shout from lower down on the hillside. No signal had been given but a man was running out from the cover of the forest with his sword drawn. I saw that it was the blacksmith. The horsemen in the valley saw him, too, and began firing arrows in our direction. At the sight of their drawn bows, the blacksmith turned around and began to scramble back up the slope into the forest, but before he could reach cover an arrow pierced his back and he fell to the ground.

From behind me, an arrow flew past my head and felled the horseman before he could draw attention to our hiding place. By now the flow of invaders had thinned to a trickle. I could see that they were in retreat when the second horn blast sounded.

Suddenly, the ground itself seemed to move as hundreds of men poured down the slopes from both sides of the valley. I watched from above as men from our village and the others of the valley fell on the invaders with all the fury remembered from suffering at their hands.

I made my way to where the blacksmith lay. I pulled the arrow from his back and turned him over. I gazed down at this man who had caused so much pain to his family; yet I could not hate him, He took me in and taught me the blacksmith's trade. Gently, I closed his lifeless eyes then looked down at the battle raging below.

I took up my bow and kept at the fight from my position on the hill. Before the sun was high in the sky, I realized that we had prevailed. The remaining horsemen were in retreat. I felt no need or desire to pursue them. They had learned their lesson and would leave our valley alone.

Chapter 99 - The Aftermath of Victory

There was a feeling of jubilation when we returned to Paramitha. We'd done it! Together we had prevented the destruction of all of our villages. This day would be remembered and celebrated as reminder of our common victory over the enemy. The immediate excitement was short-lived, though, when we returned to the valley to collect the fallen. With Jelko's help I heaved the lifeless body of the blacksmith onto the plough horse. No one else from our village had fallen in the battle. Had the blacksmith waited for the signal, he would probably have survived. We could be thankful that his foolhardiness had not been the cause of more losses among our men.

It was a grim job sorting our dead from theirs. Men from each village needed to identify and claim their fallen brothers. The dead horsemen were striped of anything of value. We had all agreed to share their horses and anything else we could salvage. After all, they had stolen or destroyed most of our possessions not many years back.

But before we could share out the loot, we needed to dispose of the bodies already beginning to rot in the midsummer's heat. Several men from each village worked with their picks and shovels to dig a big hole on the edge of the valley where the battle had occurred. Working together, it wasn't long before the stripped corpses of the enemy's dead were tossed into the depths of the cold earth.

Back in the village, their fine horses had been corralled and their arms and livery had been sorted into equal piles. The headman of Paramitha called the leaders of each village come to the fountain and draw a straw from his hand. The man who drew the longest straw would have first pick of a horse and a pile of goods, the one who drew the second longest would choose next and so on until all the booty had been shared.

I was happy when Boban drew the third longest straw. We would need to bring a cart from the village to fetch back our pile of loot to be divided amongst the people in our village. Many of the rider-less horses of the fallen enemy had turned and followed the others out of the valley but almost 40 had been caught, so after each village had chosen one there was another round and then a third.

When there were fewer horses than villages left Jelko called out, "Let's make a game of it!"

"What do you mean?" Boban asked.

"Let one man from each village ride one of the new horses and we'll have a race. The winner gets the rest of the horses for his village!"

"Good idea!" the headman from Paramitha agreed. "But to make it more interesting let the rider be the youngest from each village!"

The sound of laughter rang throughout the square as the villagers chose their representative. I looked around to see who would be the youngest of our lot. Had Victor come, it would have been my son riding, I thought.

"It's me! It's me!" I heard a voice ring out.

I looked over to see which boy was claiming the honor of riding for our village. What a surprise it was when I saw that it was no boy at all but one of the young women who had chosen to come and join us in the fight. It was Markiza, the daughter of Davko, the man with the very big horse. I had watched her growing up. She was always on the wild side, loving to accompany her father to the forge when it was time to shoe the monster.

"I'm the youngest here!" she said, laughing. "Where are the horses?"

She vaulted onto the tallest of the three and was off to join the mounted young men near the village gate.

The mounted boys looked at Markiza and laughed. "Ha! Richuka has no chance to win with a girl riding for them," one said in scorn.

Markiza smiled. "Laugh now, while you can, boys," she said, flipping her thick braid over her shoulder.

We all trooped down the hill. The riders lined up on the side of the road and we spread out to watch the sport.

"When the horn sounds, ride to that stone wall on the far side of the field, turn around and come back here," the headman said. "The first one back takes the horses! May the best man, or girl, win!"

The horn sounded and they were off in a cloud of dust. The plain resounded with our shouts of encouragement. The horses reached the stone wall and were soon heading back toward the finishing line. In the speed and the dust I could not tell who was out in front, but I could see that three horses were well ahead of the others after the turn. As they got closer I let out a cheer when I saw that our Markiza was leading all the boys!

Then she was over the line! She had won the horses for our village! I heard someone yell at Jelko, "It was your idea to have this race; you must have known that girl could ride!"

"It was my idea to have the race," he replied, "but not that the youngest person should be the rider! We were just lucky, that's all!"

"It just goes to show," Jelko called, "Richuka girls are the best; in the kitchen, in the bed and even on horseback!"

Laughing and arguing about the merits of their own girls, the men drifted away, leaving for their own villages to bury the dead and give their families the news that the enemy had been routed.

"Listen," the headman called out, "before you all go. Let's get together at the next full moon and celebrate our victory and our friendship!"

"Come to Richuka," Boban called, "It is more central and a shorter journey for many of you".

"It's very short for you!" someone yelled. "You live there!"

"Well it was my townsman's idea to fight off the enemy together," he yelled back, "so it's appropriate for us to host the celebration!"

"By the next full moon the harvest will be in and we will be ready to celebrate. See you all then in Richuka!" Boban said.

A cheer of assent rose from the crowd. We had fought together; soon we would celebrate our victory together as well.

Jelko and I went to the forest below Paramitha. We'd left the horse with the blacksmith's body in the deep shade of the woods. The ride back felt bittersweet. I was relieved that the threat of the invaders had passed but I knew that Dunia would be saddened by the blacksmith's death. When we returned to where we'd left it, I saw that Milan was there, looking at his brother's body with tears in his eyes.

I got off my horse and went over to where he stood. I lay my hand on his back to offer what comfort I could.

"I was thinking about when we were young," Milan said, quietly. "He always wanted to be a soldier."

"He made us wooden swords and we would play at fighting. He was always the captain, of course," he continued. "What fun we had, playing in the woods, pretending that the enemy was upon us".

"But then we grew up and grew apart," he said sadly. "And when Anna fell in love with me that was the end of anything good between us".

"You tried to be his friend," I said.

"I tried, but I did not succeed," he said, "and now I never will. He was the closest family I had left."

"You have Milada," I said.

"I cannot know if we shall ever meet again," he whispered.

I just nodded. "Come on," I told him, "it's time to go. We need to get back to the village and bury his body as soon as we can."

I mounted my horse and led the plough horse behind me toward the road.

We joined the other men heading west. As we rode further along, the number of riders thinned out, with men from the other villages branching out in different directions. The sun was in our faces when we turned up the road to Richuka. I waved farewell to Yion as he continued on to Havita, further to the west. True to his word, and against his father's wishes, he and a few of his friends had joined our cause. His father will be happy with the booty he's bringing to their village, I thought.

As we made our way up the hill I could hear cheering from the woods by the side of the road. As I had, years ago, boys were keeping watch from the cover of the forest.

Viktor and young Milan were running toward me, smiling and waving.

"Hurray! You are back!" Young Milan cried. "Did you kill them all?"

"We killed enough of them!" I said. "And the rest ran away."

"But who is that?" Viktor asked, pointing at the body on the tall horse behind me. "Is it grandfather?"

"Yes, my boy," I said. "He fought bravely," I lied, "and helped us all to victory."

"I'm not sorry he's dead!" young Milan cried. "He was mean!"

"He was mean, sometimes," I told the boy, "but thanks to him we have your mother and our trade. Let's remember the good things in his life. He won't be mean to us anymore but we can still enjoy the good things he gave us!"

"Run, now, and tell your mother and the others that it is safe to come home!"

Chapter 100 - Homecoming

Milan and I rode first to the churchyard to leave the blacksmith's body for burial. The priest must have stayed in the church because he was at the door when we passed on our way to the cemetery.

"You are back," the priest said; "but not all are alive."

"Yes, Father," I said, pausing in my grim task. "We chased the invaders from the pass at the eastern edge of our valley. They won't be back to bother us for a long time. But a few men fell in our defense."

"The blacksmith?" he surmised, by looking at me and Milan.

I nodded. "He fought well but an enemy's arrow found him."

"Was anyone else killed?" he inquired.

"No, Father," I replied. "God was with us. Some other villages lost some men but our losses were few compared to the enemy's."

"I will find the gravedigger," the priest said, "Tell the people to come to the church at sunset. I will offer a service for the repose of his soul and gratitude for our victory."

I nodded my agreement then tethered the tall horse bearing the blacksmith's body to a cypress tree at the edge of the cemetery.

"Let's go and find our family," I said to Milan. "They should have arrived back in the house by now."

We stabled our horses and then made our way through the crowded square where the scene resembled the happy celebration of the morning. I found Dunia and her mother settling the few things that they had taken from our home back into their places. I saw that, once again, Dunia had brought her embroideries. She blushed prettily when she saw me looking at them in her hands.

"Next to the children," I told her, "your work is the most precious thing we have. You were right to want to protect it."

At my words, she smiled and ran over to me. I held my arms open and pulled her into a snug embrace. Soon I felt warm arms on my back and small hands on my legs. All the children had joined us in a hug, young Milan pulling his namesake uncle into the embrace.

Dunia's mother looked on from the hearth. I beckoned her to come and join in the family hug. At first she didn't move, but when the children realized that I was calling her they started a chorus of: "Grandma! Grandma! Come and hug us!"

Eventually, Mother Gahla smiled and joined us. We stayed in each other's arms until we collapsed in a fit of laughter onto the divan; but once we composed ourselves Dunia looked up at me seriously.

"Where is my father?" she asked. "I told him not to go with you but he insisted. You know that he has not been well of late."

I took Dunia's hand in mine and looked at her mother, sitting with my youngest daughter in her lap, then took a deep breath.

"I'm sorry," I told them; "the blacksmith didn't make it home. We left him in the churchyard. At sunset the priest will gave a service for his soul."

I was expecting Dunia and Mother Gahla to breakdown into tears, but, to my surprise, neither of them did. Finally, Dunia's mother spoke.

"I think that he was ready to go," she said quietly. "His life was spent drinking and running away from those who loved him. He can rest in peace now."

Dunia nodded and I squeezed her hand. Young Milan jumped on my lap and, breaking the solemnity of the moment said, "Papa, tell us all about what happened!"

There was still some time before sunset so when the others joined in begging Milan and me for the story we told them all about it; from my idea of getting the villagers to work together right through to the news that there would be a victory celebration right here in Richuka at the next full moon.

By the time the tale was told the sun was had set. Milan and I needed to wash up before the service so the women and children went on to the church ahead of us.

Once they had gone, I tossed Milan and towel and said. "They took your brother's death well".

"They were relieved," Milan said.

"Do you really think so?" I asked.

"His temper and cruelty was becoming worse and worse," Milan replied. "For his wife to come to live here she must have feared for her life. I can say now that I don't know if your children were safe. He wouldn't hurt them on purpose, but when he'd been drinking any little thing could set off his murderous temper."

"I will try to do as I told young Milan," I said, rubbing the dust of battle from my face, "and remember the good things that the man did."

Milan nodded, "Holding on to the hurt and anger serves no purpose save as a reminder not to go down the same path again."

By the time we arrived at the churchyard, the blacksmith's body had been lowered into the ground and the people were filing back into the church for the service of thanksgiving.

I stood at the back, behind the other men and leaned against a wooden column, feeling the fatigue of the past few days, yet a new and unexpected strength. With the blacksmith gone, I was now the head of our family. I knew I would take good care of them and that my family would prosper in this village for generations to come. My heart was full of love and gratitude for the winding road that brought me to this moment.

As I looked up at the wall paintings illuminated by the flickering oil lamps, Mary, the mother of God, seemed to smile down at me from the dome behind the priest as he chanted the words I could not understand.

~

Remembering now the life that came before that moment and after; the sweetness of my mother's voice singing me to sleep in the little room behind the tavern; Milada calling out to me to 'see this' and 'look at that', happily exploring the forest together; the gentle cooing of my baby Gahla as I held her in my arms; dear Dunia's eyes as she bid me farewell, full of love and concern; the laughter of my children and my children's children as they grew into happy men and women.

The angels on the ceiling seem to be breathing. Yes, they are breathing. Gently they move their chubby arms and turn their heads from side to side as if waking from a long sleep. They look down from on high. They are looking at me! They disengage their wings from the plaster of the ceiling. They're fluttering down and hovering over me! I look around at the other people silently following the service. Can't they see the angels?

"Only you can see us," I hear a voice in my head say. "It's time for you to come with us, Goran."

"I cannot go," I say; "my family is here."

"Your family is waiting for you on the other side," the sweet voice calls.

I look over to where Dunia had been sitting with her mother and the children but she isn't there. Although some look familiar, I do know these people.

"Come, Gogo," the voice repeats. "They are waiting for you."

The angels reach out to me and take me by my hands. I rise with them above the congregation, up, up to the sky painted on the church's ceiling and then right through it! I look down to see the village from above, the church on the square and the familiar fountain are getting smaller and smaller the higher we rise. A golden light shines down on the green fields and forests that spread out like a quilt beneath us. The light is getting stronger and stronger as we rise above the clouds.

I close my eyes against the brightness and when I open them I am by the clear pool. I recognize it, yet it looks different. Everything is bathed in a golden light; the colors all look brighter and more sharp. On the bank of the stream I see my mother reaching her arms out to me. Beside her stand Dunia and Milada, smiling. I walk over to them and they take me in their arms. I know that I am a home, engulfed in light and love.

Epilogue

"Grandpa, Grandpa!" the young girl said, pulling on the man's sleeve. "Wake up, Grandpa! I want to hear the end of the story!"

A woman who was passing went over to the child. She gently touched the old man's forehead. It was stone cold.

"Little one," the woman said to the child, "Grandpa's tale is done."

The End

Fasoula, Cyprus January 27, 2013 - full moon

Note: Two of Mother Miriana's stories are based on traditional folktales; the story of the wastrel lad and the bird in the hand.

Francesca Pinoni is a qualified yoga teacher and has studied various natural healing modalities including Reiki (Usui & Karuka Master), magnetotherapy, and biofeedback/bioresonance and Shamanism. Her hobbies include dancing, music (Frame drum & djembe), art (painting, pastel & mosaics), poetry and traveling.

In the companion volume to this book "To the Rhythm of the Moon" (2009) Milada tells her own story.

This charming story is peopled with characters that engage the reader and a plot that will keep the pages turning. It is a book to be read at that sensitive age, the cusp between childhood and womanhood; the age when there are so many questions and no one we ask, if we have the courage to ask at all, seems to have satisfying answers. Capino's light touch belies the depth of the ideas she presents. Through an appealing story with action, suspense and romance the characters learn to rely on themselves and their own in-born wisdom to cope with the difficult situations and decisions that they must face. Through the eyes of Milada, an orphan girl living with a band of gypsies possessing profound knowledge, the plot, with suspense and romance, carries the reader through themes of belonging, growth, love and change. There are deaths and there are births. Years and seasons pass as the characters grow and develop, measured by the ever-changing phases of the moon.

www.ingramcontent.com/pod-product-compliance
Lightning Source LLC
Chambersburg PA
CBHW021119260626
47169CB00005B/1350